Isabel walked around the pond, feeling a little conspicuous as a lone woman. Everyone else in the park seemed to be part of a unit: groups of friends; couples; families.

She couldn't see the two white swans. Had they flown away? Could they fly? Then she noticed a single black swan emerging slowly from the bulrushes, a gleaming magnificent creature. She watched it glide across the water and felt chilled. A brisk walk home will do me good, she decided. She trudged off down one of the less-used paths and thought about Michael, trying to rationalise his reaction. It was understandable: she'd sprung the news on him, while she'd already had a few days to get accustomed to it. But there was something else. Why was he so angry?

Her hand went to her stomach and she kept it there, on top of her sheepskin coat, even though it was much too early to feel any evidence of a baby. A baby. It was weird, she admitted. But it could be that she'd have to get used to it – and so would Michael. Wouldn't he?

Also by Susanna Jackson

Living Other Lives

Susanna Jackson has had several careers, starting as a teacher and moving into educational writing before becoming a freelance copywriter. For a while she was the company writer for The Body Shop, working closely with Anita Roddick. She lives in London with her family. Her first novel, *Living Other Lives*, is also published by Orion.

A Little Surprise

SUSANNA JACKSON

ORION

An Orion paperback
First published in Great Britain by Orion in 1999
This paperback edition published in 2000 by
Orion Books Ltd,
Orion House, 5 Upper St Martin's Lane,
London WC2H 9EA

Second impression 2000

A CIP catalogue record for this book
is available from the British Library.

Printed and bound in Great Britain by
Clays Ltd, St Ives plc

for
Emily and Freddy

I

Isabel checked for the third time that the bathroom door was locked. No one must know what she was doing – not yet, although they probably wouldn't believe it anyway. She ripped at the packaging to get to the box, cursing in frustration, then noticed the thin white strip you were meant to pull for easy access.

At last. It was almost like a present, this neat blue pack, reassuringly designed, clearly labelled, making her think of blue skies, the sea, clear water. No doubt it was meant to. She read the instructions then scanned them again. It seemed easy enough and there would be a result in just one minute. Amazing, she thought. This had to be progress. No more carrying of urine samples in jars to clinics or the doctor's, no more lengthy waiting or anxious phone calls. She could see for herself, right here in her own home.

She arranged herself on the loo, the slim plastic wand in her hand, concentrating on trying to pee, making sure she did it correctly. God, this would be so much easier if she were a man and could pee standing up – but then men didn't get pregnant, did they?

One minute. It could seem like nothing or a lifetime, depending on which result you desired. And what did she want it to be? Positive or negative? Would she be positive about a negative result or vice versa? Now you're getting silly, she told herself. Stop prevaricating, Isabel – for she was, she was delaying the moment when she'd know, actually know, whether she was pregnant – or not.

One minute. Dare she look? She did. There it was: a distinct blue line in the square window. As she had suspected, she *was* pregnant. A rush of thoughts filled her head, tumbling over each other as if in a panic to get out: I can't be (but she could, she was); maybe the test was wrong (but it claimed to be more than 99 per cent accurate); surely I'm too old (but she wasn't) . . .

Isabel sat on the hard edge of the bath and shivered, although the bathroom was one of the warmest rooms in the house. What should she do? That was simply answered for now: the box contained another test. For unbelievers? Or those who messed up the first one?

She did the whole thing again, taking extra care, somehow managing to pee for a second time.

One more minute. Another blue line.

It was clear, it was definite.

Now what should she do? The big question. And not one she'd thought she'd have to face, not at this stage in her life. 'Oh God,' she groaned, sitting on the bath again and leaning her head against the basin. How would Michael react to this little surprise? What would those two almost-adult children of theirs say? She wasn't ready to explore that yet. First she needed to think about how she felt. Pregnant. A baby, a child, the whole damn thing, all over again. She imagined herself pushing a pram – if prams still existed – and being mistaken for a grandmother. (After all, her daughter Gemma was old enough to have a baby.) She pictured herself as the oldest mother at the school gate; becoming a pensioner as the child went through adolescence . . . Did she have the energy for this? Or the inclination?

Then there were the health risks, to her, to the baby. Could she cope with a baby that was less than perfect? She knew vaguely that older mothers were more likely to have handicapped babies (was that even the correct term these days?) but her knowledge of these things was limited. She'd have to find out all about it. There'd be so much to do, it was daunting.

She took a deep breath, trying to shake off the feeling of being overwhelmed. Her limbs felt like lead and she wanted to sleep. Perhaps I'm in shock, she thought, even though I've had my suspicions. But now I know. It's for real.

Isabel forced herself into action, collecting all traces of the pregnancy tests, placing them in a carrier-bag and tying the handles. She'd take it outside and put it in the dustbin. Secrecy didn't come naturally to her, but it seemed the best course for the moment – until she'd managed to sort the situation out in her own mind. Clutching the bag of evidence to her chest she went downstairs attempting to appear normal, whatever that was.

As she passed the hall mirror she glanced at her reflection. Of course, she looked no different – and yet she was. This whole thing was odd. What was especially odd, though, she realised, was that underneath these swirling emotions which gripped her – surprise, alarm, confusion, all that – was a flicker of something else. Joy, excitement? Whatever it was brought a smile to her face. Perhaps having another baby could be a good thing. Why not embrace the unexpected?

2

The two white swans were there, as always, coasting serenely on the pond, seemingly oblivious to the smaller birds fussing at the shore or the people tossing unwanted bread into the water, needing a purpose. They skirted elegantly around each other, their necks almost entwining. A pair, a couple.

Isabel stood with Michael, watching. She squeezed his arm, trying to draw him closer but his hands stayed resolutely in his pockets. He stared straight ahead at the water, his face obscured by his upturned collar.

'Is it true that swans mate for life?' she asked, wanting to add, Like us. But she felt a tension in him, his mood did not seem quite right. She could sense a dip in his spirits, a change in his state of mind – and so she should for they had been married . . . how long? Twenty-one years, it must be.

Michael sighed. 'Mate for life? Does anything? Or anyone?'

His tone surprised Isabel. What was the matter with him lately? But before she could respond, Michael continued 'Well, maybe swans do. I'm not sure. They certainly keep the same partner for a long time.'

'Like us!' She beamed at him and he managed a small smile back.

'Isabel you're a sentimental old thing.'

She gave him a fond push. 'Michael my love, how many times do I have to tell you? I'm not sentimental. Romantic, maybe, but isn't that good?'

He didn't reply but busied himself rounding up their spaniel, Jasper, who'd been snuffling about at the water's edge and was now barking rather too vigorously at the moorhens. They continued their circuit of the pond in silence, her arm through his, the dog trotting along beside them.

For years Isabel and Michael had gone for a morning walk in Richmond Park on New Year's Day. It had become a family tradition. They liked having family traditions, especially ones they'd created themselves. The children used to accompany them, but now Dominic and Gemma stayed in bed, for at seventeen and nineteen New Year's Eve was a time to party and go wild, or at least try to, and New Year's Day was a time to sleep.

Isabel lifted her head, regarding the day with optimism. It was sunny and cold and crisp, just the kind of weather she liked. Even the air seemed fresh. That's what she loved about Richmond Park: you could almost pretend you were in the country, if you ignored the tower blocks of Roehampton on the horizon, the crowded car parks and the Heathrow-bound jets low in the sky.

She considered the year ahead. Until a few days ago it had seemed as though it would be fairly predictable: the usual menu of family, home and her shop. Dominic would need encouragement to work hard for his A levels; Gemma needed help in finding her niche – another course perhaps, some training? But *need* was no longer the right word, she thought, as neither of them really *needed* her, not like they used to. Being a parent of children this age was rather like standing on the sidelines of a football game, Isabel decided. You watched and observed their lives unfold but only became involved if they were hurt or upset or in trouble or wanted reassurance or encouragement. It was a delicate business.

So what else? The house required attention, some redecoration, and in the garden she wanted to add a pergola for climbing roses and reseed part of the lawn . . . Then there was her work: Once or Twice, the shop she ran with her friend Angela, required a good sort-out – more and more women were bringing in their hardly worn clothes for reselling; perhaps it was a sign of the times. And they should consider getting a computer, to help make the business more professional and streamlined.

But now, of course, there was another factor to add to all this: her pregnancy.

Since doing the tests she'd said nothing to anyone. It was a secret she hugged to herself. She was beginning to get used to the idea – the idea of being pregnant rather than the idea of actually having a third child. It was ridiculous to separate the two, she knew that, but somehow it was easier to deal with one step at a time. Every now and then, as she brushed her teeth or filled the washing-machine or did the shopping, she'd try to surprise herself, asking the question, 'So how do you feel about this, Isabel?' It was an attempt to establish the truth of things, or if her feelings had changed from the day or hour before.

As she walked alongside Michael, she reviewed the position she'd arrived at (although it could still change and change again): she had not wanted or intended to become pregnant, but now she was and her instinct was to make the best of it. To go ahead, have the baby. They could afford it, they weren't that old, everyone would adjust . . . But as she presented this summary to herself, her thoughts began to fly in different directions and the inevitable tussle ensued. Her health, the baby's, its future with ageing parents. Michael?

She had to tell him. Now was as good a time as any, on this ritual New Year's Day walk – this was when they usually reflected on the year ahead.

Isabel looked up at his face and admired his profile as she always did. What would his reaction be? Surprised certainly, but then what? As they strode along she turned words over in her mind, deciding what to say. A knot of nervousness formed in her stomach.

Michael struggled to keep his irritation hidden. He felt a growing bile of bad temper rising into his chest. It was a familiar feeling. He was pissed off with Isabel, although it wasn't really her fault. He was pissed off with all these smug, comfortable people walking around them, with their Labradors and green wellies and loud, barking voices and cute children and their armoured four-wheel-drive vehicles in the car park. Ostensibly he was one of them, although he didn't feel like it. He was pissed off too with the bright, shiny day – why wasn't it gloomy, to match his mood? He was even pissed off with the dog, with its fidelity and eagerness to please.

He used to enjoy these walks, the feeling of starting again, a fresh slate, a new year. But that was before . . . Before Ellen. Before his affair. Now everything had changed and he saw it all differently. *He* had changed. And he wanted to change his life, which was what he was about to tell Isabel.

Michael looked across the pond, watching the flock of swooping, greedy seagulls, turning away from Isabel's smile. She looked cheerful, as ever. And she was keen for him to be cheerful too, he could feel it, like a physical warmth emanating from her. Or more like a pressure.

How should he tell her? And how much? What should he say? He'd been over it with Ellen – she'd even made suggestions. But the situation was an abstract problem to her: she didn't know Isabel. This was Isabel, his wife, whom he still loved – in a way. Isabel was real enough to him. So was their marriage, all twenty-odd years of it (he always had difficulty remembering the exact number). Oh Christ. But it had to be done. He had promised Ellen that he would tell Isabel after Christmas and make plans for moving out. And Ellen would expect a progress report when she returned from the States in a few weeks. She wanted action, she was that kind of girl – sorry, woman. That was one of the things he loved about her . . . And her body and her laugh, and her sharpness and energy, and the way she rode an exercise bike.

He looked at his wife, her shiny hair swinging around her face, cut in the same simple style for years (but why change? It suited her) and felt fondness and regret. He wondered how strong she was and how she'd cope with life on her own . . . Without him, without a husband. He shivered.

Isabel squeezed his arm tighter, leaned closer. 'Are you cold, darling? There is a nip in the air. Shall we head for home?'

'Good idea. I could do with a cup of coffee. Jasper!'

He whistled for the dog, who was investigating a hole in the remains of a tree, and they headed down the long, bumpy slope towards the park gate, the one that led to home. Isabel liked this stretch. The mounds of grass always reminded her of those map symbols she used to draw carefully in geography lessons at school. So long ago. Where had all the time gone? She was about to say this to Michael when he turned to her. She noticed the frown lines bunching on his forehead between his eyes as he said, 'Well, another year gone, another one beginning. Round it goes. What do you think then Isabel? Is it time for change this year?'

He thought how stilted that sounded but he was doing his best to edge towards the topic of changing his life – their lives.

'Yes, why not? I've been thinking that myself. In fact, I've –'

Her positive response took him by surprise. The last thing he had imagined was that Isabel wanted change of any kind. She liked things as they were didn't she? He interrupted her. 'Oh, really? What do you mean? And what were you going to say?'

'I've got something to tell you.'

'Go on, then. I'm intrigued . . .'

He was teasing – for how could Isabel possibly intrigue him after all this time? He tried to imagine what on earth it could be. She was smiling but sounded serious. Her cheeks were pink and it wasn't just from the cold air.

Isabel paused, faced Michael, held his arms. They were standing under an oak tree. The dog paused too.

'Michael, I'm pregnant.'

His expression froze, his mouth dropped. He couldn't speak.

'I'm pregnant. I'm going to have a baby, another child.'

'What? What did you say?'

'I said –'

'I heard what you said! But what do you *mean*?'

His voice was so loud that the dog whimpered and went behind the tree.

'Please Michael, calm down –'

'Calm down? After what you've just told me? I can't understand it. How can you be?'

'Oh, in the usual way.' She laughed. How could she? 'You know – you, me, in bed.'

'For Christ's sake, you know what I mean.' He took a deep breath, trying to control his emotions, and pushed back his hair. He always did that when troubled; perhaps it reassured him, Isabel thought, the feeling of his still-abundant hair as he ran his fingers through it.

He made an effort to sound more reasonable. 'I'm just so surprised. You must admit, it is unexpected. I never thought – well, we have our two children and they're practically off our hands now, and having another child is surely not part of the scenario, is it?'

Isabel's cheeks grew pinker. She leant against the tree.

7

'Scenario? I wasn't aware that there was one. I admit it wasn't planned, but –'

'It certainly wasn't! And, anyway, are you sure? Perhaps it could be something else.'

'I'm sure. I've done two pregnancy tests, both positive. Of course I'll go to the doctor to have it confirmed. This week probably.'

'I still don't see how this happened. I thought we were covered, well, you know, your coil.' He said it with difficulty. They hardly ever discussed these things.

Isabel came to his rescue and explained what had happened. She'd had her coil removed in October, routine stuff (it was past its use-by date), and had decided to give her body a rest, just for a while. No devices, no pills, no complicated calculations.

'So let me get this straight, Isabel, we weren't using any contraception?'

'Well, no. But –'

'But nothing! Don't you think you should have talked to me about it, or at least told me?'

She hadn't discussed it with Michael because he was at best bored, at worst repulsed, by what he perceived as women's things, all matters gynaecological, and Isabel had always accepted that as the way he was, his generation, whatever.

But she hadn't thought the lack of her coil might be a problem – after all, they didn't make love often, and then there was her age and decreasing fertility. In her defence she said, 'You've always left it to me before, you've always seen that whole thing as my responsibility.'

'Responsibility! That's a fine word for you to use now. I don't think you've behaved very responsibly, do you?' He dug his hands in his pockets, his head down, not wanting to look at her.

'Michael, why are you being like this? Is it so bad? I'm only pregnant, for God's sake!'

'But you're forty-four –'

'Forty-*three*.'

'Forty-three then, nearly forty-four and I'm almost forty-eight and . . . Well, I thought all that was behind us. There are other things to do, to look forward to –'

8

'But we're not so old. These days –'

'Oh, I've had enough of this. Can we at least go home and discuss it there? Then decide what you're – what we're going to do.' He began to walk away.

'Do? What do you mean, *do*?'

He was about to reply when he tripped over a tree root and went sprawling across the ground. For a second everything was spinning around him: branches, sky, Isabel, everything upside-down. Isabel hesitated but before she could help him up, he had scrambled to his feet, brushing earth off his suede coat. He muttered something about home then stomped off, limping slightly.

Jasper took his head out of a rabbit hole, looked from one to the other and barked, confused. Michael whistled and the dog bounded after him.

Isabel stood alone. She didn't want to hurry after him. She couldn't face an argument and she didn't want to have to pretend to Dominic and Gemma that everything was all right. By now they would probably be slumped over the kitchen table, eating an extended breakfast, leaving scattered sugar and sticky marmalade spoons and crumbs and coffee granules over every available surface, the radio blaring. Oh God, did she really want to have another child?

She called out to Michael that she'd be home soon but wasn't sure if he heard her. She decided to stroll back to the pond and watch the swans. That should have a calming effect.

Michael walked as fast as he could, away from Isabel, away from that damned tree. Falling over was as much a blow to his dignity as to his knee. It was odd falling over as an adult: you were used to it as a child, it was commonplace. But now the sudden fall, the physicality of it, was a shock. Like Isabel's news, he thought. What was he going to do now? He could hardly tell her about Ellen until this was sorted out. And what would he tell Ellen? He had encouraged her to believe that he and Isabel no longer had a sex life. They did, of course, partly because he didn't want Isabel to suspect anything. And it was still pleasant, if unchallenging.

What a bloody mess, he thought, and kicked savagely at a

hummock of grass, which was sturdier than it appeared and he stumbled, nearly falling again. He cursed the grass, cursed Isabel, cursed everything.

Isabel walked around the pond, feeling a little conspicuous as a lone woman. Everyone else in the park seemed to be part of a unit: groups of friends; couples; families.

She couldn't see the two white swans. Had they flown away? Could they fly? Then she noticed a single black swan emerging slowly from the bulrushes, a gleaming magnificent creature. She watched it glide across the water and felt chilled. A brisk walk home will do me good, she decided. She trudged off down one of the less-used paths and thought about Michael, trying to rationalise his reaction. It was understandable: she'd sprung the news on him, while she'd already had a few days to get accustomed to it. But there was something else. Why was he so angry?

Tears filled her eyes and she let them fall. She felt so alone. A woman, walking and crying in the park – what would people think? She didn't care.

Michael's words about deciding what to do reverberated in her mind. It was no use pretending she didn't understand his meaning. Thoughts of a termination had entered her mind, of course they had. But so far she had dismissed them.

Her hand went to her stomach and she kept it there, on top of her sheepskin coat, even though it was much too early to feel any evidence of a baby. A baby. It was weird, she admitted. But it could be that she'd have to get used to it – and so would Michael. Wouldn't he?

3

Isabel let herself into the house. She assumed that Michael had arrived home – yes, there was Jasper's lead hanging in the porch. Everything was quiet, there were no thumping echoes of music, so the children must still be in bed.

She paused for a moment. Sunlight spilled through the stained-glass panels of the front door, projecting coloured shapes into the hall. She loved this house. It never failed to enfold her with its atmosphere of warmth and plenty; it gave her a sense of well-being. Home.

They had moved here when the children were small, choosing the house for its square solidity, its potential space and comfort, its proximity to the park. Michael had just been made a partner, one of the youngest ever in the firm's history, so they could afford it. Isabel remembered that not long after they'd settled in she'd met an elderly neighbour in the street, who'd exclaimed, 'Oh, you're the new young family at number thirty-three!' How Isabel had relished that description. It had given her a buzz, infusing her with pride for her two bonny toddlers, her handsome, successful lawyer husband, her desirable house. She had felt more than fortunate, she'd felt blessed. Everything had seemed complete. She had wanted for nothing, wanted nothing to be changed.

Happy times, she reflected. Looking back, things appeared simpler then. Was that just because the children were younger, demanding in a more straightforward way, easier to care for, to love? And, of course, she and Michael had been younger too. There was bound to be wear and tear as you got older – and she wasn't just thinking of their bodies, themselves, but their relationship too.

Isabel sighed and went into the kitchen, which stretched across the back of the house. She spent a lot of time in here, more than she now needed to, but it was where she'd lived a lot of her life: cooking and organising and reading and thinking, talking to friends, making phone calls. And in the past the children had played at one end while she was busy at the other. She sometimes fantasised that if she were to be interviewed by a Sunday newspaper about a room of her own, it would have to be the kitchen. Where else? She would imagine the photograph: she'd be in crisp white shirt and jeans, leaning against the island worktop with its blue handmade Provençal tiles. Copper bowls and antique kitchen utensils, plaits of garlic and bundles of herbs hung from the wooden rack above. An appealing picture. Then she'd quickly dismiss the image from her head as being just too fanciful – who was she kidding, why on earth would anyone want to interview her?

The kitchen has had several lives. It had sprung from three

small rooms at the back of the house, overlooking the garden. One of the Turners' (or rather their builders') first tasks was to knock them through into one big space. Its initial incarnation was hi-tech, Italian, with a black rubber floor and shiny cabinets. Later it was transformed into pretty country-look pine, carved and decorated and embellished, with flowery cushions tied on the chairs, and a wooden floor. Now, although the wooden floor remained it was painted and stencilled, and the overall look was bleached and pale, more old Scandinavian than hearty English. Isabel had decided that this would do. No more new kitchens.

She drank a glass of water and contemplated the familiar scene. This is me, she thought, this kitchen. This and the rest of the house and the garden. And the cottage in Devon. And the shop, though that's half Angela's. My life. Oh, and the children, of course. The children. The unit of two, complete. 'How nice to have one of each,' people always said. But a third? The words 'the children' would no longer mean the same.

And Michael. Where was he? she wondered. He had probably taken refuge in the study, a small room at the side of the house, where very little studying actually went on. In reality it was Michael's den, his hideaway. Occasionally he did bring work home but not often. Isabel never asked what he did in there for the rest of the time, she recognised that he needed some personal space. She aimed to be a tolerant, easy-going person, and believed in letting people be. Whether she was born that way or learnt it from her mother, she wasn't sure, and no one in Isabel's family went in for much analysis.

A half-full cafetière of cold coffee stood on the table – a sign of Michael. Isabel rinsed it out, an unpopular task, chasing the specks of coffee grounds around the sink with a jet of water from the mixer tap, then made some more. She wondered how long he needed to digest her news, how long before he adjusted and behaved in a more civilised manner towards her. She needed to talk to him, she wanted him to tell her that everything would be all right.

'Morning, Mum. That coffee smells good – I could do with some.' Her daughter shuffled into the room, barefoot, pulling a sweater on over her nightshirt then slumping at the table.

'Hello, Gem. Happy New Year! Good party last night?'

'Oh, yeah, Happy New Year.' Even in her hung-over state, Gemma remembered that these things mattered to her mother. 'Party was good – parties, I should say, we ended up going to three . . . Oh, thanks, Mum, you're an angel.' She gave Isabel a smile before bending her head over the mug of coffee.

Isabel regarded her daughter, her first-born. The product of her and Michael, of their comfortable middle-class suburban home, of an expensive education, of ballet and piano and riding lessons, and lengthy, complicated orthodontic treatment. Still, she does have a great smile. And Gemma smiles a lot.

She gazed down at her daughter's tangled tawny hair and wondered yet again what Gemma would do with her life . . . Michael had once said – fondly and not in his daughter's presence, thank God – that hopefully she'd meet a decent chap, preferably with money, and marry him. When Isabel had protested and reminded him it was the 1990s he had claimed to be joking, only joking.

But what did Gemma want? For now, she just wanted to have a good time. She'd given up on her A levels because she wasn't really interested, and had since completed a word-processing course (just like me, thought Isabel, but it was a secretarial course then, and did my father write me off too, in the nicest possible way, because I was female?) and a cookery course and was now toying with what to do next. But Gemma didn't seem worried: she was happy as long as she had money – and she was willing to earn it through a succession of temporary jobs – and her circle of friends, and as long as no one nagged her about her future. Dominic, her brother, just eighteen months younger, was rather different, more single-minded, Isabel supposed. She frequently had to resist the notion in her own mind that the differences between her children were rooted in gender. It could just be that Gemma takes after me and Dominic after Michael, she'd think. But there you go, gender again, she'd tell herself, and would resolve to try not to limit her daughter with her own limitations.

'So Gem, did you see Dominic on your travels last night?'

'Sort of. He was at Melissa's.'

'Melissa's?'

'You know, Lucy's cousin, lives in Fulham. Dom was there, all over some girl.'

'Oh, did you know her?' Isabel tried to sound casual. She was forced to ask Gemma questions because her son did not confide in her or even really talk to her any more.

'Dunno. Couldn't see her face, what with Dom and all her hair. It was almost longer than her skirt! He was behaving like a typical sex-starved public schoolboy let off the leash.'

'Gemma, please!'

'You know what I mean, Mum. Any more coffee?'

Isabel refilled her mug and was rewarded with the smile and a squeeze of the arm. She went off to find Michael, leaving Gemma rooting around the kitchen for breakfast – she liked to create idiosyncratic concoctions. Isabel was grateful that she did actually eat and that they'd never had to worry about anorexia or bulimia, like some other parents they knew.

The study door was closed. She knocked and after a while Michael replied, 'Come!'

She opened the door gently, spoke gently too. 'Coffee, Michael? I've just made some.' She wanted to coax him out of his lair; she wanted to talk – about her pregnancy, the future, anything.

He looked up, as if he'd been in the middle of something important. 'Yes, OK, thanks.'

'And something to eat?'

'Just coffee. I'll be along in a minute.'

Isabel retreated.

Michael had been sitting and staring at the collection of objects on the desk – his Mont Blanc pen, his Psion, the stone paperweight, an Evian bottle – trying to convince himself that Isabel was pregnant. He supposed it must be true – it wasn't something she'd concoct, surely? He got up reluctantly. He didn't really have any excuse to stay in the study, not on New Year's Day, but he wanted to clear his mind, to think things through. Normally he would go to the health club, exercise it all away, but he wasn't sure if it was open today. Ellen would know. But Ellen wasn't here.

The kitchen was full of light and sound and the smell of coffee. It hummed and buzzed. There was some funky music on the radio and Isabel and Gemma were chattering like small birds, laughing about something that did not include him. The dog padded around, wanting attention. All that was missing was the cat (but no, there it was, sleeping on a chair) and Dominic to complete the family scene. The Turner family. Oh, and me, he thought.

'Where's Dominic – still in bed?'

'Probably, haven't seen him yet.' His daughter approached him, her mouth full of cinnamon toast. 'Happy New Year, Dad.'

'Happy New Year, Gem,' he said, returning her loud, messy kiss with a brush of his lips on her bulging cheek. He caught Isabel's eye. She poured him coffee and handed it to him with a small smile. She had that determined look – he knew it well.

'Gemma darling, if you're going upstairs to have a bath, can you give that brother of yours a shout? He should be stirring by now.'

As Isabel tactfully dispatched her daughter Michael scrutinised his wife over his coffee cup. Still the same slim, compact body, barely different from when he first met her. A straightforward body, a straightforward woman. No sign of pregnancy. But then how pregnant was she? She hadn't yet told him. He felt that there was a lot he didn't know.

'All right, but he'll probably curse me. I'll be in the bath then. If anyone rings, say I'll ring them in about an hour.'

She grabbed a banana and left her parents alone. They faced each other across the kitchen.

'Well, has it sunk in yet, Michael?'

'No, not really. You have to admit it's so unexpected, so unlikely.'

'Unlikely? Why? I can see it's unexpected, but unlikely?'

'Don't be petty. You know what I mean.'

'Not really but never mind. Please don't let this develop into an argument about trivia – there's no point. OK, so I'm pregnant, but it's not the end of the world, is it?'

He wanted to reply, yes, it seemed like the end of his world or at least the world he wished for. It was as if a door had slammed shut in his face, just when he thought he'd found the key to open it. Oh Ellen . . .

Michael's silence perplexed Isabel. She went to him and grasped his hands, smiling up into his face, her eyes wet. 'Is it

15

so bad, Michael? *Is* it? We can afford it, I'm healthy and strong, and lots of people have babies late these days.'

'But it's more complicated than that.'

'Well, if it is, we'll deal with it.'

He was temporarily defeated and for the moment could think of nothing to say. Nothing. He avoided her eyes by pulling her to him and holding her. As she sighed and tucked her head into his shoulder, in a familiar move, he despaired.

Dominic burst into the room. 'Now then, now then, not in front of the children, please.' He was half dressed, tucking his T-shirt into jeans, pulling on a sweatshirt, the laces on his boots trailing, his hair damp.

They parted, Isabel lifting her head reluctantly and greeting her son. 'Oh, you're up already. Happy New Year, Dominic.'

He grunted something that sounded like Happy New Year as he stuck his head in the fridge.

'Good night last night, Dom?' his father asked, regarding him fondly.

'Yeah, great. Any coffee? Then I'm going round to Ben's, meeting some people at the Anchor.'

Isabel poured him coffee, but by now he was gulping down a tall glass of orange juice. She was about to suggest, for the hundredth time or more, that he should drink water if he was so thirsty but Michael said, 'The Anchor – is that the pub by the river?'

His tone was approving and Isabel was surprised that he knew the place: Michael had never been a pub person.

Dominic drank a few sips of coffee then said he had to go. He was always in a hurry these days, Isabel thought. She said nothing about breakfast, it would be a waste of breath, nor did she ask what time he'd be back. She did notice a large red mark low on his neck. A love bite. She said nothing about that either.

Michael followed his son into the hall, delving into his wallet. There was a rustle of a note being handed over. Isabel couldn't see how much it was. She sometimes felt he indulged his son too much but that was another thing she kept quiet about. She guessed he did it because he'd never been indulged as a boy and, besides, it was something he enjoyed doing.

As Dominic left he shouted that he'd ring them later, his phone was in his jeans pocket (he'd demanded one for Christmas – 'Everyone has a mobile phone these days, Dad,' he'd said – and now he never went anywhere without it). Then he was gone and it was quiet again.

'Let's hope he works as hard as he plays,' Michael remarked as he came back into the kitchen. Not that he was really concerned, Isabel reflected. So far, Dominic had not let his father down. He performed well at school, he was competitively sporty and he was tall and good-looking (people said he looked like Michael). He seemed to be everything Michael wanted a son to be.

Isabel cleared the kitchen table. 'It's a shame he's rushed off. And I wonder what Gemma's doing today. It would be nice to tell them our news. Together, of course.'

'Our news?'

'About the baby! We've got to tell them sometime.'

'Wait a minute Isabel, hold on! We can't tell them – for God's sake, you've only just told *me*. We haven't even discussed it yet.'

For a moment she gazed at him. 'You're right. I'm sorry. That was silly – I was getting carried away. And of course we should discuss it, that's what I want us to do. I'm confused, too, Michael.' She sat down at the kitchen table and put her head in her hands.

'Let's go in the living room and talk,' he suggested – Gemma was less likely to interrupt them there.

Isabel got up slowly. 'OK. I'll just get a glass of water.'

They sat on opposite sofas in the calm, quiet room. Just the ticking of the Liberty pewter clock (one of the many fine things they'd bought together) on the mantelpiece. Michael tried to prepare himself by imagining his reaction to Isabel's news if there had been no Ellen. (But there was, there was.) How would he have reacted then? That's what he must do, what he must say, for now. The normal reaction of a man his age on being told his forty-three-year-old wife is pregnant. Think yourself into it, he told himself.

'I'm sorry, darling, I am sorry!' Isabel dashed over to sit next to him, turning sideways, her legs curled underneath her, as if she was settling in for a long haul.

'For what exactly? You don't have to be sorry.'

'Sorry for getting pregnant, sorry for feeling I want this baby –'

'Ah. Is that definitely how you feel?'

'I think so! But there's no "definite" about it. My feelings veer in one direction then another. Or perhaps my feelings say one thing and my brain says something else.'

'How do you mean?'

'Maybe it's my hormones all over the place.' She moved closer and put a hand on his knee. Twenty years of intimacy joined them, of day to day and night to night living, of ins and outs and ups and downs. It should be all right, thought Isabel, this should be all right between us. 'What I feel – my instinct is to have the baby. But rationally I know I should consider all the other things – health issues, the effect on our lives, the future . . .'

'Exactly. And not just you. *We* should consider all those things. You're the one who's pregnant, but it affects all of us, me, the children.' Michael patted her hand. 'We need to think this through. Is this what we really want at this time in our lives? How will the children react? And this baby – how will it feel having elderly parents and siblings so much older? Won't that be strange? And as for the health aspect . . . your health, the baby's health. There's so much to consider.'

Isabel withdrew her hand. 'I know that, Michael. I've already said I've been thinking about these things. I'm not stupid, just pregnant!'

'Isabel, please. Calm down. Remember you've got a head start on me here. I only learnt about this a few hours ago, I'm still trying to come to terms with it. And we still haven't discussed it.'

'I thought that's what we were doing now.'

'All right.' He took a deep breath, then exhaled. 'Let's look at the possibilities, discuss them and next we need to decide what to do.'

That was what he'd said in the park. She'd thought then that it was merely part of his initial reaction, arising out of shock and confusion. But here he was, saying it again.

'What is there to decide?'

He met her eyes. 'Isabel, you know what I'm talking about. You must have considered this already, despite your feelings, your *instinct*. We should discuss whether you – we – have the baby or not. After all, it could be argued that –'

'So you're suggesting that we get rid of this baby? *Are* you?'

'Isabel, please. All I'm saying is that we should talk about it. It's one of the options – and there are only two as far as I can see! Being pregnant doesn't necessarily mean there has to be a baby.'

'For God's sake, Michael!' She snorted.

'There's no need to get emotional.'

He was using his lawyer voice, the one that said, shut up and listen to me, I know best. It often irritated her but she usually endured it silently, nodding in the right places. Right now it inflamed her. 'Emotional! I think I have a perfect right to be emotional about this. You're talking about an abortion.'

'But I always thought you were pro-abortion?'

'Yes, yes, I am! Theoretically. No, more than that. But that doesn't automatically mean I should have one! Michael, this is *us* we're talking about here . . .' She faltered.

'I know. This is bloody difficult. Look, we're not getting anywhere. I think I'll go out for a while. Give me time to think.' He walked quickly from the room.

Isabel suddenly felt very tired, as if all the bounce had gone out of her, and she was renowned for her bounciness. She sank back on the sofa and closed her eyes, anticipating the sound of the front door closing. His car roared off.

She felt more confused than ever. His reactions had unnerved her – but what had she expected? She knew what she'd *hoped* for, but in reality that was a different matter.

4

Isabel wandered through the house, distracted and listless. Watery sounds emanated from the children's bathroom – Gemma was still in there, having one of her long soaks. She wouldn't surface for a while.

In the bedroom Isabel shook the duvet and pillows then lay

down on the bed, her hands on her stomach. Through the window she could see the bare branches of the cherry tree. In spring it would be bursting with leaves and flowers and life. And what will I be like then? she thought.

Perhaps she would no longer be pregnant. An abortion might be the best option. But every time she'd tried to confront the idea of termination she kept coming up against this instinct, this strong sense of wanting to have the baby. It transfixed her; it wired her into another system altogether.

She turned on to her side and closed her eyes, thinking of Michael. Despite this instinct of hers, she did have sympathy with his position. Of course it had been a surprise, of course it wasn't ideal ... So what was it about his reaction that troubled her? There was something just beyond her under-standing that she couldn't grasp, like that glimpse of some-thing from the corner of your eye which you were unable to identify before it vanished. Was it that she didn't know him as well as she'd always assumed? A sudden perception over-whelmed her, as she experienced the shock of the familiar turning into the unfamiliar. It had happened sometimes with a word or an object, things, but never before with her husband.

She tried to shake it off with mundane explanations. Maybe he was under excess stress at work, or missing being at work as it was holiday time, or suffering a mid-life crisis, even the male menopause, which she'd been reading about recently. Any of those was possible, or even all of them.

Or could it be that they had reached a point where they each wanted different things in life?

A disturbing thought. She buried her face in the pillow.

Isabel and Michael. Michael and Isabel. They were a couple who had always shared the same ideas, the same aspirations, who had always been in tune. How lucky they had felt to have discovered each other and how often they had said so in the early days of their relationship.

The sweetness of those times ...

Isabel remembered.

1974: she'd been working as a temp in a firm of solicitors near Russell Square: French and Sadler, a warren of oak-panelled offices in a period building, dominated by Mr French at one end and Mr Sadler at the other. For a few weeks Isabel was Mr French's secretary. As temporary assignments went, it was fine: her boss was formal and courteous and did not overload her with work. In return Isabel was quick, efficient, could decipher his handwriting and was decorative without being obviously so. One morning, in the corridor, a young man in a hurry brushed past her, knocking her shoulder. As he apologised, flicking his dark hair off his forehead, Isabel took in his brown eyes and height and rangy frame and long thin fingers clutching a file . . . She flashed him a smile and said that no harm was done. He smiled back and dashed off but he turned to look at her exactly as she turned to look at him. It was one of those eye-locking moments, they later agreed.

Isabel chatted to Mrs Harris, the tea lady, who'd been there for years and knew everything and everybody. 'Oh, that's young Mr Turner,' she told Isabel. 'Just qualified as a solicitor, he's finished his articles and he'll soon be on his way to higher and better things, you mark my words.' She leaned over her display of digestives and custard creams and whispered, 'Fancy him, do you?' Isabel giggled. 'Don't blame you,' said Mrs Harris, 'Now if I was thirty years younger . . . I was a bit of a saucepot myself, you know.'

The awareness between Mr Turner, solicitor, and Miss Wainwright, temporary legal secretary, developed with a glance here, a look there, saying good morning, a touch of their hands as he held the door open for her. Isabel sensed that he was shy and tried to think of a way to take things forward. Fate took a hand, as it sometimes does. One sunny lunchtime Isabel sat on a bench in Russell Square under those tall trees, eating a sandwich and reading the latest issue of *Nova*.

'Do you mind if I join you?'

She looked up and there he was: Michael Turner, with *The Times* and a sandwich of his own. The sun was behind him and in her eyes; she couldn't see his expression but she guessed what it might be. 'Of course not! Please do.' She moved along the bench, setting aside the rest of her egg and cress sandwich, closing *Nova* and turned to him, smiling brightly.

That was the beginning. The next night they went to the cinema – he's not that shy, after all, thought Isabel delight- edly, when he asked her out. A few days later it was a drink after work; at the weekend a walk in Hyde Park (when he took her hand) then a meal at Pizza Express in Soho (culminating in an exploratory goodnight kiss). A predictable pattern, perhaps, a steady progression, no surprises there. But what surprised them both was how well they got on, how easy it was to talk, and how much they did indeed fancy each other. During the next trip to the cinema, a Friday evening, Michael's arm slid around her and Isabel snuggled closer. His stroking fingers just happened to brush the side of her breast and as their faces turned and their lips met they knew that the film was no longer relevant. (In years to come neither of them could ever remember what it was.) As the people in the row behind tutted and sighed they stood up and hurried out into Leicester Square, taking a taxi to his flat in Pimlico and ending up in bed, as they'd hoped they would.

Isabel clearly remembered that first time with Michael. They'd stood in the hallway, kissing and kissing harder and deeper, his hands all over her slippery Biba dress, her hands running up and down his back inside his jacket. She could feel his erection pressing into her stomach. He'd paused, pulled back, looked down at her and said in a fuzzy voice, 'Isabel? Yes?' And she'd said, 'Yes, Michael, yes,' and he'd picked her up – to her astonishment, he actually picked her up – and carried her into the bedroom, one of her blue platform shoes falling off on the way. Admittedly, it wasn't far and she was very light, but the act amazed and delighted her – as did what followed. He laid her on the bed and began fiddling with all those tiny buttons on her dress until she whispered to him, 'Michael, let's just take off all our clothes. And by the way, I'm on the pill.' It happened in a rush, getting naked, and then they were together.

It had been good, so good, they both agreed. Afterwards Michael couldn't stop grinning, Isabel remembered. They spent all weekend in his flat, making love, talking, making love again ... By Sunday evening they had learnt a lot about each other. Their middle names. His ambitions, her unashamed lack of them. 'I'm just a good-time girl,' she'd joked. 'You certainly are,' he'd murmured, nuzzling her left nipple. Their childhoods (although Michael said little about his). Things they liked to do – and not just in bed. Past lovers

(Isabel: two, Michael: four), but none, they insisted, had been serious relationships. It was as if they already knew that this was going to be serious; perhaps it already was.

There we were and here we are, Isabel thought, as she stretched out on their marital bed. They had fitted like two pieces of a jigsaw, the only two pieces. After their second weekend together Michael had announced, 'You realise, Isabel, that we're compatible, and not just sexually . . .' (Love was not mentioned, not yet.) And it was true: the sex was great, but there was more than that. They just – fitted.

And we've been happy, she thought. We still are, she reminded herself. She and Michael, of all people, should be able to deal with this latest development in a civilised manner. She wasn't sure what that might be, but surely there was a way?

Isabel got up reluctantly. It would have been easy to sleep but she'd only wake up feeling guilty. She sighed and went downstairs to the kitchen. It would be good to talk to someone about this pregnancy, she decided. But who? Michael didn't want her to tell anyone, did he? She mulled it over as she made some tea, then settled down at the table with the phone, a large mug and some ginger biscuits. She'd call a friend, a female friend, someone who'd understand.

Across London, in Highbury, in a tall, thin house a bit too near the football ground for comfort, the Marcus family were arriving home, crowding the narrow hall. They'd been somewhere together for once, all of them. On the walk home Beth had felt warmly content at the success of such an outing, but it was rapidly evaporating as her children and husband began complaining that they were starving.

'That's the trouble with these pre-lunch drinks parties – that's all they are, just drinks. It's a cheapskate way of discharging your social responsibilities,' Simon moaned.

'Well, we've done it too – remember? And at least you know what you're getting.'

'Not getting, you mean. Just a few lousy so-called gourmet crisps.'

Beth watched her husband rummage in the fridge. She knew he was feeling particularly irritable because visiting the

Ropers' house always made him feel poor – and resentful. She started to go through the motions of preparing food. Always the provider. The children had vanished to their own rooms or the television, and Simon ate a chunk of cheese and fumed about the injustice of it all. Life, he meant. He compared his abundance of intelligence and qualities with Keith Roper's paltry attributes, and wondered, for the hundredth time, why Keith was so well rewarded. Bloody accountants! What is it about them? And accountants shall inherit the earth, he said.

Beth had heard all this before, and she sympathised, she really did, but right now she couldn't really be bothered and wished he'd move out of the way. She had to walk around him while trying to put together a semblance of a meal from all the post-Christmas bits and pieces left in the fridge and cupboards.

The phone rang. She didn't rush to answer it – she knew from experience that it was unlikely to be for her. She heard the rush and thumps of her three children in various parts of the house as they scrambled to get to a telephone before anyone else. Teenagers. Phone-agers, more like. Now there was shouting. Must they always argue? Then she realised it was Daniel calling out that Isabel was on the phone for her. All her children knew Isabel – they should as she was one of Beth's oldest friends.

She went to take the call in the living room. Simon looked resentful and muttered something about having to make himself a sandwich. Beth suggested he could make everyone some baked beans on toast, closed the door behind her and sank gratefully on to the sofa.

'Isabel, hi! Happy New Year!'

'Happy New Year, Beth. How are you? How was Christmas?'

'Short answer or long?'

Isabel laughed. 'Whichever *you* prefer!'

'I'll spare you the details. Let's just say I'm glad it's over and normal life – or what passes for it around here – can resume. How was your Christmas?'

'Fine. I like it when we're all together. It doesn't happen much any more, so I appreciate it.'

'Lucky you. I suppose I'll get to that stage one day!'

Isabel was used to Beth talking as if motherhood was a

sentence to be endured. How different they were – but they'd learnt to be tolerant of each other long ago. 'You will, Beth.'

'At times I yearn for some time on my own, you know, not to do anything in particular, just to do nothing.'

'You sound tired. You're meant to be on holiday, aren't you?'

'From work, yes. But there's still everything else to do. I'm sorry, Izzy, you didn't ring to hear me moan.'

'You're not moaning. But, anyway, what are friends for?'

'It would be good to see you, just us two.'

'I was thinking that. Could we meet? When does your term start?'

'Not until next week, but the trouble is I've got masses to do before then.'

'Oh. There is something I wanted to talk to you about.'

'Well, tell me, we can talk about it now.'

Isabel paused. The time didn't feel right, she could sense Beth's preoccupation with her own concerns. Beth was always busy, with her job as head of art at a sixth-form college, her children, home and, of course, Simon. Isabel had always thought that he was very demanding. She often wondered how – or even why – Beth put up with him.

'Is everything OK?' Beth spoke into the silence.

'Yes. Everything's fine. It's just that – I'm pregnant.'

'Isabel! Pregnant?'

'Yes, I know, it's unexpected and all that –'

'It certainly is! But are you sure?'

'I've done two tests, both positive.'

'Oh my God. But what will you do? Is it wanted? I'm sorry – I mean, was it planned?'

'No, not really, not planned, that is. But wanted, well, I think so, by me anyway, I think –'

'Oh Isabel. Can you face it, doing it all over again?'

'I don't mind being pregnant, Beth, I enjoyed it before, as far as I can remember. And childbirth isn't so bad.'

'I didn't mean that, I meant the whole damn thing, starting all over again.'

'You sound like Michael.'

'Why? What does he say? How has he taken it? You have told him?'

'Of course! Actually just today, I told him this morning. I've known for a few days. At the moment he's not taking it very well.'

Isabel told Beth what had happened and how Michael had reacted. As she listened Beth found that she felt some sympathy for him, which surprised her as she had never really liked him, had never felt comfortable with him. Michael always seemed too polished, too good-looking. He reminded her of those actors playing senior doctors in television sitcoms: regular-featured, tall, wearing a suit well, with a sweep of dark hair, now greying elegantly. She had sometimes wondered if his smoothness was merely a surface veneer, like plaster rendered over a rough brick wall.

Obviously the news of Isabel's pregnancy had unsettled him and she could see why. But she couldn't say that to her friend. Beth felt she'd be on shaky ground lecturing Isabel about contraception. After all, Beth was the one who'd had an abortion all those years ago. She tucked that memory away swiftly, as she had so many times before, and focused on Isabel.

'I'm sure you'll be able to discuss it with him when he's got over the shock. But you said he'd gone out – do you know where?'

'No idea. He just drove off. Can't be the health club, don't think that's open. But, Beth, I think it's going to be difficult, discussing it with him. We tried today but didn't get very far, just disagreed. Which is unlike us, we usually agree on everything – well, most things. I don't know what I'm going to do . . .' Her voice trailed off.

'Come on. It'll be all right, you'll work it out. Give him some time.' Beth tried to sound jolly and reassuring.

'But supposing I want the baby and he doesn't? What will I do then?'

'Tricky one, Izzy. If it comes to that you'd have to decide what's most important to you.'

'God, I hope it doesn't come to that. Imagine.'

They were both silent for a minute. Beth tried to imagine Isabel defying Michael and proceeding with a pregnancy he didn't want. She felt it was more likely that whatever Michael wanted he would get. Beth had teased Isabel over the years for being too conformist, too ready to play the dutiful wife to

Michael's masterful husband. Isabel invariably replied that she was merely doing what she had chosen to do and wanted to do, while privately reflecting that Beth was more dominated by Simon than she realised – or would admit to.

Beth and Isabel had often remarked that it was surprising that they'd become friends. At first they had been flatmates. Beth, a newly qualified art teacher, had somehow managed to get a lease on an unfurnished flat in a mansion block in Bloomsbury (contacts? pleading? determination? Isabel never quite knew). She considered it a rare prize: no resident landlord, no ghastly furniture or flowery wallpaper to endure. It meant freedom, a Central London address and some security, as long as she could pay the rent. As her salary was so low she'd have to share but there was plenty of room.

A friend from art school had let her down, going off to Greece with a new boyfriend to paint, so Beth had advertised in *Time Out*, hoping she'd find a like-minded soul, leftish and *simpatico*. She interviewed girls, women, for one long Saturday in the bare and empty flat, becoming increasingly desperate and decreasingly confident of her ability to judge human character. There seemed to be something wrong with all of them. She began mentally to jettison some of the qualities she'd been looking for: never mind about the politics, as long as the person seemed . . . well, normal. Then Isabel had breezed in. She sat cross-legged on the wooden floor and was so friendly and enthusiastic and refreshingly straightforward that within twenty minutes Beth had agreed that she could have the room.

Now, nearly twenty-five years later (a fact which made them shriek with amazement), they spoke on the phone regularly but met less often. The demands of families and work, especially for Beth, had a habit of getting in the way.

Isabel briskly set about tidying the kitchen. It gave her a sense of achievement to restore some order. Before Beth had to ring off, saying she could hear a family row developing and as usual she'd have to be the referee, they had made a joint resolution to see each other more this year. They knew they would have to meet alone – in the past they'd discovered that getting both families together was a recipe for disaster. They acknowledged that it was just a matter of making time for themselves and their own needs. Brave words, they both agreed.

As Isabel swept the floor she considered what Beth had said. If she had to, could she defy Michael? This was a new experience, the sense of separating herself from Michael, seeing things differently. So far, this far, their marriage had been based on consensus.

Perhaps she was being unfair. It might not come to that. She told herself she should try to listen to him and understand his point of view, whatever it was. But she couldn't help hoping that when he came back from his solitary drive, or whatever he was doing, he would feel more positively about this pregnancy. Then, who knows? They might even feel like celebrating. I am the eternal optimist, she thought, as she brought a bottle of champagne up from the cellar and put it in the fridge.

5

Michael relaxed a little once he was in his car, driving fast through the suburban streets with Tina Turner blasting from the stereo (she remained a favourite despite his family's teasing), singing about people needing heroes. It was good to be alone and to be out of the house. A small kind of freedom, he thought. He tapped his fingers in time to the music, and wondered where to go.

How circumscribed my life is, he thought. Like one of those maps you had to draw at school, a map of your life. His present one, excluding Ellen, wouldn't have many points on it. Home (London). Second home (Devon). Work. The gym. A few restaurants. That was about it. He supposed it was fairly standard for a man of his age. Standard, average, ordinary. Did anyone ever think they'd turn out that way?

Yet this life he had achieved was what he had desired, what he strove for when he was younger. Success, security, respectability. An intelligent, loyal, pretty wife, two healthy, strong children, a comfortable house in a good part of London. This was the world Michael had imagined as a child, a world glimpsed in those reading primers at primary school (*Janet and*

John . . . or was it *Peter and Jane*?, those fortunate middle-class children in clean white socks, playing in suburban gardens with wonderful mummies and kindly all-providing daddies). A distant world from his own childhood in a soot-grimed corner of South London, run-down and pitted with bomb-sites after the war. The family house he now lived in was well removed from his childhood home, although geographically it was not that distant. He felt he had travelled far. The two-up, two-down terraced house rented from a charitable foundation, with no bathroom and an outside lavatory (some charity) was still ingrained in his mind. He had consciously kept it there for years as an incentive for hard work and ambition. His mother had said, 'He's going places, our Michael,' when he passed the eleven-plus (whether it was said with pride or something else he'd never fathomed). And going places was what he had intended to do. His father had said nothing except that he supposed he'd have to fork out now for some fancy uniform. Michael had not been able to think about his father for years without a tightness forming in his chest. Anger mainly, with a selfish, mean man, who drank and gambled the money he earned from a series of menial jobs. And other sorts of 'jobs'? There had been hints from the children who played in the street that his father was involved in someone's gang, thieving, they called it. Michael never knew if it was true – if it was, he'd never been caught. Only by an early death, he thought grimly.

Soon after meeting Isabel he'd told her that he would have got nowhere without the 1944 Education Act and the eleven-plus. (Perhaps he was somewhat pompous.) She'd been puzzled: it meant little to her. He remembered she'd laughed and said that he'd got *everywhere* with her, and she'd taken him back to bed.

If education had been one gateway to the future, Isabel had been another. He'd quickly realised that her ease, her confidence, her acceptable accent (combined with her surprising lack of snobbery) would help him find his way. It wasn't just that, he thought, she'd been so unexpectedly uninhibited and sexy, but wholesome too, somehow . . . and they'd got on so well. Plus there'd been such a sweetness about her. When she'd heard that both his parents were dead (thank God, he'd thought, he didn't have to introduce her to them), she'd hugged him and called him her poor little orphan, even though he was twenty-five.

Dear Isabel. None of this was her fault, not really. It wasn't anyone's *fault*, not directly. As Gemma frequently said, 'Stuff happens, shit happens,' and he was increasingly inclined to agree with her (while not approving of her language).

Michael turned into the main road, cursing the traffic and glaring at hesitant bank-holiday drivers. As he headed towards Central London he realised he was on the route to his office. Hardly surprising really, as it was where he spent most of his life. He could go there as he had his office keys in the car. It wasn't unknown for partners to go in to work on official holidays – it was accepted that sometimes the office served as a refuge from home. The quiet and calm appealed to him now as he needed to keep a clear head and concentrate on Isabel, this baby, the whole damn thing. What a bloody disaster. All he really wanted to do was think about Ellen, the next best thing to being with her. Oh Ellen.

Stuck in a jam at Hammersmith, he indulged in a few moments of pleasure, closing his eyes, thinking about the first time they had met. Her long legs stretching on the machine in the gym, her arms pumping, shining with sweat, her face closed and focused, a damp patch down the middle of her leotard . . . He had watched her, although he did not make a habit of watching women in the gym (who wanted to be considered a creep?), and when she paused, relaxed, and lifted her head, she had caught his eye. And grinned. She eased herself off the machine and he slowed down on the exercise bike, noticing how tall she was, how lean, yet seeing the round outline of her breasts, the central points of her nipples, like the stylised drawings of children.

Who had started it, smiling and saying, 'Hi'? When they reminisced like lovers do, he thought that he had spoken first, but Ellen insisted that it had been her. Whoever. Perhaps they had spoken simultaneously. Whatever. It had led to a friendly chat about the benefits of the different machines and the facilities at the club, then they had drifted to the café and sat in a comradely way, towels around their shoulders, drinking iced mineral water, eyeing each other up and down, their thighs close . . . The conversation edged towards the personal – their names, her American accent. It had certainly been attraction at first sight.

Michael groaned aloud. Why was she so far away? Why was he married? Why was Isabel pregnant? This was ridiculous, his thoughts swerving from Isabel to Ellen then back to Isabel again. It was really no way to live, was it? He banged his fist against the steering-wheel in frustration, and as the traffic started moving he decided against the office and turned in the direction of Ellen's flat.

Since meeting Ellen and starting the affair – although he didn't like to call it that, it sounded so . . . so commonplace – he had tried not to do too much soul-searching. It sapped his energy and he needed more of that than ever, running these two parallel lives. He'd read an article in a men's magazine which said that the secret for successfully maintaining a marriage and a mistress was to *compartmentalise*. He disliked all that clichéd mistress stuff – and he knew Ellen would be furious to be described as one – yet the compartments strategy seemed sensible. But it was bloody difficult to put it into practice. And he couldn't help a certain amount of soul-searching, it was inevitable. He'd be a monster if he didn't sometimes agonise about the situation, he thought.

Michael had asked himself, 'Why?' many times, perhaps anticipating the moment when Isabel would ask him the same question. There seemed to be more than one answer.

He'd got to the point – when? Maybe a year ago – where he looked at his life, the very life he thought he'd always wanted, and he'd wondered, 'Is this it? What now?' More of the same, possibly less of the same. Getting older, approaching the downhill slope. These thoughts, these feelings, began to seep into everything he did. Did Isabel feel the same? She showed no signs of it (but then maybe neither did he) and she was younger than him, and her life was and had been different . . . He didn't discuss it with her; he didn't discuss it with anyone.

So did that mean he had been looking for distraction? he reflected. Not consciously, he decided. He had not gone looking for it, as they said.

But he had met Ellen. And that was it. The first time he had been unfaithful to his wife. But why Ellen? he asked himself.

That was easy to answer. Not because she was there (although she was) but because she was Ellen.

Michael sat in his car outside Ellen's empty flat. He felt very alone. The inner-city streets were deserted, there was that unnatural bank-holiday silence. He gazed up at her windows, wishing he could go inside, sit on her sofa, lie on her bed, smell the echoes of her perfume, be among her things. But she had never offered him a key – not yet – and he had felt he couldn't ask.

She lived on the top floor of a converted school near Holborn, a solid Victorian building with the old crests of the London School Board still in place, resolutely part of the brickwork. What faith they'd had in the future, assuming the permanence of the school, the perpetual flow of small children through entrances marked in terracotta: *Girls, Boys, Mixed Infants.* The playground was now the car park, hidden behind the original high wall newly equipped with security gates. A year or two ago Michael had seen an advertisement for this conversion in one of those glossy property magazines that came thudding through the door every month. 'Loft-style apartments,' it had said. 'Manhattan living in Central London.' It had seemed strange, for as a small boy he had attended a primary school just like it. These double- and triple-decker red-brick buildings still dotted the landscape of London, once beacons of learning and dependability. Another distance travelled, Michael thought.

He remembered the first time he had come here, the first time he and Ellen had made love. Her apartment must have been created out of two classrooms knocked together. The tall windows still remained, but set high enough in the wall so that small children could not have looked out. Her bed was on a mezzanine floor constructed over the open living space below. As they'd climbed the wood and metal stairs together he felt as if he were entering the magical kingdom of a princess. He had felt transformed. And more alive than he had felt for a long time.

He tried to drag his mind back to Isabel. She seemed to have no idea that he was involved with someone else. There was never any sign of suspicion. His excuses were unoriginal, he thought – working late, seeing clients, going to the gym . . .

But, then, Isabel was relatively innocent of the world of work, his kind of work, and she had a trusting nature. She not only trusted him, she thought well of him too, he knew. Oh, shit.

I must try to be fair to Isabel, that's the least I can do, he told himself. But was it only this morning that he had stepped out on that walk with her, planning to tell her about Ellen and his desire to leave? It seemed so far away and long ago, frozen in time like a fly trapped in amber. What *was* he going to do?

He clung to his idea that he should react to her pregnancy as he would have done if there had been no Ellen. He would still have been angry, he knew, as she had got them into this situation without consulting him. And he knew, too, that he would not have wanted another baby. His two children were enough, more than enough. But this was Isabel, this was *us*, as she'd said so poignantly. The familiar us: marriage, home, family. His problem – *one* of his problems – was that there was another 'us': Michael and Ellen.

He sighed wearily and reluctantly started the engine. Time to go home and face Isabel. One step at a time, he told himself. Try to convince her that this baby was not a good idea, then take it from there.

6

They were getting nowhere. Late one night Michael sighed and said, 'We seem to have reached an impasse.'

That sounded misleadingly like an achievement, thought Isabel, for of course they had not actually reached anywhere. As they'd talked – *again* – an image had come into her mind of one of those executive toys (Michael used to have one on his desk in the eighties) with chrome balls on wires. You hit one against another, *clunk*, and that was it. Perpetual motion but getting nowhere. Like their conversations, which were turning into confrontations. What it now came down to was Isabel saying that she didn't think she could get rid of the baby – *clunk* – and Michael saying he didn't think he could handle having another child. *Clunk*.

They may have approached each other with good will

(remember, this is *us*), they may have begun these discussions with good intentions (Isabel trying to be fair to Michael, Michael trying to be fair to Isabel) but somehow it wasn't working. It was as if they took up their positions and faced each other from opposite corners. The distance between them grew day by day.

Isabel had told herself to be patient with Michael: his initial response was understandable. She was prepared to sympathise with his feelings, but when he showed no signs of adjusting or shifting his views she became less and less understanding. As the depths of his aversion to the pregnancy were revealed her own feelings crystallised. If he could be so entrenched, so could she.

Michael ran out of ways to challenge her. Last night in bed he had turned to her – for a second Isabel had a wild hope that he was about to hold her or kiss her – and said solemnly, 'Here it is, then. It seems that you want this baby and I don't. So what do we do now? Who decides, Isabel? Who decides?'

She did not know the answer.

Isabel was due at the doctor's in an hour, to have her pregnancy confirmed. There was no rush. She sat alone at the kitchen table, slowly eating a bowl of live natural yoghurt and a chopped banana for breakfast. Lately, at moments like these, she found herself thinking more and more about the past.

She tried to remember what her first two pregnancies had been like in the early stages. Had she been nauseous with Gemma, yet not with Dominic? And the tiredness that kept overwhelming her, at what stage had that happened before? Had it been less when she was younger? The experiences were clouded by a fog and she could not think her way through it clearly. Where did all those memories go? She sometimes wondered why you couldn't remember the whole of your life, second by second, minute by minute, instant and total recall. Yet if you could, you'd go mad.

Isabel cleared away the breakfast things. As she put the tub of yogurt back in the fridge, she saw the unopened bottle of champagne. She began to feel a little sorry for herself, something she rarely did. Her mother used to say, 'Feeling sorry for ourselves is something we don't do, not in this family. Best just to get on with things.' Isabel sighed. Even now – especially now? – she missed having the sort of mother whose shoulder you could cry on, who'd give you a hug and say, 'There, there, it will be all right,' however old you were. Hilary, her mother, had always been firm and brisk with Isabel and her older brother John. Kindly but distant. She had encouraged her offspring to be strong and independent, although as Isabel grew up it occurred to her that maybe it was for her mother's benefit as much as theirs. Well, we're certainly independent now, independent of each other anyway, she reflected. Any closeness to her brother had diminished when he was sent away to boarding-school. Now a research scientist, he'd lived in Toronto for years with his Canadian wife and children, and Isabel's main contact with him was through Christmas cards. Her parents had moved to Menorca, to enjoy a comfortable retirement with their house and boat and the social whirl of the expatriate community, fuelled by the excellent local gin. 'There's life in the old sea-dogs yet!' her father had said when he left his desk job in the navy and announced their decision to live abroad.

Distance, more distance, thought Isabel. It seemed to permeate her life.

Her father being in the navy had been the dominant factor throughout Isabel's childhood: she never really became accustomed to the frequent moves, the many different schools, the repeated making and breaking of friendships. There had been no getting around it, no complaining or rebelling. When she tried to protest, her mother would give her a good talking to, as she termed it, dismissing the sacrifices that had to be made if you were a naval family . . . The sense of duty, the idea of service to queen and country had to be cultivated. Her father would extol the admirable traditions of Wainwright vice-admirals stretching back through time . . . Isabel learnt not to listen. What a relief it was when she and Angela (also a product of a naval family) discovered each other at their girls' school in Devon, the final school for both. They became allies and their friendship was sealed with the shared confession that every time they heard the word naval it conjured up the confusing image of a belly-button. Together they giggled at protocol, dismissed the idea of rank, rejected hierarchy. None of it was too serious but it gave them a space to find – and be – themselves.

Isabel wondered if she was as strong as her mother had trained her to be. Strong enough to go through with this pregnancy, despite Michael's objections?

It was Michael who had always represented strength to Isabel; once, soon after they were married, she had referred to him self-effacingly as her rock, the one she'd cling to in stormy seas . . . He'd been puzzled. It took her a while to realise that Michael regarded *her* as rock solid: he saw her as the one with the secure background, the respectability, the established middle-class family, the right accent, the conventional upbringing. That's how it appeared to an outsider, but how could you explain the shifting sands of her childhood and the particular sort of insecurity it caused?

So together she and Michael had carefully created their own security, their own mutual safe haven. Marriage, the home, children, his career. Material comforts, success. A straightforward, satisfactory life. And so far it had seemed watertight. Now she wasn't so sure.

Isabel walked briskly home from the doctor's surgery, glad to be outside in the cold air. The waiting room had been filled with the typical January crowd, coughing and sniffling loudly. She'd felt out of place, having no ailments and being merely pregnant, and had tried to immerse herself in *Country Life*. At least it was a fairly recent issue.

Her attention was caught by a mother and baby. The woman was young and becoming increasingly anxious about the cries of her child. She resorted to pacing the room, up the corridor and back again, jiggling the baby on her shoulder, attempting to soothe it with words that were actually directed at the adults trying to ignore the noise. 'What's the matter? Is your tummy hurting? You can't be hungry again!'

Isabel caught her eye and smiled sympathetically but could see that she was too exhausted and preoccupied to smile back. As she turned for another circuit Isabel glimpsed the back of the baby's neck, that special place, soft and creased above the towelling collar. Sensations came flooding back to her, how she had loved to nuzzle and kiss Dominic and Gemma there, breathing in their smell and sweetness, experiencing the almost damp quality of the satiny skin.

How could Michael not want this baby? she thought. Be fair, she told herself, he had probably never felt that intense physical closeness, those delights of a baby, or she assumed he hadn't. But, still, how could he be so against the idea? It wasn't just that he lacked enthusiasm – that she could live with, she even felt it herself at times. It was his antagonistic attitude that perplexed her. By now she'd thought they'd be, well, making the best of it.

Now the baby in the waiting room was really crying, with that desperate and insistent squeal Isabel recognised. Nothing less than feeding would suffice, she knew. The mother probably knew that too but seemed reluctant to acknowledge it. Perhaps she was too shy to breastfeed in public, or had not brought a prepared bottle. She too was desperate, Isabel could see, with that need of new mothers for someone else to take over, to shoulder the baby and the responsibility. Isabel had been wondering if she should offer to help when she had heard her name called at last.

Dr Finch was friendly and efficient as usual, examining her internally with the minimum of fuss and confirming the pregnancy, saying that she seemed to be nine weeks. They'd conferred on dates and it looked as though the baby was due about the end of August. She checked Isabel over briefly and took her blood pressure. Everything was fine. Then she sat back in her chair, looked Isabel straight in the eye and asked, 'So how do you feel about this pregnancy?'

Isabel looked back, noticing the shadows under the doctor's eyes. 'How do you mean?'

'Your reaction to the pregnancy.' Her voice softened. 'Was it a surprise?'

'Yes, it was, at first. I – we weren't exactly anticipating this.'

'I remember I took your coil out . . . When was it?' She scanned her computer screen. 'Ah yes. October.'

'That's right.' There was a pause as Isabel recollected what they had discussed at the time: another IUD, or other options, the advisability of using protection – condoms? – until she had decided. She realised that Dr Finch was probably recalling the conversation too. But I haven't done anything wrong, thought

Isabel. I don't owe my doctor an explanation. She added quickly, 'I must – it must have happened a few weeks later. And as you said, a surprise, but I *am* pleased about it.'

Dr Finch smiled. 'Good, that's fine. But if you want to talk about it, any aspect of it, don't hesitate. That's what I'm here for.'

There was a pause.

Did Dr Finch think that she was too old to have this baby? Or even that she might not want to go through with it?

'Mrs Turner?' The doctor inclined towards her. Isabel blinked, trying to banish the tears that were (ridiculously, pathetically, she thought) filling her eyes. 'Would you like to talk about it now?'

Dr Finch leant back in her chair, a sign that she was ready to listen, other patients could wait.

Isabel swallowed. 'When I said I was pleased, well I am, most of the time. I mean, I know it's not ideal, I – we didn't intend it to happen. I realise my age is a factor and of course the health issues concern me but despite all that – Oh God, I'm sorry.' She blew her nose. The doctor pushed a box of tissues to Isabel's side of the desk and waited.

'You see my instinct is to go ahead,' Isabel continued. 'If I felt that I couldn't cope or really couldn't face it then perhaps I'd – I'd have an abortion.'

'Is anyone saying you *should* have a termination?'

'No, not exactly. But Michael, my husband, is not pleased about this news. I thought he'd come round to the idea but so far he shows no signs of doing so.'

'You've talked about it, obviously.'

'God yes! Over and over again. He just seems so hostile . . . And the more negative he is about the whole thing, the more positive I am. Isn't that odd?' Isabel tried to smile.

'Maybe not. Look, I think the best thing I can do as your doctor – apart from listen – is to give you all the facts about pregnancy at your age, any risks associated with the baby, and so on. And I can talk to you about termination, if you'd like that information too. You have a bit of time. You have choices –'

'But only two. Have the baby or not! There's no middle way, is there?'

38

'I know, Isabel. It's not easy.'

She must feel sorry for me, thought Isabel. She's using my first name now.

Dr Finch suggested that Isabel made another appointment for Thursday afternoon, her antenatal day, when they could go through it all in more detail. Isabel agreed, while reflecting that the doctor could say or do nothing about what seemed to be her major problem: Michael.

Isabel stepped carefully over an icy patch on the pavement and turned the corner towards home.

'Isabel! How are you?' her neighbour called from her front garden, appearing from behind some shrubs.

'Oh Jenny, hello. Sorry, I didn't see you.'

'You looked deep in thought.'

'Probably! But what are you doing? Not gardening at this time of year, surely?'

'Er – no, not exactly, although there are usually things you can find to do if you're a mad gardener like me! I was just seeing if any snowdrops are out yet. The sight of them always cheers me up.'

Her voice faltered. Isabel knew from experience that Jenny was never far from tears these days.

'How are you anyway?'

'Oh, you know. Staggering on. Come in for a cup for coffee, Isabel.'

'OK, just a quick one. I've got to go and sort out the stock at the shop today. We reopen next week.'

Jenny's house was quiet and dusty. She lived alone, but not from choice. Graham, her husband of twenty-five years, had left last September. Her two adult sons, the twins, were in Australia, either travelling or working, she wasn't sure which as their communication with her was minimal.

Isabel followed her into the kitchen and watched as Jenny scooped up a mess of books and papers from the table.

'Looks as if you're studying, Jenny.'

'No, no. Just reading up on a few things. Got to find something to do!'

'How's the job search going?'

Jenny filled the kettle, hiding her face from Isabel, reluctant to reveal her despair. Isabel gazed at Jenny's bulk. She wore her unhappiness like an extra layer.

'Pretty hopeless. All the temporary shop work that was available before Christmas has gone. I'm going around the agencies but let's face it, who's going to want a middle-aged woman who's spent most of her life as a wife and mother?'

'Jenny! Come on, you know you've got things to offer. You used to help Graham with his business, didn't you? And you're not middle-aged!'

'I'm older than you, remember. I'm fifty-one this year. That has to be at least middle-aged in my book!'

She placed two mugs of instant coffee on the table and brought out a packet of chocolate digestives. Isabel took one to keep her company.

'Have you thought of taking a course – retraining, computer skills or something like that?'

'Yes, I'm looking into it. But it's a matter of confidence.' Her voice faded.

Isabel saw the tears welling in Jenny's eyes. She was reminded of that childhood rhyme, 'Poor Jenny lies a-weeping'. How did it go? She had a snatch of a memory: standing in a circle of small girls in a school playground, singing seriously, pointing at a figure in the centre. She reached over and squeezed Jenny's hand. 'If there's anything I can do . . .'

'Oh Isabel, you've done more than enough already. You've been such a support since – since Graham left. It must be tedious for you, me always in a state, I'm sorry. I know I've got to pull myself together.' She blew her nose and looked at Isabel brightly. 'Let's not talk about me. How are you? And the family?'

'I'm fine. We're all fine.'

'Good. You're looking well.'

'Am I? Actually, Jen, you probably won't believe this, but I'm pregnant.'

Oh God, it had slipped out.

'Isabel, are you really? Pregnant?' She reached for another biscuit. 'I don't know what to say!'

'I know, it is a surprise.'

'But I didn't know you wanted more children.'

'Well I didn't, not exactly. Or I thought I didn't. This wasn't planned, I must admit.'

'But are you pleased?'

'Most of the time. It's still all a bit confusing.'

'So how pregnant are you?'

'Only about nine weeks. That's what the doctor said, I've just come from there.'

'Anyway, congratulations. Are congratulations in order?'

'Sort of. Do you know, Jenny, that's the nicest reaction I've had so far. Oh shit.'

'Isabel, what's the matter?'

'Bloody hell. I shouldn't really have told you. You see, Michael – oh damn. Look, the children don't know yet, no one really does, so I'd be grateful if you kept this to yourself if you don't mind.'

'Of course. Don't worry – after all, who on earth would I tell?'

Isabel hurried home. Why did she have this need to announce that she was pregnant as if it was wonderful news? Perhaps because part of me feels it is, she decided. But she had to think of Michael and the children too. Who else had she told? Only Beth so far. She'd better ring her, swear her to secrecy, just in case. Beth would probably think she was mad, making a big deal out of nothing. And maybe I am, she thought, maybe I am.

7

Jenny made herself another mug of coffee and continued to work through the packet of biscuits. Lucky Isabel, she thought, not for the first time. Jenny had always liked her, for she was unfailingly friendly and supportive and *nice* – the word could have been invented for her. But she had often envied Isabel too, she couldn't help it. Isabel appeared at ease with herself, a quality that Jenny valued enormously – she'd never managed to achieve that state of grace. How wonderful to be comfortable in your own skin, she thought. Isabel had a certain lightness of touch too: everything she had, everything around her seemed to *work*. Her whole life was enviable. She still had a marriage for a start – Unlike me, Jenny lamented. Michael might be intimidating (so good-looking, so urbane), although he was perfectly pleasant to Jenny on the rare occasions they spoke, but he and Isabel complemented each other, they were a couple, anyone could see that. They seemed happy.

And now Jenny felt an extra twist of envy because Isabel was embarking on something new. A new baby. A late baby. An adventure. What a contrast to me, whose life is over, she thought.

She picked up the books and papers she'd been looking at earlier and spread them across the table. She had been researching the bridges over the Thames, trying to establish which would be the best one for jumping off. Or for throwing herself off – she preferred that image. This had become her secret purpose in life: finding the best way to end it. She'd been through all the arguments as she lay in bed awake and alone, night after night. Did suicide have to be a selfish act? In her case she couldn't see that it would be. Who was there to need her or even to mourn? Her sons barely acknowledged her existence; to Graham she was an embarrassment. She realised she was awash with self-pity but she'd come to view killing herself – and she practised saying it, *killing myself* – as a positive step, the only way forward.

After the shock of Graham's desertion she had at first taken to her bed. It was a kind of hibernation: all she did was sleep and eat and watch television. Eventually she had roused herself enough to try to reassemble her life but had discovered there was nothing left to rebuild it with. No foundations, no building blocks. Days passed slowly to the thudding accompaniment of her inner voice: who am I? What am I? It was hard to come up with any satisfactory answers. All she did know was that she was an overweight middle-aged woman, of no use to anyone. Her husband had flown, her children were gone. To reinvent herself, to get a job and earn some money, to become independent, would take reserves of energy and optimism that she did not possess. She couldn't look to the future for she did not feel that she had one.

What had finally convinced her of the true course of action were the conversations she'd had, or not had, with Graham before Christmas. She had dared to ring the number of his flat in Edinburgh, although he'd informed her threateningly that it was for emergencies only. What exactly was an emergency? she'd wondered, as she'd hovered over the phone. Was his idea of one the same as hers? Unlikely. As he'd said when he'd told her he was leaving, they no longer shared anything, their interests were different, so were their views and ideas, *everything*. They'd grown apart and he wanted – no, he *had* to move on. She had listened open-mouthed as he declared his need to find some space for himself, to discover who he was. Which was why he had accepted the job in Edinburgh. Scotland, the land of his grandfathers, was where he wanted to be.

She had rung – oh, why had she rung? To say hello, to make contact, to share the fact that she'd received a Christmas card from Australia – the boys had actually been in touch and who else was there to tell? She had wanted to hear Graham's voice, partly just to hear it, partly to test her own reaction. And this female voice had answered, a young female voice saying the number.

Jenny stumbled over the words, they would not come.

'Hello? Hello there?' The voice was Scottish.

Jenny eventually managed, 'Is – is Graham there?'

'No, Gray is away just now. At a meeting. Who's that?'

'Jenny.'

The girl, for surely she was a girl, said crisply that she'd tell Gray Jenny had called.

Jenny replaced the receiver. It was wet. She was hot and sweaty, she was trembling. *Gray?* When had he ever been called Gray?

She was a fool, she told herself. She should have known. The signs had been there. She remembered Isabel remarking ages ago that Graham was looking different, he was changing. At some point he had stopped trying to disguise his thinning hair by careful combing and had had it cut really short, close to his head. His clothes had altered too: he'd started wearing polo shirts, or shirts buttoned up without a tie with his suits. And he'd acquired a black shirt and a suede jacket, and replaced his large glasses with small, oval Armani frames. He was looking rather trendy, Isabel had said. Jenny had noticed the visible

43

modifications to her husband, of course, but she had not considered their significance. She had put it down to the new directions he was taking in his work. Towards the end of the eighties Graham had found that being an accountant had become almost fashionable. His skills were in demand, even in unlikely places. His new clients were theatre and dance companies, freelance designers and copywriters, a small fashion house. One thing led to another and he began to call himself a financial consultant, moved his office out of home into a courtyard development in Richmond, and took on staff. He didn't have to rely on Jenny any more for help with paperwork, and it was just as well that clients no longer had to come to the house as Graham felt that Jenny didn't present the right image. Image was everything, he now realised, and he had set about changing his.

What Jenny had not grasped was that Graham was actually evolving into something or someone else. The process was completed last year when he shed his former self and accepted a prestigious (he said) post in arts management in Edinburgh. Now he'd obviously found not only himself but a young female companion too. It all fell into place.

Jenny groaned. It was too, too predictable – so why hadn't she seen it coming? Maybe she really was as pathetic as Graham had said she was. Isabel may have guessed something was happening – perhaps she'd been hinting at it in their chats over coffee about men facing up to fifty. Jenny remembered wondering if there was such a thing as the male menopause. Isabel had snorted and replied that men were bound to muscle in if they thought it would get them the sympathy vote. Jenny thought now that, if anything, Graham was experiencing a second adolescence. It seemed he even had a *girlfriend*.

He had eventually rung her back a few days ago.

'So who's the girl Graham?' She had tried not to ask but it spurted out, she could taste the bile in her mouth.

'Her name is Laura. And she would prefer to be called a woman.'

'Oh really?' Pompous as ever, Jenny thought. 'And you'd prefer to be called Gray now, is that right?'

'Not by you.'

The dislike in his voice made her catch her breath. He used

44

the pause to get down to business, as he put it. It was about the house – he thought it was time they sold it. After all, it was too big for her on her own, wasn't it? Anyone could see that, especially as Mark and Tim seemed keen to stay in Australia – oh yes, he'd heard from them too, hadn't he mentioned it?

Jenny was holding on to the phone so tightly that her hand began to feel numb. She heard the words but they hardly registered. Half share. Estate agents. Improving market. His voice grew distant as she slowly replaced the receiver.

That night in bed she cried for hours, the effect of this latest bombshell. So she was to lose her home as well as everything else. He'd said she could buy him out, of course. Bastard, she'd thought, he knew she had no money and no prospect of any but she hadn't argued or challenged him. Throughout their marriage she had rarely disagreed with him. She'd thought that was what he'd wanted, yet when he'd broken the news that he was leaving he had called her passive. He said her passivity drained him, it sucked away his energy.

She wondered what those years of passivity had done to her. All that time trying to be a good wife and mother, trying to do things right, trying to please. She'd read in a magazine recently that excess weight could be a sign of repressed anger. Was that it? Had she swallowed her own views, her own ideas, her own self, and turned them into flesh, into all this extra baggage that she carried?

She was too tired to work it out. Tired of bothering, of getting up in the morning and trying to face the day and the world with an appearance of bravery. There were times when she had tried to make the best of it, stretching out across the bed and listing all the things about Graham that had annoyed her. How pleased she was not to hear him clipping his nails at night, knowing the pieces would fall on to the carpet for her to hoover up; how good it was not to have him criticise how she looked, her hair, her clothes, her shape. What a relief not to listen to those words 'You should do this', or 'You ought to do that'. There were so many things she knew she would not miss. But what had replaced them, what had replaced him, was this hurt, this confusion. This despair.

When Isabel had seen her in the front garden Jenny had been hiding a For Sale sign under the holly bushes. It had been erected ten minutes earlier. The man was in a rush, the back of his van a felled forest of signs. 'Nothing to do with me', he'd said when she'd protested. So as soon as he'd roared off she took direct action and ripped it down. Graham had obviously gone ahead and instructed the estate agents to put the house on the market, as he'd said he would. No doubt they'd soon be in contact, wanting to photograph and measure and hype this ordinary home into something else.

Jenny was more sure than ever that she was right to choose to end it all. Other women did it, she read about them in the newspapers: wives betrayed by celebrity husbands, wives who felt they had outlived their usefulness, wives who could not face getting old. Jenny had kept the cuttings. She would leaf through the file, weighing up the advantages and disadvantages of their methods of suicide. Overdose? But which pills and how many? Shotgun? Possible if you were a farmer's wife or a member of the hunting set, but where on earth would *she* get a gun? Hanging? She wasn't sure she was competent enough. And they were all messy and relied on family members or friends to find you. *To find the body*. That wasn't fair, Jenny decided. Who would find her? Isabel, perhaps. No, it wouldn't be right.

She needed something more impersonal. That's why she was attracted to the Thames, to the dark, silent water. She imagined it closing over her, protectively, finally. And she'd be found by a professional, one of those policemen who patrolled the river and was used to fishing out bodies and dealing with the whole thing. She'd make sure she had some identification on her so that they'd know who she was. Funny, she thought, identity won't be a problem for me in death as it is in life. Nothing will be a problem! And she turned almost cheerfully to her map of the bridges over the Thames.

8

Isabel let herself into the shop, thinking that the door could do with a new coat of paint – something else for her list of things to discuss with Angie. She kept the Closed sign up – they weren't reopening until after the weekend. It would be busy next week with women bringing in the outfits they'd worn at Christmas or on New Year's Eve and knew they wouldn't – or felt they couldn't – wear again.

It was chilly and smelt a little stale after the long break. She switched on the lights and the heating, plugged in the kettle in the tiny kitchen at the back and looked around.

The shop needed tidying – they'd left it in a bit of a mess when they closed at lunchtime on Christmas Eve, when Angie had had to rush to Heathrow to catch a plane and Isabel had run out of energy, her mind full of all the things she had to do at home, worrying if she'd bought enough food and presents and wrapping paper. And, as always, she'd over-provided in her efforts to make everything as perfect as possible. There were still a few carriers scattered around the house, filled with tissue paper, silver string and bags of mixed nuts. Next Christmas she'd buy less – but, as Michael had pointed out, she said that every year.

Coffee first, then down to work, Isabel thought automatically, but she didn't feel like coffee. She hadn't managed to finish the mug Jenny had made her: it had left a metallic taste in her mouth – was it because she was pregnant? She pressed her stomach, reflecting on the changes that were happening to her body, *in* her body, right now, right this minute and the next one and the next, and how it went on regardless of what she or Michael or anyone thought about it. She felt a little giddy. The idea was alarming – but exciting too, she had to admit.

Rosehip tea, that would be good. There was a jar in the cupboard with assorted herbal tea-bags in little paper envelopes – one of Angie's occasional enthusiasms. Now, first she'd go through the stock book, Isabel decided, to check on what had been sold and what remained unsold, what needed reducing or returning. There was a set of procedures to which they adhered strictly; that way there were fewer hassles and misunderstandings. It had taken her and Angie a while at the beginning to sort out all the conditions of sale and get them right, but now they were clearly stated on a card in the window for all to see. Most of the time the system worked, but they had to be meticulous about record-keeping – hence the stock book. It was a large accounts ledger with ruled columns.

They filled it in by hand – 'We're like Dickensian clerks', Angie said. It had become a running joke between them, but they were reluctant to consider computerisation – why waste money? they both agreed. Now it was time to start a new book, preferably with a different-coloured cover from last year. Isabel began to write all these things down. A list of things to do was a comforting sight, she always thought, it brought a degree of order to life. Not that her life was disordered, it was just that lately she had been feeling rather adrift. Her emotions skittered all over the place, when she allowed them to.

She took her tea and notepad, settled down in the wicker chair by the counter. (It was so important, she and Angie had decided at the start, to make the shop friendly and comfortable: they had provided a couple of chairs and a children's corner with a toy box, and gentle music.) It would be good to get organised by the time Angie came back, as they'd probably spend more time talking than sorting out the shop. There would be a lot of catching up to do. Isabel wanted to hear all about the mystery lover in Spain – she was sure there was one, knowing Angie. And then she'd have to tell Angie her own news.

The shop had been Angie's idea. She'd found herself (or rather *not* found herself, as she'd self-mockingly said to Isabel) reaching forty, feeling she was approaching a dead-end. It was time to take stock. One brief failed marriage in her twenties, an acting career that seemed to have fizzled out (her only work the occasional voiceover), no children (although she'd never really wanted any, had she?), lots of ex-lovers and a worryingly increasing overdraft. But she had her cottage in Mortlake and her cat Desdemona, and her health and her looks, more or less. (More of some bits, less of others.) And good friends like Isabel. She knew that what she had to do was find a new way of making money, a different direction. She'd give up on acting before it gave up on her – although she wouldn't actually announce it and she'd never refer to herself as an ex-actor, she'd just start doing something else. Even regularly working actors had to do that sometimes. Most of her actor friends had part-time jobs, working in galleries or restaurants, cleaning houses, interviewing the public for market-research companies; one ran a flower stall.

Once she'd made the decision she experienced a sense of relief for she was tired of going to auditions and not getting parts, being made to feel old when she wasn't; she was weary of hassling her agent for action.

The question was: what to do? Angie had had the idea while sorting through her wardrobe, trying to create some space. As ever she was reluctant to throw anything away. She hoarded clothes and shoes because they reminded her of good times, or because they were trophies hunted down in charity shops, or because she thought that some day they might be valuable. She had a special section devoted to original Biba: little stripy stretchy dresses, a fitted tweed maxi coat with a velvet collar, a dusky plum shirt with narrow shoulders and full sleeves and tight-buttoned cuffs . . . Her wardrobe was a reliable source for those fancy-dress parties where the invitations said, 'Come as you *were*'.

She told herself she should be strong and get rid of stuff (but not the Biba) in line with her new start. There was a shop in Fulham that took in your clothes and sold them for you – she occasionally went there to buy and had picked up a few designer items, hardly worn. That was it! Who wanted to struggle through traffic all the way to Fulham? There had to be a demand for a shop locally. All those women in Richmond, East Sheen and Barnes with bulging wardrobes – surely they'd like to offload things and even buy too? After all, the recession had hit everyone and no one had as much money, these days.

The next day Angie had insisted Isabel met her for lunch in Sonny's. The menus lay unread as she outlined her plan. She'd even thought of a name: Once or Twice. The waiter kept returning, eyebrows raised, pencil poised, but Angie repeatedly waved him away, talking, explaining, leading up to persuading Isabel to join her in the venture. It turned out that Isabel required little convincing: she told Angie it was a wonderful idea and asked when they could start. It was just what she needed, she thought. Now that Dominic and Gemma were in their teens, she had more time on her hands and had been privately wondering what to do with her life. She had liked being at home all these years – that was what she'd wanted, to be there for Michael, to be with her children. A career had never figured in her plans when she was younger – anyway, a career as what? She'd had no serious education, no encouragement, no training, unless you counted shorthand and typing and how to look after your boss, and she'd certainly had no vocation – except, perhaps, as a wife and mother. And no regrets – but Angie's suggestion was well timed. They had ordered champagne and toasted each other, their friendship and, of course, the shop-to-be. Two hours later, they staggered out of the restaurant, giggling and excited.

That had been four years ago. We've done pretty well, Isabel thought, as she sipped her tea. People had been sceptical at first, thinking Angie too impractical to run a business and Isabel too inexperienced. Michael had been amused at the idea and rather patronising about it, but had let her get on with it. He didn't voice his doubts to Isabel, but he had never thought it would last.

He had been wrong. Other people's lack of belief did not deter Angie and Isabel: it strengthened their belief in themselves. They were determined to make it work. It was like being fifteen again, they laughed, us two taking on the world.

Once or Twice had become something of an institution. They'd placed a few ads in the local newspapers at the beginning but the shop took off through word of mouth. Some women relied on it as a way of raising money, selling off their mistakes or things they shouldn't have bought or that didn't fit any more, or unsuitable presents from husbands or lovers who didn't really know their size or taste. Angie and Isabel got to know their regulars, and often found that they were doing more than reselling clothes. They provided a sympathetic ear for customers when redundancy or bankruptcy struck, or a husband left, or children went off the rails. Lately these events seemed to be happening more and more and the box of tissues they kept under the counter was often in demand. Angie said that Once or Twice seemed to be turning into a community service – perhaps they should apply to the council for a grant?

Someone was knocking at the door. Isabel tried to ignore it but some customers were so persistent, and a Closed sign was no deterrent. Reluctantly she went to see – and there was Gemma, smiling, wearing her mad five-pointed purple hat. Michael said it made her look like a jester; Isabel was quite fond of it.

'Gemma! I didn't realise it was you, come in.'

'Hi Mum. I've been knocking for ages. You looked as if you were in a dream. Anyway, I thought you might want some help. Angie not back?'

'No. Some time over the weekend, I think. I expect she'll ring. It's sweet of you to drop in. I'm just going through the stock and there are a few things you could do. The carpet for a start.'

Gemma took off her long fake-fur coat and dumped it on a chair. She was wearing a shrunken orange sweater and seventies flared velvet jeans, both second-hand from Portobello market. 'Why do you have to look so – so alternative?' Michael had once demanded. 'Alternative to what, Dad? This only seems alternative to *you*,' Gemma had replied calmly.

It was hard to concentrate on the stock book as Gemma thrust the vacuum cleaner over the carpet, banging energetically into the corners. Isabel regarded her affectionately.

'Mum? Are you all right? You're looking dreamy again.'

Isabel watched Gemma wind the lead of the Hoover around its handle: she had been far away, trying to recall the details of her daughter's birth, remembering Michael arriving from work, dashing into the delivery room, then being removed so that he could take off his jacket and tie and put on a gown and mask. His efforts to help her with her breathing, his calm voice telling her, no, it wasn't a good idea to get off the bed and go home, she was going to stay here and have the baby, wasn't she? Gemma arrived soon after. As Isabel had held her for the first time, overwhelmed with joy, relief and other emotions she couldn't yet identify, the sun had streamed through the tall windows and Michael encircled them both in his arms, saying huskily, 'My two girls.'

Isabel blinked. 'Sorry, was I? I was just thinking about when you were born, darling.'

'Mum! Whatever brought that on?'

Isabel wanted to confess, to say, 'I'm pregnant'. She had a desire to embrace her daughter and to feel Gemma hug her back; she imagined the two of them talking about baby names in this quiet, female place. My place, thought Isabel, and Angie's too, of course.

She turned away from the temptation, seeing in her mind

Michael's disapproving face, knowing that she mustn't tell Gemma, not yet. Get a grip, she told herself. 'I'm not sure. Something hormonal, I expect. Oh God, I sound like –'

'You sound like Dominic! Do you know what he says whenever I'm pissed off with him? PMT, he sneers. It's such a cop-out, it's so easy for him, for men, to dismiss everything that way.'

'I know, I know.' Isabel felt weary suddenly and couldn't face a discussion about the shortcomings of her son and men in general. She agreed with Gemma, but what could she do?

Gemma was forcing the Hoover into the small cupboard, pushing and cursing. All she needed to do was to turn it the other way. Isabel showed her, gently.

'I think Dominic has a really dodgy attitude to women, you know, Mum. You should try to sort it out. Sort *him* out!'

Isabel smiled. Gemma liked to display what she saw as her street cred, the result of time spent at the local mixed sixth-form college, after many years at a private all-girls establishment. She regarded her brother as some kind of Neanderthal, the product of his hothouse male public school. It was funny, thought Isabel, that other people considered him a success, a prime example of young manhood. Michael did.

'And talking about Dad . . .'

Was it telepathy? Isabel wondered, not for the first time. Her daughter often surprised her like this, she always had, even when she was little. 'Were we?'

'You know what I mean. Anyway, is there something wrong with Dad? He seems so grumpy lately. Or is it just me? Do *I* put him in a bad mood?'

'No, Gemma, it's not just you.' It was true that Michael didn't entirely approve of his daughter's attitude to life. Her lack of direction and drive, as he perceived it, could irritate him, but Isabel wasn't going to talk about it. Neither was she going to disclose what she thought was the real nature of his discontent. She pulled Gemma towards her. 'It's probably his age, something like that. Don't worry.'

Gemma's smile returned. 'I won't.' She held her mother tightly.

'Right, then, do you want to help me with the stock? I'll call out the items from the book and you can check the rails.'

'OK, you're the boss.'

They worked steadily for a couple of hours, interrupted by Gemma's occasional shrieks of 'Isn't that gross?' or 'Who would wear that?' or sometimes even, 'Actually, that isn't bad, in an ironic sort of way. Can I try it on?'

Isabel sat down with relief – she was definitely getting more tired these days – and looked around. Everything was under control.

'Well, Gem, it looks pretty shipshape, as your grandfather would say. Thanks for all your help, I really appreciate it.'

'That's all right. Anytime – well, almost! Do you mind if I shoot off now? I said I'd go round to Lucy's.'

'Of course not. Off you go.'

Gemma pulled on her coat and kissed her mother's cheek. Isabel couldn't avoid inhaling the musty odour of the fake fur, the hint of previous owners, a contrast with the freshness of her daughter's hair and skin.

She sat for a while in the shop, the sky darkening outside. Her hand strayed to her stomach; it was becoming a habit. Was it her imagination, or was her waist beginning to thicken, the skin to tighten? It was all so strange. Isabel closed her eyes and struggled to make sense of it all. There was Gemma, outspoken, herself, all grown, *alive*. Twenty years ago she had been right here, inside, a tiny bud, a beginning. And Dominic too. Now there was another. A fact of life, whatever Michael thought or said.

9

Michael leant back in his office chair – padded black leather, top-of-the-range, ergonomically sound – his arms stretched out above his head. He yawned, and yearned for some coffee, but his secretary Janice hadn't arrived yet and he couldn't be bothered to make it himself. God, he was tired, but the day had hardly begun. Last night he hadn't slept at all well – again. It was becoming a habit. He'd woken in the early hours and had lain listening to Isabel breathe until he could bear it no longer and had to get up. Downstairs he'd wandered from room to room, restless, thinking about Ellen, then about Isabel and this bloody baby, finishing up in the kitchen with the brandy bottle. Eventually he'd gone back to bed, feeling hopeful, surely now he'd sleep, but just as he felt himself slipping into drowsiness the first jet of the day had droned overhead, followed by another then another. He'd cursed, unable to understand why assurances of no night flights to Heathrow meant that these planes still shuddered over his house before dawn. In the end he thought he might as well get up and make an early start at work.

He looked through the entries for the day in his diary, then at the files of work on his desk, each pile representing a different case. He couldn't summon up the energy to get stuck into it.

It was quiet, he could get some peace in here until the rest of the firm kicked into life nearer nine o'clock. He surveyed his office: everything was as it should be, as he'd wanted it to be. There was some satisfaction in that, but less than there used to be. He gazed at the shelves of law books and leather-bound law reports, the props of his profession. God, how he used to get a buzz from it all. *His profession, his office, his secretary, his law firm* . . . (Well, partly his.) What was it with him? Was this another of those creeping-up-on-you things, those corny mid-life events or non-events over-analysed in the media? Maybe. He'd become jaded, that was for sure. Energy had to be summoned up, enthusiasm had to be faked instead of coming naturally to him . . . Even the intellectual challenges of the copyright cases he handled were diminished – or, rather, his satisfaction in meeting the challenges was diminished. He'd misplaced the thrill of solving legal problems, of finding a different angle – all that. He was once able to say that he honestly loved the law. But now?

He stroked his tie, smoothing it between his fingers from top to bottom, again and again, soothed a little by the soft, undemanding feel of the silk. It had been a Christmas present from the children, although he suspected that Dominic had had little or no involvement in its purchase. A busy design of clocks, lots of clocks, in shades of yellow: at first he'd been unsure but now he was becoming quite fond of it. 'Good to have a change, Dad,' Gemma had said, on seeing his face as he unwrapped it. How right she had been, he thought, but it wasn't going to stop with a tie.

Ellen, Ellen. Michael missed her, he wanted her. Why the hell hadn't she called him? When was she coming back? Soon, it must be. She could ring him here, at work, she knew that. He glared at the phone as if it were to blame, but he knew that if she did ring she'd ask him *that* question, the last thing he wanted to hear: 'Have you told her yet?' He sighed, his thoughts swerving to his wife, their predicament – no, *his* predicament, for it seemed that, as far as Isabel was concerned, there was no problem. God, what am I going to do? It was like being on that rope swing the kids used to love, tied to a tree that hung over the stream on the common. I've launched myself off, thought Michael, but am I going to make it without falling into the water?

Someone moved on the other side of the glass in his door. Great. If it's Janice, it will be coffee-time, he thought. But the shadow was too tall for his secretary.

'Morning, Michael! And how are you today?' James stuck his head in, his voice overloud as usual, his ego begging for exercise. Ever since he'd been made a partner his confidence had soared off the scale. He was younger than Michael, and junior to him, but Michael didn't entirely trust him. James was ambitious – like I used to be, he thought. What do I want now? Just a different life, with Ellen. Perhaps that's ambition of a different sort.

'Fine, James, though I could do with a coffee.'

'Me too, but that infernal machine – who can work it? And those infernal girls, where are they? But let's go over to Pret à Manger and grab something. How about it?'

'Why not? It's still ridiculously early. I'll just be a second – meet you downstairs.'

What is wrong with me? Michael asked himself, as he carefully arranged his desk so that anyone looking in would be able to see that he'd already been in the office. Shuffled some papers, opened his diary, put his coat over the back of his chair, opened his briefcase. Pathetic behaviour, he told himself. He was a senior partner, after all, yet still he did it. What did he have to prove?

As he strode along the street next to James, matching his

stride, it continued to niggle him. James was enthusing about the health club (membership came as one of the perks of a partnership) but Michael wasn't really listening. The old insecurity lurked within him, like a dormant volcano – no, an underground stream, eroding his idea of himself. Background, schooling, accent, class. Why the hell did these things still matter? It was people like James who reawakened in him the feelings of being the wrong class, in the wrong place. The feeling of being an impostor, that he would be found out. Look at James, thought Michael, a typical specimen of the English ex-public schoolboy, tall and blond, looking as if he was born to wear a three-piece pin-striped suit, who wouldn't know what self-doubt was if it suddenly swept up from the pavement like yesterday's newspaper and hit him in the face. Yet James has no idea how I feel, or I hope he doesn't, thought Michael.

For most of his life he'd tried to make himself impregnable. He was bolstered by education and qualifications, he'd been buffered by his nice, acceptable wife, as middle-class as they come. He'd provided his children with all he never had, especially a private education. Although at times he'd dreaded being asked, 'And what did your old man do, Michael?' or 'Where did you go to school?' and he'd worried his worked-on accent would not pass muster, on the whole he'd been good at covering up, but sometimes he felt so tired of it all. He'd like to be himself – but who was that?

Now he was doing a different sort of covering up, hiding his life with Ellen, the beginnings of a life. It occurred to him that perhaps it was no accident that she was American. He didn't have to pretend with her, did he? She was outside all this – this Englishness, this ingrain of class and privilege. It hadn't changed, not really, despite all the stuff politicians liked to churn out.

James moved fast between the crowds pouring out of the tube station towards their offices, flicking his hair back out of his eyes. He was saying something. Michael paid attention: it could be a snippet of gossip about the firm that he should know.

'. . . this new girl who works there. Delicious arse. I wait for the moment when she turns to work the cappuccino machine, you can see the line of her panties.'

James laughed, Michael laughed too – well, you had to, didn't you? Play the game, keep up appearances, be one of the lads.

'But you're not interested, are you Michael? Happily married man, all that?'

Michael stepped sideways. 'James, all I'm interested in right now is a good cup of coffee.'

Isabel picked up the post from the doormat and rifled through it. A couple of credit-card bills, a card for Gemma from Thailand – one of her friends who was travelling, no doubt. She couldn't read the signature: every available space was covered in scrawly writing in biro. A fat catalogue sealed in plastic – a mother-and-baby catalogue. She'd requested it, feeling a little foolish, but she couldn't help it. She'd better hide it from Michael, for now. Another postcard fluttered to the floor, a seductive photograph of a white hilltop town in Spain. It was from Angie. Bloody Angie, thought Isabel, when *is* she coming back?

The message, in Angie's distinctive black handwriting, was brief. Sorry, sorry, sorry that she was still in Spain but it was hard to tear herself away. (Bet I can guess why, Isabel thought.) She promised to return on Wednesday with news to tell!

Intriguing, reflected Isabel. Or not. Angie was pretty predictable, really. Met some man, adored him, got to know him better, then it all went wrong. Time and again, although it happened less frequently these days. The supply of men was drying up, Angie had said a few months ago, 'And perhaps I am too,' she'd added, shrieking with laughter.

Wednesday – the day after tomorrow. Not long, Isabel thought. Good. For she had news to tell as well – could she tell Angie? She was Isabel's oldest friend, although she'd never been very good at keeping secrets.

This was becoming ridiculous, thought Isabel, with a flash of irritation. This feeling that she shouldn't tell anyone about her pregnancy, for if she did Michael would be cross ... Pathetic behaviour for a woman of my age, of any age, she decided. They had to resolve this, and resolve it soon. Fine words, she told herself, although how the hell they could satisfactorily resolve it without one of them changing their mind, she had no idea.

10

The view always took Ellen's breath away. Standing as close as she dared to the window, twenty-seven floors up, she gazed at the lights of Manhattan below her, around her and beyond, with the two rivers framing the scene, East to the left, Hudson to the right. Everything was shiny and bright against the sky and the strips of dark water.

She stood very still, breathing deeply, enthralled, pressing her palms against the floor-to-ceiling glass, knowing that it was double thickness and reinforced, but there was still a feeling of danger, of taking risks. Whenever she stood here she could understand how people jumped from buildings believing they could fly.

This was her father's showpiece. He would lead first-time guests into the cloakroom, then leave them for a minute or two to take in the revelation of the view. It invariably had the desired mesmerising effect. Ellen wondered if anyone ever used the loo, apart from her father. It was too inhibiting, like being in an aeroplane toilet but with a revealing window to the skies.

He was calling her. 'Ellie! Come and eat.'

She dragged herself away.

The circular stone table was set just for two. Martha, her father's lover, partner, whatever, she was never sure what to call her, was away at a retreat of some sort in Colorado. Josh had prepared the lasagne himself, he said proudly (but not *made* – it had been sent up from a restaurant on 83rd Street). Ellen tossed the salad and sat down across the table from her father.

He ate quickly, talking at the same time, pausing only to swig wine from the tall Mexican glass. For as long as Ellen could remember he had always seemed to be in a hurry, doing several things at once, as if they were about to be taken away from him. She had sometimes wondered if her mother's early death had been due to exhaustion, worn out by her husband.

'So, sweetheart, what's new with you?'

'Well, you know about the work.'

'Sure, it's good. I read that piece of yours on the English aristocracy at play. Amusing.'

'It was a bit frivolous, I know, but that's what the magazine wanted.'

She bent her head, forking over her salad. Just because her work wasn't serious or political she often ended up feeling silly and of little consequence in her father's presence. Did he intend to have that effect?

She looked at him now, enjoying his lasagne. As he regularly remarked, he was what he was, and other people could go fuck themselves. He had always been uncompromising, both in his behaviour and his principles. Here was Joshua Linden, prize-winning writer, anti-war campaigner, crusading journalist, subject of countless profiles by lesser writers, who usually resorted to describing him as larger than life.

Ellen smiled at him. No, she didn't think he meant to make her feel inadequate. Indeed, more than once he had said he was proud of her. She was his adored only child, his special daughter, all he had left of the beautiful wife who had died young.

'Well, listen Ellie, it pays the rent. We can't always choose what to write, can we? It's a luxury to be able to write what you want.'

'Are you, Dad? Writing what you want?'

When they were alone together she slipped into calling him that, even though for years he'd encouraged her to call him Josh.

'I'm trying! But hell, it's almost too much – you know, the blank piece of paper, the hours stretching ahead, the freedom! I sometimes wonder if I'm cut out to produce a novel. Perhaps I'm strictly a thousand-words man!'

A few years ago, on reaching sixty-five, Josh had announced that he was going to stay home and write fiction. Since then he'd produced a few short stories, but he wouldn't let anyone see them. That was partly because he loved to tease. Meanwhile there was a sense of waiting – the non-appearance of the novel was a topic of conjecture among his friends and acquaintances. Whenever the dwindling circle of fellow ageing writers – Josh's crowd – met in a bar or deli, they joked that perhaps he'd lost it, his gift or nerve or whatever. Yet if an editor called with a request for a commentary on the state of the union or asked for his view of the latest political scandals he always agreed and managed to turn in work that was punchy and insightful – and on time. He could still do that, and Ellen admired him for it. She didn't think he'd lost it.

'Dad, you just need to have patience. Stick with it.'

'That sounds familiar. You're turning into me! That happens you know, children become parents to their parents!'

They both laughed. Then a pause, silence. *Parents*. Each knew that the other was thinking of the parent who was missing, Ellen's mother. Josh could recall Celia, the actual physical person, but as Ellen could barely remember her, she could feel only the reverberating loss, the lack of her mother then and now.

There were a few minutes of silence. Josh finished the salad, poured more wine, then asked his daughter, 'Tell me more about your life in London, I know so little about you these days.'

Ellen told him about her apartment, the hassles of decorating it, the neighbourhood. He demanded details. She gave them, trying to avoid the moment when he would ask her about her love life, which he always did. She told him about plays she'd been to lately, and exhibitions, and added a few she hadn't actually seen, delaying the inevitable. It came.

'So Ellen, what do you think of English men? Are you seeing anyone?'

'English men? I'm not sure. I don't think I'm an expert.'

'Come on Ellen, you're holding out on me!'

'No! Not really. They're like all men. Some I like, some I don't.'

'What's happened to your powers of observation? Your professional insights?'

Ellen groaned. 'You won't leave it alone, will you, you old monster?'

Josh had gone into the kitchen area, buried his head in the freezer and was extracting several tubs of Ben & Jerry's, so she wasn't sure if he'd heard. No matter, he'd get his way, he usually did. He returned with bowls and spoons. 'Have some Rainforest Crunch. So, what aren't you telling me?'

'Oh, OK. I am seeing someone. And he is English.'

'Now we're getting somewhere. What's his name? What does he do?' Josh spooned ice-cream straight from the tub, bypassing his bowl.

'Michael Turner. He's a lawyer. And no lawyer jokes, please! He's older than me –'

'How much older?'

'He's in his forties.'

'Well, that's not such a difference. I was older than your mother.'

'I know that, Dad.' Ellen put her head down, studying her spoon.

'What is it, Ellen? Are you serious about this guy?'

'Yes, I am. And he cares about me.'

'That's great! So what's the problem? There is a problem, isn't there?'

'Dad, let's just leave it, shall we?'

Ellen stood up and began putting the lids back on the ice-cream tubs, concentrating, not wanting to meet her father's gaze.

'Ah. Is he married, is that it?'

'Yes, as it happens, he is.' She looked at her father defiantly. 'Before you start lecturing me –'

'Who says I'm about to lecture you? I'm not a heavy moralist, you know that.'

'Yeah, OK. It's just that whatever you say I've already said it to myself, believe me.' She slumped back down on her chair. 'It's not ideal. I would rather not have got involved with a married man, but I've got involved with Michael ... His children are more or less grown, he and his wife have drifted apart ...' Her voice trailed away, waiting for his reaction, for a bellow of 'Bullshit' or 'How original', but her father remained silent. His expression and raised eyebrows said it all.

Ellen looked away, wondering why the hell she still needed his approval.

Josh leant forward and took her hands in his. 'Ellen honey, you can tell me to mind my own business, but whatever I say is not because I want to interfere – you're thirty, for God's sake, I'd be crazy to try.'

'Thirty-*one*, Dad.'

She was accustomed to him forgetting her exact age. To him she was probably for ever a little girl, his little girl, although to his credit he never actually used those words, not any more.

'Oh yeah, so you are. Anyway, this is only because I care about you, I don't want you to be hurt. Christ, this situation is stuffed full of clichés!'

They laughed, and Ellen withdrew a hand to wipe away a tear. 'Sweetheart,' Josh said softly. 'You surely realise that if he cheats on his wife he could cheat on you. He could lie to you – think about it.'

It was one of those New York winter mornings that Ellen loved: bright white light, crisp cold, a wind that whipped around corners and between buildings, catching you unawares. She crossed over into Central Park – it was safe at this time of day, plenty of walkers and joggers and even a couple of the NYPD's finest on horseback, managing to look benign. There was an air of joviality about it all – either it was her mood or the new reality of New York that she'd been reading about back in London. She strode along the winding paths, smiling at the elderly women in heavy makeup with tiny dogs on long leads, pausing at the Wollman ice rink, wondering if she could still do it, the backward skating, the fancy twirls.

Ellen headed down Fifth Avenue, deciding she'd continue on foot as far as she could before the cold froze her nose. People walked by fast and furiously, heads down, collars up, in an array of headgear – woolly hats, fluffy earmuffs, baseball caps, hurrying into buildings and the welcome assurance of heat.

It felt good to be out of the apartment, alone and away from her father. Her time was her own, she could do what she liked. She was due to meet her friend Grace later, downtown at Dean & DeLuca in Prince Street, but that wasn't for a few hours. If she had the energy, and could bear the cold, she might even walk all the way to SoHo.

Ellen pulled her fake-fur hat further down over her ears and lengthened her stride, curving through the office workers and early shoppers. Steam rose up from beneath the streets, the archetypal New York scene. As she stopped for a Don't Walk sign (surprised as ever how many people obeyed) she remembered her father crouching beside her on the sidewalk, answering her question about the steam. How old must she have been? Five, six? He'd told her it came from the trolls who lived under the city, that when they got angry, when they got all steamed up, their breath escaped through the holes in the roads. She had believed it for years, treading carefully on the sidewalks to avoid upsetting the trolls.

'Hey lady, move it will ya?'

The light had changed, she was in the way, and a guy in purple earmuffs glared in her face as he pushed past her.

'Welcome home, Ellen,' she said to herself. Or what used to be home. And she walked as fast as she could, arms swinging, head up. The trolls wouldn't get her, no one would.

This walk is as good as a morning in the gym, Ellen told herself, but she needed a break. The Barnes and Noble superstore on Sixth Avenue would be perfect and was just a few minutes away. She'd stay there a while, relaxing, catching up on magazines and the latest books, and have a coffee too. She turned down a side-street, hurrying past a tall dishevelled man who sang a hymn as he pushed a supermarket trolley filled with what she assumed were all his worldly goods. Ahead of him was a petite blonde in an ankle-length fur coat and fancy black and white patent shoes, walking a cream poodle. The woman's steps seemed as small as the dog's. Only in New York, Ellen thought.

She entered the bookstore with a sigh of relief and a sense of pleasure, pausing inside the doors in the rush of warm air to remove her hat and gloves. She wandered, gathering hardbacks in her arms, between the neo-classical pillars, past the students at the small tables, books spread out, using the place as a library – there were even trolleys for books for reshelving. Music played softly. Brahms? Mendelssohn? An elderly man in a black beret slept in a chintz armchair. Amazingly she found an empty sofa and settled down among the floral cushions with her pile of books.

'May I sit here?' She looked up. A guy in a long black overcoat stood over her.

'Oh, sure. Sorry, I'll move these.' She shifted her books

along, making space for him. He smiled and said thanks, folding himself elegantly into the other corner. He wasn't bad-looking, nice haircut, stubbly chin, deep brown eyes. What are you doing Ellen? she asked herself. Thinking about other men? You have Michael, remember. Or, rather, you don't have him. Not really, not yet.

She concentrated on her book, trying not to give out signals of availability. This was probably a pick-up place for singles but she wasn't part of that scene any more so what did she know? Was he looking at her or did she imagine it? She got up abruptly, taking her books with her, and made for the stairs to the mezzanine café. Time for a coffee. As she relaxed over a latte and a kugel she gazed down past the art deco lights. He was still on the sofa, deep in a book. Perhaps that *was* what he was here for, after all.

The aisles of books immediately below, with headers proclaiming *Relationships*, *New Age*, *Self-improvement*, were crowded. People sat cross-legged on the floor, heads down, reading intently. Ah, surprise, surprise, thought Ellen, they're all female. Why is it that women are prepared to make the effort, put the time in to change themselves, improve things, make it work? Her thoughts flicked back to Noah, the man she'd lived with for two years, the shit who'd decamped to California to further his script-writing career, who'd pretended to be surprised at her distress when he announced the news. She rubbed her hand across her forehead, as if to remove all memories of him. How she'd worked at that relationship! All that summoning of patience, all that soothing and succouring and supporting . . . It had seemed natural at the time, normal when you loved someone. She'd fled to London soon after he'd left, vowing she'd never debase herself in a relationship again, never put the man first, never set her needs aside, as she'd done with Noah. And it *was* different with Michael, more equal, even though he was older. There wasn't that tremble of fear she'd so often felt with Noah, when she'd failed to anticipate his mood, trying to predict the unpredictable. But no more Noah, she determined. Think of Michael, or even herself.

'Ellen – it is *so* good to see you. I can't tell you how good!'

'And it's so good to see *you*, Gracie!'

Ellen leapt up from her seat and they hugged each other hard, shrieking and almost dancing, ignoring the looks from those around them. The guy by the wall continued playing the cello.

'Great! You managed to get us a table, Ellen. It gets so crowded in here, these days, with tourists.'

'Like me?'

Come on! You – a tourist? Please . . .'

Ellen watched her friend divest herself of layers: vintage velvet beret, suede gloves, black nylon rucksack, camera on a red strap, long stripy scarf, old leather coat. Then Grace insisted on dashing off to the counter to get the coffee. Ellen relaxed, leaning against the giant plant pot next to her chair. Their table was right at the back – a good place to observe any comings and goings. It was wonderful to be here with her oldest friend, tourists and all.

Ellen observed Grace's progress on her extreme platform-heeled moc-croc boots, balancing coffee and carrot cake on a small tray. She made it back to the table, laughing. One of the things that Ellen loved about Grace was that she laughed a lot.

'Now, Ellen, I want to hear all your news, and I mean all of it.' She picked up her camera, ready to fire off some shots.

'Grace, I'll tell you, but no pictures, not yet.'

The shutter clicked anyway, several times. Grace had been a compulsive photographer since she was fifteen and now it was her work.

'Why so shy? You're looking great, you know. Very sleek. Something suits you – is it London?'

'Could be.' She sipped her coffee. 'And what do you mean *sleek*? Sounds like an insult to me.'

'I'm just admiring how you're turned out, Ellen dear. You put an old ragbag like me to shame.'

'You're a tease, Grace Irving. We both know how much care goes into that look of yours, the research, the hunting, the bargaining. What did that article call it? Eclectic expressionism? Or was it expressive eccentricity?'

'You should know, Ellen, you wrote it. More like excessive bullshit!'

They grinned at each other.

'Now, gossip time.'

'You first. You said you'd tell me all your news. So how is London?'

'I like it – well, I always have, but I do like living there.'

'Do I detect a secret? Come on, tell Auntie Grace. Is it a man?'

Ellen paused. 'You sound like my father.'

'So? There's worse things. But come on, who is he?'

'All right. He's called Michael, he's a lawyer, I met him at the gym.'

'Sounds *very* New York, not London! Sorry, go on.'

'There's not much to tell. I've been seeing him for about six months or so.'

'Not much to tell? You're kidding! Why didn't you say something about this before? You never mentioned it in your e-mails. Secrets, secrets!'

'I'm sorry. I've hardly told anyone.'

'I'm so pleased – must mean you're finally over Noah, Mr No-no. Can we stop spitting now when we say his name?'

'Yes!'

'He did you wrong, sweetheart. But one thing you'll enjoy – I heard on the grapevine that Noah is *not* doing so well in LA. Still hawking round that sitcom script of his – but enough. This new man, is it l-o-v-e, lurve?'

'Oh Grace . . . Yes, maybe. It's complicated.'

'What is it Ellen, are you going all English and reticent on me?'

'No. It's just that . . .'

'Let me guess. Is he married?'

'Yes.' Ellen sighed. 'He is.'

'A bitch, isn't it? Don't feel bad. We've all been there. There are so few guys around who are straight and available, what's a girl to do?'

'I don't feel bad, not in a guilty way. I feel sad – for me, because I want to be with him.'

'That's an honest assessment. But where is it going? *Is* it going anywhere? And do you care?'

'Yes, I care! Here's how it is. Michael wants to be with me.

He says he's going to leave his wife – I'm hoping he's going to tell her while I'm here. That's partly why I came, to give him a bit of space, let him get on with it.'

'I see.'

'What, Grace? What?'

'Oh Ellen, what can I say? I hope it works out for you. It never has for me. Remember that guy I wrote you about – Adam, the artist? I was crazy about him, he said it was mutual, and he went back and forth between me and wifey for months. He actually left her at one point and moved in with me, even though there wasn't really room – especially for his ego – you know how small my place is.'

'What happened?'

'When he was with me he began to miss his wife! He agonised about her, kept calling her, he met her secretly. It was weird, everything was turned on its head. Bizarre. In the end he went back to her, but wanted to go on seeing me. Can you imagine?'

'Oh Grace. What a bastard.' Ellen was sympathetic but told herself this had nothing to do with her and Michael: he was different, they were different. 'Did you – do you see him?'

'Like hell I do. My sense of self-preservation kicked into play. So at this point in time I'm more or less celibate.'

'Well, being celibate is fashionable these days, so I hear.'

'Depends which circles you move in. I have the occasional fling – hell, who am I kidding? Occasional one-night stand, I mean, when I get lucky. One good thing is I'm getting so much work done – I'm using all that effort and energy that I'd pour into a relationship!'

'I haven't seen any of your work for ages.'

'Well, why don't you drop by the studio tomorrow? But right now I think I need a drink. We haven't toasted this New Year yet, you and I. How about it, girlfriend?'

'Why not, Gracie? Let's go. Lead me to a bar.'

It was getting dark outside, as dark as the city lights would allow. They linked arms and Grace steered them towards West Broadway, she knew just the place, she said. They agreed that they'd have a damn good time, men or no men, and Grace shouted to the sky, 'Men! Who needs them?'

Angie kissed her lover goodbye at Málaga airport. 'As soon as I've sorted everything out in London I'll be back with you.'

'Don't take too long.'

'I'll try not to, but you know there are loads of things to deal with – my house and the shop. And the cat.'

'I've told you, bring the cat!'

'If I can. Now, I'd better go.'

They hugged and kissed again and Angie hurried through the barriers, her shoes slipping slightly on the shiny marbled floor, turning once to wave. Then she headed for the duty-free shop. She wanted to buy some cigarettes and vodka, and some perfume for Isabel. That was the least she could do. How would Isabel take her news, she wondered. Would she be cross at being left in the lurch – would she see it like that? Or would she be happy that Angie had found love and was moving to Spain to live with her lover?

Probably a mixture of both, thought Angie as she sniffed at the perfumes she'd sprayed on each wrist. Knowing Isabel – and she had known her for a very long time – after the initial irritation she'd be delighted. She always did have a generous nature, Angie reflected, and she's been a good friend. Now, was it Trussardi on the left wrist and Tuscany on the right? She sniffed again but couldn't remember and decided on the Tuscany because she preferred the packaging.

The plane to Heathrow was half empty and Angie had two seats all to herself. Good, she thought, I won't have to talk to anyone or accommodate their knees or elbows or be aware of their eating. She closed her eyes and tried to relax while deliberating on what to do about Isabel and Once or Twice.

She was going to have to tell Isabel that she wanted to disentangle herself from the business, she wanted out. She hoped it wouldn't be too complicated: she had her new life to organise and wanted to shed the old one as easily as she could. Surely Isabel would understand?

The plane lowered itself noisily over south-west London. Angie looked out of the window, trying to spot familiar places.

There was Richmond Park, an island of green, even in winter. That meant her house was down there somewhere on the other side. Home. It would be dusty and cold. At least there was Desdemona – although she'd be distant and cross because she'd spent all this time in a cattery. Angie decided to treat herself to a taxi from Heathrow and then they could take a small detour to pick up Desdemona on the way home to Mortlake. She didn't have much English cash but she had her credit cards. What the hell.

She flicked on the hall light and looked around quickly. Everything seemed fine: the lights worked, no sign of leaking pipes or burglars. Usually she loved this moment of re-entry into the world she'd created, back in her small, cosy cottage – and it *was* a cottage, she always insisted to sceptical friends, even though it was in London. Originally a railwayman's cottage, admittedly. But then she even found the sound of the nearby trains romantic, especially late at night. But right now she wasn't experiencing the reassuring embrace of home. There was a musty smell of rugs and clutter, of books and more books and the magazines she stockpiled for too long. Her mind filled with cleaner images of expanses of old terracotta floors and rough white plastered walls, of brown hillsides and twisted olive trees. And the lean lines of her lover's body, long legs stretched out on a white linen sheet, bare skin and the clarity of sharp hip bones . . .

'OK, Desi, I'll let you out, hold on.' The cat howled in protest from inside the travelling basket. Angie opened its door and Desdemona rushed into the kitchen, looking for her food bowl. On finding it empty, she rushed through the cat-flap into the back garden to re-establish her territory.

Angie shivered. It was a cold night, much colder than Spain, but what did she expect? She clicked on the heating then picked up the scattered mail on the doormat. Nothing of importance. A private view she'd missed, some bills, a few late Christmas cards. No surprises. That's what my life would continue to be like here, she thought, no surprises. That's why I'm going to move to Spain. That's a surprise. A bubble of excitement rose in her chest and she smiled to herself. She was going to say goodbye to all this and hello to something new, something wonderful. She could hardly wait.

'Isabel! It's me, I'm back. How are you? Have a good Christmas?'

There was no need to announce who it was – Isabel recognised Angie's voice immediately. She'd always had a great voice, low, husky, sexy. Isabel's mother had once remarked years ago, 'That girl's voice could get her into trouble.' Whether it had or not was debatable, but it had got her into acting.

'Angie! Good to hear you at last! Oh, Christmas was fine, the usual. How was yours?'

'Wonderful, absolute bliss. I'll tell you all when I see you. How's the shop?'

'Busy at the moment. And there's lots that needs doing, and things we need to talk about.'

'Of course. Look, I'll be there in the morning, bright and early, never fear! And then we'll talk, OK?'

'Fine. You'll open up, then?'

'Yes, I will.'

'See you tomorrow, Angie. I'm glad you're back. Goodnight, then.'

Angie wished Isabel goodnight too, but she had already rung off. She'd sounded tired, thought Angie, not her usual cheerful self. And normally Isabel would have demanded immediate details of what Angie had been up to. Perhaps she's already a bit pissed off with me, thought Angie. And this is just the beginning. Bloody hell.

She searched the house for a drink, discarding the half-drunk bottle of burgundy left from before Christmas. I'm not that desperate, she decided. There was a bottle of cheap champagne she kept in the fridge for emergency celebrations – perhaps now was the time. And there was no damn food in the house so she might as well get sloshed. The cork took a while to negotiate, but she eventually settled down with the bottle next to the phone and dialled the number in Spain.

Isabel could see Angie through the shop window, cleaning the counter. Making amends for lingering on holiday, she thought, smiling. Angie was always so transparent: it was part of her charm. It worked most of the time. And she had missed her.

'Izzy!' Angie rushed forward to hug her friend with the Mr Sheen still in her hand. 'It's so good to see you.'

'You too, Ange. Let me get my coat off. Get down, Jasper! Leave Angie alone. In your corner. Sit!'

'Is he pleased to see me? Or can he smell Desdemona? She spent the night on my bed, having eventually decided to forgive me for putting her in the cattery.' Angie watched Jasper trot obediently to the back of the shop with some relief. She was more of a cat person herself.

'So how are you?' Isabel asked. 'You're looking really well. Whatever you got up to in Spain suited you.'

'I told you, Izzy, it was a painting holiday.'

'Yes, yes. I've known you a long time, remember?'

'You're right. I'll tell you all about it, we need to talk. I'll put the kettle on. Let's have some coffee.'

'OK, but no coffee for me. There are some herbal tea-bags.'

'No coffee? Are you all right, Izzy? You look a bit tired.'

'Thanks! That's usually a polite way of saying that someone looks lousy.'

'No, no, you don't. Just tired. Sit down. I'll be back in a minute, then we can catch up.'

Isabel flicked through her notebook and ran her eye down the list of things to do. Hopefully she could offload a lot of them on to Angie who, after all, didn't have a husband and children – she didn't have to perform as a wife and mother – and who wasn't pregnant. Angie's energy levels should be high after her fling, whatever it was, in Spain and that's what the shop needed: a boost of enthusiasm.

'Here we are.' Angie set the tray down on the counter she'd just cleaned and got out the extra folding chair. She handed Isabel a mug of tea.

'Thanks, Ange. We probably won't be interrupted by customers until eleven or so.'

'Good – well, not good, we love our customers, don't we? But you know what I mean. So fill me in.'

Isabel informed Angie about the stock situation, the figures since Christmas, and began to work through her action list. She could sense Angie beginning to fidget – honestly, she had the attention span of a child. 'Angie, what is it? Am I boring you?'

'I'm sorry, sweetie, it's just that I remembered I brought you a present. Can I give it to you now?'

'Yes, of course, but you shouldn't have –'

'I hate it when people say that.' Angie rummaged in her straw basket and handed over the duty-free bag. She watched as Isabel unwrapped it.

'Perfume. Angie, that's lovely, thank you.'

'Aren't you going to smell it? Oh, damn – have you got some already?'

'No, no, I haven't. I'm sure it's wonderful, I've heard it is. It's just that . . .'

Angie leant towards her friend. 'Isabel, what *is* the matter? There is something, isn't there? You don't seem quite yourself. Remember, I know you nearly as well as you know me.'

Isabel sighed. 'OK. It's just that I can't take strong smells at the moment, any sort of smells, even nice perfume.' She shrugged and turned her hands upwards. 'I'm pregnant, you see.'

Angie went to Isabel and put her arm around her friend's shoulders. 'Izzy, are you all right?' But Isabel kept her head down. 'Hey, this isn't like you. What is it?' Angie hesitated. 'Don't you want it – the baby?' Being childless, she felt on uncertain ground. It was hard to cross that divide between mothers and others: there was so much you could only imagine. She was reluctant to trespass.

Isabel looked up. Her eyes were wet and bright but she seemed to be making an effort to smile. Good old Isabel, thought Angie, putting on a brave face as usual. 'Yes, I think I do. I think I do want this baby. If I let myself I am excited about it, in a way. But Michael isn't . . .'

'Ah. Is that a problem? Surely he'll come round?'

'That's what I'm hoping. But he's very stubborn. Oh, I know I can be stubborn too. Perhaps I am being – look, I'm sorry. You don't want to hear all this. It shouldn't affect you much, or the shop. Obviously I'll continue, although you may have to take over more for a while, when the baby's born and so on. Angie?'

Angie crossed swiftly to the door and turned the sign to Closed. To give her determination she summoned up the image of that delicious afternoon in Spain when her lover had taken her to bed for the first time. She pulled her chair close to Isabel's and took a deep breath. 'Isabel.'

'My full name – must mean something serious! Sorry, go on.'

'There's something I was going to tell you – *am* going to tell you. God, this is difficult, especially now after hearing that you're pregnant. I'm afraid I won't be able to take on more here. You see, I'm planning to move to Spain – I'm *going* to move to Spain. I've met someone –'

'I knew it! That was the reason you were reluctant to return.'

'Well, yes. You see, I think this is *it*. Don't look at me like that, Izzy. I know you've heard that before. But this is different. Really, it is!'

They both laughed. Angie could see Isabel struggling to say the right thing.

'Angie, I'm pleased for you, I really am. But isn't it a bit sudden? And it's a big step, moving to Spain. It's not just the shop – what about your house? What about Desdemona? You can't leave her!'

'I can take her with me. And I'll probably let the house.'

'Yes, don't sell it. I mean, don't burn all your bridges – you may want to come back.'

'I don't think so. But I know I should be sensible, keep my options open. And I'm so sorry about the shop, Izzy. Just when you need me, I'm letting you down.'

For a moment there was silence between them. Then Isabel sighed and said, 'Never mind. You weren't to know. I'll manage. That's life – and this is your life. You've got to seize the chance of happiness when you can.'

'Exactly! Oh Izzy, thank you for being so understanding, I knew you would be.' Another hug, kisses on the cheeks. 'And I'm so happy.'

'It shows! So tell me about him. Did this all happen over Christmas? Did you meet him at the painting course?'

'Max runs the painting course.'

'Max? Is he Spanish or . . .?'

'Australian originally. And Max is short for Maxine. You see, Izzy, Max is a woman.'

Later Isabel took Jasper for a long walk on Barnes Common before she went home. Her head was throbbing. She kept rerunning her conversation with Angie through her mind, like a loop. Was she shocked? Not in a moral sense. It was just a surprise. What a surprise. She trawled through memories to see if there had ever been any clue that Angie's sexuality might be ambiguous. She couldn't find anything, not really. Angie had always seemed energetically heterosexual. There had been that time at school when both she and Angie – aged twelve? – had a crush on a prefect called Tessa and would find any excuse to ask her questions and admire her dark glossy plait, which hung almost to her waist. It didn't mean anything at that age. It was normal. But, as Angie had said when they'd abandoned the shop to go out to lunch at the Depot, what is normal, anyway?

She had told Isabel about Max, how interesting and beguiling she was, how she'd done so many things in her life and had ended up in Spain, restoring the *finca* and starting up the business of art holidays. Max had two horses and was going to teach Angie to ride. Max cooked a great authentic paella. Max . . . As Angie spoke about her lover, Isabel tried to suppress the questions that leapt into her mind mischievously, like imps in a fairy-tale. How did it happen? What did they do to each other? How did it work? Was sex with a woman better than sex with a man? Could you even make comparisons? Isabel felt a little ashamed of herself. After all, she thought, if Angie had a new male lover, I wouldn't dream of asking her what they did in bed.

Angie was looking at her, smiling. 'I expect you're curious, Isabel,' she'd said. 'I know you're avoiding the dreaded L word. I don't know if this makes me a lesbian. I suppose it means I'm bisexual. All I really understand at the moment is that I'm in love and it's great and the person I've fallen in love with happens to be female.' She'd reached across the table and squeezed Isabel's hand. 'And you don't have to worry, Izzy, nothing's changed between *us*. I'm not about to jump on you or try to seduce you!'

She had laughed and Isabel had begun to giggle, both unaware that the people on the next table were straining to hear more.

Isabel called Jasper and set off towards home. It would soon be dark. God, this was all so confusing. She was pregnant. Angie was in love with a woman and leaving London for Andalucía. Change and change again. Briefly she wondered what Michael would say but she realised that she would not tell him, not about Angie's new love life. He'd only sneer or laugh, and then she would feel she'd betrayed her friend. I'll keep quiet, she decided. Who says wives have to tell husbands everything?

12

Isabel stood outside Covent Garden tube station, shifting her weight from one foot to the other, waiting for Beth. They often met here as it was roughly half-way between them. Beth was late – So what's new? thought Isabel – and it was starting to rain. She turned up her coat collar and made for a shop doorway.

'Isabel, I'm so sorry – bloody trains! Have you been here long?'

Beth came rushing towards her, they kissed each other on both cheeks.

'Five minutes or so but don't worry.'

'Hey, it's good to see you Izzy!'

'You too. I'm glad you could get away.'

'I had to if I wanted to remain sane.'

'Do you want to tell me about it over a coffee? Or shall we hit the shops? Or did you say you wanted to go down to the National Gallery?'

'Coffee first, I think, don't you? Let's get out of this weather.'

They headed for a café they knew in Monmouth Street, walking quickly together under Isabel's umbrella, the drops of rain growing larger by the second. Inside it was steamy and untrendified, smelling of bacon sandwiches. They were in luck – a table wedged in the corner was empty. Beth took off her big black felt hat and released her curly hair over her shoulders, fluffing it out with her fingers. When they had first met Beth had hated her curls, passionately envying Isabel's straight hair. Isabel remembered those times in the flat when Beth would conduct her experiments in hair-straightening, involving sticky tape or giant rollers or attacking it with a brush and hair-dryer. Ironing her hair through brown paper had been the worst – Isabel had been coerced into helping and could still recall the stink of scorched hair and hot brown paper. Or was it the other way round? Not long after that Beth had had her hair cut really short, and then at some point – it must have been post-children, Isabel thought – she'd decided to let it grow and live with her curls. Now Isabel envied Beth's hair. It seemed to have a life of its own and gave her an air of insouciance.

'I told Simon I had to do some research at the National Gallery for one of my classes. It was a good excuse.'

'Beth! Why do you need an excuse?'

'Oh, you know, he likes me to be around. He feels he can't cope with everything on his own, especially at the weekend.'

'Cope with what exactly?'

'The kids, the house, food, the cat being sick, paying the milkman, anything, everything, you name it!'

'Oh, really!'

'I know, it's pathetic. Pathetic of him, and pathetic of me, especially with my feminist principles.'

'Well, things are never easy or straightforward.'

'God, you can say that again!'

'But I'm pleased you're here. It's been ages since we met like this.'

'We should make the time. Oh, I'm sorry, I haven't even asked how you are and you're the one who's pregnant!'

'I'm fine, physically that is. A few minor things, you know, feeling tired, a bit nauseous and so on.'

'You're fine physically but what? There is a but, isn't there?'

'There is. It's Michael mainly.'

'Has he come round to the idea or not? Hell, it's more than an idea! What's he saying now?'

'He hasn't come round. And I don't think he will. We keep talking and talking about it but we keep repeating the same things.'

'So he's against having the baby and you're for it, is that it?'

'In a nutshell. But, as I said, nothing is ever straightforward. I feel – I feel so confused, Beth. I don't get it, I really don't. I thought I understood him, I thought I knew him. I really thought that by now he'd have adjusted and said, "What the hell? We're having another child, it'll be all right." You know what I mean?'

'You feel he's let you down.'

'I suppose I do. And he probably feels the same. But I think there's something else, something he's not telling me, which makes him so against having this baby. He's so moody, almost withdrawn. I don't know what's the matter with him. I can't quite put my finger on it . . . Which makes me more confused.'

'What could it be?'

'God knows. But the weirdest thing is – if he'd been more positive and supportive and said, "OK, let's go ahead," then *I* might not have been so keen –' Isabel broke off while the elderly Italian waitress, one of a dying breed, manoeuvred their cups on to the table.

'You mean you might have considered not having the baby?'

'I might. But as it is, the more Michael seems against it, the more I want to go ahead. Quite contrary.'

'It's probably a protective response.'

'Could be.' Isabel exhaled. 'This – this struggle is making me so tired. I feel as if I'm in a tug-of-war. I even had a dream about it the other night. Being tugged one way but me tugging the other, towards having the baby . . .' She bent her head down over her hot chocolate.

Beth reached across, placing her hand on Isabel's arm. You know if there's anything I can do . . . How pregnant are you now?'

'About eleven weeks. And I am beginning to *feel* pregnant.'

'Eleven weeks? So there's still time –'

'For an abortion? I suppose so. But, you see, there's no real reason for me to have one – except to please Michael! I can't do it.'

'I understand, Izzy, but I want you to know that if you decided to follow that route I'd be there for you as you were for me.'

*

Beth scooped froth off her cappuccino. Flickers of memory infiltrated her mind but she'd long since trained herself to ignore them. A large Victorian house near Epping Common; the nurse who'd told her to pull herself together as she awoke weeping from the anaesthetic; Isabel collecting her in a borrowed Triumph Herald, turquoise it was; the chestnut trees in the road outside bestowing conkers on them as they'd walked slowly to the car. She had never regretted the abortion – it was necessary: she'd been deliberately sleeping around after Simon had insisted they had a break from each other; she'd been confused and in a mess and certainly not ready to have a child. And Isabel had understood and seen her through it. All those years ago . . .

They did not speak of it now.

Isabel smiled and squeezed her friend's arm. 'Thank you, Beth. But if I'm going ahead with this and having the baby – as I seem to be doing – I may need your support in other ways.'

'Whatever you want, just ask. And Michael? What will you do about him?'

'God knows. Although I do know that I don't want him to start telling me what to do, or trying to. Part of me just wants to go ahead and get on with it, whatever he says or feels. Does that sound awful?'

'No, it doesn't. It's your choice.' Beth turned and peered through the steamed-up windows. 'It looks like it's still raining. Do you want another hot chocolate? I'll have another coffee and let's have a pastry – one each or share one?'

'Let's go mad. One each!'

'It's strange, isn't it, you spend all this time married to someone and you wonder if you know them at all?' Beth stirred sugar into her cup. She was ostensibly referring to Michael but Isabel recognised it as a cue that Beth wanted to talk about Simon. She asked, 'So what's Simon up to?'

'He's going through some kind of crisis, he says. And nothing his therapist can help him with, apparently.'

Beth ran her fingers through her hair. Isabel knew that Simon's years of therapy were a source of conflict between him and Beth, especially as they needed the money for other things. But he claimed that his grandmother, a doyenne of post-war liberal Hampstead society, had left him money specifically for his therapy to continue as long as he felt it necessary. Which he did, and he'd now notched up over twenty years. 'Honestly, his therapy – you know, I think it's turned into a hobby. Why the hell can't he take up fishing or golf like other men?'

Isabel laughed. 'But if he needs it . . . And maybe he'd be even more – well, difficult without it.'

'That's what Simon says. Who's to know? Anyway, what he's thinking about now is a complete change of direction. Wants to give up teaching, says he can't stand struggling with bored sixteen-year-olds any more, trying to inspire them to read poetry and Shakespeare. Says it's a battle already lost, so why bother? You should hear him, Izzy, he's beginning to sound like an old reactionary! Goes on and on about the horrors of the age, all this crap about *communications* – he hates that word – when people are forgetting how to simply talk to each other.'

'So what is he going to do? If he's giving up teaching.'

'He wants to become a storyteller. Don't laugh, Izzy, please.'

'I'm not . . . I won't. But, Beth, a *storyteller*? What does that mean exactly?'

'Well, he wants to revive the oral tradition, not single-handedly, of course, there are other people doing this, but he says he'll become a human library of folk tales and myths, stories from other cultures.'

'And do what? Go to schools and festivals and things?'

'I suppose. God only knows. But we haven't really got down to the nitty-gritty of it yet, especially to the part where we discuss money – how he's actually going to earn any!'

'Perhaps there is a need . . .'

'Perhaps. But schools, these days – *state* schools, anyway – can't even afford textbooks and roof repairs and teachers, you know, *basics* like that, so how are they going to afford storytellers?'

Isabel said nothing, merely nodded. She recognised Beth's fierce tone, which implied, it's all right for you, Isabel, with your children's privileged private education. What do you know of the deprivations of the state system? How could you possibly understand what it's like to work in it? There was a silence but then they grinned at each other. Beth accepted that Isabel didn't share her interests in political issues, or her views, so they usually avoided talking about such things. What she didn't realise was that Isabel valued Beth's passion and her principles, even if she didn't always agree with them.

Isabel steered the conversation back to Simon. 'So what happens now? How's he going to do it?'

'Who knows? No, that's unfair. He's worked out a plan of sorts. He'll work until the end of the academic year and meanwhile he's sussing out if there are any offers of early retirement. I'm sure the powers-that-be would be pleased to see the back of him – they regard him as an awkward sod, always rocking the boat . . . Anyway, he's collecting stories, he's into Native American stuff right now . . .'

Beth paused to finish her coffee. Isabel was about to say something about political correctness but then she remembered that Beth and Simon considered it a good thing, not something to be mocked. Isabel was accustomed to the people she knew, her neighbours and Michael's colleagues and the people she met at dinner parties, sneering at it. She wondered if it was a North London/South London thing, but didn't feel like discussing it with Beth, not now.

'Simon's begun to practise,' Beth continued. 'I hear him in the study, performing into a tape-recorder – he's bought himself one of those tiny ones. Actually, he sounds rather good, I have to admit.'

'Well, he always liked performing his poems, didn't he?'

Simon had had two volumes of poetry published in his twenties and had progressed around the college circuit, reading them aloud. He had been briefly fashionable but had published nothing since. Later he claimed he'd only done it to meet women.

'Of course . . .' Beth looked thoughtful. 'I hadn't connected this new idea with his poetry readings.'

'And it's not such a bad idea, you know. Maybe he has a point. Traditional things like fairy tales and nursery rhymes, how many people teach them to their children, these days?'

'Yes, you're right.' Beth leant back and sighed, then seized her hat and biffed it into shape. Maybe she was imagining it was Simon, thought Isabel. 'Anyway, enough of all that. I could do with some air, Izzy. Shall we brave the elements and walk down to the National Gallery?'

The rain had almost stopped. Beth squashed her hat down over her hair and put her arm through Isabel's, as she often did, and Isabel, as ever, felt both fondness and slight embarrassment.

'So how is everything else, Izzy? How are the children?'

'Fine. I hardly see Dominic – he's either studying or out with his friends. Gemma's still deciding what to do with herself.'

'It's good you're so relaxed about it.'

Isabel wasn't sure what her friend meant but let it pass. 'And how are your three?'

'The usual ups and downs. Always arguing, if not between themselves then with me or Simon. But they're OK really.'

They were both happy to leave the subject: comparisons of their children, their differences, the schools they went to, their academic successes (or not) were further potentially sensitive issues.

She asked Beth about work, tentatively. As Beth launched into a tirade against new curriculum initiatives; the marginalisation of art; her doubts about what she was doing and was it all worth it; the problem of getting good life models these days, Isabel recognised the divide between them. Funny, she thought, there's a gap between me and both of my closest friends. With Angie it's to do with me being a mother and her not; with Beth it's the fact that she's always worked, she has a career, and I haven't. (The shop didn't seem to count.) For all the talk about female solidarity, we can still be separated by basic differences of experience . . .

Beth was laughing, saying it was time for another change of subject. Isabel began to tell her about Once or Twice and how it was doing, but she kept it brief as, after four years, she was still unsure of Beth's views about it, whether she approved or not. Did she think it frivolous, something Isabel merely played at? Which brought Isabel to Angie. How much should she tell? Did it matter? Angie and Beth rarely met, and when they did, they were polite, even amiable, but they would circle each other warily, as if rivals for the position of Isabel's best friend. Angie didn't swear me to secrecy, thought Isabel. In fact, she seemed almost proud of her new adventure, so here goes.

'I'm going to have to manage at the shop on my own soon, which is a bit of a bore.'

'Oh, is Angie backing out?'

'Sort of. To be honest, I'm not sure if it's permanent, but she's going off to live in Spain, with her new lover.'

'How romantic! Lucky her. Though it's a bit mad, isn't it, giving up your life for love? What's he like? Hope he's not a rogue.'

'Actually, Beth, he's a *she*.'

'What?' Beth shrieked and stood still on the narrow pavement of St Martin's Lane. Tourists and others pushed past her, looking at her with momentary curiosity. 'Oh my God. So Angie's become a lesbian?'

Isabel grinned, enjoying the expression on Beth's face and the opportunity for once to seem to be the worldly one. 'I don't really know. And I'm not sure that she does.' This time, she linked her arm through Beth's to move her on. 'Perhaps she's bisexual. Isn't there a theory that we all are, to a certain extent? Anyway, she's with this woman – Max, short for Maxine – for now. Says she fell in love with the person rather than the sex.'

'Does that make sense to you, Izzy?'

'In a way, yes. But don't ask me – I lead a very sheltered life!'

'I'm beginning to think I do too. But, you know, although I am surprised about Angie, there seem to be lots of women doing this, becoming gay, whatever.'

'Lots? Really?'

'Well, it's fashionable, isn't it? And I've heard of several women, friends of friends, that sort of thing, who after years of marriage have gone off with another woman. Or decided to have relationships with women instead of men. Maybe it's easier or cosier . . . Better? Or perhaps women get fed up with men, they've had enough.'

'Or perhaps it gets harder to find men as they get older so they turn to women instead.'

'Isabel! That's a cynical view!'

'No, no, I didn't mean it like that. It's just that . . . Take

82

Angie, for instance, she's had lots of unsuccessful relationships with men and she's said herself how hard it was to meet any decent unattached ones, so women are an alternative – after all, we all need love and affection.'

'I can't disagree with that.'

They climbed the steps to the National Gallery and Isabel let Beth choose the five paintings they'd look at today. This was a thing they did, limiting themselves to five works or sometimes just one artist. Isabel was beginning to feel tired but she daren't say she wanted to go home as Beth might be upset or offended. As they crossed the mosaic entrance hall Beth was talking about Dégas, enthusing about his painting of a woman drying herself after a bath. Isabel followed her, half listening.

Isabel closed her eyes. Luckily the bus wasn't full and she had the seat to herself. She'd decided to go home by bus – it took two buses, in fact – as she couldn't face the tube. The descent underground was unappealing in her present mood. Her body, her mind, wanted some peace and she found it temporarily on the number 9 bus. Beth was a dear friend but nevertheless Isabel found her wearisome at times. She didn't want to think about Simon or the lack of funding for state schools or the portrayal of the female nude in Western art, she wanted to think about the baby. As the bus stopped and started and crawled through the traffic she indulged in imagining this third child, this little surprise.

Beth sat squashed in a seat on the tube, trying to establish some room for her elbows. Just her luck to be stuck between two oversized men. Why did they have to sit with their legs wide open? Why did they assume a proprietorial position on the arm-rests? She delved into her bag to retrieve the postcards she'd bought in the gallery shop: looking at them would take her mind off things. And what things . . . This business with Simon. He'd do whatever he wanted despite her views or the children's. At first they'd been incredulous when he told them of his plans to be a storyteller, then they began to find it a bit of a joke. Now he was on a mission to explain it to them, earnestly and at length, so they avoided him as much as they could. And I'm stuck in the middle, as usual, thought Beth. Holding the centre. What if the centre cannot hold?

She thought of Angie and her new lover. She envied her. Other people's lives were changing, even Isabel's ... What about me? she thought. She needed change, something new. From the outside it might look as if she had everything: career of sorts, three lively, healthy children, a husband, a comfortable home ... All this around her, all she had, banked up and solid, could not dispel this empty feeling, this awareness that it could all turn out to be hollow at the heart.

13

Jenny stood on Putney Bridge and gazed down at the Thames. The water was a strange khaki colour. She remembered reading somewhere that rivers and the sea reflected the colour of the sky above them. Could that be true? Today the sky was a typical London colour, a non-colour, really, greyish, either cloudless or solid cloud. Featureless. It certainly wasn't any sort of brown. The river beneath her looked as if it were picking up colour from its depths, from the centuries of mud and silt. It did not attract her: she would rather wait until it was a better colour, on a better day. She imagined sliding into deep midnight blue water, like thick ink, which would welcome her softly. Perhaps night-time would be best.

Today wasn't meant to be the actual day anyway, although she sometimes wondered if the impulse to jump would take her by surprise. There were still preparations and plans to make. What would she wear? Should she remove her shoes first, or leave them on to encourage her to sink? Would she leap from a bridge or wade in from the riverbank? She favoured a bridge, but still hadn't found the right one. Putney was a possibility, with an easy parapet to climb, but it was busy with too much traffic, too many people. As she'd been standing here an elderly woman with a fluff of stiff white hair, waiting at the bus stop on the bridge had said, 'Watch out, dearie, you don't want to go over.' Jenny had smiled and moved further on, thinking, Oh yes, I do.

She should have replied with some pleasantry, she thought

afterwards, for no doubt the woman had meant well. And it was an opportunity to talk to another human being – so why had she passed it up? Days went by when she spoke to no one, unless you counted the few words in shops when she bought a newspaper or some food. It didn't bother her too much although she liked to talk to Isabel when she could. Lately that hadn't happened much – Isabel seemed so preoccupied. The other morning they passed each other in the street, Isabel hurrying to the doctor for a check-up, looking tired. She had told Jenny it seemed more complicated being pregnant this time – so many decisions to make, so many things to sort out, which tests were available, which ones she should have . . . Then she'd rushed off and Jenny had barely said a word. It was unlike Isabel: she was normally prepared to be understanding and patient and to listen. Jenny had always regarded Isabel as one of those few selfless people who genuinely had time – or made time – for others. Oh, well, it can't be easy being pregnant in your forties, Jenny thought charitably, even if you happened to be Isabel.

Jenny did have things of her own to do. Over the past few weeks she'd been systematically trying out bridges for size, working her way downstream from Richmond. This act of hers, her last act, involved a great deal of thought and organisation. All that walking along the river had convinced her to buy some trainers. She'd braved the sports shop in Sheen – her? in a sports shop? how Graham would have laughed – and come out equipped with a cushioned, padded, white and silver, fat-tongued pair, especially good for walking, the assistant informed her. He added that walking was the best form of exercise, so they said. How kind of him to omit to say, 'particularly for overweight middle-aged women', she thought.

The trainers were serving her well. Every morning she'd put them on and stride out towards the river with a bottle of water and a map. She wore tracksuit trousers and warm layers under her Sloppy Joe sweatshirt. How Graham had hated that! She recalled the day she'd bought it, from that shop in Barnes village, when she'd been so pleased she could get it on with room to spare. OK, so it wasn't so sloppy on her, not like on all those young skinny blondes you saw around, wearing them in pastel shades as their daytime uniform. Jenny's was darker, in navy, and she'd had it on when Graham came home that night. He'd glared at her, at it, and had said, his voice dripping with disdain, 'What *are* you wearing? Sloppy Jenny, more like.' He'd laughed at his own joke while she'd rushed upstairs, crying, to stuff the sweatshirt at the bottom of her wardrobe. That had been near the end, just a few weeks before he left. Yet another sign she hadn't noticed, or wanted to notice.

The sweatshirt was sloppier on her now, she realised. Perhaps it was all this walking. Exercise – surprise, surprise. Plus the fact that she was out of the house more, removed from the temptation of food. Her quest for the perfect suicide site wasn't the only thing keeping her away from home: she wanted to avoid the estate agents and the eager couples in search of a new family nest. She could see the logic of selling the house – it was too big for one person. And, besides, she wasn't going to be around much longer, although no one else knew that. Graham had strongly suggested, in a curt note (mainly a list of instructions relating to selling the house, obvious things that she already knew), that she should look for a flat, so she pretended to do so, even letting the agent send her details of places nearby. What a farce, she thought. If she really was going to move why would she stick around here? With her half of the proceeds from the house she could buy a cottage in the country with a lovely garden to spend her days in . . . She actually began to fantasise about it, but then firmly put the dream away, determined not to be deflected from her main purpose in life: ending it.

Meanwhile she sorted through clothes and books and the debris of family life, ruthlessly discarding, filling rubbish bags and boxes to take to charity shops. She steeled herself not to be emotional or sentimental by pretending that she was clearing out the house for someone else, a dead friend or relative, so that none of it affected her: these were no longer the artefacts of *her* life.

She gave the estate agent a set of keys and a list of times when the house could be viewed, then made sure she was absent. That was for the best. Before this arrangement there had been one awful occasion when she had hidden as the agent showed a couple around the house. She'd been gardening – unnecessarily pruning a shrub – with her head down, refusing to look up. When it had started to rain suddenly, she'd taken refuge in the shed, leaning her weight against the door so that no one could come in. No one had tried.

Now, apparently, there were several interested purchasers, so the agent had said when he rang yesterday. He had waited for her to be enthusiastic, but her mind had been on her own plans: this meant she had to end it, *do it*, before the house sale was concluded and she was expected to move out. How long had she got? How long?

Jenny turned off the bridge on to the embankment to begin her walk home. She walked away from Putney, past the boathouses in the direction of Barnes. She'd check out a spot she'd seen beyond Hammersmith Bridge and past the Swedish School, where the path narrowed through bushes and trees and came close to the river. A bricked bank sloped into the water under a twisted tree with low, thick, overhanging branches. Could that be the place? A gentle roll or slide? She'd investigate further.

She paused, leaning over the railings to inspect the river for she wanted to know it, to understand it. It was, after all, to be her final friend. My God! Such melodrama – she almost laughed at herself. The water was flowing fast, as if it too had a purpose, trying to get somewhere. She looked for birds she could recognise but there were only the ubiquitous seagulls circling overhead. Even though it was winter she often saw different birds by the water. There was a heron, a frequent visitor to the stretch at Barnes near the police station: it would stand on the stones and mud that resembled a beach when the water was low.

She shivered – it was getting cold. As she started to walk briskly towards the towpath she noticed a lone swan paddling energetically close to the shore, almost desperately, against the currents. It was a bizarre sight: swans were usually so elegant, gliding smoothly and effortlessly across the water. This one was working hard, she could see its webbed feet moving backwards and forwards, fast, practically lifting its body out of the water. What was it doing?

Jenny watched, mesmerised. As the swan battled towards Putney Bridge, it seemed to be making progress despite the force of the water. She measured the distance it was travelling by markers she picked out on the embankment – a lamp-post, a litter-bin, a bare tree . . . It was getting there, wherever it wanted to go.

The effort and determination of the swan tired her. Why couldn't it just go with the flow? She turned away and carried on walking.

14

Fatigue rooted Isabel to the sofa. This was happening every night: tiredness overtook her at about ten o'clock and she yearned for sleep. Lately she'd been surrendering to it and going to bed an hour or two before Michael, but that meant they hardly saw each other. This had been going on for weeks. She suspected that he didn't care, that he wanted to avoid her. Not just her, but the question of the baby, the whole thing.

Tonight she had resolved to stay awake and was waiting for him to return from walking the dog. This couldn't go on. Surely they had to try to resolve the situation? It was so unsatisfactory, this feeling of being in limbo. And Michael couldn't keep ignoring the fact that she was pregnant and hoping it would go away.

The sound of his key in the door roused her. She sat up quickly, not wanting to be found dozing and supine.

Jasper trotted in, pleased to see her, licking her hand. Michael followed. 'Isabel! I thought you'd be in bed.'

'I wanted to see you. We seem to keep missing each other lately.'

'Well, you're always tired, and I'm always busy.'

'That's not fair, I'm not *always* tired. Anyway, we're both here now, so can we talk?'

'OK, OK. I'm going to have a Scotch. Do you want one?'

'No, thanks. I'm –'

'Of course, you're off alcohol, aren't you? How could I forget?'

He went into the kitchen, the dog padding after him. Isabel clenched her teeth, resisting the urge to match his sarcastic tone with a comment about *his* drinking. She breathed deeply to keep calm. He returned with a large glass of whisky, swirling ice cubes round and round. Strange, Isabel thought, he never used to take it on the rocks – American-style, he'd called it dismissively.

'I took Jasper on the long walk tonight, up to the Thames and back. You'll never guess who I saw by the river. It was rather odd.' He gulped his drink.

'I've no idea. Tell me.' Isabel was convinced that he was trying to delay discussing real concerns.

'Our neighbour, Jenny. She was leaning over the wall, gazing at the water. In a world of her own. Didn't seem to hear me when I said hello, didn't respond anyway.'

'Oh. Perhaps she felt like some fresh air.'

'It's not exactly fresh air out there tonight, it's a bit foggy. And bloody cold. I didn't see a dog.'

'Jenny hasn't got a dog, you know that.'

'Hasn't she? Even odder, then. And it's not exactly wise for a woman to be out walking late at night on her own, is it?'

'If you say so.'

'Why that tone? What's the matter, Isabel? I thought you were her friend. You always seemed so worried about her after Graham left.'

'Michael, why are you suddenly so concerned about Jenny? It's unlike you.'

'What does that mean exactly?'

'It means – oh, never mind. Look, I don't want to squabble, all I want to do is talk about us.'

Michael looked at her, wearing a severe expression which he put on at times like these like a suit and tie. She met his glance, determined not to be intimidated. Eventually he shrugged and said, 'Very well. I'll just get another drink.'

Isabel sighed, making an effort to conceal her irritation. She didn't really want to do this now any more than he did – she was so tired – but it had to be done. She stood up and stretched, thinking about Jenny and wondering what the hell she was doing walking alone by the river at night. She must make a point of seeing her soon.

Michael watched Isabel from the doorway. She was yawning, stretching her arms over her head, unaware of him. Her long loose sweater moved against her body and he thought he could see a new roundness at her stomach, a fuller profile of her breasts, her nipples visible. Could the pregnancy be showing already? It must be that, Isabel never put on weight. Surprisingly, he felt desire, he wanted to take her to bed and explore the changes in her body . . . A sudden vision of Isabel when she was previously pregnant, quite heavily pregnant, sprang into his mind. He remembered one night when she was expecting Gemma, it was still a novelty and her enormous enlarged nipples were too. How they'd giggled as they compared them to fruits. Strawberries? Raspberries? Loganberries? And how they had aroused him. Isabel had eased herself on top of him, murmuring reassuringly that it was all right, really it was. Their love-making had been slow and prolonged: Isabel moving precisely and deliciously on his penis, her eyes closed and head tilted back; his hands spanning the full mound of her belly, while he gazed up at her swollen breasts with their newly appeared faint blue veins, almost too solid to bounce, shifting and rising, and those nipples – he'd had a sudden urge to nibble at them . . . He didn't, he held back, as he held back the need to thrust high and hard into her . . . The restraint he demonstrated was exquisite, practically painful. It had been extraordinary, this pregnant sex, he thought afterwards, as he had held Isabel against him, the curve of her bump pressing against him. Their baby. He remembered feeling emotional and reflecting that all was right with his world. Oh Christ.

Everything was so mixed up, *he* was so mixed up. While walking the dog tonight he'd spent all the time thinking about Ellen, yearning for her, counting the hours until her return, planning what to say to her. She had rung him at work today from New York – she had actually rung him – and said she'd be back in a few days' time. He'd almost slobbered over the phone with excitement. Talking to her, prolonging the call, not wanting her to go, making jokes, alluding to sex, swerving the conversation away from any difficult area where she might ask, 'Have you told your wife yet?' all served to make him late for a meeting. He'd kept clients waiting. That wouldn't do. Even his secretary had looked disapproving. Recklessness kept overtaking him: he'd take risks for Ellen, he *did* take risks. For Ellen, for himself.

Yet now the sight of Isabel moved him and affected him in

a myriad of ways, despite his efforts to distance himself from her, to exclude all thoughts of a baby and the continuance of family life as they'd known it. He had promised Ellen he would tell Isabel that he'd leave her, but now it really didn't seem so straightforward. Perhaps it never had been.

'Michael?' Isabel was regarding him from across the room, her arms folded.

'Yes, yes. I know, talking time.' He went over to the mantelpiece, leaning his elbow on the marble next to the smiling family photos in silver frames.

'Why don't you come and sit down?' Isabel guessed what he was playing at: standing up was more authoritative. He wanted to be in control.

'I'm fine here. By the way, where are the children? I don't want them overhearing all this.'

'It should be OK. Gemma went out with Lucy and won't be back until half-eleven or twelve. Dom is in his room revising.'

'All right, then. Now what did you want to talk about?'

'Michael, please! Don't play games. You know full well what I think *we* should talk about. The baby. Although maybe we shouldn't go on talking, perhaps it's decision time now.'

As Isabel said the dreaded word 'baby', she noticed his expression and saw how he tried to conceal it by gulping his whisky. Why *was* this so difficult for him?

Michael turned and faced her. 'Quite honestly, Isabel, I'm not sure what else there is to say. And as for a decision, you've already made up your mind, haven't you?'

'Well, I *think* I want to have the baby. I can see no reason why we can't.'

'We? What is this *we*?'

'What do you mean?'

'This is about *you*. You got pregnant. You want to have the baby. You've decided –'

'That's unfair. It's not quite like that.'

'It is. There's been no room for my feelings here.'

'That's not true! You just haven't expressed them.'

'Now *that*'s not true! I've made it clear all along that I did not want another child. This was a complete surprise. You

91

sprang it on me out of the blue. How did you expect me to react, for God's sake?'

Isabel struggled not to cry.

'Well? I'm waiting for an answer.'

'I suppose I thought you'd change your mind.' She looked down at her lap, away from the force of his gaze.

'No tears, please, Isabel. Why are you getting upset?'

'It's a sad situation. You, me –'

'Yes, it's bloody sad, but you got us into this mess.'

'Mess? Is it a mess?'

'From where I'm standing it seems so. You did this with no consent from me, there was no discussion . . .'

For a moment Isabel let his voice wash over her. She tried to focus inwards, to find a place of calm and safety. It was difficult, Michael was in full flow. This had happened before on the rare occasions when they disagreed, when it was an issue he felt strongly about: his argument took on a life of its own, growing and swelling to its logical (to him) conclusion. She had always supposed it was related to his profession, his legal training. Silence was the easiest strategy: if anyone dared interrupt he would not be diverted but would continue on track regardless with 'Yes, but . . .'

He seemed to be bringing his discourse to an end, Isabel recognised the tone of his voice: his closing tone. She wasn't listening – she didn't need to as he invariably ended up where he had started, restating his point of view in subtly different words.

'Michael, all I can say is that I didn't intend to get pregnant.'

She waited for him to claim that she hadn't been listening to a word he'd been saying, but this time he snorted at her in disbelief. 'Are you sure? Maybe this is an attempt to hold off the advancing years, a way of keeping yourself young.'

'What a nasty thing to say! And it's not fair – I'm not old, I'm only forty-three, for God's sake! I still feel young! I did *not* do this deliberately.'

He raised his eyebrows.

She was determined to make him understand and continued, 'Look, I explained about my coil.'

'Yes, you mentioned that.'

'I *was* going to tell you at the time so that we could take precautions or whatever.'

'Get to the point, please.'

'But soon after – well, you know that party in November?' He looked blank. 'The Colemans' fireworks party – remember? When we both drank rather too much?'

Michael sat down wearily in the leather armchair in front of the fireplace, running his hands through his hair. He did remember that night. The Colemans lived round the corner and frequently gave what they called neighbourhood parties, marking events on the calendar such as New Year or English Apple Week or Guy Fawkes' night. Planning for their Millennium party had long been well advanced. Michael didn't particularly like the Colemans but he admitted that their parties served a purpose.

That night he'd been tired and reluctant to go but Isabel had jollied him along. There had been a huge bowl of hot punch in the Colemans' conservatory and they'd both drunk a lot of it in an attempt to keep warm. It was typical November weather – depressingly damp. Everyone was encouraged to stand outside while the finishing touches were made to the bonfire and the fireworks were ignited. Isabel had snuggled up to Michael during the obligatory oohs and aahs and later they'd walked home arm in arm, pleasantly tipsy, laughing and gossiping about their neighbours. The feeling of togetherness lasted and they ended up rolling over the bed, half undressed, making love. Isabel had unzipped his jeans, easing his penis out of his boxers, calling it a Roman candle, encouraging his erection with her fingertips. Had he tried to resist? He'd wanted to, for Ellen's sake, but then had thought, sod it. Isabel was here, she was his wife, and he had to keep up appearances. And he'd wanted to. He'd helped her pull off her knickers, unbuttoned her shirt, pushed up her bra and pulled her to him.

'I think that was the night I conceived.'

'So?'

'So surely we were in no fit state to discuss whether I still had my coil in or not?'

'I wasn't *that* drunk, Isabel. You could have explained.'

'I didn't mean our drunken state. I was referring to our state of – of arousal.'

They were both silent for a moment. Michael got up and walked around the room, not looking at her as he spoke. 'A brief flare of passion – like a fucking firework – and this is what happens!' He heard her gasp, as if his words had struck her.

'What now, Michael?'

'What now indeed? It's not up to me, is it?'

'It's up to both of us. It's our baby.'

'No, Isabel, it's *your* baby.' He was standing over her. 'If you insist on going ahead with this, I can't guarantee what my role will be.'

Isabel stood up and faced him. 'That sounds like a threat.'

'I'm merely telling you how I feel, although so far it hasn't done me much good, has it? You're going to have this baby, aren't you?'

'Yes. I am. And as I'm twelve weeks now and all seems to be well, I suggest we tell the children. How about on Sunday, when we're all together for lunch?'

'Do what you damn well like!'

He slammed out of the room.

Isabel sat very still. She felt dizzy and hoped that it would pass if she did not move. It wasn't a physical thing, she realised. She was reeling from Michael's onslaught, for that was what it felt like. The force of his feelings and the unpleasant way he'd expressed them made her feel ill. She wished she'd lied to him and said that she'd got pregnant despite her coil, that no method was foolproof, perhaps he'd have accepted it then. What *was* the matter with him? She was becoming convinced that it wasn't just the pregnancy: there must be something else, something wrong, to make him react like this. Otherwise he wouldn't be so unfeeling and unforgiving. But what could it be?

She didn't want to think about it.

All she wanted right now was a cuddle, for someone to soothe and comfort her. But it didn't look like it was going to be Michael.

She pressed her hand to her stomach. 'There, there,' she

said. 'Everything will be all right.' But the reassurance was more for herself than for the beginnings of the baby inside her.

Michael sat in his study in the dark, the blinds open, with only the delicate light of the moon coming through the window. His feet were up on his desk next to the whisky bottle. A small ache of shame was creeping through his body. He suspected he'd behaved like a bully. A memory of his father shouting at his mother came into his mind. The things we learn, he thought uncomfortably.

He poured himself another drink. All right, so he was angry with Isabel for getting pregnant but why had he deliberately puffed himself up like one of those prickly fish defending itself? And then gone on the offensive? His own pompous tones echoed in his mind. His cruel, dismissive words. What had he been trying to achieve? To make himself so objectionable that Isabel would not want him? To turn himself into the kind of person who could do this to his wife – be mean to her, cheat on her, reject her? Especially when she was vulnerable, being pregnant. Was he trying to push their marriage to the edge of some sort of precipice?

How could he be such a shit?

He buried his head in his hands, resisting turning his thoughts to Ellen. That would be too easy. Thinking about Ellen would distract him and make him feel better, but he didn't deserve to be released. He didn't deserve Ellen. Neither did he deserve Isabel.

Truth time. He tried to examine himself as he would a dodgy client. If he were honest, if he dared to be, he knew that the scene with Isabel would have been very different if his relationship with Ellen had not existed. He would have behaved more decently. Isabel was right, she knew him well enough, for Christ's sake, he would eventually have caved in. He would probably have said, 'Never mind, what's done is done, number three it is,' or something like that. He might even have found solace in this obvious evidence of his continuing virility.

He could still do that now, he thought. He could go to Isabel and be merciful and throw himself on her mercy, he could say he was sorry – was that so hard? He'd say he had a shit-awful

day at work, with difficult clients, all that believable stuff . . .
Excuses, excuses. He'd say he wasn't used to surprises but
perhaps he could get used to this one. Isabel would fling herself
into his arms and she'd cry then laugh and they'd go to bed.
And he was reminded again of that other time twenty years
ago – perhaps they could recapture some of that, he could
explore her body and see how far the baby, this baby, had
changed it . . .

But then what would he do about Ellen?

Michael took another swig of whisky. A cloud obscured the
moon and the room darkened. He thought about what he
should do, he considered what he *could* do.

A rising sense of panic kept him fixed to his chair, and he
remained sitting alone in the dark looking up at the sky,
waiting for the moon to reappear.

15

Isabel surveyed the kitchen. Everything was almost ready. It
had been difficult to know what to cook as the family rarely
sat down and ate Sunday lunch together these days. Eventually
she'd opted for something traditional and simple: a corn-fed
chicken, with sprigs of thyme, cloves of garlic and half a
lemon stuffed inside and roast potatoes with steamed vegeta-
bles, broccoli and French beans, which she was leaving until
the last minute to cook. She'd hesitated over a starter but
ruled it out – this wasn't a dinner party, merely a family lunch,
and she mustn't make too big a deal of it, she knew that. It
was as if she were walking a high-wire, edging towards doing
what she wanted, what she thought was best – having the
baby, telling the children – while trying to deal with Michael
too. No wonder she felt wobbly.

There was apple crumble for dessert. Everyone liked that, as
far as she could recall. The table was laid: she'd put a cloth
over the long oak table, a piece of old French linen she'd
picked up at a market in the Loire valley years ago. Should she
open some wine or leave that for Michael? She decided to wait.

Waiting. That's what she had to do now. And remain calm.
Where were they? She'd told everyone this morning that lunch

was at one thirty. She couldn't decently delay it any further – after that and it wouldn't really be lunch, would it? Michael had barely responded and returned to the living room with the newspapers. Dominic hadn't staggered up until nearly twelve. He'd looked at her with disbelief over his cereal bowl. 'Lunch? But Mum, I'm just having breakfast and then I was planning to go –'

'We are all having lunch together, Dom. I don't often insist but I am today.' Her firm tone must have surprised her son as he said no more and disappeared upstairs to have a shower. It had surprised her too. Gemma had been easy-going as ever, taking Jasper out for a walk – that way she'd work up an appetite, she'd said. But she wasn't back yet.

At one, Isabel switched on the radio, but barely heard the news as she was listening out for sounds of Michael approaching or Dominic clattering down the stairs or Gemma's key in the door. Then she told herself not to be so ridiculous, so pathetic, sitting and quivering with anticipation. She filled the steamer with water and put it on to boil.

The meal wasn't a success. Dominic toyed with his food, obviously not hungry. Michael was mostly silent. Isabel tried to keep up some sort of conversation with Gemma, aware that it sounded twittering and trivial, then gave up and concentrated on finding the right moment to tell the children the news. There wasn't one. She wanted to catch Michael's eye to give him a clue – a nod, a look – something to show him that she was about to speak but he avoided her gaze. As she served the apple crumble Dominic pushed back his chair and said he really couldn't manage anything else so would they mind if he went upstairs? Isabel was pleased to see he still had some remnants of the manners they'd taught him but knew that she had to grab the moment now.

'Actually, Dom, I'd – we'd – rather you stayed put. There's something we need to tell you.' She glanced at Michael, willing him to join in, be at her side in this. He stared back. Silence dominated the table.

Dominic pushed his hair back from his face – that sweep of hair so like his father's – and suddenly looked very young, Isabel thought. His expression – one that she saw infrequently, these days – revealed that he felt unsure, unsettled. When he was small he'd turn to me with that look and I'd reassure him, make everything all right, thought Isabel. He must still feel like that but he's learnt to hide it. Or he doesn't turn to me any more.

'Mum?' Gemma's voice. She looked puzzled. 'Is everything OK?'

'Yes, darling, everything's fine!' She tried to make her voice sound bright and cheerful, which she was, wasn't she? So why did she feel tearful? 'But we have some news to tell you both –'

'Oh God, you're not splitting up, are you?' Gemma interrupted.

'Everyone's parents are splitting up. Not you too?' Dominic joined in. He and his sister looked at each other, their habitual animosity set aside.

Michael took control, throwing up his hands, assuming his professional voice. 'Children, please! It's not that. Your mother –'

'Dom, Gemma, don't worry, it's something positive, not negative. What I have to tell you is that I'm pregnant. We're going to have another baby.'

Silence. A gasp – from Gemma? A sigh – from Michael?

'Bloody hell. A *baby*? Oh, no! Do you have to? What will everyone think?' Dominic looked from one parent to the other.

Isabel could sense Michael preparing something to say, carefully gathering an acceptable word here, another there, something that would calm the situation without betraying what he himself felt – for, after all, didn't he agree with Dominic, in essence?

'What other people think isn't of prime importance here, it's not really an issue.' Michael had found something to say.

'Oh, really? Perhaps not for you, but it is for me. A baby – who wants a baby around? We don't need this . . .' Dominic stopped, as if suddenly tired of the whole thing, even though it had barely begun.

'Gemma? You haven't said anything.' Isabel spoke gently to her daughter.

'I'm gob-smacked. Shocked, I suppose. It's weird though isn't it? Must be for you too.'

'You could say that!' Michael gave a little laugh.

'Obviously it was a bit of a surprise when I found I was pregnant, I can't deny that.' Isabel tried a laugh too.

'Oh really? What did you think, Mum? That babies were found under bushes?' Dominic smirked but he was flushed with embarrassment. This was too much, being forced to admit that his parents actually had sex and having to think about it.

'Dominic! That's enough! There's no need to be rude to your mother.'

He glared at his father but mumbled an apology, then said he was going upstairs. As he left the room he threw a remark over his shoulder about not wanting to play happy families any more.

Michael rose from his chair. 'Let it go,' Isabel said quietly, and turned to her daughter, who was examining the embroidery on the tablecloth with great attention.

'Gemma?'

'It just seems so odd, Mum. It's come out of the blue.' Now she too looked embarrassed. 'You know what I mean. And what about your health – and the baby's? Doesn't it get more dangerous the older you are?'

'I'm fine and healthy. And plenty of women my age have babies these days. I know what the statistics show – more risk of Down's syndrome, and other things.' She paused, sensing Michael becoming rigid with tension. 'But there are tests that I can have.'

Neither Gemma nor Michael would look her in the eye. The unspoken questions hung over the table: What if? What then? Isabel didn't want to discuss it. She hadn't even confronted the possibility of having a disabled child herself, not seriously, although she knew she must. What *would* she do?

'Does anyone want some more crumble?'

'No thanks, Mum. I've got to make some phone calls. Shall I stay and help?' She looked eager to get away.

'No, it's OK. You go and make your calls.'

Gemma quickly left the room.

Isabel began clearing the table.

'Well Isabel, I wouldn't say that went very well, would you? But then, I didn't expect it to.'

'They'll adjust. Of course they're surprised –'

'Surprised? That's putting it mildly! And as for *adjusting* – God, you make it sound so easy. They'll have to, won't they? Like me. We don't have any bloody choice.'

He slammed out of the room. Isabel bent over the dish-washer, plate in hand, and let the tears fall.

16

The room was full of darkness. Momentary bewilderment. Isabel slowly came to and remembered coming upstairs to lie down after lunch. Everything had been so fraught, not at all how she'd wanted it to be, although she realised she'd been naïve to expect anything else. Bed offered an escape, and she was so weary. She hadn't meant to fall asleep, she'd just needed to rest – and to be alone.

She got up stiffly and went to the window. The street-lights glowed dimly and it was very quiet: no one was about out there. The beginning of another long winter evening. She had no idea what the time was – how long had she been asleep? The luminous dial on the bedside clock said five thirty. A vague feeling of guilt came over her.

After splashing her face with cold water, determined to ignore the start of a headache, Isabel ventured downstairs. She had a small sense of dread at the thought of seeing Michael – or Michael as he was at the moment. It was like a science-fiction fantasy, she thought, as if the real Michael had been snatched and his body invaded by this other being who showed no sign of humanity whatsoever, especially towards his wife. She kept wishing and hoping that would change, that the next time she saw him he would be his old self, that he would hold her and everything would be all right. Meanwhile she continued to struggle to understand the way he was behaving.

Gemma seemed to be the only one at home. Isabel found her watching *The Clothes Show*, curled up on the sofa with a mug of tea, the cat by her side.

'Mum! There you are! Are you OK?'

'Yes, I'm fine, I had a lie-down.'

'Shall I make you some tea?'

'No, don't worry. You watch this. By the way, where's Dad?'

'Not sure. He just said he was going out for a while. In the car, I think.'

Isabel went into the kitchen and switched on the kettle. Although she thought she'd cleared up after lunch the room still looked messy. Crumbs on the table, a saucepan on the hob, a dead tea-bag nestling in a spoon on the worktop, an empty milk carton left by the sink. 'Shit,' said Isabel, aloud, and Jasper looked up at her from his basket in the corner. She glared at him: she wasn't in the mood to walk or feed him. Did I leave it like this? she wondered. If I did, why couldn't someone else finish the job? And if I didn't, why the hell can't they clear up after themselves?

A woman's work is never done: one of her mother's clichés. How Isabel used to smile to herself when her mother said it and sighed as she washed or tidied or ironed or cooked or swept. 'I'll never be like that,' Isabel had declared. 'My life won't be so conventional or obvious, I'll be different.' Yet look at me now, she thought. Despite technology and progress and feminism, what's changed? It still seems to be down to me, all this household stuff. If I didn't do it, would anyone notice? Or care? And Isabel thought, perhaps my mother wasn't mouthing a cliché, maybe she was telling the truth.

She turned her back on the kitchen, the place that usually soothed and welcomed her, where she felt especially at home. Right now it seemed a lonely place. Isabel had a sense of things fragmenting, of cracks appearing in the whole, and it made her uncomfortable. Perhaps she'd been taking things too much for granted: Michael, their marriage, happiness, stability . . .

She picked up the phone and tried Beth's number. Constantly engaged. Probably Beth's wild children phoning their wilder friends. What is the matter with me? Isabel wondered. I'm not usually like this. She punched in Angie's number.

Angie answered at last, sounding breathless. 'Oh, Isabel. Hi.'

'How's everything going?'

'Chaos. Can you believe I'm up a ladder decorating? Or I was.'

'I'm sorry to interrupt.'

'Don't be daft, Izzy, you weren't to know. You see, if I'm to get a good price for my house, whether selling it or letting it,

I've got to smarten it up, the agent says. So you should see me now! Brilliant white emulsion all over the place. It may not be fashionable –'

'Isn't it?'

'Shouldn't I be experimenting with Tuscan terracotta tones or baby blues or something like that? You read *Elle Deco*, those interiors magazines, don't you?'

'Sometimes. But I don't take them too seriously or put that stuff into practice. Most of our house is white.'

'Anyway, I've got to get this finished and I can't afford to pay someone to do it. The sooner it's done, the sooner I can go to Spain. God, it's bloody frustrating, I miss Maxi like hell!'

'I'd better let you get on with it, then.'

'I should really. Oh, I'm sorry, Izzy, did you ring for anything special?'

'Not really. Just a chat.'

'Well, look, I'll see you at the shop tomorrow, OK?'

Isabel said it was, although it wasn't, not really.

'Gemma! Gemma?'

'Yes?'

'I'm going round to see Jenny. Won't be long.'

'All right Mum.'

Isabel threw on her coat and hurried to Jenny's house. Her usual visits were made in the spirit of good neighbourliness – Isabel being a good neighbour to Jenny, wanting to make sure that Jenny was all right, whatever that meant. Tonight was different.

The hall light was on. She rang the bell several times and eventually Jenny appeared, looking dishevelled.

'Isabel! This is a surprise –'

'Hi Jenny. I'm sorry – you don't mind me popping round, do you? As I haven't seen you much lately I thought it would be nice to have a chat.'

'Of course I don't mind. Come in, come in. Sorry about the mess.'

The hall was full of cardboard boxes, stuffed with – as far as Isabel could see – clothes and books and bits and pieces. A lampshade stuck out here, an old tennis racquet there.

'Looks as if you've been busy.' Isabel stepped over a box and followed Jenny to the kitchen.

'Yes. I was up in the loft when you rang the bell. So difficult to get in and out of! And there's so much to clear out –'

'It's a good idea, a new start, that sort of thing.' Isabel sat down at the table, watching Jenny warily, knowing she must be careful what she said or Jenny might crumble. But as she turned from washing her hands at the sink, Isabel was relieved to see that she was dry-eyed.

'It certainly is,' she spoke briskly, 'And it has to be done. Ah, but you don't know, do you?'

'What don't I know?' Isabel leaned forward.

'Some people want to buy the house, they're very keen and it's a good offer.'

'But I didn't even know you'd put it on the market!'

'Graham's idea, of course. He insisted. But I can see the sense of it.'

'But what will you do, Jenny? Where will you go?'

Jenny looked across at Isabel and felt an impulse to confide in her, to tell her everything in a great rush of words and emotions. But how would it help? It would probably resolve nothing and besides, it wasn't fair to involve Isabel, who was looking pale and puffy and tired, and didn't seem her usual perky self. Perhaps she had her own problems. Anyway, where would I start? thought Jenny.

As she tramped towards the fate she had chosen, confusion was setting in. Her purpose was still clear, she thought, but her mind was becoming muddied. How could she describe it to Isabel? I'm determined to end my life; I've decided on drowning; I'm working on it . . . But there are still too many imponderables (and unthinkables?). How could she possibly plunge into the depths of her soul – for that was what it felt like – and come up with an acceptable explanation, a neat and tidy account of her situation?

Yesterday she had stood on Hammersmith Bridge, the wind whipping her hair over her face. This was the place she favoured – for the moment. She liked the atmosphere of the river here, the sweep and curve of it, the Victorian grandeur of the bridge itself (although she was not so sure about the

Harrods green of its paint job). And how appropriate, she thought, that the seemingly robust structure was in fact fragile and not adequate for the demands of the late twentieth century? (Like her?) At present it was closed to most traffic, with just buses and the occasional motorbike passing, but still she'd have to choose the right moment, avoiding any rowers near the banks and commuters walking home. She had stared down into the water, leaning her breasts on the rail. (A reasonable height to get over easily.) Not that she could see anything – the river was its usual muddy colour, shifting in tone as the wind created ripples on its surface and the light changed. Behind her she heard a bus trundling over the bouncing boards, laid on top of the original roadway. Then it was peaceful. There was no one about. Concentrating on the water, Jenny asked herself, Can I do it? What if someone dives in to save me then loses their own life? (That happened once below this very bridge: she'd read the memorial plaque.) Suppose she changed her mind as she hit the river, as it enfolded her, as her clothes and shoes combined with the force of the water to drag her down . . . Into that awful darkness, into the unknown?

She was not quite ready yet.

'Jenny?'

'Sorry, Isabel. My mind was elsewhere. What was it you said? Oh, yes – I'm not sure where I'm going yet . . . Something will turn up. Now, what can I offer you? There's not much in the house I'm afraid.'

'A cup of tea would be nice. Oh God, does that sound pathetic?'

'It's all right, I know what you mean. Sometimes tea really is just the thing. I'll join you.'

Jenny could feel Isabel watching her as she moved around the kitchen. 'You're looking well,' Isabel said. 'Have you lost weight?'

Ordinarily Jenny would have wanted to retort that you could look well without losing weight, the two didn't necessarily go together, but today she replied calmly, 'I think so. I haven't weighed myself lately but my clothes are looser. Odd, isn't it? For once in my life I haven't been actually trying to lose weight, yet I seem to have managed it.'

'Bit like me. I didn't try to get pregnant but here I am!'

Jenny smiled and said nothing, not quite sure of the connection. She went to the fridge to get the milk. It was nearly empty and she was pleased with its bareness. The kitchen cupboards were like this too: she'd attacked them a few days ago, throwing out tins with smudged best-before dates; jars of mustard and relishes (Graham's favourites); half-full packets of flour and dried fruit; birthday-cake candles and unopened boxes of icing-sugar; an ancient Marks and Spencer's Christmas pudding still in its Cellophane . . . She'd filled three black rubbish bags. Shopping had changed too. Resenting anything that took her away from the river, she no longer lingered in delicatessens or strolled leisurely around supermarkets. These days, when she went into Waitrose she picked up a wire basket and kept the items to a minimum. When Graham had first left she had continued to take a family-sized trolley at the entrance as she couldn't bear the idea of shopping just for one. And she'd fill it with unnecessary things like crisps and ice-cream and chocolate and fizzy drinks, pretending they were for the teenage boys she'd once had at home, but were in reality treats and comforts to fill her lonely evenings. But no more.

'Sorry, I haven't got any biscuits or anything.'

'Don't worry, I'm not hungry.'

They sipped their tea in silence. Jenny sneezed. Then again.

'Bless you!'

'It must be the dust in the loft. There are some things that haven't been touched for years – the boys' Scalextric sets, stuff like that. God knows what I should do with it all.'

'Ours is the same. I ought to have a look up there, see if there's any baby stuff, although I'm sure I got rid of it all – I never thought I'd have another one!'

'No, I'm sure you didn't.'

'Michael thinks I did this on purpose, you know, Jenny. He's got some mad theory that I did it to keep myself young.'

'But does having children keep you young? I suppose there are pros and cons. In some ways it ages you more, I think – Isabel, what is it?'

Isabel's face was crumpling before Jenny's eyes.

'I'm sorry, I'm so sorry. It's just that I need to talk, I feel so overwhelmed.' And she sniffed and tried not to cry.

Jenny knew those feelings only too well, although her distress had been caused by different factors. But it took her a moment to respond, for she had to adjust to seeing Isabel like this. In all the time she'd known her, from when the children were small, she had never seen Isabel upset. Irritated, yes, a bit pissed off, yes, but not really upset or distressed. She had sometimes wondered if it was because Isabel kept things to herself and vented her feelings in private, or was it because she actually had no reason to get upset, with her seemingly perfect life?

But right now, thought Jenny, something is going wrong in Isabel's life, or it appears to be. She went to Isabel and put her arm around her, as Isabel had so often done to her in recent months.

Isabel wailed, 'Oh, Jenny,' and it all came tumbling out: Michael's continuing opposition to the pregnancy, her confusion, her decision to go ahead – was it the right one? – the children's reactions, Dominic's contempt . . .

So it's all to do with having the baby, Jenny thought. Poor Isabel, what a difficult position to be in, and the changes to her hormones probably didn't help . . . No wonder she was weeping. But then Isabel blurted out more about Michael: how cold he was being, even cruel, so distant, and a chill came over Jenny as she thought she recognised the familiar symptoms. Michael, an errant husband? Was that possible? One thing I've learnt in the last year, she thought grimly, is that anything is possible. But had it occurred to Isabel?

A great wave of doubt and anguish streamed from Isabel. Jenny tried to contain it, holding her and hushing and murmuring words of comfort. This is strange, she thought, not just because our situations are reversed and it's Isabel who needs a friend, but also because it's ages since I was this close to another human being. Now that's sad.

'What am I going to do? What am I going to do?' Isabel sobbed.

'None of us really knows, Isabel. None of us knows what we're going to do.' Then Jenny calmed her, saying all this upset was bad for the baby and reassured her that everything would be all right. For wasn't that what everyone wanted to hear? And she promised, 'I'm here for you, Isabel. I'll help, I'll do what I can.'

Isabel began to quieten down.

Jenny's vision of the Thames was fading. The prospect of the river started to slip away, sliding sideways until it was like a picture on a wall, a misty, liquid landscape that she could admire but not enter. For now.

17

Ellen kicked off her shoes and lay down on the pale wooden floor, stretching out her arms and legs and gazing up at the high chalky-white ceiling, enjoying the feeling of space. The flight from New York hadn't been too bad, she'd even managed to doze a little, but the crowded tube journey from Heathrow had been horrendous. Standing most of the way, squashed between other people, their luggage and protruding backpacks, she wished she'd taken a taxi.

It was great to be home. She loved this apartment – and it was all hers, thanks to the windfall left her by her grandmother. It had been a shell when she'd bought it and she'd kept it as empty as she could. Even Giles, the architect she'd employed for his minimalist reputation, had been surprised by her ideas. Once the work was under way he'd admitted that he'd envisaged she'd want something more girly, a folksy kitchen or walk-in closets for all her clothes. Ellen had drawn herself up to her full height of five feet ten, told him that she wasn't paying him for his pathetic sexist views and had walked away to check on the plumber, who was installing her power shower. She guessed that Giles fancied her – that may have been his clumsy way of flirting, acknowledging that she was a *girl*. Ugh. She still couldn't quite fathom English guys – except Michael, of course.

She closed her eyes and relished the thought of him. God, they were good together. Sex with Michael was probably the best she'd ever experienced . . . Was it because their bodies fitted so well? Or was it because he was older? He was the oldest lover she'd ever had. (Not that he was *old*.) But that didn't necessarily explain his sensitivity and patience and all-round general wonderfulness. They were a couple. It was just such a fuck-awful thing that he was married to someone else.

She wasn't going to think about that, not now. The situation. The wife was part of it, of course, she knew that, but she chose to push her to the edges, marginalise her. Ellen knew her name but preferred to think of her as The Wife: that way she remained less real. A shadowy figure loosely attached to Michael. He had always been reluctant to talk about her and usually that suited Ellen, but sometimes she felt a desperate need to know: what did she look like? How did she dress? And her voice? Her sense of humour? Why was he originally attracted to her? How did they meet? In the absence of answers, not that she ever voiced most of the questions, she created an image of The Wife in her mind. Mousy, middle-aged, quiet, boring, reserved in that English way. Ellen knew she was constructing a stereotype but it suited her, it was easier to deal with. And hopefully the situation was near some sort of resolution. He had promised to tell her, he had promised.

Ellen planned what she was going to do. A shower, wash her hair, unpack, check her phone messages and e-mails, then call Michael. Or perhaps she'd allow herself to call him *first*? He'd better have some free time today – or could make some – she needed to see him. No sex and no Michael for nearly a month. He must be desperate to see me too, she thought.

She rang him.

A brief conversation, a hurried arrangement. As always. But he'd be here in a few hours. 'Yes, yes, yes!' she whooped, pirouetting down the length of the room. But now what? She wandered through the apartment. There was a light layer of dust over everything – where had it come from? Maybe she'd spruce things up a bit before Michael came over. And there was nothing to eat or drink – the fridge boasted a bottle of champagne, that was all. Ellen felt the stirrings of domesticity, something that she usually declared did not come naturally to her – why should it? But Michael had that effect on her. Early in the relationship she'd realised that he presumed her fridge would be full, that her cupboards would contain jars and bottles and boxes from which she could conjure up something delicious. He expected it just as he expected water when he turned on a tap. It was a generational thing, Ellen decided. She'd try to re-educate him when they were together for real. Meanwhile she blamed The Wife for providing for him so well. Too well.

There was no way she was staggering out to some distant supermarket, even by taxi, so she found the Food Direct catalogue (why was everything *direct* these days?) and scanned it quickly, making a list of basics like toilet tissue, olive oil and coffee beans plus extras such as ready-to-eat lobster. And there had to be snacks and finger-food – stuff she classified as after-sex food. She and Michael had got into the habit of having picnics on the bed after making love and before making love again. It could be messy but Ellen had to admit there was a certain primitive appeal to the whole thing. She was thinking of writing a piece on it: *post-coital cuisine? Ten other things to do with your fingers.* Would Michael care if she used their activities as material? She guessed he wouldn't. Not that he'd ever know: he didn't read the sort of magazines she wrote for; he barely acknowledged their existence.

Ellen sighed, feeling her excitement seep away and a weariness slip into its place. Must be jet-lag, she decided, despite her in-flight use of aromatherapy oils and careful doses of melatonin. She sat at the beechwood kitchen table with the phone and a credit card and ordered the food, stressing the urgency, pleading for speed. Two hours was the best they could do, and for that she was grateful. Hopefully the delivery would arrive before Michael, and not when they were making love . . .

This is crazy, she thought. Here she was, an independent woman of the nineties, la la la, juggling important issues such as getting food in and trying to make everything perfect for her lover. Grace would laugh at me, she thought. *I* should laugh at me.

But her resolutions after Noah still held firm, didn't they? She retained her independence, her self-respect, her dignity. And Michael wasn't Noah, he was a far superior specimen of manhood, and she'd learnt her lesson, hadn't she? Except that she wasn't sure what it was.

She checked her messages – nothing that couldn't wait –

then searched for the pink fluffy feather duster that she'd bought as a half-joke and rarely used. It was in the coat closet. She flicked her way around the apartment, telling herself that this was an ironic duster, it was ironic dusting. (Another article, she wondered? *Ironic housework . . . How to avoid serious domestication* . . . Perhaps not.)

Now, time to get herself ready, make herself irresistible, although Michael always said that he could never resist her, she was perpetually gorgeous. His Amazon. The first time he'd called her that she'd laughed and pointed out that she had *two* breasts and no experience with a bow and arrow. 'Only love's arrow,' he'd murmured. 'Now, about these breasts, I'd better check . . .' His hands had moved seriously over her.

Ellen turned the shower to massage mode and surrendered herself to the water, letting it pummel her neck and shoulders. Afterwards she rummaged in her luggage for the Kiehl's moisturiser she'd bought in New York – she always stocked up, it was cheaper there. Steady strokes all over, rubbing and smoothing. Damn – did her legs need shaving? She could probably get away with the way they were. What were Michael's views on untouched female hairiness? So far she'd never put them to the test, always presenting herself plucked and shaved and hairless – she guessed that was what he preferred.

She turned the heating up even higher, wanting to wear the minimum of clothes, to be ready for him. No bra, no knickers. Just a loose linen-mix sweater and some Muji grey cotton joggers. The look that said, I'm cool, I haven't made an effort, not really. She repainted her toenails and slicked her hair back. A few squirts of Acqua di Gio, a touch of mascara and lip balm and that was it.

The door buzzer sounded as she was finishing putting the food delivery into the fridge. She kept most things there – it always amused Michael, he found it very American. 'Cold coffee beans? Chilled apples?' he'd say, with a smile. But she knew that he relished what he perceived as her differences. She sometimes even accentuated her American-ness to entertain him (never mind that her mother had been English).

The buzzer sounded again as she sprang to the entryphone. It was him. A few moments later she opened the door.

'Michael.'

'Ellen.'

He flung his briefcase on the floor, attempted to shrug off his coat, his arm got stuck, she tugged at his sleeve and they were at each other. No time to look, to talk, to ask, 'How are you?' He kissed her face all over, quick urgent kisses, until her mouth found his. Their tongues met, their bodies collided. His hands slipped up under her sweater and claimed her breasts. She sighed, he groaned.

'Where, Ellen?' he asked, as she pulled at his tie and shirt.

'Anywhere, here.'

Their voices shared that throaty aroused interrupted tone.

Her sweater was off, her breasts bare against his chest. Shivers of anticipation as their skin made contact. Walking backwards into the living space, taking him with her, she unbuckled his belt and dipped her hand down inside his trousers.

They reached the Persian rug in the middle of the floor. She quickly stepped out of her jogging pants and he gazed at her nakedness, but only for a moment, there was no time. Off with his trousers, out of his boxers.

'Oh, Michael,' she said, 'you *are* pleased to see me.'

Afterwards they lay together on the rug, stretched out naked, facing each other. Their smiles matched.

'Are you cold Michael? Shall I fetch a quilt or something?'

'No, I'm fine. Nicely warmed up – just had all that exercise. And your heating's up high as always.'

Ellen propped herself up on one elbow. Michael did too. They laughed. He watched her breasts jiggle slightly then said, 'Look at us, we're like bookends.'

He stroked the length of her body, down from shoulder to thigh, enjoying the taut quality of her skin (not flesh – not Ellen), the line of her hip bone, everything in its place, just so. He appreciated the pared-down quality of her, from the short, boyish haircut to the trim shape of her bush, a perfect triangle. (He'd once asked her if she snipped it – she'd said no but she would if he wanted, how about a heart?)

'We're a pair.' She arched towards him. He thought, not for the first time, how feline she could seem.

'A matched set . . .'

'Not quite, not quite matched, Michael. Look how you're different.'

Her hand skimmed over his stomach muscles and lifted his penis. It rose to her touch. Her head went down, her tongue flicked into action and he gave himself up to pleasure, to her.

They made love more slowly. That was their pattern: passion in a rush, then after an interval of love talk and circling and playing (if there was time) they would do it again, with more precision and deliberation, each knowing how to please the other. Yet there were still surprises, when they discovered new things to do or new ways of doing them.

They ended up on Ellen's bed, which was wide and elongated (American-sized, she insisted, British beds were so small) with plenty of room for manoeuvre. Crisp white sheets, to start with, quilt thrown on the floor. Naked to the air, the light, open to each other, they rolled and explored and appreciated these bodies of theirs. Long, lean, muscular. Made supple by exercise, perfect for experimenting with different and difficult positions. Michael marvelled at the places Ellen could put her legs.

If they had been tackier people, or lived in an earlier time, there would have been mirrors on the ceiling, on the wall. As it was, they basked in their mutual glory, revelling in the reflection of themselves in each other.

'Shall we open some champagne, Michael? And are you hungry?'

Ellen waited for him to glance at his watch and say he had to make a phone call. This time he didn't.

'Yes, to both. But would you like to go out to eat?'

Ellen turned to him in surprise. They rarely went out together, that was the nature of the relationship. She'd learnt to accept it.

'Bold words! I'd love to say yes, but I've actually got all this food in.'

'Really? And you whose cupboards are usually bare! Don't look like that, Ellen, I'm only teasing. Come here.'

He pulled her to him, tucking her head into the place where his shoulder met his neck, a strong, safe place, she thought.

She sighed. He smoothed her wet hair (they'd showered together, splashing and messing about like kids) and murmured, 'Whatever you want, my love. Let's stay here and have one of our picnics.'

Ellen laid out food – bread, olives, salads, the lobster – on the beech table. She didn't feel like carrying it all up to bed. Everything was pre-prepared, all she had to do was unwrap it.

'This looks wonderful, Ellen. And I'm starving.'

'Good. Oh, open the champagne, will you? I'll get the glasses.'

She watched him ease out the cork with his thumbs. As the champagne rushed into her outstretched glass she wanted to ask him if they had anything to celebrate. The question of whether he'd told The Wife had been kept at bay by her joy at seeing him, by the distraction of delicious sex, but now it was bubbling under the surface like an underground stream, searching for an outlet into the open.

'To us,' he said.

They sat close at one end of the table, Ellen in a little cotton vest and knickers, Michael in the spare towelling robe. (He was the only one to use it, but she resisted calling it his.) He attacked the lobster. It was noisy, this breaking and cracking and sucking the meat from the claws. She toyed with some bread, her appetite waning, the voice in her head drowning out other sounds: He said he'd tell her, he promised. So has he, has he?

'Ellen?' He was wiping his mouth, pushing the hair back off his forehead, looking a little anxious. 'You're very quiet. Not hungry after all?'

'I'm OK. I'm a bit tired, perhaps it's jet-lag. I'll eat something later.'

'Now, come on, what is it?'

You must know, thought Ellen. What else is there? She stood up. 'Let's talk, Michael. Leave all this.' She gestured at the mess on the table and went over to the sofa.

'Ellen, I think I know what you want to talk about –'

'You should know. You promised to tell her. So have you? Have you told her about us and what you're going to do?'

He leant towards her, carefully enfolding her hands in his. At that point she knew the answer.

He said it wasn't that easy, he said Christmas, all that, was a difficult time, a family time by its very nature, he was sorry, but that's how it was. But that wasn't all. When she tried to interject he begged her to listen, to understand. It was complicated. There was a problem – Yes, you're married, that's the problem, she wanted to shout. A problem with – with Isabel. His voice faded. Holy shit, thought Ellen, he actually used her name. She waited. He said Isabel was ill, that's why he couldn't tell her, not *now*. Ellen demanded details. He faltered, saying something about tests, investigations, hinting at trouble with her womb, suggesting it was serious. He passed his hand over his face and once more said he was sorry.

Ellen could see that his distress was real enough – but was it because he'd let her down or because his wife was sick?

'Michael?'

His eyelashes were wet. Why the hell did he have to look so appealing? She reached out to him, stroking his hair. It reminded her of feathers, sleek raven's-wing feathers. Comforting him began to calm her.

Michael settled his head between her breasts. 'Ellen?' His voice sounded as if it was struggling.

'Yes?'

'Whatever happens, I love you. I want you. Can we continue, please? Please?'

'Oh Michael.' She held his face in her hands, looked him over for a moment or two, then kissed his eyes, his nose, his mouth. Then she pushed him back on the sofa. This was one way she could take control.

18

A line had been drawn between Isabel and Michael. It was that little push in the night that did it. No, not such a little push, more of a shove, a sudden definitive poke in the shoulder. From Michael. It had woken her with a jolt, leaving her feeling trembly and confused. Isabel and Michael lying in their marital bed but everything was not as it should be. What had happened? What had she done? She spoke his name, but he was asleep or pretending to be. Had she imagined it? But she could feel it still on her shoulder, not pain, not exactly, rather an after-trace of ill-will. It felt as if Michael had pushed her with malice.

In the morning, in the rush of the kitchen at breakfast-time, she'd confronted him. He looked up reluctantly from *The Times* and said he couldn't remember, but perhaps she'd been lying on her back snoring, she had done that a lot recently, and if he'd *nudged* her – *if* – it was probably to get her to turn over so that he could get some sleep. Then he'd returned to the newspaper. Dominic kept his head down over a bowl of cornflakes, spooning fast. Isabel left the room, her emotions lurching from distress to anger. What he'd said may have been superficially true: she did sometimes end up sleeping on her back because her breasts had become tender. She could have been snoring . . . Yet there was more to it than that. She was not overreacting, this was not just her hormones. *When push comes to shove*, she thought. This was it.

The symbolism was not wasted on her – it was like a push over the edge. It moved her into unexplored territory, into the unknown, away from him. Was that what he wanted?

Michael hurried to catch the train to Waterloo. Long strides, almost running. He'd rather not do this, he'd rather be cocooned in his car but he only drove to the office if he managed to leave really early, before seven. Only then could you dodge the traffic – like catching a wave – zooming into London before the masses. But this morning he'd got up late, he'd left late. Last night had been a nightmare, tossing and turning, unable to get to sleep, but when eventually he did, waking up again. It was tempting to blame Isabel and her spasmodic snoring but if he were honest he had to admit it was more his own state of mind preventing him from sleep.

What he'd told Ellen troubled him particularly. Isabel's 'illness'. Was he a complete bastard? No, not complete, there were remitting circumstances. And what he'd said wasn't entirely lies, more a sort of version of the truth, a twisted version, maybe. But what else could he do?

Honesty. Now there's a thing, he thought. He'd always thought of himself as an honest man but now here he was lying to Isabel, lying to Ellen, in a way lying to his children by default, lying to everyone who mattered.

He made determinedly for an empty seat towards the end of the carriage. Something's going right then, he thought wryly as he sat down. Torn in two, torn in two, the wheels of the train seemed to say. Torn in two, torn in two . . . And no doubt everyone in this train can find a meaningful message in the sound on the tracks, he reflected. Shaking open the second section of *The Times*, he tried to concentrate on the business news and clear his mind of all this emotional stuff which threatened to engulf him.

It was hard. As images flashed past the train window – back gardens, graffitied brick walls, goods yards and Portakabins, neglected anonymous spaces of south-west London – images flashed through his head. Images of the past. Isabel. The way she brushed her hair, head tilted to one side. That blue bikini she used to have. The first time she made spaghetti Bolognese. Buying their bed in Selfridges, her unabashed bouncing to test it. His life with Isabel: the ease of it, the familiarity. How they had clicked, how they had always been in step. When had that changed? For Isabel, perhaps it hadn't, until recently. And when had it had changed for him? He couldn't put his finger on any particular time, not exactly. More of a slow wearing down, as familiarity replaced the rest. Had loving Isabel become a habit?

Michael glanced at the news of legal judgements and the words fused. The train stopped at Putney and he watched a young woman with a buggy struggle off a train at the opposite platform while her child continued to sleep. Getting Gemma into her buggy had often been a trial, he remembered: she'd been a lively toddler and had always needed persuading to be strapped into it. It had given him backache as, being tall, he'd had to stoop to push it. 'Carry, Daddy, carry,' she'd say, holding up her plump little hands, twinkling her fingers at him, and he invariably ended up carrying her, pushing the buggy precariously with one hand. Dominic had been the same, insisting on walking as soon as he could, at his own pace, investigating ants on the pavement, stopping to stroke a cat, finding a stick to bang about with . . .

Why do I keep thinking of these things? Michael asked

himself. Wandering off through these fields of memories when there are so many other things I could be thinking about . . . He could abandon himself to thoughts of Ellen, her body, her laugh, how it had been between them last week when she returned from New York. Escapism. Yet he couldn't lose himself entirely· there was that ever-present undertow he was trying to avoid, the whole thing of telling Isabel (or not telling her), of disappointing Ellen yet somehow keeping her believing in him . . . Of what to say to Ellen about what he had not yet said to Isabel. Then there were the things he *should* be thinking about. Preparing for the day at work, thinking about clients and their cases – after all, he had to perform, he had to keep things going. Otherwise he, it, the whole shoot, was in danger of being derailed.

He was distracted by the slurpy sound of kissing from the couple opposite. Ah, that's why this seat had been left empty, he realised, as he tried not to watch them. Eight thirty in the morning and they were cuddled up together in the corner, their hands inside each other's coats, their faces close. Murmuring and giggling between kisses, oblivious to the other passengers and the rest of the world. There was a languorous looseness about them, which irritated the shit out of him. They sprawled out towards him, one of the girl's legs hooked over the guy's . . . They had that look – in their twenties, fashionable haircuts, layers of expensively *faux*-shabby clothes, both wearing identical obscure workers' boots – which proclaimed that they were here, they were now. Probably film editors or computer buffs or graphic designers, Michael thought. Or entrepreneurs. Thin cats with fat-cat salaries . . . Bloody hell, he thought, I'm feeling old. I'm getting old. And he shook *The Times* more vigorously and hid behind it.

19

Jasper surged forward on the lead. Lately Isabel had been combining walking the dog with going to Once or Twice: it saved time and energy. It wasn't ideal having Jasper there – some customers were wary of dogs and Angie wasn't too keen either, not that she'd be around for much longer – but what was ideal? And who could attain it?

I used to think I had the ideal, everything in the garden was rosy, Isabel thought, but not any more. Perhaps I've just joined the real world, the one everyone talks about where compromises are made and things are less than perfect. Life, that's life.

Angie worked her way along the rail of shirts and sweaters, smoothing the sleeves so that they hung straight. She was going to miss this: the shop (it was *her* creation), its satisfying calm and order . . . And Isabel, she'd miss her too. Angie could hear her right now, humming as she sat at the counter doing some paperwork. Isabel humming was a sign that something or someone was worrying her, Angie knew. Strange to know someone that well, she thought, and for so long. That's what I'll miss.

There had been no customers, or potential customers, for over an hour. It was like that sometimes. In the early days they'd found it scary: the awfulness of waiting and waiting for the door to open and someone to enter. That was the thing you could never get away from: with a shop you relied entirely on the whims of others. Whatever you did, however good your stock was or however realistic your prices, however inviting the window display or however welcoming the ambience of the shop itself, however much you smiled and tried to be patient, it could only work if people actually came through the door and then decided to buy. In the beginning they used to play a game, 'Spot the Customer'. They'd sit and gaze out of the window and as a woman approached they'd take it in turns to guess whether she'd enter the shop or not. In the end they had to stop doing it, realising that from the outside they could look desperate, even threatening. For it had mattered to both of them that their venture succeeded: they might have joked and played games but they were serious about it, deadly serious. And it had worked, so far.

'Izzy. You're humming,' she said gently.

'Oh, was I? Sorry.'

'I didn't mean that – I don't mind if you hum! Though I wish

Jasper wouldn't snore.' The dog was sleeping at the back of the shop. 'But what is it, Izzy? What's up?'

Isabel put down her pen and sighed. 'There are some things on my mind. Obviously.'

'Thought so. Look, why don't we shut up shop for an hour and go and have some lunch?'

'Actually Angie, if I'm honest I don't really feel like going out.'

'Well sweetheart, if you can't be honest with me! Now, how about I go and get some sandwiches from that new place round the corner? What do you feel like?'

Angie flipped the sign on the door to Closed as she hurried back inside, shaking her umbrella. They spread out their sandwiches on the counter on some kitchen paper. Angie paused in tackling her ciabatta packed with rocket and Brie and said, 'So, what's the matter? Tell Auntie Ange.'

Isabel finished her mouthful. 'Oh, what you'd expect – being pregnant, Michael, what to do about the shop without you.'

'One thing at a time! I thought you were happy to have the baby?'

'I am, mostly. But I can't help feeling ambivalent at times. There's so much to think about. It's not straightforward. I went to the doctor last week – antenatal appointments have started, all that. Because of my age there are tests to check whether the baby is normal – I've got one later this week. And what would I do if there was something wrong with it?'

'I suppose you worry about that *if* it happens.'

'Well, I can't help worrying about it now! And Michael's no help.'

'I was wondering how he was.'

'Things aren't that good between us. I just wish I had his support. He still seems so pissed off with me. I get the impression he thinks I'm being selfish.'

'Pregnant woman are allowed to be selfish, aren't they? That's the only part of it that ever appealed to me! You know, being pampered and treated as special.'

'Well, I'm not getting much of that. Michael's certainly not in the mood to pamper me, he's just about polite to me at the moment. I do sometimes wonder if there's something else the matter with him. I mean, me being pregnant isn't such a disaster . . .' Isabel played with the remains of her cheese and cucumber sandwich – she'd kept it simple as she'd been reading an article about the health dangers to pregnant women of unpasteurised cheeses, uncooked eggs (no mayonnaise, then). Was there no end to things she should be worried about?

Angie dredged her mind for a reply. An obvious one, in other circumstances, would have been to ask if Michael was showing any signs of the much-touted male mid-life crisis. Could he be playing around? But she didn't feel she could say that to Isabel, not in her present state, and anyway, she thought, not Michael surely? Instead she said, 'You know Izzy, perhaps he's jealous.'

'Jealous? Of whom?'

'Well, maybe not jealous exactly, more resentful. Of the baby. Perhaps he was looking forward to having you to himself, now that Gemma and Dom are nearly grown-up. He could have had plans for the two of you. But now . . .'

Isabel reached over and touched Angie's arm. 'What a romantic you are! That's an optimistic way of looking at it. If only it were true . . . But somehow I don't think so. If it were that, surely he would say so?' She began to gather up the rubbish from their lunch. 'Whatever it is, Angie, I can't do anything about it. There's a part of me that thinks, Well, damn you, Michael, I'm just going to have to get on with this by myself.'

'Sounds like a bit like mutiny to me, Izzy!'

They laughed, as they always did, at anything with a naval flavour, this long tradition between them, and turned their attention to the shop, going over the stock book together, although everything was in order and there was no real need to do so.

Isabel sat back. 'So what am I going to do without you?'

'I'm sorry, I really am, leaving you in the lurch. But I've got to give this a shot – going to Spain and living with Max.'

'I know you have. It's OK, I do understand. About most of it, anyway.'

'I know! Let me guess which part you understand least!'

They grinned at each other.

'I'm going to miss you, Angela,' Isabel said, in a pretend-stern voice. 'You are irreplaceable.'

'No one's irreplaceable! Well, as a friend, maybe. But with the shop . . .'

'I know. I suppose I'll have to get some help – someone part-time. I could advertise.'

'That's such a hassle. But you know I still want to keep my stake, or whatever you call it, in the shop.'

'Of course. I'm not looking to replace you in *that* way. This is our joint baby, I haven't forgotten! But we don't need to discuss it formally, do we? Shall we just see how it goes?'

'You mean, how it goes with me in Spain? With Max?'

'I suppose I do. Look, I'm not suggesting that it's not serious –'

'I know you're not, Izzy. And you're right, it's wise not to rush into things – although I am rushing in, sort of, aren't I? But I'm not burning my boats . . . Don't laugh, Iz, another seafaring term, God help us. Anyway, that's why I'm going to *let* the house, not sell it.'

'What's happening on that front?'

'I'm waiting for the agents to contact me with prospective tenants. Apparently my dear little house isn't quite top-notch enough in the letting game – they say I can't expect to get corporate clients like German brokers or Swedish business-men or Japanese bankers.'

'There are quite a few of them living around us.'

'In houses like yours, maybe. But I haven't got enough bathrooms or high-tech showers or fancy kitchen equipment or whatever, which is a shame in terms of money. But as long as I let it to someone who'll care for it, that's my main concern.'

'Not students?'

'Preferably not. Hopefully someone suitable will turn up quickly. I want to leave for Spain as soon as I can, but I'd like to get the business of the house settled first.'

Angie went to the back of the shop to switch on the kettle and Isabel watched the rain run down the window. It was dark and gloomy outside, even though it was the middle of the day. Then the idea hit her like a shaft of sunlight. *Jenny!* Why didn't I think of her before? she thought, appalled that she'd so nearly missed the obvious. Because I've been so preoccupied with my own concerns, she decided. But this could solve all our problems.

'Angie! Guess what? I've had a brainwave. Listen to this!'

There was a Sale Agreed sign planted in Jenny's front garden. That must have gone up this morning, thought Isabel. And she prayed, to no one in particular, Please let Jenny be there, please make this work, please make her say yes . . .

'Isabel, hello! Come in.'

'Are you busy? Can we talk?'

'Of course. I'm just sorting out more stuff. But how are you? I was worried about you.'

'I'm all right. Thank you anyway. I'm sorry about the other day, breaking down like that.'

'Oh, don't be sorry. I've done it to you enough times in the past.'

Isabel followed Jenny into the kitchen. The table was covered with piles of papers and photographs and albums. Jenny began moving them to one side, apologising for the mess.

Isabel sat down. 'This looks like the family archives.'

'It is, in a way. I'm trying to sort things into three piles. One for me, one for Graham, one for Mark and Tim – theirs is a joint pile, for the moment. There are certificates, GCSE and A levels, things like that – they're the easy part. But then what I want to do is divide up the family photos, so that everyone has some . . . That's more difficult.' She sighed and shuffled through some holiday snaps.

Isabel waited, picking up a photograph of the four of them together: Jenny and Graham, looking tense, standing behind the twins, who were grinning mischievously at the camera. The twins looked more of a couple than their parents, Isabel thought. Behind them were tall masts of yachts in a harbour. She turned it towards Jenny, who smiled grimly and said, 'I think that was in Menorca. The boys must have been eight or nine. I remember asking a woman who was passing to take our picture. Graham was cross because he saw himself as in charge of the camera.'

'Oh, Jenny.'

To Isabel's surprise, Jenny gave a snort of laughter. 'God, he was impossible! He could be such a silly little man. It's taken me this long to see it. Anyway, that's the past.' And she put the photo down carefully on a pile.

'This may be a good moment to ask you something. It's about the future. How's that for a link?'

'The future. God knows about the future. Sorry, what is it Isabel? Do you need some help or –'

'In a way. I think this is a great idea but you can say no.'

'This is intriguing – tell me!'

'You know Angie's going to Spain? I have told you that, haven't I? Well, how would you like to work for me, *with* me, at Once or Twice?'

'Isabel! Are you sure?'

'Don't sound so surprised! I'd really like you to. I think it would work out well . . .'

'I'm touched, I truly am.' Jenny wiped her eyes. There was a pause.

Oh bugger, have I blown it? thought Isabel. Did I sound patronising, all Lady Bountiful and lady-of-the-manorish? I didn't mean to. 'But?'

'There is no but! I'd love to, I mean, yes. A job in your shop would suit me very well.'

'Great, I'm so pleased. What a relief.' Isabel reached across the table and squeezed Jenny's hand.

'And I'm so glad you asked me, you've no idea.'

'We'll need to talk about money and hours and –'

'There's plenty of time for that, don't worry. I trust you! But when would you like me to start? When is Angie going?'

'Ah, well, that's the other thing I want to put to you.'

'You mean there's more? I don't think I can take all this excitement!'

'Course you can. You see, Angie wants to go to Spain as soon as possible but first she needs to let her house. So we thought – Angie and I – we wondered if *you*'d like to rent it. You know where it is, don't you? In Mortlake. It's a cosy little cottage, wonderful for one. You don't have to say yes or no yet. Obviously you'd have to see the house and discuss rent and all that with her . . .'

'Wow. Angie's house. Say no more! Yes, yes! It sounds like a great idea. I've got to leave here in a few weeks anyway so –'

'So is this the answer to all our prayers?'

'Isabel, I would say it is!'

Later, after Isabel had left, Jenny sat for a while at the table doing nothing but finger the piece of paper with Angie's phone number written on it. Isabel had said she'd set things in motion. A new life beckoned. A different life. Was this, Jenny wondered, what her mother had always meant by 'things falling into your lap'? It had never applied to Jenny before, or her mother: it was the sort of thing that happened to other people. The refrain had echoed throughout her childhood: her mother would observe a friend or neighbour or relative and remark, in a tight voice, 'It's all right for her, things just fall into her lap.' When she was very small Jenny would scrutinise people's laps, which you could only do if they were sitting down, of course. She was disappointed never to see anything falling from on high, no jewels or riches or treasures or manifestations of good fortune.

Some things have changed, she thought. Perhaps I'm becoming the kind of person to whom things happen – Isabel's offer of a job, Angie's house. She perceived that it would be preferable if things didn't happen *to* her but if she made them happen herself. Still, this was a start. Never mind that someone like Graham or her mother might sneer that this was just for convenience – Isabel's convenience, Angie's convenience. This was convenient for her too. Never mind that it might seem as if she were merely taking over the discarded bits of Angie's life – that way of thinking was unproductive. It was negative, she would indulge in it no longer.

As Jenny sat and listened to the rain she shivered, and decided she'd had her fill of water. She hadn't visited the river for a few days, not since before Isabel's visit in distress on Sunday. It would always be there if she ever needed it.

River, rain, tears: enough.

20

Isabel was immersed in pregnancy books and guides and magazines. She read them in private: during the day when no one was home; in the shop when it wasn't busy; in the bath. She firmly believed that the more she knew the better; the more information she had the more she'd be in control. But this was beginning to make her nervous, all this stuff about older mothers (without doubt she fell into that category). Apparently she had an elderly uterus: she learnt that at her age it was ageing faster than her other organs. So did she have a grey, wrinkled womb? Hardly, under the circumstances, she thought. Statistics told her that there was a higher risk of premature birth or Caesarean section or stillbirth, plus she was more likely to suffer from high blood pressure, varicose veins – the list went on. It was daunting. Plus there was more chance of having a Down's syndrome baby . . .

Which was why she was having this test today, a simple blood test that would screen for what they called abnormalities. There might, of course, be nothing to worry about. And her GP, Dr Finch, was sanguine. 'I think you're becoming overloaded with information, Isabel.'

'Well, I think it's a good idea for me to find out as much as I can.'

'Oh, I agree. I'm not one of those doctors who disapproves of patients – people – searching for knowledge. It's just that you seem to have become rather anxious.'

'I suppose I am. But isn't that natural? All these facts about what can happen to older mothers and their babies . . .'

'Yes, the statistics are there, we know what *can* happen, but that doesn't necessarily mean it *will* happen to you. And there's a lot of data showing many positive things about being older.'

'Oh, please, do tell me!'

'Well, let's see. You're less likely to suffer morning sickness.'

'That's true, I haven't, just some minor nausea.'

Dr Finch continued to count off her fingers. 'Better at coping with stress, less likely to suffer from post-natal depression, less likely to have an episiotomy and stretch marks.'

'I've got stretch marks already.'

'Haven't we all! But remember, Isabel, that most of the threatened troubles you've read about *don't* materialise. For you or the baby. Most babies are born perfect. And this is a good time – there's been a revolution in antenatal screening and testing over the past twenty years.'

'I'm relieved. And this test I'm having today?'

'The quadruple test, it's called. Don't look like that – nothing to do with having quads! It's a routine blood test with four functions. If it shows any cause for concern we consider amniocentesis, but we won't do that unless we – and you – think it's required. Now, I'll have a quick look at you first then you can pop along to the nurse who'll take some blood.'

'OK. When will I get the results?'

'About a week. Pop up on the couch so I can examine you.'

Funny how doctors always say that, thought Isabel. Pop up on the couch, pop your clothes on the chair, pop along . . . Even someone as straightforward and un-twee as Dr Finch. Perhaps they learnt it in medical school.

'You know, Isabel, you're doing fine. Everything is as it should be. The baby's coming on nicely, your blood pressure is OK, your weight gain is just right. So why don't you relax and enjoy this pregnancy?'

'I am, I do, most of the time.'

'Good. After all, you probably won't do this again.'

'Probably not!'

'And a thought for you to consider. You know many women over forty have difficulty in conceiving, you've probably read that in one of your books, so –'

'So think myself lucky?'

'Not quite what I was going to say, but never mind. Now, at your next visit we'll discuss your birth plan.'

'This is like having homework!'

'You could say that. Then you'll meet one of the midwives, who'll take over much of your routine care. OK? And you've been sent an appointment for an ultrasound?'

'Yes. It's next week. And everything *is* OK. Thank you, Dr Finch.'

'Oh – and this might amuse you. Did you know you're going to be a MOM?'

Isabel looked confused.

Dr Finch grinned. 'I read it in some literature recently – American, of course. M-O-M – it stands for Moneyed Older Mom!'

They groaned in unison.

The nurse inserted a needle into Isabel's arm. She watched the syringe filling up – her blood was a very dark red. Extraordinary stuff. The stuff of life – and from this small sample they could discover crucial things about the baby. Her baby.

Strange, though, Isabel reflected, that all a blood test would do was establish the facts. Whatever existed, existed already. If there was something amiss, having a test wasn't going to put it right. One drop of her blood would change nothing. Except what she knew.

She pressed the small plaster to her arm like a talisman for luck. All she could do now was wait and hope that everything was all right – no, that's too much, she decided. Maybe not everything, just the baby.

Isabel lingered over a mug of honey and ginger tea: she was working her way through a repertoire of fruit and herbal varieties. As she sat at the kitchen table she thought of all the things she should be doing. Household tasks like sorting out washing, or watering indoor plants, or ironing. Looking around the kitchen, she could see various things that needed cleaning or tidying. As always.

She felt listless. There seemed to be no reserves of energy to draw on. Yet physically she was fine, hadn't the doctor said so?

Something was dragging her down. Michael. The lack of him. Oh, sure, he was around, sometimes, but he wasn't with her in spirit. If only she could share the pregnancy with him, especially all this stuff about the health of the baby . . . There was probably no need to worry, but it would be good to be able to talk it through with him. If only he were involved, she could tell him about the test, the implications. Lonely, that's what she felt. Angie had gone to Spain. Beth barely had time to talk even on the phone – and when she did Isabel would hear the usual litany of work, kids, stress, Simon, more work. Isabel didn't try to introduce the subject of her worries, her pregnancy: she felt a little foolish. In fact, she experienced something of what Michael had objected to, a sense that it was somehow *inappropriate* for her to be pregnant. And not just on the phone to Beth. At the Thursday afternoon antenatal clinic at the surgery all the other women in the waiting room were much younger than her. Unlined faces, with a bright, enthusiastic air about them. They weren't even what would be considered young mothers (no teenage mums here) – she supposed they were all in their late twenties, early thirties – but, nevertheless, they made her feel old. Poor baby, she'd thought, growing in this elderly womb of hers. She'd known it would be like this, she kept telling herself, but facing the reality was sometimes harder than she'd thought it would be – and this was just the beginning. But how could she express her feelings? And who to? Even Jenny, dear Jenny, who'd taken to the shop like a duck to water, didn't need to be burdened with her concerns – at least, Isabel presumed she didn't. Jenny had her own difficulties to cope with, like moving out of her family home, settling things with her estranged husband. Major events.

So who else was there? Isabel still hadn't informed her parents that they were going to have another grandchild, not that they'd care one way or the other, she thought. At times she was tempted to confide in Gemma but she always held back. It wouldn't be fair just because she was female and her daughter and a captive audience. Anyway, while Gemma appeared to be adopting a neutral stance towards her mother being pregnant – she wasn't actively hostile like Dominic – she didn't seem particularly interested either. Why should she be? Isabel told herself. This is my life, she has her own to lead. And Gemma was busy, helping a friend of a friend run a sandwich-delivery service in Hammersmith, getting up early for work and still going out to socialise most nights. Isabel saw her less and less.

No, it was Michael she needed, Michael she wanted to talk to. He was, after all, her husband and the father of this baby. She missed his support, she missed that warm, comfortable feeling of having someone at your side, *on* your side. Without it, worries were magnified, fears grew out of all proportion, and vulnerability became her companion.

Isabel remembered how Michael had been when she was expecting Gemma and Dominic. The first time round he'd been even more excited and interested than she'd anticipated. He'd skimmed through pregnancy books, he'd rest his head for ages against her stomach waiting to feel the baby move ... When he rubbed her back it became a sensual experience, not just a relief from aches and pains. He'd accompanied her uncomplainingly to antenatal classes – she'd expected him to shy away from such public participation. Being Michael, he wanted to do this father-to-be business thoroughly and well, she realised, as he always did everything. And it wasn't just a novelty: when she was pregnant with Dominic he'd continued to be involved. OK, so he didn't read the books or come to the classes this second time (she did less of that, too) but he still rubbed her back and at weekends did the shopping and took Gemma out so that she could rest ... The contrast with his present behaviour saddened her immensely.

Isabel put her head down on her arms on the table and closed her eyes. What had gone wrong? They had always been such partners. She yearned for their old closeness. She needed it now more than ever. Why couldn't he show her some compassion?

Dominic came in from school, the front door slamming behind him. The sound of his bag being dropped on the floor made Isabel start. Jasper barked and went padding into the hall to greet him.

'Mum! I'm home,' he shouted.

Isabel sat up, feeling fuzzy-headed. Had she been crying? Had she dozed off? For a moment she couldn't remember. There was Dominic standing in the doorway with a look of alarm on his face. She smiled, stretching her eyes wide, trying to look cheerful and welcoming, a professional-mum type expression.

'Hello, Dom. How was your day, darling?'

'It was all right.'

He turned to the fridge and wrenched open the door. Isabel winced. One day it would come off its hinges.

She persevered with questions about school, about his history course, and geography (avoiding his third subject, maths, as she was really out of her depth on that one). They managed to have a kind of conversation as he stood by the sink eating yogurt from the carton but his replies were brief. It was a struggle. Silly, really, she thought, having to make small-talk with your own son. Maybe it wasn't personal, maybe his responses weren't to do with her being his mother or being pregnant; he was at *that age*, as everyone called it. They'd come through the other side of this eventually, wouldn't they?

He seemed keen to get away, to go upstairs to his room. Unlike when he was little, she thought, when he wanted to be with her and was always pleased to see her. She had a sudden vision of Dominic standing in his cot shouting for someone to come, jumping and gurgling with his arms held up as she approached, a big smile of delight creasing his chubby baby cheeks.

Dominic closed his door and flicked on his sound system so that his room filled with noise. Insulation from the rest of the world. He lay on his bed with his phone in his hand, trying to decide whether to ring Sophie or not. Ever since New Year's Eve she'd been dangling him on a string, that's what it felt like. Sometimes she encouraged him, sometimes she didn't, backwards and forwards they went. His friend Ben said she was a tease, everyone knew that, but Dominic wasn't sure. There were lots of things he wasn't sure about these days.

Nothing seemed simple. His mother being pregnant, that complicated things. He kept looking for signs of her state, he couldn't help it. She appeared much the same so far, perhaps a bit heavier, a bit thicker round the middle. Had she noticed him looking? Sometimes she caught his eye, like just now in the kitchen. And she'd looked – what? Disappointed? Upset? He got the feeling she wanted to talk, but he didn't know what to say to her and when he spoke it often came out all wrong. Oh shit. As if he didn't have enough of his own worries.

And what was the matter with his bloody parents? When he saw them together, which wasn't often, they hardly spoke to each other. There was an awkward atmosphere. Yet they must have been close enough to have sex to get pregnant.

Sex. This bloody baby – *a little sister or brother*, yuk – was proof that they still did it. But he didn't want to think about *them* having sex, he wanted to think about having sex with Sophie – or anyone, although preferably someone with long legs and long hair . . .

It should be *him* having a sex life.

He turned over on to his stomach, clutching his phone to his chest. Girls. So difficult to understand. Gemma said it was because he'd been cut off from girls all his life (apart from her!), cloistered in an all-boys school. It wasn't natural, she said. Perhaps she was right. He couldn't get to grips with Sophie, in more ways than one. And he thought about her so much, he thought about *sex* so much, and he knew A levels were looming and he had to get stuck into his school work . . . If only she'd agree to go all the way. It was odd, she still said no, even though she seemed to get as worked up as he did. But then she'd pull away and the last two times that happened she'd bent over him and given him a blow-job. Which was fine by him, as far as it went. But was she giving him a consolation prize? And why did she think that oral sex was OK but not the real thing? What was the big deal?

It was a mystery. Sophie was a mystery. He wanted it to be straightforward: take her out and talk to her and go to bed with her and have a good time . . .

Dominic wished that there was someone he could talk to. There was only so much you could say to another bloke, like Ben. Gemma? But if he confided in her she might use it against him later when they had an argument . . . Whom could he trust? Sometimes it was tempting, momentarily, to let it all hang out and talk to his mother but he knew in reality that would be *too* embarrassing.

He envied Sophie and her friends, always chattering and whispering and giggling and hugging. He bet they told each other *everything*.

Oh God.

Thinking about her had made him feel hot and horny. He'd ring her, that's all he could do. It would be another lengthy labyrinthine call, driven by her, when they'd gossip about what was happening and who was seeing whom and who fancied whom and who was wearing what and eventually she'd dissect what he'd said and what he'd done the last time they met and why and how she felt about it . . . They'd get nowhere. Still, Dominic thought, what else was there? And he punched in her number.

21

Angie leant back in a rattan chair and surveyed the view from the terrace. The valley dipped away towards the coast – the sea wasn't visible but she knew it was there. On the hillside a goatherd walked slowly, stick in hand – or was it a crook? – his goats scampering around him, nibbling here and there. His silhouette was distinctive: small and bow-legged with a wide hat. Angie assumed he was elderly, but she had only ever seen him from a distance. He was there most days, always about this time in the morning, then later in the afternoon as dusk approached. Where did he go in between? she wondered. At first she'd imagined pastures over the hill – *the grass is greener* – but having begun to explore she realised that one hill followed another, curves and hollows and ridges, brown and bare or grey-green with low-growing shrubs and twisted olive trees, interspersed with occasional pines or poplars. Her eyes were becoming familiar with the Andalucían landscape and she liked to sit here and gaze upon it. Then there was the sky – so much of it, you could drown in it. At night it was so very dark, real night-time, unlike that semi-permanent orange glare that eclipsed the night in London. And the air was not just fresher, it seemed emptier: no dust or dirt or traffic fumes or vapours of aircraft fuel. There was space to breathe.

Angie sighed, the only sound apart from the faint tinkling of goat bells. A pretty sound. Oh, and she could hear muffled noises coming from the stable on the other side of the house – horse noises. Max was seeing to the horses, Dali and Rocco. Angie wasn't quite sure what that entailed, but no doubt she'd find out sooner or later as Max was keen to get her involved in *everything*.

Angie sipped her coffee, wishing her lover would hurry up. She'd brought a tray out here and arranged breakfast on the stone table. Breakfast with Max in the early-spring sunshine

. . . Bliss. Or it would be if she were here and not with her precious animals. The coffee was getting cold, the juice would no longer be freshly squeezed. She lifted her hair off her neck and held it on top of her head as she watched the goats recede into the distance. She wondered if she should have it cut. Was she getting too old to have it falling around her shoulders, in pre-Raphaelite red?

Footsteps behind her, a vigorous kiss on the back of her neck. Max, smelling slightly of the stable.

'There you are – at last!'

'Sorry, Angel. Rocco was being difficult. Let me just go and wash my hands and I'll be with you.'

Angie studied Max as she walked into the house. She was wearing a white T-shirt and jeans, pulled in by a wide leather belt with a silver buckle. Her jeans were tucked into tall riding boots of the same brown Spanish leather (anything leather she had handmade by a guy in Seville – she said she'd take Angie there soon). She always wore the same sort of thing, jeans or trousers, sometimes jodhpurs (and not just for riding). She looked wonderful in jodhpurs, Angie thought. The way they fitted so snugly over her bum and across her taut stomach . . . And on top she wore T-shirts or crisp cotton or linen shirts, usually white, occasionally black or khaki. She never wore a bra. 'Why would I need to?' she'd asked. For her breasts were small and set high on her chest, the sort of breasts that never got in the way, Angie thought.

Max reappeared and sat down opposite Angie, pushing her glossy dark hair out of her eyes. It was long at the front and cropped into her neck at the back, like an early Vidal Sassoon cut. It suited her – but, then, everything Max did or wore or created seemed right. And not just because I adore her, thought Angie, she happens to be one of those fortunate people who is comfortable in their skin; she knows who she is.

They smiled at each other over their coffee cups.

'So, Maxi, what needs to be done today?'

Max tore into an orange and offered Angie a segment. 'I'm going to sort out the studio – clean the easels, chuck out useless paints, all that stuff.'

'Shall I help you?'

'It would be a bigger help if you could tackle that pile of mail in the office.' She leant forward and patted Angie's knee.

'OK. Sure.' Angie would have preferred to work alongside her in the studio.

'Then, tell you what, Angel, why don't we drive over to Ronda for some lunch? Treat ourselves. Then back here for a siesta together?'

'Now that sounds good.'

The small room designated as the office overlooked the courtyard. Angie sat at the desk, the pile of mail pushed aside, and stared out of the window. Everything had been white-washed last week: the flagstones, the walls of the stable and the studio. It had to be done annually, Max said. Huge terracotta tubs stood outside the window with deep red flowers – what were they? – bursting into bloom. Angie wondered if the daffodils were out in her window-box in London. Or would they have been and gone already? She was losing track of time without the familiar triggers to remind her.

She looked around the room, at the wall calendar dotted with coloured stickers indicating each art course from April through to September, at the noticeboard covered with lists and telephone numbers and postcards, at the framed land-scapes painted by Max . . .

Perhaps it was useful to have some time on her own – she needed to get her head together, as Max would say. In some ways it was so wonderful to be here; in other ways she was finding it difficult.

It had taken a few days after arriving for her to grasp that she was not on holiday. Of course she *knew* she wasn't but being in Spain with the sun, the different light, the food, the sensual delights – everything conspired to make her feel that she was having time off. But Max had a business to run, and it was obvious that Angie should help her. Max explained that in these weeks before Easter, the start of her busy season, there was loads to do. Redecorating and repairs on the farmhouse, getting the garden in shape and the pool serviced, checking bed linen for the guest rooms, plus the equipment and supplies for courses – it went on and on. Then there was all the

administration: placing ads, answering queries, making bookings . . . Angie understood. After all, she had run the shop with
Isabel. So what had she expected?

One afternoon, as they lay in bed after one of their siestas,
after making love, Max had stroked her hair and asked what
was wrong.

'Nothing. How could anything be wrong? I'm here, with
you.'

'Brave words, Angel. But there's no need to act with me.'

'I wasn't acting!'

'Don't get cross. Come here.'

Max had enfolded her, breast to breast, and kissed her. They
became engrossed in each other – again – and there was no
need to talk about anything being wrong.

Angie flipped through the mail, dividing it into bills,
inquiries, bookings. There were a couple of personal-looking
envelopes for Max with Australian stamps, which she left
unopened. A few things that looked like Spanish junk mail she
put in a pile – she really must learn the language, and quickly.
She'd talk to Max about it.

That was the trouble: she had to refer to Max about
everything. It wasn't anyone's *fault*, it was just the way it was.
She had come here to be with Max, to live in Max's house,
become part of Max's life, it was natural for her to feel strange,
having lived alone and been independent for so long. Going
over it in her mind she questioned whether she would have
felt more or less uncomfortable if Max had been male. Would
she have been so ready to move in and leave everything behind
if this involved a man?

There were no easy answers. She did know that if she'd
moved in with a man she would probably have slipped into a
certain role: nurturing and cooking, housekeeping, shopping,
taking over that side of things. The female role. Pathetic,
really, but she'd have done it – she *had* done it in the past –
more or less willingly. However she may have objected,
intellectually, theoretically, that there should be no such
thing as a female role, she had usually assumed it in a
relationship with a man because it made life run more
smoothly. Sometimes she had told herself to see it as an acting

135

role: playing the female, being a woman. The things we do, she thought.

Now, surely, there was a chance to do things differently, to throw away the unwritten rule book. They could be open with each other, no strategies or subterfuge, no secrets. Max had already told Angie about her past, her teenage experimentations with boys that left her determined to follow her instincts and love women. Angie in turn had recounted brief details of boyfriends, lovers, the failed early marriage to Barney, fellow thesp; the difficulty of meeting people, the dissatisfaction with her love life as she knew it. All her experience had been with men. She did reveal an incident, or near-incident, with a young actress, Lisa, in a theatre dressing room in a northern town – Bolton? Barnsley? She couldn't remember. They were near the end of a tour with a Chekhov play and Angie had got used to Lisa's lack of inhibition, sitting half-naked in vintage cami-knickers to put on her makeup, wearing a loosely belted antique kimono with nothing on underneath. After the last performance, undressing in their cramped space, Lisa had turned to Angie and asked, 'Hold me.' Angie complied, in what she thought was a friendly big-sisterly sort of way, but then Lisa had kissed her ... The next moment the stage manager had burst in. Max had laughed on hearing this, and called the girl a little minx, a temptress. 'Just how I used to be,' she said. And then she grinned and told Angie, 'I'm so glad you saved yourself for me ...'

So most lovers shared tales of their past sexual encounters, didn't they? Angie thought. That was what lovers did. What she wanted now was more openness, no barriers or obstacles. As no men were involved, no one would need to adopt this role or that, they could create a safe place where they could both be themselves *and* be together. Surely two women could achieve that?

She was finding things were not that simple or straightforward. This thing about helping Max was that at times she couldn't avoid feeling, well, subordinate, like a little wifey.

Dear Max, thought Angie, it wasn't her fault, she did try to be sensitive. Last night, after supper (cooked by Angie) they'd stood entwined on the terrace and looked up at the stars together.

'So are you glad you're here, Angel?'

Angie liked being called that, although she still wasn't sure whether Max called her 'angel' as a general endearment or whether it was Angel because of her name. Did she call other people angel? Angie would have to listen out for it.

'You know I am. It's wonderful, you're wonderful.' She squeezed Max closer to her.

'But? I do sense a but. Are you missing that cat of yours?'

Angie laughed. 'There is no but. And I'm not missing Desdemona, not really. It was best she stayed at home. Jenny will look after her. I think she needs someone – or something – to love.'

'Don't we all?'

They hugged and gazed up at the stars, taking it in turns to spot constellations and name them, as new lovers often do.

'It's strange to think that these are the same stars that are over London, not that you can ever really see them there!'

'So do you miss London, is that it?'

'No, I don't think so.' Angie hesitated. She wanted to share her anxieties with Max, but it was difficult to put them into words, even to herself. 'What it is –'

'I knew there was something.' Max played with a strand of Angie's hair.

'Oh, it's nothing important. It's just me. I feel a bit odd, a bit displaced, sometimes. I'm not sure of what I should be doing.'

'But, Angie, you're here to be with me, for us to be together.'

'I know, I know.'

'And I admire you for doing it, for leaving your home and everything for love! Seriously, that's one of things I love about you, your spontaneity, your capacity to grasp the moment –'

'My lust for life? Or my lust for you?'

They fell on each other giggling, then hurried to bed.

Sex with Max was delicious. It was exquisite. Angie threw herself into it with abandon but then she supposed she always had, even with men. It still surprised her sometimes, as she lay next to Max, both of them naked on the bed, that here she was with a *woman*. Breasts. Smooth soft skin, neat triangle of pubic hair. Vagina. Like her, yet not precisely the same. At intervals they had fun comparing and contrasting parts of their bodies, like children playing doctors and nurses. Angie's breasts fuller and lower than Max's . . . The hair under Max's arms darker and lusher than Angie's . . . It went on. Their commentaries became erotic. *You feel . . . This is . . .* Sometimes they played games, like trying to touch nipples to nipples. Or they attempted to do the exact same thing to each other at exactly the same time, although it didn't always work – their arms would become entangled, it wasn't physically possible, the angles were all wrong . . . They laughed a lot. They came a lot.

Angie couldn't help comparing it to sex with men. The dynamics of it were different, the rhythms were different. There was no rush towards the inevitable conclusion of ejaculation, none of that tender reverence required for an erection. Their intimacy was based on equality. Love-making was intricate and sensual. Tongues, fingers, delicate work. And circular: you could start in one way, in one place, and end up there too. It was like having endless foreplay, except that there were no boundaries between what was foreplay and what was not. And there were no boundaries between them, not in bed.

The attraction had started last September, when Angie had come on a painting holiday – she had needed a break and this seemed a good way to go on holiday alone. She'd anticipated, correctly, that she'd meet some *simpatico* people. They were mostly women, older women, who were easy to be with. But Max had been the most *simpatico* of all. Their leader, everyone had teasingly called her. To her surprise Angie found herself being flamboyant, wanting to grab Max's attention. And it worked. Nothing had actually happened between them but connections were made: a brush of the arm as Max leant over her easel; a touch of the hand over the dinner table; the nudge of a breast (Angie's) in a crowded market . . . Eye contact, which became more intense as the week had progressed. On the last day Max had whispered, 'Let's keep in touch. Come and visit me.' Throughout the autumn they'd phoned each other and written, at first amusing notes or postcards, later long revelatory letters. It was a kind of courtship. Then came the visit at Christmas. There had been no art course, as Angie had told Isabel. It was just the two of them. Max and Angie. On that first afternoon in bed, as it rained outside, they had discovered and explored each other. Old world, new world. And Angie had experienced the extraordinary first-time feeling of holding another woman, naked. She had found a new kind of pleasure – and joy.

Angie turned her attention back to the stuff on the desk. Max had said this was where she could be of most help. 'I'm hopeless with paperwork, Angel, I'd be so grateful if you could handle all that.' Angie recalled the good old stock book at Once or Twice with fondness – I'm getting sentimental, she thought. And she missed Isabel, who had, after all, been a constant presence in her life for so long. She wondered how Isabel was, and resolved to phone her more regularly – Max wouldn't mind, surely?

The computer made a friendly noise as she switched it on. Something else Max had confessed she was hopeless with, this new computer system. It had been installed last year in order to make her life easier, in theory, and allow her to concentrate on the more creative side of the business. She'd failed to come to grips with it. I'll be the rescuing angel, thought Angie, as she read the manual, it can't be that difficult. After all, she was becoming used to trying new things.

So get on with it, Angie told herself. What was she worrying about? There was bound to be a certain surrender of self in any relationship. Meanwhile, she still had her cottage in London, she hadn't given up her share of the shop. Things were on hold, for now (thanks to Isabel and Jenny). There was a safety net – she could return. But she might not want to . . .

She imagined growing old with Max, still giggling.

22

Gemma burst noisily into the kitchen. 'Oh bugger, is that the time?' She thrust some bread into the toaster and thwacked the switch down, *clunk*.

Isabel gave up reading the paper. 'Would you like some tea, Gem? There's some in the pot.'

'Please. You're an angel. Can you do my toast for me while I find some socks?'

'What do you want on it?'

'Just honey, please,' her daughter shouted from the utility room as she rummaged through the laundry.

Dominic yelled out goodbye from the hall and she heard the front door slam. Yet again he was leaving for school without any breakfast, Isabel thought. But what could she do? There was no point in nagging, as he called it.

She assumed that Michael had gone to work already but as she'd been sleeping in the spare room she wasn't sure. There had been too many nights with them lying self-consciously alongside each other in the marital bed, each taking care not to touch the other. Double beds were fine when you were operating as a couple but once you'd become separate in one way or another – that invisible line between them – you were acutely aware of how little space there was. So last week she'd announced that she'd sleep in the spare room; that way they'd both sleep better. She'd implied that it was because she was pregnant, that was the problem – and in a way she supposed it was. Michael had merely shrugged and said, 'If that's what you want.' Gradually she'd been moving her things in there, her alarm clock, cleanser, tissues, moisturiser . . . It was becoming her nest.

Gemma sat on a chair, pulling on her socks. Isabel placed some tea and the toast in front of her.

'Oh thanks.' And she beamed at her mother. 'Is it just you and me, then?'

'Yes. Dominic's just left – didn't you hear him? And Dad went earlier.'

She wondered if the children were aware that she was sleeping separately from their father. Neither of them had said anything, which probably meant that they were too wrapped up in their own lives to have noticed. Or that they were being sensitive and avoiding asking potentially embarrassing questions.

The mail thudded through the letterbox. 'I'll get it,' Gemma said, through a mouthful of toast, dashing into the hall.

'For you, Mum.' She handed over some bills and a letter.

Isabel tore it open. Could it be the results of her blood test? It was over a week since she'd had it done. The last few mornings had been filled with anxiety as she waited for the post. Yes, it was from Dr Finch. This was it. She scanned the contents quickly and saw the words, *Low risk established . . . No further tests considered necessary . . .* She read them again. Thank God, good news! Such a relief. However much she had tried to be sensible, this had been preying on her mind.

She seized Gemma and whirled her around the kitchen, laughing.

'Mum, wait, what is it?'

They came to a stop by the back door. Isabel needed to catch her breath. 'Sorry, Gemma, did I take you by surprise? But I've just had some good news.'

'Must be really good to make you do that!'

'It is. The results of a blood test – you know the one I had last week?'

'Did you? I don't remember.'

'Well, anyway, I did. It tested the baby for abnormalities – especially important at my advanced age. And everything's fine! I can't tell you how relieved I am.'

'Oh, good. That's great Mum, I'm glad. And guess what? I've had some good news this morning too.'

Gemma was waving a letter, which had got a little creased when Isabel had grabbed her for dancing.

'Really? What is it?'

'I've got an interview for a summer job with Mark Warner – you know, at one of their holiday beach clubs. It's next Monday. I'm so pleased! God, I hope I get it! I don't mind what I do, cooking, or looking after children. It will be wonderful to go away.'

'I didn't know you'd applied.'

'Oh, I thought I'd mentioned it. Perhaps you forgot. You have been preoccupied recently with your own stuff, Mum, this baby and everything.'

'Gemma –'

'Oh Christ. I really must go – can't be late again!'

Her voice receded as she bounded up the stairs to get ready for work. Isabel sat down again at the table, trying to hold on to the feeling of exaltation she'd experienced five minutes ago. She suddenly felt very alone.

Half an hour later Isabel was still sitting at the kitchen table. She didn't have to be at the shop until lunch-time – thank God for Jenny, she thought, not for the first time. Shopping first, if she could rouse herself.

It was quiet and peaceful. The cat slept in one corner of the conservatory, the dog in the other. She had been trying to keep them out of the house as much as possible, especially the kitchen – she'd read about this horrible disease you could pick up from their bacteria and pass on to the baby . . . Another anxiety.

But the baby was all right. The test had shown that, the letter had said so. She stroked the gentle swell of her stomach. What's going on in there, baby? she wondered. A lot, she knew. Even as she sat here the baby was growing and developing, bit by bit. Muscles, eyelids, nails, hair. Awe-inspiring. Miraculous. All those sort of words really did apply.

'So, just you and me, babe,' Isabel said, as she patted her stomach. 'Let's make the best of things, shall we?' (The saying, a favourite of her mother's, reminded her that she should phone her parents in Menorca.) 'You're making the best of my so-called elderly womb, I'll make the best of – of everything.'

The window display of Gap Kids in Richmond tempted Isabel. What the hell, she thought, and entered the shop. Why shouldn't she look at baby clothes, indulge herself a little? Smiling, she squeezed past a sleeping baby, eyelashes resting onits plump cheeks, in a buggy laden with shopping. Its mother, holding up a small blue sweater, smiled back.

Isabel lingered in the baby section. *Newborn*, the header said. Newborn. Isabel felt a lurch inside – surely not the baby, it was too early to feel it move – and her head spun. She tried to focus on the tiny white towelling socks – bootees? – in front of her, hanging in rows like votive offerings. She envisaged this baby, her baby, as a newborn. Naked, innocent, vulnerable. She was overcome by the purity of this vision. And by the responsibility.

This is odd, she thought. It's not as if this is the first time,

I'm a mother already. But motherhood as she knew it now, of two fledgling adults, seemed distantly related to the experience of renewed motherhood of a newborn. That's me, recycled mother, she thought, and almost laughed.

She concentrated on looking at the clothes, otherwise the assistant might assume her to be some sort of weirdo. But she was feeling pretty weird . . .

The labels were momentarily confusing then she suddenly understood: the clothes were sized by the weight and length of babies. Some of this was coming back to her. Three kilograms. How much was that in pounds? She worked it out, which made her remember how much Gemma and Dominic had weighed when they were born. Six pounds ten ounces and eight pounds one ounce respectively. Some things you never forgot.

She began to relax, lulled by her surroundings. The shop was filled with light and colour and she let herself enjoy playing with the idea of dressing her baby. That overwhelmed feeling was replaced by delight, for the clothes *were* delightful. Soft dungarees, tiny jackets, stylish hats, little knitted sweaters that were light years away from the pastel cardigans Isabel's mother had knitted for her grandchildren. She was charmed. This shop hadn't even existed when she had Dominic. As Dr Finch had said, so much had changed. Increased availability of cute clothes was the least of it.

Resisting buying anything (*Not yet, wait,* a voice of caution told her) Isabel reluctantly left the rainbow reverie behind and headed for WH Smith's. She picked up the latest issues of the magazines devoted to pregnancy and childbirth and glanced at the book section, although she thought she probably had enough books already. Could she have *too* much information? There were still things she had to research, for that's what it seemed like: how and where she wished to give birth; how to come up with a birth plan. She found a book she hadn't seen before, celebrating the experience of childbirth. And that's what I'm going to try to do, thought Isabel, celebrate my pregnancy, childbirth, the whole damn thing.

As she made her way to the sales desk she seized a book of names too – another whim to indulge, thinking about what to call it – him? Her? They'd had one years ago, of course, but it

143

had been thrown out when they'd no longer needed it. Then she added a hard-covered notebook in which to write her lists of things to do, questions to ask Dr Finch, ideas for her birth plan, those possible names . . .

The woman at the till scanned the items. Isabel wondered if she registered what they were . . . or was it all the same to her, whether it was *You & Your Baby* or *What Car* or *Loaded*? If she does notice, will she realise I'm pregnant – do I look it? – or will she think they're for a pregnant daughter? How old *do* I look?

The transaction was completed with few words and even less eye contact so Isabel was left wondering. The assistant was probably too involved in thinking about how long it was until her lunch hour to be curious about me, she thought, clutching the carrier-bag to her and walking back to the car park.

She was getting organised, she was on her way. Now that she knew the baby was all right (touch wood), she felt she could move forward. And if there was one thing pregnancy did, it was to move inevitably forward. It was as if she was coming out – coming out as a pregnant woman. Was this how Angie felt, she wondered. (If, in fact, Angie had come out as gay, Isabel still wasn't sure.) She knew it wasn't really the same, but she did experience a sense of feeling comfortable with herself, and even some pride.

It still seemed strange to find Jenny in the shop rather than Angie but Isabel was getting used to it. And Jenny had slipped into Angie's place fairly easily and painlessly, Isabel had to admit.

As Isabel was about to open the door a woman came hurrying out, head down, almost colliding with her. She muttered apologies and Isabel could see that she had been crying.

'Hi Jenny. Who was that?'

Jenny put the box of tissues back under the counter. 'Oh, sorry, Isabel. That was Liz Stanford. Do you know her? She lives round the corner.'

'No, I don't think so. She wasn't a dissatisfied customer, was she?'

Jenny flushed. 'No. It was nothing to do with the shop.'

'Jen, I was only teasing. Relax. I'll put the kettle on then you can fill me in on everything.'

As she went towards the back of the shop she glanced quickly over the racks and shelves of clothes. Everything was in order.

The shop was quiet so they sat and sipped their tea and talked.

'So how has it been, Jen?'

'Fine. A few customers this morning. A woman wanted a wedding outfit, her sister's wedding. She bought that Max Mara suit.'

'Yes, I thought that would go quickly.'

'Someone brought in a couple of Ghost dresses. I said I'd ring her with the selling price, I'd like you to have a look at them.'

Isabel sat back and listened to Jenny. It was good to see her so animated. It did wonders for her face.

'We'll look at the stock book when we close up.'

'Ah yes, the stock book!'

They laughed.

'But Jenny, you haven't told me about that woman just now – Liz, was it?'

'The usual story – husband's just left her. Look, I'm sorry I was spending time with her.'

'Jenny, please, that's all right. Don't worry. It's good for business, making the customers or would-be customers feel at home. Anyway, it's always been like that in this shop. Perhaps because they find it non-threatening, I don't know, but Angie and I have often had people crying on our shoulders – not literally, of course, although there was one time . . .'

'Liz needed to talk. She knew about me and Graham, you see.'

Isabel was pleased to see that the mention of his name didn't change Jenny's expression. Maybe she's really on the mend, she thought. 'It seems to be happening so much. Do you think it's particularly prevalent around here?'

'Why? What do you mean, Isabel?'

'Well, it's a relatively affluent area. Husbands can afford to leave, couples can afford to divorce, run two households.'

'I hadn't thought of it like that. But there's certainly a lot of it going on. Only yesterday I bumped into someone in Waitrose, Sally Vickers.'

'Oh, I know Sally. Plays a lot of tennis.'

'There we were in the cereals aisle and she told me her husband had abandoned her and burst into tears and I found myself crying as well. Two women crying together in Waitrose! It was awful.'

Isabel made a sympathetic noise and reached over to pat Jenny's hand, keeping one eye on the door for customers.

'It's OK, Isabel, I'm all right. Surprisingly.' Jenny smiled. 'I am getting over the bastard. I'm even beginning to find it hard to believe that I was married to him for all that time. It seems so bloody unreal. And, in a way, it helps to hear about it happening to other women – it's not just me, so perhaps I shouldn't take it too personally!'

'That's one way of looking at it. But what happened with Sally?'

'She was still in a state of shock. Her husband – Rob, isn't it? – was posted to Kuala Lumpur to set up a subsidiary, something like that. Anyway, after a few weeks he writes to her – *writes* to her – and says he's not coming back, the marriage is over.'

'Bloody hell. But they must have been married . . . how long? Fifteen years or so?'

'Eighteen, she said. And there are the children. Imagine having to tell them! He said he'd be in touch with them but so far . . .'

'What a shit. I can't believe it. They always seemed happy. Certainly as a family they were very *together*. All that playing sport and doing things in unison.'

'You're right, it happens to the most unlikely people. But it's always the men, isn't it? They make it happen, to women, to their children.'

'So what *is* it with these men?'

'God knows. I'm still trying to work out why Graham left. But there does seem to be a pattern, Sally and I were talking about it. Her husband, and Graham too, and all the others I've heard about lately.'

'You make it sound like an epidemic!'

'Perhaps it is. The four or five men I've heard about in the last few months have all been in their late forties, approaching fifty. There hadn't appeared to be problems. It wasn't a question of splitting up, more the man leaving, saying he needs more space. And going. Just like Graham. They all claimed there was no one else –'

'I suppose they would say that, wouldn't they?'

They turned as the shop door opened. A woman entered with two children in tow and Isabel and Jenny stood up, smiling.

Isabel removed the tea mugs and went to the kitchen, leaving Jenny to talk to the customer. When she peeped out a few minutes later she saw Jenny settling the children in the toy corner while their mother picked out some shirts to try on. Jenny had switched into professional mode. Friendly, helpful, capable. She was definitely a safe pair of hands, Isabel decided, and the thought occurred to her that maybe she, and others, had made the mistake of underestimating Jenny in the past.

As she rinsed the mugs she thought about the men who'd left their wives. It was tempting to lump them all together and create a social trend. Perhaps it was, yet Isabel knew that every relationship was different, every marriage unique. Who really understood what went on inside the comfortable homes of people like her? We all appear so similar, she thought. Our houses resemble each other, we drive the same sort of cars, shop in the same places, dress alike, go on the same sort of holidays . . . But what do we know of other people's emotional lives? We don't talk about such things with the people we regard as friends, not until something goes wrong.

It occurred to her that even husbands and wives didn't seem to talk about their emotional lives much either, if the evidence Jenny presented was true. Which made Isabel think of Michael. He was approaching fifty. But if he was restless or unhappy that was more to do with her being pregnant than anything else, wasn't it?

23

The Turner family were about to have supper together: a surprise event. Isabel no longer planned for this to happen and didn't cater for it, not exactly. Lately she'd taken to cooking quiches, pasta bakes, casseroles, or buying ready-made versions, things that could be eaten hot or cold, by one person or four, on one day or the next. Flexi-feeding, she called it, dignifying it with a name. Gemma was usually out, Michael tended to arrive home late, Dominic would grab something and eat in front of the television. Often Isabel ate alone while listening to *The Archers*. Sometimes she felt as if the families of Ambridge were more real than her own.

But tonight here they were, suddenly, in the kitchen at the same time. She grilled some chicken breasts while Gemma cooked some rice and made a salad. Michael was opening a bottle of white wine and talking to Dominic about rugby.

Isabel had a sense of everything winding down, like a slow-motion sequence in a film. Michael's hand as he turned the corkscrew. The flick of Dominic's hair as he put his head back, listening to his father. The mixed green leaves, glossy with dressing, as Gemma tossed the salad. A vision of how things should be. The moment could not last, she knew. She tried to hurry things along before they all disappeared.

Gemma told her brother to lay the table – twice – and he complied, making a lot of noise about it. Then they sat down to eat.

'Well, this is nice. All of us together for once,' said Isabel. Little response.

They ate in silence, apart from requests to pass the salt or the salad.

She tried again. 'I've had some good news. Gemma knows already. About the baby.' As no one asked what it was, she continued, 'I've had a screening test. For abnormalities. And everything's OK – the baby is fine.'

Isabel caught Michael's eye. He had the grace to say something.

'Well, I suppose that is good news.'

Oh, Isabel thought, why couldn't he be more enthusiastic? Why couldn't he just be *nice*?

The children glanced from one parent to the other and then at each other, watching, waiting.

Isabel made another effort. 'Gemma, aren't you going to tell Dad and Dom about your good news?'

'Mum, it's not exactly good news – well, it is, but nothing's really happened yet.' But Gemma told them briefly about her application for a summer job and getting an interview. She seems reluctant, thought Isabel. I shouldn't have used her to oil the wheels of family life. Oh dear. And Isabel could see Michael frowning; he was unlikely to approve.

Michael was thinking of the one time the family had gone on a Mark Warner holiday, in Italy. The children had loved it, disappearing all day with kids their age for supervised canoeing or volleyball or watersports. Isabel had liked it too, playing tennis or swimming or reading by the pool. He'd pretended to like it but had become increasingly depressed, surrounded by families just like them, mixing with people just like them, yet feeling he didn't fit in. Isabel had joked and said it was South-west London-on-Sea, as if that were no bad thing. To him it seemed just a puffed-up holiday camp for the middle classes. (It made him think of the few holidays he'd had as a child, when his parents had managed to find the money to go to a Pontin's camp in Kent or, when they became more adventurous, Devon. Memories of attempts to create a respite from post-war austerity. A poky chalet with thin walls. Brown soup served at long, long tables in a huge hall. Crackling Tannoy announcements. The novel excitement of table-tennis tournaments. His father entering a knobbly knees competition.) At the beach club Michael was expected to compete with all the other middle-aged men – and how they did *compete* – in sailing races or archery contests or telling anecdotes or talking loudly. Continual jostling for position. Doctors, surgeons, accountants, lawyers like him having to prove how successful they were at everything, even on holiday. He'd done it, he'd played his part, but he swore that was the last time. In future summers he had come up with different ideas for holidays. But now Gemma wanted to work in one of those places. But then, she was different from him, she didn't carry the same emotional baggage.

Dominic's voice, getting louder, interrupted his thoughts. 'So now is it my turn? *Mum's good news. Gemma's good news.*' His tone was sarcastic. 'This is like Show and Tell. Let's go round the table and see –'

'Dominic! What is the matter with you?' Isabel looked upset.

'Well, all this stuff about *babies*. And Gemma's little job. Some job! What about me? I've got important things to do – I've got my exams in a few months, remember? I've got to get those bloody grades, haven't I? And all I hear is this shit.'

He pushed back his chair and rushed upstairs. Gemma swore under her breath.

'Couldn't you say something, Michael?' Isabel asked, her eyes filling with tears.

'What can I say? It's his age. And perhaps it's understandable. Dom *is* under a lot of pressure, he really wants that university place at Bristol – so, as he says, he's got to get the grades. It's a difficult time.'

'That justifies his awful spoilt-brat behaviour, then, does it? Honestly!' Gemma snorted and left the room.

Isabel stood up. 'I give up,' she said. 'I'm exhausted.'

She put her hands behind her, rubbed the small of her back and stretched. The gesture pushed her breasts forward and Michael could see how they had grown heavier, her nipples bigger. Her belly was fuller, rounder, her shirt clung to it. How pregnant she looked, he thought, and words tumbled into his mind: fecund, full, female. Part of him couldn't help being moved, part of him wanted to go to her and hold her. The rest of him was confused.

After supper, he took refuge in the study with a glass of wine and closed the door. His confusion came with him.

This is like being on a roller-coaster, he thought. My life. Hurtling downwards out of control surrounded by screams and noise, unable to get off, then chugging slowly upwards in calmer mode, enjoying a brief moment of joy at the top before the familiar swoop towards earth . . .

He swore and drained his glass, trying to resist the urge to ring Ellen. So much for compartments. He usually avoided calling her from home, but tonight he felt desperate. Not particularly desperate for Ellen – although to a certain extent that was always there – but just desperate. He picked up the phone. She answered quickly.

'It's me,' he said.

'A nice surprise.'

'What are you doing, Ellen?'

'Actually I'm working, I've got a thousand words to finish by tomorrow. What are you doing?'

'Phoning you.'

'Funny guy. So where are you?'

He hesitated. 'At home.'

'Ah. That explains why you're whispering.'

Isabel retreated to the bathroom: it had become a sanctuary, a place where she could be alone and undisturbed. She did this most evenings now, around nine thirty.

She passed the study on her way upstairs, moving slowly as her back was stiff and aching. In the absence of back rubs from Michael a soak might do it good.

Michael's voice drifted through the door. He seemed to be murmuring. She couldn't actually hear what he was saying but his tone interested her. It sounded warm, personal. Probably not a work call, although he'd been known to schmooze clients when he had to. But not at this time of night.

So who was he talking to?

Not family – he didn't really have any. A friend? Unlikely. His friends were their joint friends and it was usually Isabel who rang them and kept in contact.

So who could it be?

Isabel sat down on a stair, listening but trying not to hear. Murmur. Pause. Murmur. Laughter.

She gripped a banister tightly as a wave of awareness flooded over her. No, it can't be. He couldn't, he isn't. No. Please, no. A cataclysmic shudder reverberated through her. Momentarily she felt something of what it must be like to be swept up in a major natural disaster: earthquake, tornado, hurricane, lava flow. Tossed and buffeted by destructive forces outside your control, helpless, unprepared.

She squeezed her eyes shut as if that would divert the great tumble of ideas and images whooshing through her mind like so much flotsam and jetsam in the wake of a catastrophe. Michael working late, Michael absent from the office when she rang, Michael off driving alone, Michael at a distance, Michael's puzzling behaviour, the mystery of Michael, all accompanied by an undertow – Michael and another woman?

There, it had surfaced.

But what was she going to do with it, this possible revelation?

A simple question: 'Who were you talking to, Michael?'

Or a not so simple question: 'Are you having an affair?'

Even framing the words in her mind made her wince. And supposing she asked him, he could always lie. He may be lying already.

Silence from the study. Isabel got up and climbed the stairs to the bathroom. Imagine if he'd found her sitting there. How undignified.

She turned the taps full on and sat on the stool, watching the bath fill, letting the steam and the fragrance of geranium oil surround her. The noise of water began to calm her; it always did. Try to relax, she told herself, think of the baby. There was enough turmoil in her life already, she didn't need any more. All she had was a suspicion, probably fuelled by her conversation with Jenny about all these unlikely men leaving their wives and families. Michael wasn't like that, was he? And there was probably a perfectly ordinary explanation for the phone call she'd overheard – probably – but she wouldn't ask him about it, for then she'd have to reveal that she'd been listening.

As she lay in the tub she swished the water back and forth, again and again. There was some reassurance in it, in the sound – *splosh* – it made as it hit the end under the taps. She remembered her childhood game of making waves in the bath, trying to sink her toy boat. Which one was it? The plucky little tug, the wooden sailing boat? Ships and boats and water had always featured strongly in her early life, with her father being in the navy, although much of his time had been spent on shore at the naval college or in a desk job. 'A navy man, that's me. All you need to know,' he would say. As a small child she had assumed it was something to do with the colour of his uniform. It became a family joke when her lack of understanding was discovered.

She thought of the sea, the English sea off Devon. How you never really knew it. Unfathomable. How the colour changed. Sometimes steely grey, cold and grey, sometimes with a greenish hue, sometimes startlingly blue. The hugeness of the sea.

Big things, little things.

This thought she'd had, this suspicion, she couldn't deal with it, not now. She would not look it in the face. Pushing it down, down in her mind, she consigned it to the very depths of the ocean.

Finger-in-the-dam time.

And time to turn inward, look to herself – and her baby. It needed her energy and attention; she would not dissipate them elsewhere.

Her stomach rose satisfyingly above the water if she lay at a certain angle. She couldn't understand those pregnant women who wailed and complained about being fat. This wasn't *fat*, this was a baby. And its support system. She massaged the tight skin gently with the sea sponge then drizzled water over its warm flushed surface, imagining the baby inside her, secure in its own watery world.

'There you are, little one,' she murmured, 'safe and sound. We'll be all right, you and me. Yes, we will.'

She reached out for her pregnancy handbook and propped it on the bath rack. There were remarkable *in utero* photographs of each stage, showing the development of the foetus month by month. What was she now? Nearly sixteen weeks? Imagine: the baby was already completely formed, it should even have eyebrows. That, in particular, amazed her. Eyebrows: so specific, such a small part of the whole picture. And, thank God, the baby was all right, it was normal and healthy. *Some* things she could relax about.

24

Jenny was curled up on Angie's sofa with Angie's cat purring beside her, half watching Angie's television. As so often happened, she'd turned on a programme, this time a documentary about penguins, creatures she usually found irresistible, then her mind began to roam over recent events, her gaze wandering over Angie's things. The pictures on Angie's walls, her sepia photographs in old silver frames (Victorian ancestors? 'God no,' Angie'd said, she'd got them from Bermondsey market as a job lot), her collection of mismatched blue and white china, the hotchpotch of furniture, which somehow looked so right . . .

Jenny was fascinated by Angie's taste and sense of style. It had all been put together on a shoestring, Angie had told her, much of it accumulated from jumble sales and charity shops. Angie had laughed and confided that some of it had even been 'borrowed' from props departments of theatres or TV studios. The odd thing here, the odd thing there. She reckoned it was justified by the low wages she'd been paid as a humble bit-part actress. But that was all in the past . . .

It was enjoyable sitting here, savouring the results of Angie's efforts. All this had been assembled by Angie alone, she realised. And without fear. No compromises, no asking permission. If Angie had wanted old chenille tablecloths as curtains, she got them. If Angie had wanted to throw giant gypsy-like shawls over the sofas, mixing floral and Paisley patterns, she did.

It could not have been more unlike her own house, her *ex*-house, which she'd recently left behind. That had been bland and unadventurous, the product of her timidity, she now acknowledged, and Graham's idea of what was tasteful.

As she stroked Desdemona, murmuring, 'We're getting on fine, aren't we?' provoking even deeper purrs from the cat, she reflected on the leaving of her house – *home* – and the manner of it. It had been easier to relinquish than she'd expected. Leaving the place where she'd spent most of her marriage, where she'd raised the twins, should have been a traumatic event. However, when she'd paused at the gate and looked at it for the last time she realised that any happy times she'd had there had been erased by the more recent and dominant unhappy memories. Now it was occupied by builders, hired to remake it in the image of its new owners. She'd never met them, had managed to avoid it – wasn't that what estate agents were for?

The contact she'd had with Graham had been surprisingly civilised too. They'd been speaking over the phone for weeks, agreeing their acceptance of the offer, discussing timing, all the financial implications of the house sale. Jenny had managed to keep calm, be businesslike, as if this were a neutral transaction and not the disposing of the family home. She kept repeating to herself the simple advice she'd read recently in a self-help book (she'd been buying quite a few of those – and actually reading them): if you can't change the situation, change your attitude towards it. So she'd tried and found it began to work.

The seemingly more abstract things were easier to resolve than all the physical stuff that surrounded her. She had already made a good start – throwing lots away, or giving it to jumble sales and charity shops, but there was still . . . all this. Perhaps she was avoiding closure, as one of her books called it.

Every day she stepped over it or around it, avoiding the issue. Big items like pieces of furniture, pictures, bikes; smaller ones, photographs in frames, tapes and CDs, books, the boys' things . . . She'd abandoned the idea of making separate files of photos and mementoes for Graham and the twins. The would-be family archives remained in one large box. She figured that if anyone wanted anything they would soon ask her (and expect her to know where it was).

When she'd dared to raise these practical questions of sorting and disposal with Graham on the phone he had said blithely, 'Do what you like. Get rid of it all . . .' How predictable, thought Jenny, and became increasingly flustered as she looked around the house and found it impossible to make decisions. Isabel had been appalled. 'Graham should help you, Jenny. For God's sake, this was his home too – his past! It's too bloody easy to say get rid of everything, like it's so easy just to leave and walk away. It's his responsibility too – so ring him, get him down here!'

Jenny had been surprised at Isabel's vehemence – but she was right. After practising what she was going to say she rang Graham and told him – *told* him! – as straightforwardly as she could that his presence was required as soon as possible. He agreed to come the next weekend.

That had felt like an achievement, and she experienced a burst of optimism and energy. She finally told Angie that she'd take up the offer and rent her house for an initial period of six months. She sorted out suitable storage – they were bound to need it; she wrote to the boys, care of their latest *poste restante* address, in Sydney, informing them of what was happening. She took action, she made decisions. For some women, she thought, this would be nothing special. For Jenny, who was beginning to think she might have slumbered through most of her life, it was significant. Nevertheless, she was glad she was working at Once or Twice: it would help her to avoid agonising over how it would be with Graham. It was now nearly six months since she'd seen him.

He arrived on the doorstep late on Friday afternoon and rang the bell. Perhaps he thought she'd changed the locks? Or was he being uncharacteristically sensitive? She checked her appearance in the hall mirror – she'd do, she thought, fluffing up her hair. She put a smile on her face and opened the door.

'Graham. Hello.'

'Jenny. Well, here I am.'

There was a pause as they regarded each other. He was wearing a long dark overcoat she hadn't seen before. Did he have a little less hair? He looked tired. And he seemed smaller than she remembered, not just shorter but smaller all over. Diminished.

'Graham? Are you coming in?'

'Oh, sure.' Over the threshold, reluctantly.

'Don't you have a bag or anything?'

'Er – no. Well, yes I do, but I left it at the hotel.'

'Hotel?' She had assumed he'd be staying here, in Mark or Tim's room.

'Yes, I've booked into a place in Richmond, near the station. I'm staying until Monday. That should be enough time, shouldn't it?'

Time enough to dismantle what was left of their marriage, their life together. Yes, three days should do it easily, she thought.

They worked efficiently alongside each other all weekend, saying little. Every evening Graham went back to the hotel and Jenny felt a great relief. It was a strain, being with him, doing this, but it was less difficult than she'd anticipated. So far she hadn't made a fuss or broken down or screamed at him. She could tell he was surprised and she sensed him waiting for her to become emotional, as he'd always called it. That strengthened her resolve not to. She would remain in control even when they divided up family photographs, disposed of holiday souvenirs, things they'd bought together . . . Occasionally Jenny would feel him watching her and she'd catch his eye, then he'd look away. She would not deliver the reactions he was expecting.

After a while it occurred to her that perhaps he was scared of her, of what she might say or do. That could be why he escaped to the hotel every night. Or perhaps his girlfriend was there waiting, keeping an eye on him.

On the last day they toured the house, checking that they'd covered everything. Graham hovered over the boxes piled on the upstairs landing and brought up the subject of money. They'd already agreed over the phone that the proceeds from the house sale, after legal and other expenses and clearing the mortgage, should be split straight down the middle. Jenny had suspected that Graham thought he was being more than fair; she thought it was her due. Now he said, 'Of course you'll have a decent sum. Have you decided what you'll do with it?'

'Not yet.'

'Well, you don't have to buy anywhere immediately, do you?'

She'd already told him about renting Angela's house.

'No, but I expect I will eventually buy a place of my own.' She enjoyed the ring of those words and found herself smiling.

Graham looked uncomfortable. 'Anyway, what I wanted to say, Jen, was that if you'd like any assistance or advice about what to do with the money – you know, investing it, that sort of thing – let me know.' He cleared his throat. 'I'd be glad to help.'

She could see that he meant it. In his own way he was trying to be nice. And he did look a little upset. Perhaps this house clearing had affected him more than her. Or maybe he was just feeling guilty.

She paused before replying. 'I don't think I'll need your help. But thank you anyway.'

There. She was learning to say no. A little late, but it was happening. She was going to stand on her own two feet. A small step for womankind but a giant one for her.

Desdemona nudged Jenny's hand with her forehead, demanding more attention. Graham had always frowned upon pets – think of the mess, the trouble – and despite the boys' pleas for a dog or a cat the most they had ever been allowed was something small. A succession of mice, hamsters, gerbils came and went. Creatures that could be caged and kept upstairs in their bedrooms, with the excuse that taking responsibility was good for the boys. The little animals never lived long. They – their bones now – were buried under the pear tree in the garden. Ex-garden, Jenny reminded herself. Looking back, she wished she'd protested on her sons' behalf. Why had she deferred to Graham all the time? What was – no, what *had* been the matter with her? He had dominated her, bullied her, even, until she had not known who she was. And she had let him.

Enough of all this raking over the past, of using Graham as a frame of reference, even in her memories. Out of the window with it all.

She did miss her garden. (Although Angie had given her *carte blanche* with her small patio and profusion of pots, saying she'd heard Jenny was a brilliant gardener. That might help.) The day before she left Jenny had walked around it, saying goodbye to the forsythia in bloom, that wonderful splash of yellow, precursor of spring. Every shrub she'd planted, every bulb, every rose, every herb, everything, even those lying dormant underground, all received a whispered farewell. There was a clump of snowdrops near the house, almost past their best, heads drooping heavily as if they had a lot on their minds. One stalk was snapped, the flower lying on the earth. She picked it up, cupping it gently in her hand even though it could not be saved. In the house she rinsed it and laid it on kitchen paper. Snowdrops were amazing. They seemed so delicate, yet they were toughies, she thought, raising their heads while winter lingered, unafraid. And as they opened up they became a different flower. Tapering outer petals spread wide, revealing inner petals decorated in green: delicate stripes inside and tiny horseshoe shapes on the outside, as if painted by a steady hand with a minuscule brush. As she examined it closely Jenny experienced a sense of wonder. She placed it gently between the pages of her plant encyclopaedia and pressed hard. The book, with the fading snowdrop inside, was one of the few things she had brought with her.

Jenny eased herself away from the cat and went into the tiny galley kitchen – perfect for one. She made some coffee in the old chipped enamel pot (French maybe?) and wondered where Angie had picked it up. There seemed to be a story behind everything to do with the woman, including Angie herself.

She wandered back into the living room, barefoot, mug in hand, and idly read the titles on the bookshelves. Shakespeare, poetry, thrillers, art, travel. She selected a Patricia Cornwell and settled back on the sofa next to the cat. It occurred to her that she could do what she liked – drink coffee or wine or hot chocolate, watch any television programme she wanted, read or do nothing, have a bath any time she felt like it . . . There was no one to consider but herself.

Why wasn't it like that in her old house, she wondered, when she'd been living there alone? Something had always held her back. Echoes of family life perhaps, the ghost of how things used to be? But now she'd been set free. She stroked the cat under the chin. 'Do you know, Desdemona, I feel like purring too?'

A rush of gladness came over her. Everything was all right. She was going to be all right. Angie's house was proving to be a magical place: it was like a nest, somewhere she could put herself back together. Making a life, that's what she was doing. A life of her own. She had money in the bank – and it was quite a lot of money, to her anyway. She had a job, a home, for six months at least, depending on whether Angie decided to return. She could do all sorts of things. Enrol on a garden-design course, join a reading club, try line-dancing, buy a car, go away for weekends to places she'd always wanted to go but Graham hadn't, Vienna or Dublin or Copenhagen . . .

Meanwhile, she realised that she felt content. No more thoughts of the river, of abandoning herself to its darkness, of letting herself be overwhelmed.

She remembered – she was doing it again, *remembering*, but so what? – it was only natural – the motivational posters Graham used to have on his office wall. To inspire him? Impress clients? Embarrass them more like, she thought.

Anyway, there was one, a rather good photograph of a rolling sea, waves hitting a beach. The caption said: 'Embrace change.' She had actually quite liked it; it would be good on her wall right now. For that was what she was doing: embracing change, learning to love it. No more fear.

25

The night was illuminated by the double helping of the lights along the Thames and their reflections in the water. Michael and Ellen sat at a window table in the Oxo Tower restaurant, gazing at the view. Wasn't this what people came here for? The gleam and curve of the river; the buildings lining its banks, some shimmering with strategically placed spotlights, others in darkness clad in scaffolding. Grand Victorian chunks standing next to bigger but less grand contemporary structures, interspersed with an occasional art deco block. And, despite being hemmed in by its surroundings, the dome of St Paul's managed to make itself known.

Ellen was feeling distanced from everything. It wasn't to do with being up on the eighth floor – to her, a New Yorker, that was nothing. She felt distanced from Michael too. This view, this expensive view, somehow made her think of her father. That was probably to do with the views from his apartment. Was this feeling homesick? she wondered.

Michael was talking about the name of the building. O-X-O. Ellen was thinking of New York, thinking of her dad. She remembered that old friend of his – Frank? Saul? – bending down to her level when she was seven or so and asking if she knew that her pa was a man of letters. For a long time after that she'd imagined her father being made up of the letters of the alphabet, seeing a T in the shape formed by his eyebrows and nose; a V in his beard; each ear was a D ... And it concerned her that at any moment he might deconstruct into a tumble of As and Bs and Cs, like a character in *Sesame Street*.

'Ellen? Are you with me?'

'I'm sorry. You were saying?'

'Did you know I was born not far from here? The hinterland

of South London.' He sighed. 'Places you don't know about, Ellen, and won't ever need to . . .'

She wondered what he meant. Before she could ask he continued, 'We used to see this building on our trips into town, to Oxford Street – that was a treat, "up town", we called it. Anyway, it was a landmark and when I was small I thought it was something to do with noughts and crosses.'

'Noughts and crosses?'

'Oh, now what would that be in America? Zeros and crosses?'

'I've lived here long enough to know what a nought is, Michael.'

'Sorry. Let me explain about noughts and crosses.'

If the napkins had been paper he would have drawn a diagram on one. As it was he used his hands. Ellen got the picture but let him finish. She'd never seen him or heard him like this, so garrulous and talking about his childhood, of all things. He couldn't be drunk, they'd only had a couple of martinis.

'I know what you mean. That game. Tic-tac-toe, we call it.'

'Oh, do you? Tic-tac-toe. Ah. But then I found out it was nothing to do with that anyway.'

He started to say that as a child he'd never made the link between Oxo and this building because at home his mother had used Bisto and – then he saw the puzzled look on Ellen's face. What did these things mean to her? Why was he talking about his working-class childhood in a poor part of London, which he usually never discussed with anyone? God, he was being pathetic. And, really, Oxo, Bisto . . . Even if they had them in the States she was hardly the sort of girl to spend time in supermarket aisles in search of gravy powders . . . Did she even know what gravy was?

He thought of his mother and his grandmother in the kitchen. The holy significance of gravy. What an accomplishment it was, he'd come to realise, just when everything else for the meal was ready, that last minute heroic production of a steaming jug of gravy . . .

'Michael, I said, shall we order?'

They concentrated on the menu. Back on safer ground, he decided.

She wondered if all this chat was an effort to keep off the subject she really wanted to talk about: the state of his marriage, the state of his wife. Perhaps he was just nervous.

'Acorn-fed pigs?' He laughed. 'What do you think, Ellen?'

'Well, what about sole with sea-urchin butter? Maybe not a good idea, sounds as if it will have spiny bits in it.'

They tossed items of amusement back and forth across the table until it became difficult to choose anything. Ellen was becoming bored with it all, all this elaborate food, all this discussion, all this *choosing*. She and Michael had been eating out a lot lately and at times it seemed as if the restaurateurs of London were engaged in a game to see who could come up with the most outlandish ideas, the most bizarre combinations. Even those chefs who claimed to serve peasant cuisine from far regions of Europe added unlikely twists to the food, which would make said peasants turn in their humble graves. Perhaps she should write an article about it: 'Let them eat fake'.

It wasn't only restaurants they'd been visiting. They never used go out like this. Why now? Ellen asked herself. Did he want to be seen or was this a step forward, some progress in their relationship?

'Do you realise that we're stepping out together?' Ellen had asked Michael wryly. For it was like that, stepping over the threshold of her apartment, taking their relationship into the outside world. At first she'd worried that it might not stand up, it might be frail out in the light, but so far it had survived.

There was a flurry of activity, of arrangements. Nearly every week Michael would ring and say he had tickets for the latest play at the Almeida, or for the opera or ballet. Ellen sometimes got the feeling that he was working his way through reviews, ticking items on the listings page, seeing what should be seen. She wondered if the tickets were corporate hospitality that had come his way – not that he was mean, far from it, as these expensive meals proved. He invariably refused when she tried to pay or split the bill. That could be a generational thing. She hoped it wasn't anything else: every so often the idea slipped into her mind that this was how men of a certain kind treated their mistresses. *Mistress*. How she hated that word and all it implied. Or was he trying to compensate in some way? For not telling his wife, for not leaving her?

Michael pushed aside his plate and took Ellen's hand, turning it over and stroking her palm. 'It is so good to be with you,' he whispered.

She looked at him. He had the capacity to move her. There was a hint of vulnerability about him tonight, he seemed tired. Above his shirt collar his neck looked strained. At times like this he looked his age. That did not deter her, it just made her all the more impatient to have him – why waste time?

'By the way, Michael, how do you explain all these evenings out to your wife? What do you tell her?'

'It's easy. I just say I have to wine and dine clients, which I do on occasions.'

'*Easy*?' Her feeling of distaste must have shown on her face, for he added quickly, 'I mean it's not *easy* exactly –'

'No, it isn't easy, Michael. Nothing is easy. For any of us. And surely it's more difficult now that she's ill?'

Ellen removed her hand from his. She sipped her wine, stopping herself from probing into how ill his wife was, what was actually wrong.

'In some ways, yes, it's harder. In other ways it's – it's easier because she's very wrapped up in herself. I mean she's focusing on her – on her illness. She has to . . .'

'Oh Michael.' She reached across and stroked his cheek.

They decided to skip dessert and coffee and hurry back to her flat. It wasn't far.

'Do you have time, Michael?'

'Yes. I have time.'

His car was parked nearby. Ellen's hand rested on his thigh while he drove. As they crossed Waterloo Bridge she remarked, 'You know, the sight of Big Ben always gives me a thrill, to see it in the flesh, as it were. It's such an icon, so familiar from postcards and all those old British films.'

'I suppose it's a bit like the Empire State Building for us, or the Statue of Liberty.'

'Michael, listen! Wouldn't it be great to go to New York, the two of us, just for a few days? I'd love to take you. Could you get away?'

'I'd like that. I'll try. Let me think about it.'

She turned her head away from him and said no more.

Michael wondered if this was the moment to tell her he was going away soon, for a week's skiing. He couldn't get out of it and, in a way, he didn't want to. Every year, around Easter, the family went to Switzerland. They'd been doing it for years and had a regular booking at the same small hotel in Zermatt. A few days ago Isabel had announced she'd decided not to go because of her pregnancy, she didn't think it wise to ski. To be honest, what with everything else going on, he'd barely given the holiday any thought. He supposed she was being sensible, he could understand. But when he'd asked about him and the children, she'd said, curtly, that surely there was no problem, they could manage without her, couldn't they? So that's what was happening. He'd been having fantasies of asking Ellen to come, striving to fathom a way of fixing it, of explaining her to the children. He hadn't yet worked it out and part of him knew he shouldn't even be trying.

'Actually, I'm going away for a week at Easter. Skiing.' He told her about it.

'So you want me to come as a substitute, is that it?'

'Ellen! I didn't mean that. I just thought it might –'

'Please! You know it's not possible. How would you explain me to your kids? Just forget it. Anyway, I don't ski.'

'You don't? Really? I assumed –'

'Never assume.'

He stopped the car off Aldwych and turned her face towards him. 'I'm sorry, Ellen. I don't know what I'm doing half the time, these days.'

She sighed. 'It's all right. Don't let's argue. Take me home.'

They hurried up the stairs of her building, she fumbled with the door key, he held her as she opened it. Now there was no need to talk, no problems to overcome. They reached for each other in silence.

Clothes half off, entwined, mouths clamped together, reluctant to part even for a second, they lurched as one to a corner of the room. He eased her up and back against the wall and pushed her skirt up. She guided him inside her, straddling the corner, arms stretched out for balance. It was fast and frantic, leaving them leaning on each other gasping for breath.

They nuzzled and kissed gently before stepping apart.

'Look at us,' Ellen laughed. 'Feel like a shower?'

Later they lay in her bed, a linen sheet over them. It was cool and calm. They'd fooled about in the shower then made love again in bed. Though Ellen wasn't sure if it was making love: sex seemed a more appropriate word. For what was happening between her and Michael, this physical stuff, was at times becoming wilder, rougher. They played games, they talked dirty, they tried this . . . then that. Biting and squeezing hard and holding a little too tight – they both did it. Everything exaggerated. They never referred to it, to this new way of doing things, or discussed it afterwards. There was a certain darkness about it.

Ellen thought that it was probably a release from the frustration and dissatisfaction they felt. Maybe it was a way of liberating themselves from the constraints of their situation. It wasn't that they wished to hurt each other – she knew what *that* was like, she'd been there with Noah, when cruelty beckoned. Never again.

What she wanted was an easy, happy relationship between equals. Nothing tortured, nothing difficult. Was that so much to ask? In different circumstances, if he wasn't married, she thought she could have it with Michael. Hopefully she still would.

She looked at him now, lying beside her, his eyes closed, his arm around her, fingers resting idly on her breast. This was good. Isolate the moment, she told herself, don't think of anything but this, now.

Michael stirred. Ellen guessed he was fighting sleep, wondering what the time was. Then he turned, sliding his arm from beneath her and murmured that he had to go.

She sat up suddenly, her breasts exposed. Anger rose in her throat like bile. She hated being in this position, of not being able to get mad at him, of having to feel grateful for his time and attention. It wasn't fair, but how could she say so? The bloody wife, the poor sick wife. It was if as she lay between them, pale and ill.

Michael began to pull on his clothes. She stayed in bed and

watched him. As he stepped into his boxers she saw his long penis, freshly limp against his leg. Then it was enclosed, tucked away. How intimate we are, she thought, yet we haven't done ordinary things together like shopping for clothes or going on a plane or sleeping all night in the same bed . . .

He looked down at her. 'What Ellen? What?'

He continued to dress, zipping up his trousers decisively.

'You know what, Michael. You know.' She bowed her head in case she was looking needy, she couldn't bear that. And he wouldn't be able to cope with it.

He sat on the edge of the bed and put his arm around her. 'Listen, darling, I want us to be together, I know –'

Ellen wondered if he called his wife darling. Of course he did. She drew away from him and wrapped the sheet around her. 'Michael, there is so much you don't know. No, hear me out. Look, we agree that we want to be together, but we're coming from different directions. We won't go into that. One thing that worries me is that all this, the way we have to conduct our relationship, is going to wear it out, wear *us* out. There may not be anything left by the time you can –'

'Ellen, don't say that! Don't, please.'

'I'm just being realistic.'

'And be patient too, please try to be patient.'

'What else can I do? And that's what I find hard to take. I have so few choices here!'

He pushed his hair off his face in that familiar gesture, apparently at a loss for words.

Ellen moved closer to him and stroked his cheek. She couldn't stay mad at him for long. 'I'm sorry, Michael. I don't want to pressure you, I know it doesn't help. It's just that sometimes it gets too much.'

'I know, with me too. But how can I make it better, apart from the obvious? And you know I –'

'OK, OK ... Let's focus on the can-dos. It would be wonderful to go away together, just for a couple of nights, perhaps? Forget New York – for now. Couldn't we grab a weekend away in the country somewhere, some discreet little hotel? It would be so good for us. Imagine, all that uninterrupted time together.'

'In the same bed together all night.'

'You said it! So how about it? Do you think you can?'

'I suppose I could. Yes, why not?'

'Great! Aren't there weekend conferences, stuff like that you could use as an excuse?'

'There are. I'll think of something, I promise.'

'So we'll do it soon?'

'We will.'

And he wrenched himself away, kissed her goodbye and left.

As Michael drove home he adjusted his clothes and mentally adjusted his face and attitude – although he wasn't sure why: no one paid much attention to him at home, not even Isabel lately. That much was true: she was preoccupied with herself or, more accurately, with the pregnancy. But lying about her being ill was beginning to leave a sour taste in his mouth. Luckily he wasn't superstitious. Perhaps it hadn't been such a good idea, after all. He was feeling pretty ill himself, exhausted and nauseous. What a mess this was. And then there was the other mess, the one Isabel had got them into. He couldn't begin to see a way out of any of it.

Ellen sprawled across the bed. Sometimes when she was with Michael, when he was fucking her, when she went down on him or simply when they kissed, in her mind she'd be framing the words, Tell her, tell her, and hope that they'd be transmitted to him by sheer force of feeling. Lately, she realised, the words in her head had changed to Tell me, tell me. For she had a sense that he wasn't telling her everything – but what was it?

She stared up at the ceiling, trying to work out what it was she felt for him, give it a name. Was it really love? Desire yes, need yes, but love? Everyone always said that if you had to ask the question then it couldn't be. With love you knew. Well, I think I know, Ellen told herself.

She got up, wrapped herself in her robe and made some hot chocolate. She'd ring Grace in New York – she'd done that quite a lot lately. But then, as Grace herself said, what are friends for?

It was hard to make friends in London – she had hardly any. Be honest, Ellen, you have none. Partly because she was freelance so she had no access to that office camaraderie, no gossiping at the coffee machine, no going for drinks after work or eating sandwiches together and moaning about the boss. She rarely even went into magazine or newspaper offices, these days – so much of her work was done via e-mail or fax.

Admit it Ellen, you're lonely, she thought. She'd originally anticipated she'd get to know people at the health club – and then she'd met Michael.

That was the trouble. This situation with Michael, it made it seem as if her world was shrinking, as if she had fewer prospects. The immediate outlook was not good.

If she'd been someone else she'd be saying, 'Get a life.'

26

Isabel massaged cleanser into her face, slow, rhythmic circles up and round, up and round. It took several cotton pads to wipe off all the lotion and the London grime. Just one day's worth of emissions from cars and planes, of tiny particles of debris from people, pets, everything, floating through the air. Disgusting, thought Isabel, and wondered if there was any fresh, clean air left anywhere.

She brushed her hair, as she did every night before bed. I'm well trained, she thought. And a creature of habit. She sighed and blew her hair upwards off her forehead. It settled back down again, falling into place as it always did. The sort of hair, straight and obedient, which lent itself to being neat and tidy. Unlike Angie who had often been reprimanded at school for having unruly hair ('As if I can do anything about what I was born with,' she'd protest), Isabel's smooth, shiny head had never attracted attention. She remembered Angie's frantic attempts to keep her school beret on, involving complicated arrangements with hair pins and clips. Isabel smiled, thinking how things had changed, trying to imagine Gemma putting up with any of that sort of interference from teachers.

Thoughts of school uniform and petty rules faded as she confronted the fact that her hairstyle had barely changed since she was a teenager. Same old cut, the classic bob, through the years, sometimes with a fringe, sometimes without if she could be bothered to grow it. And more or less the same old natural colour, although now she was more mousy, (with a few grey hairs) rather than the blonde she had been as a child. This wouldn't do. It really was time for a change. Tomorrow she'd make an appointment at the hairdresser's and surprise everyone, including herself.

Pulling back her hair, trying to imagine it differently, she regarded her face in the bathroom mirror and took stock. Small clusters of lines, keeping each other company, radiated from her eyes – she could live with those, laughter lines, weren't they? That made them more acceptable. Pregnancy seemed to have plumped out her face a little, easing the frown furrows forming on her forehead (now, those she could do without) and the suggestions of lines to come running from her nose to her mouth. What was it she'd read once: at fifty you have the face you deserve? Well, she wasn't near fifty yet. And she wasn't sure what sort of face she merited. Her life had been comfortable and fairly ordinary, so she supposed that's the face she had, or would have . . .

It was also said that if you wanted to know how you'd look when you were older, you had only to look at your mother. Isabel wasn't so sure. For a start, physically she had always been more like her father's side of the family. And what about all the variables, like better nutrition and increased awareness and differing styles and social change? Looking at her face now she couldn't see any signs that she was becoming her outdoorsy ruddy-faced mother. Maybe she didn't want to.

She'd rung her parents this evening. It was about time: she'd been putting off telling them her news and it was beginning to assume rather more importance than it should. As she dialled she'd wondered for the hundredth time why they so rarely called her. Was it that they didn't care or that their generation didn't feel comfortable using the phone for long conversations, or was it simply that they liked to save on their phone bill?

After hearing about the painting and servicing of their boat, something they did every spring, and their health niggles (nothing serious) and the difficulty of finding a dentist they liked, Isabel eventually announced that she had some news. 'I'm expecting another baby,' she'd said. There was a long pause, then her mother had responded, 'Oh. That's a surprise.

But is it wise, dear?' Isabel had laughed and said, 'Probably not, but there you go.'

The conversation had quickly moved on to the subject of Isabel's brother John in Canada, a favourite topic of her mother. The latest breakthrough in his research project, his trip to Japan, the sporting achievements of his son Rick ... Isabel only half listened, wondering as she had so many times before if her mother ever boasted about Isabel to her brother. Probably not, was the conclusion she usually arrived at. After all, what does she consider my achievements to be, if any? Got married, stayed married. Then, when her father came to the phone his offering was, 'Up the spout again, then?' Bizarre, she thought. Peculiar phrase. Perhaps he felt awkward or else was trying to be jocular, that was the image he liked to cultivate. She put her hand on her bump – it definitely was a bump now, even though a small one – and said, 'Well, baby, your grandparents don't seem too excited about you. Never mind, we don't need them, do we?'

Speaking to her parents always left her feeling dissatisfied but tonight she felt lonely too. If only she could reach out to Michael. If only he were *here*. Nine o'clock. Surely he should be home by now? The phone was still in her hand so on impulse she dialled his office. His voice-mail answered. An empty sound.

She had no idea where he was. He may have mumbled something about working late as he left this morning – but did she even see him this morning? Maybe he was out with a client. Perhaps he'd gone to the gym – he said it relaxed him after an arduous day at the office. *Maybe ... Perhaps ...* There were other possibilities, she knew that, but she was not going to entertain them. She had made the decision not to open the floodgates of suspicion and for now she was sticking to that. Questioning Michael, doubting him, would be an ordeal in itself, let alone what he might reveal. She didn't have the stomach for it.

She climbed wearily up to the bathroom to steep herself in warm water and try to unknot the tension that had taken up residence in her neck. As the bath filled she knocked on Dominic's door. No response. Hardly surprising, considering the music thundering from his room. She knocked again and called out his name. He shouted that he was on the phone (How could he hear anything, she thought, and what about the essay he'd claimed to be doing?) and Isabel shouted back that she was going to have a bath. One of the basic safety measures she'd always drummed into her family (now *that* was from her parents): always inform someone if you were having a bath or shower, in case . . . In case of what exactly was never spelt out. Fainting, falling asleep, tripping over . . . Or being overcome by fumes of geranium bath essence, Gemma had once suggested. Whatever, it was a habit, another habit, thought Isabel, although she could hardly imagine her son breaking down the door to rescue his mother.

Ten thirty. Ten forty-five. She sat in the kitchen in her towelling robe, flicking through *Good Housekeeping* to see if there were any hairstyles she fancied trying. So far there weren't. In fact, some of the models or so-called 'real women' featured had haircuts just like hers.

The sound of a key in the front door. It wasn't Michael. Gemma came in, flushed and smiling. 'Mum! You're still up.'

'Living dangerously for once, darling. How was the film?'

'Oh, we didn't go in the end. Couldn't be bothered. Just went to the pub instead. Like some tea?'

Gemma went upstairs, saying she was knackered, and still Isabel sat at the table. She was determined to see Michael. Not for any specific reason, not to argue with him or interrogate him, just to be reassured by his presence. To have him here, at home.

It was well past midnight when Michael got home, but Isabel was still in the kitchen.

'Isabel – I thought you'd be in bed. You weren't waiting up for me, were you?'

'Not really. I –'

'Are the children both in?'

'Yes, for once.'

'I'll just put the chain on the door, then.'

He went back into the hall, hanging up his coat, taking his time. It had been a shock to find her still up: she usually went to bed so early, these days. And if the children were both in, surely she must have been waiting for him. Christ! Perhaps she suspected something. He checked in the hall mirror for any giveaway signs that he'd been with Ellen, although he was unsure what they'd be. None of that lipstick-on-your-collar crap applied, not to Ellen. Or him. But he might smell of her . . . He dived into the cloakroom to wash his hands and splash his face. That would have to do – he could hardly dash straight upstairs for a shower.

As he returned to the kitchen for a drink, he thought, Suppose Isabel asks me where I've been. Should I tell the truth, just let it out, and damn the consequences? Can I do it? Is this it? But she did not ask. As he gulped a glass of water all she said was, 'How was your day, Michael? Certainly a long one.'

Her tone was straightforward, sympathetic, even. The moment when he could have confessed had not happened. He drew a deep breath and said, 'Yes. I'm sorry I'm so late. It's this Tom Springer case – have I told you about it?'

'No, I don't think so.'

'I won't bore you with it all.'

'I'm sure it isn't boring.'

'Some of it is. Tom Springer is an inventor, electronic gadgets mainly, with some success. He's convinced that a multinational is ripping him off, wants to take the company on. I'm not sure it's a good idea – intellectual property law is a difficult area, it'll be a complicated case. Anyway, he needs a lot of support so I had to have a meal with him tonight.'

There, another lie. But Isabel seemed satisfied with his story. She was smiling at him, reaching out for his hand. He remembered evenings like this in the past (though obviously *not* like this, no Ellen, no lies), sitting here at the end of the day, the children in bed, catching up over a glass of wine, winding down in the comfortable security of Isabel, his home, his family.

'Michael, are you OK?'

'I'm all right. Just tired.' He rubbed his eyes. Why did she have to look so damn appealing, so ridiculously young, sitting there in her soft blue robe, her face clean and shiny, looking at him sweetly. And hopefully.

There was a long pause. Not a particularly comfortable silence.

'Me too. Time for bed, I think.' She got up slowly and he saw how pregnant she was looking, the belt of her robe tied neatly across her bump.

He got up too, to refill his glass. They looked at each other. There was some tenderness between them and he felt he should acknowledge it; he owed her that at least.

'So how are you feeling, Isabel? With the – the baby?'

'I'm fine. I feel well, really. Bit more tired than usual, my back aches sometimes. Minor things.'

'Good. I'm glad. Well, glad they're minor.'

She came and stood close, looking up at him. 'Michael, are you getting used to the idea of this baby at all? I so wish you would.'

'I know, I know you do. So do I. And I suppose I am, in a way.'

He couldn't say any more. It was odd, he realised, that he could lie about all sorts of things but he couldn't lie to Isabel about the baby and pretend that he'd changed his mind, that he was pleased, that it was wonderful.

She was still looking up at him, her eyes moist. 'That's something,' she said. And she waited.

He stroked her hair. 'Why don't you go on up to bed? I'll lock up.'

'OK. Goodnight, then.' She leant upwards and kissed him on the cheek.

'Goodnight.' He kissed her lightly back.

As she was leaving the room he said, 'Isabel?'

'Yes?'

'I – I'm going to speak to Swissair tomorrow about cancelling your ticket. Are you sure you won't change your mind, just come with us and not ski?'

'I don't think so. And it will be good to go to Devon. The house needs airing.'

'If you're sure. It won't be the same without you.'

'I'm sure. And no, it won't be the same, I know.'

As Isabel climbed the stairs to the spare room she bit her lip, telling herself she would not cry, she wouldn't. Though, God knows, there were plenty of things to cry about ... Her marriage and what had gone wrong (what has gone wrong?). Feeling rejected. Feeling lonely. And tonight, watching and listening to Michael, searching for signs of rapprochement, imagining a thaw, however fragile. Waiting for a hug, some reassurance. Being pathetic and desperate and letting it show. Being needy. Letting her resolve slip, bypassing her decision to just get on with it come what may, whatever he felt . . .

She cried in bed anyway, just a little. Silently.

Michael stayed in the kitchen with a brandy. He had been drinking more lately – not surprising, in the circumstances, but he must keep it under control. Enough in his life was out of control already.

He studied the golden liquid in his glass, thinking, This is what drinkers do: gaze lovingly but perplexed at the alcohol they're about to consume.

The sight of Isabel in her robe, ready for bed, looking vulnerable, stayed with him. God knows what he was going to do. Right now, all he could come up with was a sense of seeing things through.

27

Isabel sang along to the stereo as she travelled down the motorway in the Volvo. Some unfamiliar radio station was broadcasting sixties and seventies sounds, which suited her fine. 'R-E-S-P-E-C-T' she yelled. The sun was shining, she was on her way to the cottage for some time on her own – and that felt surprisingly good. She wouldn't have dared sing like this if Michael or the children had been in the car.

The family should be well on the way to Zermatt by now, probably on the hyper-efficient Swiss train from Geneva up to the mountains. She'd deposited them at Heathrow this morning before heading west on the M4. It had been strange, driving off and leaving them there outside Departures. She could see them in the rear-view mirror, wrestling with skis and snowboards, boot bags and luggage, balancing it all on trolleys. The farewells were brief as she was double-parked but she'd hugged both the children (even Dominic surrendered quite willingly), then had turned to Michael. They kissed each other quickly on the cheek, their eyes met. At that moment she could see he was feeling regretful, perhaps more than she was.

'Well, have a good time, all of you,' she'd said briskly, smiling determinedly. 'And take care!'

Gemma rushed to hug her mother one more time. 'Oh Mum, it'll be so weird without you!'

'You'll be fine, darling. Now, off you go. And I must too – look, I'm about to cause a traffic jam!'

She *had* felt wistful. The three of them going off together and her alone. They'd been going skiing as a family for – how long? Twelve, thirteen years or more? It had become one of those punctuations of family life, woven into the very fabric. The rituals: checking the ski clothes and equipment, seeing who had grown out of jackets or salopettes; what needed to be updated; going to the dry ski slope to 'keep their legs in', as Gemma had called it . . . The anticipation and excitement, finding out about the levels of snow, the packing, then the holiday itself . . . Isabel sighed. They would come to a natural end at some time anyway, she knew, as Dominic and Gemma left home. But will we start going skiing with child number three? There's a thought.

As she'd negotiated her way out of the airport she renewed her resolve to be positive about things. *She* had made these choices: having the baby, not going skiing. And it was good to break the pattern, initiate change. Like her new haircut. If she moved her head there was no more hair swinging around her ears. The classic bob was no more. It was shorter, spikier, with blonde highlights on top (she'd checked that the chemicals wouldn't harm the baby). And it had surprised everyone. Good, she thought.

She pulled into the service station near Exeter. This place was always crowded with coach parties and school trips and everyone else, but she needed to pee and so, probably, did Jasper. She lifted the rear door – he was still asleep on his blanket. 'Come on, old thing. Time to stretch your legs. Want some water?' He opened one eye and made it clear that he did not want to move. She let him be. He was used to this journey and had slept his way through it before. Reluctantly she'd had to bring him. She couldn't ask Jenny to have him – Desdemona would have rebelled. Besides, Jenny was already committed to popping into the house every day to feed the cat as well as being responsible for the shop. There was a limit, although Jenny seemed to be flourishing on having lots to do.

She joined the queue of mainly elderly women with hair newly set for their holidays, handbags over their arms. Why did women always have to queue to go to the lavatory? Why were there never enough loos? And right now she wished there was a fast track for pregnant women.

Emerging at last she avoided the café and the smells of burgers and fish and chips and hurried back to the car. A cup of tea could wait until she got to the cottage.

Jasper was still asleep. 'Not long now,' she said, as she started the car, more to herself than the dog. An hour and a half, maybe less. She turned the radio on. 'Continuing our Soul Sisters Special,' the DJ announced.

'Yes!' whooped Isabel, and began to sing once more. 'Rescue me!' She loved this final part of the journey.

It was goodbye to the motorway at Exeter, roaring off down the A38, anticipating the moment she cherished – round a bend, then the sudden appearance of an empty bare field of rich red earth. It curved across the gentle hills bordering the road. Inevitably there was one, but whether it was the same field or it rotated she didn't know. Yes, she spotted it. The colour, deep blood red, meant she was really in Devon.

The road skirted around Dartmoor. Even with the sun shining it had an air of stillness and mystery. She kept sneaking sideways glances at the landscape: purply grey-green hills in the distance, with an occasional rocky tor visible. A cloud or two was clinging to the moor – wasn't there always?

She turned off, heading south now. Past Dartington, towards Totnes. A stony stream ran next to the road, weaving between tall trees. Around here Dominic and Gemma used to recognise places and signs and begin to chant, 'Nearly there, nearly there.' She turned off again, thinking that the Volvo was a bit like an old carthorse, knowing the way. The roads became progressively narrower. She remembered showing the children this on a map spread out on the cottage table: motorways were blue, then green for major roads, then red, then yellow, then white – and their cottage was on a white one, more of a lane than a road. She'd intended it to be educational but they ended up being confused, having taken it literally. After that they'd demanded to know why the motorway didn't *look* blue? Had the cars worn away the paint?

The last turning. High hedgerows lined the lane, their mossy banks dotted with clumps of primroses, masses of them. They looked so much brighter and more robust than the pale, delicate versions you sometimes saw in London, she thought. The sight of them made her smile.

Buildings appeared through the trees ahead, chimneys, a roof.

'Here we are, Jasper. Stone Cottage – home,' said Isabel, driving carefully off the road, through the gap in the dry-stone walls and parking next to the house. She got out of the car and stretched. That lower backache had been troubling her again – and the long drive hadn't helped. Jasper started barking. She let him out and he rushed happily around the front garden, tail wagging, sniffing everywhere, lifting his leg, renewing his acquaintance with familiar territory.

Isabel stood for a moment and looked around, checking it over. No one had been here since before Christmas but it seemed fine. The garden required attention, the clematis around the front door needed cutting back, the paintwork was looking a bit shabby . . . But it looked wonderful to her, this unpretentious square cottage, showing its age, surrounded by its overgrown country garden. She loved it, she always had. It was so good to be here, and to have it all to herself was an extra bonus, she had to admit.

Jasper was waiting. Isabel let them both in. From inside the front door you could see straight through to the back porch where they kept wellingtons, Barbours, walking sticks – country walks paraphernalia. They had opened up the ground floor, knocking down walls to get rid of the narrow hall and tiny rooms so that light could flood in from all sides. Isabel could remember how different it had been when her great-aunt had lived here: full of old oak furniture – they'd kept a few pieces – and a lifetime's clutter. Books and ornaments and photographs and plants and half-completed embroidery. But she remembered it fondly, and she remembered Great-aunt Beatrice particularly fondly, not least because she'd left Isabel the cottage.

Everyone in the family had been surprised when they learnt of the bequest, which came a few months after Gemma was born. A birth then a death. Isabel's mother, Beatrice's niece, had been very sniffy about it. She'd had hopes of it herself, or at the very least had thought it might be left to the whole family to share – such a useful holiday place, after all. Isabel hadn't been so surprised: she'd been close to her great-aunt, especially when she was a teenager and they'd been living nearby at Dartmouth. Beatrice was unexpectedly tolerant, and she was a good listener, unlike Isabel's mother. Isabel had been the one who visited the elderly woman, the one who hadn't minded kissing the whiskery face, who had found her amusing and interesting. Sometimes she'd brought Angie along, and Beatrice welcomed her too, understanding that they needed somewhere as a place of escape from what they saw as their over-regimented lives.

So when the time came Isabel had unquestioningly accepted Stone Cottage and her good fortune.

Isabel had a small ritual, which she tried to perform every time she came down here. Standing still, closing her eyes, thinking of Beatrice and silently saying thank you.

She sighed and looked around. It felt warm and welcoming. There was a jug of daffodils on the mantelpiece and another on the window-sill. Signs that her next-door neighbours had been here. They had a spare key in case of emergencies, like burst pipes or whatever, and she'd rung them a few days ago to say when she'd be arriving. They must have put the heating on – good, there'd be hot water too. Dear Connie and Erica, she thought. And there on the kitchen table was another of their touches: a willow basket covered with a blue and white tea-towel. It looked like something from an illustration to *Goldilocks* or *Little Red Riding Hood*. Inside was a box of fresh farm eggs, some home-made blackberry jam (Connie's), a loaf of soda bread (Erica's department) and a note telling her there was milk, butter and cheese in the fridge, and that she must come round for tea.

'We'll do that Jasper. I'll take you for a walk first, then we'll pop next door, shall we?'

Isabel filled a bowl of water for the dog then took her bag – she hadn't brought much – upstairs. The bedroom smelt a bit musty. She opened the windows and stood for a moment looking out at the view, fields and woods and gentle hills for as far as she could see. I'll sleep well tonight, she thought. No planes churning overhead, no sounds of traffic.

Then she felt it. The baby moved. Unmistakable. That flip inside her stomach, then again. A liquidy flip deep inside her. The strange yet familiar feeling, quite unlike anything else. It was magical, wonderful. 'Oh,' said Isabel. 'Oh.' She sat down on the bed, hands on her stomach, tears in her eyes. My baby moved! 'Hello, little one,' she said. 'It's so good to feel you.'

Connie poured from a big yellow teapot, one finger carefully on the lid. Erica filled a striped jug with milk. The table was laid with a white linen cloth covered with all the ingredients for a traditional tea-time, Devon style. Scones and bread, several kinds of jam, clotted cream and butter. Connie and Erica were the only people she knew who actually had cream teas in their own home. 'Why deprive ourselves of essential pleasures?' Erica once said.

Isabel sat in her neighbours' kitchen, enjoying the attention.

'So, Isabel dear, tell us all about it. How you came to be in this pregnant state of yours . . .' Connie demanded, laughing. These two laughed a lot.

They'd noticed immediately when she knocked on their door. First they'd remarked approvingly on her new haircut then, as she was thanking them for the provisions, Erica interrupted, 'Isabel, you look pregnant! *Are* you?'

They always came straight to the point, that was one of the many things about them that she liked. Michael never felt comfortable with them, disparagingly calling them the old biddies, although he admitted that they were useful to keep an eye on the cottage when it was empty. He couldn't understand why Isabel spent any more time with them than she had to.

Isabel no longer tried to explain it. It occurred to her that perhaps Michael was frightened of people whom he couldn't easily pigeon-hole. When the women had first moved in, about eight years ago, Isabel herself had made assumptions about them, which she had had to revise.

Connie and Erica, recently retired as teachers, looked alike but were not related. At first only Connie wore glasses but now Erica did too. Both were short and roundish with sturdy legs and crisply cut no-nonsense grey hair. Typical spinsters, Isabel had thought, expecting them to be reserved and rather prim.

How wrong she'd been.

In some ways they were more worldly and less narrow-minded than her. They took an intelligent interest in so many things. You name it, they had an opinion or a relevant piece of information. Their books overflowed from shelves on to the floor: biographies and philosophy politics and poetry and feminism. Early on Isabel had used the term 'headmistress' and Connie had become indignant. 'Please, not that awful word. Such outdated language, so sexist! We were both *headteachers*.'

They talked passionately about education, about the inner London primary schools they had run – Connie in Vauxhall, Erica in Southwark. They had known each other for years but had lived in separate flats. 'When we decided to move down here we thought we'd give living together a try,' Erica had said, and Isabel could have sworn she winked. After that she'd begun to wonder if theirs was a sexual relationship. She didn't know for sure, but she guessed it was. And good for them, she thought.

Tough old townies they claimed to be, yet Isabel was amazed at how they'd taken up more pastoral pursuits. Erica even wove willow baskets, such as the one they'd left in her kitchen.

It would be easy to underestimate them, Isabel had decided. Michael did. But she didn't.

As she sat drinking their strong tea and eating a scone oozing with jam (they'd insisted) but no cream (she'd insisted), she told them about being pregnant, how it had been a surprise. There wasn't much to tell, she said. They asked bluntly about the risks at her age. She told them but gave the reassuring news about her test results. 'Marvellous!' they both said. She revealed how she'd felt the baby move for the first time just this afternoon.

'Wonderful!' Erica said.

'How exciting that must be,' said Connie, almost wistfully.

'And what about that husband of yours?' asked Erica.

'Yes, how does Michael feel? Is he pleased?' asked Connie.

Isabel drank some more tea and attempted to express what Michael felt, which was difficult as she didn't know, not exactly. But then, neither perhaps did he. However, she gave them a flavour of how he was behaving.

The two women did not seem surprised.

'Men can be miserable buggers,' said Erica.

When Isabel said goodbye a few hours later – they'd insisted she stay for supper – they made her promise to ask if she needed anything. She promised, and hugged them both.

As she walked the short distance home she realised that there was something about them, or her experience of them, that reminded her of Great-aunt Beatrice. The quality of kindness. 'We can all do with some of that can't we?' she remarked to Jasper, who was waiting in the hall.

As she undressed for bed she stood before the mirror and had a good look at herself. Her waist had disappeared and in its place was this rounded belly, sweeping from her pubis up towards her breasts. One unbroken line. She followed the curve with her hands. It was satisfying, solid, vibrant. Lifting her breasts she felt the weight of them, so much heavier, and the shape had changed: they were fuller (literally, she supposed) and rounder. Everything was rounder. Except her nipples. Looking at them sideways their profile was dark and elongated. Like nuggets, she thought. Strange that they have these tiny openings for milk to come through . . .

All this sprouting and growth. No wonder she was feeling tired.

When she went to bed Isabel left the curtains open. Michael hated that, he liked to be cocooned in complete darkness. So often in the past, a compromise meant that he got his way. But right now she could lie in the middle of the bed with double pillows and look out at the night sky. There was some moonlight. It was quiet, very quiet. She heard an owl. Another noise, an animal noise. Probably a sheep coughing several fields away – sounds carried dramatically in the country at night.

'Goodnight, Great-aunt Beatrice,' she said. 'I'm lying here

like you did, alone but cosy in this big brass bed, in my white cotton nightdress.'

And goodnight, little one. She wondered when the baby would move again. When it wants to, no doubt, she thought. It has a life of its own already.

Goodnight, baby.

28

Michael sat on the bench in the ski room under the hotel, aching and weary, releasing his feet from his boots. He'd been in a group with a ski guide today and at times he'd found it hard to keep up with the pace, although he hated to admit it, even to himself.

Neither of the children's snowboards were in the rack, so he assumed they were still up the mountain or having a drink half-way down or in the village. That's what he and Isabel usually did at the end of the day, discussing snow conditions or the state of the runs, lingering over a beer or a brandy, before returning to the hotel for a shower and, sometimes, sex. It surprised him to remember that. Yes, he and Isabel indulging in vigorous late-afternoon sex, energetic and good-humoured after a day on the slopes. But that was before he had met Ellen, before all this.

Up in his room he pulled off his jacket and salopettes, left them in a heap on the floor, and stretched out on the bed, closing his eyes. The shower could wait. Everything could wait. Why did he feel so tired? A hard day's skiing was usually invigorating.

As he lay half asleep Michael couldn't help remembering previous skiing holidays he'd had with Isabel and the children. Family holidays, happy ones. The experiences rolled into one. Memories turned in his mind, like one of those mirrored globes that hang above disco dance-floors. A snatch of Isabel laughing, gliding slowly down a nursery slope with a much-younger Gemma on small skis; there was Dominic shouting in triumph as he won a ski-school downhill race; Isabel eating a sandwich at a mountain restaurant, wearing her lilac all-in-one suit, her teeth very white against her tan . . . And there was more, so much more, all of it illuminated by the brightness of sun on snow. Too many memories, Michael thought, and buried his head in the pillows.

'Dad! Dad!' Michael was woken by the sound of Gemma at the door. 'Are you in there?' The children had the room next to his.

He rose unsteadily and opened the door. 'Oh, God, what time is it? I must have fallen asleep.'

'It's after seven. You said we'd go out to dinner tonight, remember? You OK? You look a bit groggy.'

'I'm all right, a bit tired and I think I'm coming down with a cold or something. Look, I'll meet you downstairs in half an hour.'

Michael forced himself under the shower and tried to summon some energy. He would have been happy to eat in the hotel restaurant and then have an early night, but he'd promised Dominic and Gemma that they'd go out together, and he'd booked a table at the Old Spaghetti Factory in the Hotel Post. His offspring were quite capable of going out without him but he and Isabel insisted that it was important to do things as a family, even if it was only occasionally. But Isabel wasn't here. The family wasn't complete.

Michael sneezed, several times. Bloody awful time to catch a cold, he thought. He rummaged through his suitcase to see if he had any vitamin C tablets, not remembering if he'd packed them. Isabel usually did that sort of thing. She could always be relied upon to have a remedy for whatever might befall you. It had been something of a family tease among them, calling her Medicine Woman because of the plastic bags of pills and powders and boxes and tubes she always stuffed in the suitcase. He'd scorned her in the past and said it was mad, especially in Switzerland of all places, where here in Zermatt smart clinical pharmacies were dotted along the main street, cornucopias of cures. But, as she'd said, what if it's the middle of the night? What if they're shut? What if you can't face going out to buy throat lozenges?

She was often right.

Michael revived a little over dinner. The place was buzzing as

183

always, the food was good enough. He told himself to relax, after all he was on holiday, and tried to ignore his headache and the tickling in his throat. A decent bottle of red wine helped. He looked across at Dominic and Gemma, both dressed in baggy fleeces and trainers and combat-type canvas trousers, a look that said, we may be off the mountains but we're still snowboarders. Their faces were flushed from a day out on the snow. Healthy, strong kids, who knew how to have a good time. That was something.

And they weren't squabbling or bickering, as they so often did. Over the years he'd been continually amazed that they could find so many things to argue about. It was like a compulsion. But tonight they were laughing, messing about, talking about bands ... The music playing in the restaurant seemed to amuse them.

Gemma suddenly looked at him. 'Dad – are you OK?'

'Yeah, Dad, you look a bit dodgy.'

'Oh thanks, Dom. Actually I am feeling a bit rough. Think I'll go back to the hotel. What about you two?'

He noticed that he'd drunk the whole bottle of wine. The children had been drinking Budweisers straight from the bottle.

Outside the cold night provided a welcome blast of fresh air – and here the air was really fresh. The walk back to the hotel should help clear his head. After repeatedly asking if he was going to be all right on his own, Dominic and Gemma had gone off in the opposite direction to find a disco or special dance night or wherever the action was.

A light scattering of snow began to fall. There had been a time when that would have excited him. But it wasn't enough to settle. Strange the way it filled the air yet left barely a trace on the ground.

Few people were out in the village. It resembled a Christmas-card scene – in April. Impressive icicles, looking as if they were trying to prove that size did matter, hung from under the eaves of older buildings. Ahead of him a couple strolled slowly, arms linked, her ankle-length fur coat swaying, the feather in his hat trembling. Some kids hung about outside McDonald's – it still surprised him to see it here. It had an Alpine-chalet timbered effect: they had made some sort of effort. And apparently it served a McRösti.

He walked briskly past the shops devoted to watches and expensive jewellery, the ski-hire places, clothes shops, banks, the pharmacies, of course. The same names cropped up again and again over the doors: the old families of Zermatt, the original Zermatters. Familie Julen. Perren. Aufdenblatten. Seiler. Biner . . . Some names were joined together, Perren-Julen, he assumed so that the names would not be lost when people married. He envied them their pride and sense of identity.

That 'What am I doing here?' question flashed over him. It had been a regular visitor throughout his life, usually prompted, he'd come to realise, by feelings of not belonging. He'd experienced it at grammar school on the very first day, sitting in his stiff new uniform, shirt collar like cardboard around his neck, tie bright and unstained, blazer much too big ('Got to make it last,' his mother had said), feeling like an alien. And then at university, surrounded by accents more elevated than his, revealed by more confident voices. And at work. Meeting Isabel's parents . . . He'd managed to deal with it by answering the question superficially: I'm here to learn; I'm here to study; I'm here to earn my living and enter a profession; I'm here to meet my prospective in-laws. And he always knew the multi-purpose reply: I'm here to remove myself from my background, to rise above my station (a phrase of his mother's – she felt everyone should know their place), to reinvent myself. And along the way he practised telling himself that he was as bright as everyone else, if not brighter; he was as good as everyone else, whatever that meant.

And who could answer the deeper question of why are we here? He wasn't alone in finding that difficult. Mustn't get depressed, Michael thought. He was here to ski, which he loved; he was on holiday with his children – how many more times would they do this? He was privileged to be here. So enjoy it, you miserable bugger, he told himself.

Back in his overheated room he peeled off his layers of clothes, decided against a brandy nightcap and thought he'd just go to bed. Or should he ring Ellen first? He opted for sleep. Much as he'd like to speak to her their conversation would inevitably gravitate to how much they wanted each other, what they'd do, how it would feel . . . That had happened one night when he'd called her from the office. She was adept at telephone sex, he had to admit, but right now he didn't have the energy or the appetite for it – or even for pretending.

The next day he stayed in bed.

'God, he must be feeling ill,' Dominic said to his sister.

'Yeah, Dad never normally misses a minute's skiing, he's such a fanatic.'

Gemma found some aspirin in her bag and took them to her father. It was odd seeing him lying in bed, stubble on his chin, looking lousy. She brought him a glass of water and watched him swallow the aspirin. 'Is there anything else I can do, Dad?'

'You could get me some stuff from the chemist's – you know, garlic capsules, vitamin C, things for a cold. There are some francs over there on the table. I'll just stay here.'

'That's probably for the best. OK then, see you later. Wish you better.'

She hurried after Dominic. Typical, she thought, she was the one who had to play nursey-nursey. Now she'd have to make sure she came down from the slopes before the pharmacies closed. Responsibilities, who needed them? She wished her mother was there.

The day passed in a haze. Michael was hot then shivery then hot again. Perhaps becoming ill was inevitable, he thought, as he churned about on the unfamiliar bed, what with the additional stress and the agonising he had been going through lately. He'd been feeling lacklustre for a while, suffering from vague stomach pains, frequent headaches, which he rarely had in normal circumstances. But what was normal now? It was no wonder that a virus had leapt on him, seizing the opportunity while he was low.

As he dozed on and off he couldn't avoid thinking about his predicament. It was a situation he'd played a large part in creating, he recognised that. But what should he do? What could he do? He wanted to tell Isabel about Ellen and he wanted to tell Ellen the truth about Isabel. The reality of actually doing so frightened the shit out of him. He kept coming to his usual conclusion, like a train hitting the buffers: there was no decent way to resolve it.

His head hurt. How he wished there was someone to hold him and soothe his brow and say, 'There, there.'

The next day, to his relief, and Gemma's, he felt a lot better. No more self-pity, he told himself. Get up, get out there.

Expert Off-piste, the group was called. It was due to meet up at the Klein Matterhorn station. Michael joined the tramp and trudge of skiers in the streets, ski boots clunking on the cobbles, like an army on the march. Snowboarders shambled along, treading more softly. Periodically someone on a mountain bike – usually a ski instructor in distinctive red jacket – would weave through in a hurry. Electric cars buzzed and whined – you had to listen out, they came pretty close – delivering bread, crates of Coke and beer, plumbing materials, supplies to keep it all going. Some served as taxis carrying lazier skiers. Rush-hour, thought Michael.

It was a grey morning: grey sky, grey buildings, grey streets, contrasting with the brightness of the skiers' clothes. Hopefully it should be sunny up the mountain, thought Michael, blowing his nose, determined to be optimistic.

Their ski guide introduced himself as Heini. It was hard to tell how old he was: his face was deeply tanned and weathered, the skin had a leathery texture, but his eyes were a clear and piercing blue. His hair was the yellow-white of a blond growing old. What was he? Late fifties? Sixty or more? Michael had encountered local men like this before, who were often much older than you thought. Living in the clear air, going up and down the mountains all their lives kept them fit. Only their skin seemed to age.

Heini checked that the group were all there, then put out his thin brown cigarette. He spoke of his plans for the day, where he'd be taking them, and emphasised safety precautions, in excellent English. They followed him to the cable car. Michael usually avoided groups if he could, preferring to ski with friends or with Isabel, but it seemed the best solution this year. A guide like Heini could take you places you couldn't, or shouldn't, otherwise go.

He tried to check out the others surreptitiously. Five of

them: four men, one woman. He looked and listened. One man he guessed was Japanese, another was American, there was a Dutch couple, he thought, and one other English guy. Let's hope they're all serious skiers, he thought. It could get pretty hairy up there.

They skied hard all morning. The pace was relentless, the group was competitive. No one spoke much: there were too many other things to think about. The sun was out, the snow shone, the scenery was breathtaking, but at times all Michael could concentrate on was just getting *down*, negotiating steep gullies, steering through close-spaced trees.

They stopped at last for lunch at a small mountain restaurant. Heini and the owners were obviously well acquainted, laughing and joking while everyone else caught their breath. The group began to loosen up a little as they sprawled on the wood-decked terrace facing the sun. There was a clear view of the Matterhorn rising to one side – Michael never tired of looking at it. Today it stood out crisply against the blue sky with just a wisp of cloud trailing across from the peak, like a ghostly flag, as there often was.

The other English guy settled down next to Michael clutching a beer and his plate piled high with food. Michael stuck to mineral water – this kind of skiing needed a clear head – and ate a simple rösti.

'I'm Ian.'

'Michael.'

'That was a damn good morning, eh, Michael? Extreme! I get a real kick out of this high-altitude stuff. And I never ski *on*-piste myself, too tame, don't you think?'

Michael closed his eyes and lifted his face to the sun. He still felt a little fragile and the last thing he needed was a bore like this Ian, whoever, going on in that macho way about skiing. He enjoyed doing it but he didn't necessarily enjoy hearing about it all over again. The experience was enough.

The voice stopped. Thankfully, Ian was now occupied with eating.

Michael sipped his coffee. Heini's cigarette smoke wafted over and it smelt good, as cigarettes sometimes did in the outside air, even to a confirmed ex-smoker like Michael. He caught Heini's eye and asked him if he was a mountain guide too. Heini put down his beer with an air of deliberation. Great, thought Michael, perhaps he's in the mood for talking. He always enjoyed hearing mountain stories from guys like this.

'Yes, I am. As was my father before me, and his father and so on. It is a family occupation.'

'Have you climbed the Matterhorn a lot?'

'Many times. Every summer. Approximately three hundred times in fact.'

He paused, and expressions of amazement were heard around the table.

'I guess you must be pretty familiar with it by now?' the American asked.

'In some ways. But I respect the mountain. The Matterhorn is a tricky climb, you know. These people who wish to *conquer* it! You can never *conquer* it. It can *conquer* you – look in our graveyard and you will see. It can also take you and may never give you up.' He paused, lighting another cigarette and taking a deep drag. The group stayed very still, wanting to hear more. 'Let me tell you a story. A true story. It concerns my cousin Otto, who is seventy, same age as me.'

Gasps from everyone. Seventy? Incredible!

He nodded, then continued. 'Last week he had to go to the chapel of the dead to identify his father.'

'How old was *he*? Ninety odd?' interrupted Ian. The others glared at him.

Heini raised his hand. 'Listen, my friend, or you will miss the point. Otto went to view his dead father . . . *whom he had never seen before.*' He paused for effect. 'You see, seventy-one years ago, when Otto was in his mother's womb, his father Franz went up on the mountain to guide a party of Germans. The weather had turned atrocious, they think there was some problem with one person's equipment. Anyway, there was an accident and they all perished. All the bodies were found – although some not for a while – except for Otto's father Franz, he was never found. It was a tragedy, as you can imagine. Poor Greta, Franz's wife, became a widow at twenty-four with a child in her belly. Although, of course, mountain guides' families have to bear these things. And some months later she was delivered of a healthy boy. Otto.'

He drank some beer and continued in the silence, 'Then last

week, seventy years later, a body is found on the mountain. The snows shift – and they are melting faster than ever – a crevasse was uncovered. The body was brought down and laid in the chapel mortuary. It had been well preserved in the ice. There were things to help identification, a piece of paper, a mountain-guide badge. They quickly guessed it was Franz, for all of us in the village knew of him and what had happened. The mountain had given him up. Otto was summoned to see the body. Otto, who is seventy, stood in the mortuary looking down on his father, who is for ever twenty-eight. The son, an old man, looking at his dead father, the young man.'

The Dutch woman stifled a sob.

'Bloody hell,' said Ian.

Michael gulped and rubbed at his eyes.

'Now, shall we ski?' Heini smiled and stood up, pulling on his red woollen hat. 'Ready, everyone?'

That afternoon Michael skied more slowly. He didn't care if he wasn't the fastest in the group. The story weighed upon him. How he wished Isabel was here so that he could tell her about it. As he swished and swooped down towards the village, in need of a brandy now, he realised that he was missing Isabel. How strange, he thought. He had expected to be yearning for Ellen but here he was missing his wife.

Michael was about to have a shower when his door buzzer sounded, incessantly, as if someone was leaning on it.

'Gemma? Jesus Christ! What happened to you?'

His daughter leant against the doorframe, her hair matted with blood, a thick trail of blood across her forehead and down the side of her face. Dried blood dotted her jacket. She was very pale. 'Bit of an accident, Dad. I – I –'

'Here, let me help you.'

He put his arm around her and steered her to a chair. Gemma closed her eyes momentarily. As Michael tried to push her hair gently off her face she winced. 'Where are you hurt, darling? Tell me.'

'I'm all right, really. A bang on my head, in my hair, that's where all the blood's coming from, I think.'

At least she's talking coherently, thank God for that, thought Michael. 'How did it happen?'

'A group of us were coming down a slope. Someone came from behind and crashed into us. He hit a rock, we think, under the snow. There was a bit of a tumble, and I think a board got me on the head.'

'How did you get back down to the village? Did anyone fetch help? And where the hell is Dominic?'

'Relax Dad, it's OK. Dom's been very sweet. He was with me, he helped me down. Right now he's putting the boards away, he'll be up in a minute. And luckily no one was hurt but me, so it didn't seem worth calling the crash team or blood-wagon or whatever they're called.'

Michael sighed, relieved that Dominic had done his bit. But how could he relax? Here was his daughter looking like a casualty, covered in blood, with a head injury of sorts. How he wished Isabel was here.

'Right. Now, let's get you sorted out. Ease your jacket off gently, that's it. I'll have a look at your head. Keep still.'

He hesitantly parted her hair, feeling awkward. 'Well, there's a gash just above your hairline. It's hard to see how deep it is, but you might need a stitch or two.'

'Oh no, surely it's not that bad.'

'Gemma, don't fidget!'

This was familiar ground, it came flooding back to him. Gemma falling off her bike and wanting to get back on in spite of the gravel stuck in her knee; Isabel rushing home from the park, shaking and ashen-faced, carrying Gemma in from the car with a split lip and bloody nose after she'd got in the way of a swing. Even then, he remembered, she'd struggled and wanted to watch her favourite TV programme rather than go to the doctor. She hated a fuss of any sort. But it was down to him to fuss over her now.

'Dad! I'm OK. Please –'

'It's probably wise for me not to try to clean it up or anything. I'll leave it for the doctor. You've also got a nasty-looking bump coming up on your forehead.'

'Ooh, let's see. I'll be an egghead yet!'

He followed her into the bathroom. 'See, Gemma?'

She was staring at her reflection, horrified. 'God, what a sight I am! No wonder people were giving me funny looks as we staggered through the village.' She started to splash water on her face to rinse off the blood.

'Mind you don't touch the cut – you don't want to open it up.' Michael hovered over her. 'When you're done, we'll go along to Dr Lutz at his clinic, get him to look at it.'

The door buzzer sounded and Michael went to open it, avoiding her protests.

Dominic hurried in. 'Where's Gemma? Is she all right?'

'She'll be fine, but we'll have her checked over. Thank you for helping her, Dom.' He patted his son on the back. They both looked a little embarrassed.

Gemma came out of the bathroom, clutching a once-white now pinkish towel to her face. 'Dom, there you are. Don't worry, I'm in one piece! Sorry, Dad, looks a bit like *Psycho* in there. I was going to clean up but my head hurts when I bend down.'

'Don't worry about it. I'll deal with it.'

Michael looked at his children: Dominic sprawled on the floor, exhausted, still in his snowboarding gear, his nose and cheeks red; Gemma, leaning back in the chair, smiling bravely. His children. He found himself feeling misty-eyed. 'I think a quick shot of brandy is called for,' he said. 'We've all had a shock, especially you two. Then I'll call the front desk, make sure there's a taxi to take us to the clinic. OK?'

'Way to go, Dad! So you've got secret supplies?' Dominic teased, as he got up slowly.

'Strictly for medicinal reasons,' grinned Michael, as he fetched glasses from the bathroom.

As they sipped their brandy he resisted the urge to hug his children. In fact, it had been him who really needed this drink. He was sure his daughter would be all right but she had given him – all of them, well, all *three* of them – a nasty shock. There was no Isabel here to help absorb it, to take charge, smooth everything out. Right now it was down to him: he had to be mother and father rolled into one.

He experienced a small tug, like a reminder that he'd forgotten or mislaid something but didn't quite know what it was. So how could he look for it? It dawned on him, literally, like a glimmer of light, that it was to do with Isabel. Missing her. And something else. Had he lost sight of her, was that it?

29

The phone in the cottage was ringing. Isabel dashed inside, dumping the shopping on the floor. She'd been to Totnes for food and hadn't bought much – it was so easy catering just for herself. Eating when she felt like it, simple meals with a minimum of effort. She was enjoying the novelty of being alone.

It was Beth.

'Isabel, you don't mind me ringing, do you? I know you said you were going to Devon for some time on your own but I'm desperate.'

'Beth, what is it? What's the matter?' Isabel imagined all sorts of awfulness.

'I've just had it – had it with the lot of them, Simon, the kids. Everyone's so self-centred they wouldn't even notice if I was on fire, which, in a way, I am.'

'But what's happened?'

'Oh, nothing really, it's all the same as usual. I can't take it any more – I suppose *that*'s what's happened. The reason I'm ringing is to ask if I can come down for a few days, join you at the cottage. Is that an awful cheek? I'd keep out of your way, I won't impose.'

'Please! Don't be daft! I'm not some mad recluse.'

'I wish *I* was.'

'Listen, of course you can come. When are you thinking of?'

'Tomorrow? I'm just going to announce that I'm going away and I will not be persuaded otherwise, whatever they say.'

'Tomorrow's OK.'

'Oh Isabel, thank you so much. This means such a lot to me. Do you know you're saving my sanity?'

'That's good.'

Isabel put down the phone and sighed. What else could she do? A friend in need and all that. Beth's distress seemed real enough, although Isabel wasn't entirely sure what had caused it. Family life, she supposed. No doubt she'd hear the full details when her friend arrived.

For the moment she was determined to enjoy her last

evening by herself. At dusk she took Jasper for a walk down the lane, pausing when he did to investigate the hedgerows. How complicated they were, she thought. No wonder people wanted to save them. Plants and bushes and low trees intertwined, seemingly growing out of the chunks of stone underpinning the hedges, existing together like a family. Here and there spaces between leaves and stone revealed pockets of soft red earth hollowed out – by mice or voles or rabbits? 'Wouldn't you like to know, Jasper?' she murmured. Rustling in the undergrowth suggested the presence of birds or the makers of the holes, concealed in their own world.

It was good to wander, Isabel thought, and notice things you normally rushed past. There was a slight breeze and a faint smell of woodsmoke in the air. And it was quiet, so quiet.

As it began to grow dark she returned to the cottage for supper, walking briskly now. She made a green salad and cooked the fresh ricotta and spinach tortellini she'd bought from that wonderful shop in Totnes. After setting the table and lighting a candle, she put on a CD of new-age music, something else she'd bought in Totnes, which was intended to be relaxing and also good for pregnant women, or so the girl in the shop had said. It was very pleasant: piano and flute and acoustic guitar. Soothing and unchallenging. 'I could get into this,' she said, whether to herself or Jasper or the baby she wasn't sure.

Eating took hardly any time when you were on your own, she'd discovered. Washing up her few plates and dishes was over quickly too. She flicked the TV control but could find little to watch, although she enjoyed the regional ads for tractors and farm machinery – they made her feel a long way from London. Another early night, she decided. She'd need lots of energy just to listen to Beth tomorrow.

As Isabel was locking up the phone rang again. A small part of her hoped it was Beth, cancelling because of her family's adverse reaction to the idea of her going away. But it was Michael.

'Isabel, how are you? You sound ridiculously near.'

'Michael! I'm fine, it's so quiet and peaceful here, I'm enjoying it. But I didn't expect you to ring. Is everything all right? The children –'

'It's all right, everything's all right. I didn't ring to alarm you.'

'So there *is* something wrong?'

Her mind leapt ahead: if she had to go to Switzerland, how quickly could she get there? What would be the best way from Devon?

'Really, there's nothing to worry about. Gemma had a slight knock when she was snowboarding, but we've been to Dr Lutz. She's got a few of those butterfly stitches –'

'Where? Where was she hurt?'

'Her head.' Michael heard her sharp intake of breath. 'Isabel, it's OK. He even took an X-ray, mainly to reassure me, I think. It's all on the insurance, anyway. But she's fine, honestly.'

'If you're sure. And I suppose she can always go back to the doctor if you're at all concerned. He is wonderful.'

Isabel had been to see Dr Lutz a few years previously when she'd hurt her thumb while skiing.

'He is indeed. I think Gemma was quite taken with him too!'

'Can I speak to her?'

'She's just gone to bed. I insisted on an early night – it's been a while since I could do that! We've had a quiet evening playing rummy.'

'Oh lucky you! Did Dom win as usual?'

'Actually I did, surprise, surprise. Dom's just gone out for a while, to see some friends. Now don't worry, you can speak to Gem tomorrow. She won't be snowboarding, not if I can help it.'

They talked for a few more minutes. Exchanges about skiing, Totnes, the children, the hotel, Jasper chasing a squirrel in the garden . . . The currency was the familiar – and they shared a lot of that. And it was easy, easier than it had been between them for some time, almost as if nothing had changed.

Beth had been to the cottage before. She, Simon and the children had spent a few holidays there, especially when they were short of money, which was often. Isabel refused to charge them a proper rent, despite Michael's suggestions otherwise, and only allowed Beth to give her a cheque to cover the phone bill and the electricity they'd used. Isabel felt she could insist, although nothing was said between her and Michael, because the cottage was hers and hers alone.

A roaring exhaust outside announced Beth's arrival. Her old Volkswagen was practically falling to pieces.

'I never thought I'd make it. Damn car.' She kicked it, then turned to Isabel. 'Izzy! Look at you, look at that tum! It's getting quite substantial. Let's have a feel.' She ran her hand over Isabel's bump.

'I felt the baby move for the first time on Monday.'

'Oh, wonderful! That's one of the best bits, isn't it?'

She dragged her old canvas holdall into the cottage and went back for a box, which she thumped on to the kitchen table.

'I love this.' She stroked the old oak surface. 'I always imagine it was a monastery table, rows of monks eating in silence in the refectory.'

'Hey Beth! Why not nuns in a convent?'

'All right, you have me there! Why not indeed?' She started to unpack the box. Cartons of gourmet soup, tins of tomatoes, garlic bulbs, bottles of wine, a chunk of Parmesan, gnocchi, oranges, a head of green celery with its leaves trailing, packets of rocket . . .

'I thought I'd bring a few things, save us shopping too much. And don't worry, I'll do the cooking, you don't have to treat me like a guest.'

'That's sweet of you, Beth.'

'No, Isabel, it's sweet of you to let me come and stay.'

Isabel sat down and gave Beth directions for where things should go. 'That cupboard, bottom left . . .' She felt tired already.

Later they sat on the rug in front of the wood-burning stove. Isabel rested her back against the sofa. The baby moved inside her – this was beginning to happen more often. She rubbed her stomach and silently said hello.

'Are you sure you won't have some wine, Iz?'

'Well . . . Perhaps just one glass, then.'

'That shouldn't do any harm, surely?'

'No. And I mustn't get too frantic about it. After I discovered I was pregnant I began to feel guilty because I missed all the *pre*-conception care that everyone talks about, these days. You know, how you're meant to prepare yourself, get yourself in tip-top condition ... Then I thought, Well, it's too late now, and I eat healthily, I don't smoke, so why give myself a bad time about it?'

'Exactly. That's the trouble with motherhood, it's one long guilt trip – or it is if you let it be. Anyway, cheers, here's to you and the baby!'

'Thank you. Cheers – here's to you too. And friendship.'

'I'll drink to that. So tell me, are you actually ploughing through all those?' Beth gestured at the pile of pregnancy books on the coffee table.

'Sort of. Dipping into them, more like. I still haven't done my birth plan.'

'Anything to help you be in control. All those male doctors thinking they know what's best. How many of them have ever seen a normal natural birth anyway?'

'I won't be having a male doctor, Beth. My GP's a woman, and the midwife is too.'

'Well, she's crucial.'

'She certainly is. Although I haven't written it out yet, the plan is that as soon as I think I'm in labour I ring her, day or night – isn't that good? – and she arrives and checks me out and cares for me at home. We decide when to go to hospital.'

'The later the better.'

'Hopefully. Then she comes to hospital with me and delivers the baby. If everything's fine, I – we – come home the same day.'

'Sounds sensible.'

'I think so. And I have great faith in her, the midwife. Her name's Sheila, she's very down-to-earth and straightforward. You should hear her on the subject of pelvic-floor exercises!'

'All that stuff about doing them while standing at the bus-stop?'

'Sort of.'

'So, is Michael getting involved yet?'

'Not really. I'm still not sure how he feels. Lately I've been thinking that his attitude might be changing, that there's a bit of a thaw ... But, oh, hell. I don't know. I've given up challenging him about it, it just gets me stressed, so we avoid the subject.'

'Hard to avoid, I'd say,' and Beth gestured towards Isabel's bump.

They laughed and Beth refilled her glass. Isabel was still sipping her wine.

'So tell me about it, Beth, what made you run away?'

'I haven't run away – I wish! Not really. I just felt that something had to happen, something had to give. Everything had reached boiling-point, or perhaps it was me, I had.'

Isabel put a cushion behind her lower back. She knew this would be a long listening session.

Words came tumbling from Beth about Simon, how his storytelling project was beginning to take off, to her amazement. He'd dressed it up as research, which it was in a way, and persuaded the college to give him a sabbatical – so he'd be having the autumn term off, paid, thank God, they couldn't manage otherwise. Lucky him, Beth said. That was just what *she* needed . . . Incredible the way Simon had become so *energised*. Busy, busy, busy, reading so much stuff, recording his voice, spending time in libraries digging up stories: contemporary urban myths, ancient folk tales, country yarns, stories that crossed international boundaries . . .

Forget schools, he'd decided, no funding available, no money in it – 'Yes, this is Simon we're talking about here,' said Beth. And stories were not just for children, were they, as most people assume?

What he was really excited about was infiltrating the corporate world. It was quite the thing, apparently, he'd been reading about it in American radical-business magazines. 'And yes, they do exist,' Beth said, with a sigh. Hiring a poet or storyteller was becoming fashionable – it encouraged self-expression and creativity among staff, supposedly, and furthered the corporate culture. He'd heard that Marks and Spencer had even hired a poet. And Simon was so excited about the power of storytelling, he believed it could lift tensions and create understanding . . . Beth said that was ironic really, because that's just what was needed in their household. And he enthused about 'dilemma stories' in which a questing hero is confronted at every turn with awkward questions – 'Aren't we all?' asked Beth. 'Isn't that life?'

Isabel interrupted. 'Hold on, Beth, this is fascinating but it's all about Simon.'

'That's the point! I'm glad for him, it *is* exciting, things are happening for him – or they will, I'm sure. And he's happier, he's less moody and irritable and – wait for this, Izzy – he's stopped going to therapy!'

'Wow, that *is* a change! Progress even. But? But?'

'But I envy him. I resent him. What about me?' asked Beth. '*I* need a change. *I* need time off.'

Work was wearying – well, work was, wasn't it? Things had changed, there was so much admin and paperwork on top of teaching, and no one seemed to care about education any more, it was becoming a marketplace like everything else. And she had to deal with adolescents all day long, just like at home. She described life *chez* the Marcus family. Daniel wanted to leave school – what was the point? he said. He just wanted to earn some money. Hannah looked eighteen, or tried to, even though she was only fourteen, and would not listen when Beth tried to warn her about dressing provocatively or wearing too much makeup. Hannah said it was not her problem if people got the wrong idea, she dressed to please herself. Beth questioned if she'd been a feminist all these years for *this*? Then Leo seemed to suffer from being the youngest and took refuge in computer games, she was worried that he was becoming withdrawn.

Isabel dared to suggest that this was all quite normal, this was family life in the nineties, but Beth persisted. It was continual conflict, with egos clashing, the children arguing and fighting. Isabel said that hers were the same, all brothers and sisters fought. But Beth said her three were so ferocious. Maybe it was her and Simon's fault, they'd always encouraged the children to express their feelings, not bottle things up. But things were so – so raw. And she felt as if she were the referee, she had to stand in the middle of them all and somehow sort it out. She groaned and put her head in her hands.

Isabel reached across and put her arm around Beth's shoulders. 'I know, I know. Being a mother is rather like being a sponge at times.'

Beth lifted her head and snorted. 'A sponge? Sounds like one of those ghastly embroidered cushion covers, "To be a mother is to be a sponge." A commemorative gift for Mother's Day. For that special sponge.' She said this in a passable American accent, like one of those voices on a movie trailer.

They got the giggles. At last Isabel managed to say, 'You know what I mean, Beth. We have to soak things up, don't we? Men's whims and moods, children's tantrums and difficult stages . . . Mop it all up. The everyday flak, the negative stuff that's thrown around. It's about absorbing it all.'

'Now you sound like an ad for sanitary towels or disposable nappies!'

Giggles again. When they'd recovered Isabel said, 'But seriously –'

'I thought you were being serious, Izzy, a serious sponge.'

'Enough! Beth, what I wanted to say is that everything shouldn't be down to us, should it? What I mean is, down to you . . . So when it gets bad at home, can't you just leave them to it?'

Beth looked up, pushed her hair off her face and smiled. 'I suppose I just have.'

The next day they planned things to do together and separately. It was, they said, just like old times. They'd walk on Dartmoor, weather permitting; stroll on a beach (ditto); indulge in a cream tea; visit Connie and Erica; go to Totnes . . . Beth wanted to take some black and white photographs, perhaps do some sketching. Isabel had to do some gardening. It was pleasant, companionable.

That morning, walking from Dartmouth towards the old castle at the mouth of the river Beth said, 'You know, when you talk about the baby you don't seem worried about how it will interfere with your life.'

'Oh. That's the one thing I don't think about much. But, then, I'm not exactly a high-flying career woman, am I?' She laughed.

'Well, you have the shop. But, anyway, who is?'

'*You* are, Beth.'

'Sadly I don't think so!' retorted Beth. 'Think about it, though. Who do we know of our generation who's had a *real* career, a real serious career with power and money? Do you know anyone like that?'

They walked silently, mentally scrolling through women of their age, women they knew.

'Patchwork lives, Izzy. We all have patchwork lives. Compromised, interrupted by children.'

'But I never really wanted a career.'

'Perhaps you weren't encouraged to. *I* did. Oh, I've got a job, I've made progress, but I don't think I was single-minded enough.'

'But how can you be single-minded with kids? We have to be double-minded, triple-minded.'

'Or more! Anyway, let's hope it will be different for our daughters.'

They marched on towards the sea, both thinking that although it might be different it would never be easy.

When a drizzling rain defeated them, they turned back to Dartmouth, agreeing it was time for that cream tea.

They squeezed into a corner of a tea shop (or shoppe, so the sign said), crowded with people coming in out of the rain. There was a pervading air of dampness. They arranged themselves on oak wheelback chairs and Isabel carefully shifted the table to accommodate her bump. Beth grinned and raised an eyebrow. Delicate china cups sat upside down on saucers, awaiting their moment. The tablecloth was thick and white. They gave their order – the full works, why not? – to an elderly waitress wearing a black dress and frilly apron and something lacy pinned into her hair.

'God, this place can't have changed in years,' Beth said, looking around.

'It hasn't. Does a good cream tea, though.'

'Of course, you spent some of your adolescent years down here, didn't you Izzy?'

'I did indeed. Though not actually in *here*, not the bits that counted.'

'Ah, which bits counted? Let me guess, boys, sex, exploration.'

'You're right.' laughed Isabel. 'And discussing it afterwards with Angie. Sometimes that was the best bit!'

They walked slowly up the steep hill to where the car was parked, Beth groaning about eating too much. Isabel pointed out that you had to eat too much with a cream tea, it was part of the deal.

She drove steadily back to the cottage, down the high-sided lanes, their surfaces glistening with rain. It was cosy in the car with Beth, lulled by the sounds of the windscreen wipers and some swoony opera on the radio in the background.

'It's funny though, isn't it, Izzy, how at a certain juncture we stop talking to our friends about our sex lives, about our relationships?'

Beth often did this, picking up on an earlier conversation as if there had been no interruption. It was possible between good friends, Isabel thought.

'How do you mean?' She pulled into a curve in the lane to let a tractor pass.

'You mentioned talking to Angie about teenage sex, all that, how important it was. But at some point it stops. We no longer talk that way, no longer share.'

'Well, I suppose when a relationship gets serious our loyalty shifts. Allegiance to a boyfriend or lover or husband then takes precedence, doesn't it?'

'I suppose it does. As we grow older, as we stop experimenting, we stop confiding.'

'So did you want to talk about sex with Simon, is that it?'

'Not really!' Beth laughed.

'Well, if you wanted to –'

'Thanks, Iz. Actually sex is not our problem. It's always been good, though now it's less frequent – inevitable, I suppose. Too tired, too busy, too preoccupied. Or we've had a row. That's changed: in the past, if we'd argued, we'd make up in bed, with sex. We don't do that any more. Disagreements are either solved by thrashing it out with words – and, God, that's exhausting – or if we have no energy, through silence.'

'Mm. Marriage isn't easy, is it?' A bird suddenly flew low across the front of the car – a blackbird, a thrush? Isabel had noticed they did that more in the country. Was it a way of claiming their territory or were they merely not so accustomed to cars?

'Is it marriage or just life in general that isn't easy?' Beth turned sideways in her seat to look at Isabel. 'But you and Michael are OK, aren't you? Despite your present state.'

'I used to think we were. I *still* think we are . . . but he puzzles me.'

She stopped the car outside the cottage. Jasper barked from behind the front door. They stayed where they were as Isabel continued, 'Do you ever get that feeling that you think you know someone so well then suddenly you have a sense that you don't, after all? It may only last a second or two, a flash, but it's strange.'

'Yes, and disturbing. I do get that, with Simon. And you with Michael?'

Isabel nodded. They were silent for a minute. 'Jasper's getting frantic. We'd better go in.'

As Isabel got out of the car she gasped and held her back. 'Izzy, are you all right?' Beth hurried to her side.

'Yes, yes, I'm fine. Just backache, the usual!' She straightened up and rummaged in her bag for the door keys.

Beth leant against the porch and remarked, 'It's obvious that you and Michael have sex, anyway!'

'Do you mean me being pregnant? All that shows is that we had sex once.'

The dog rushed around them as they went inside. 'Down, Jasper, down!' Isabel said sharply. 'God, I must pee.'

She came back and sank on to the sofa with relief.

'Do you know Beth, Michael and I haven't made love since I told him I was pregnant? We haven't even got near it. And I've avoided thinking about it until now.'

'Well, some men are wary of pregnant women. They think they're fragile.'

'It's not that. We made love when I was pregnant before. Perhaps it just reveals how strongly he feels about this baby.'

She was about to add that she didn't mind about not having sex, it was the cuddles she missed and the physical closeness and being held, when that thought, that suspicion she'd had, unexpectedly resurfaced, thundering into her mind like a runaway horse. She headed it off and turned to Beth, who'd come to sit beside her.

'Isabel? I was saying that I've always thought that you and Michael had a really strong marriage. A real marriage. I still think of me and Simon as having a relationship – I actually find it hard to use the words wife and husband, all that stuff. You and Michael have something concrete, something solid.'

'I'd always thought so. We fitted so well, shared the same views, wanted the same things. And there was passion, certainly at the beginning. Hopefully this phase is just a temporary hiccup.' She smiled and looked down, stroking her bump. 'That's what you are, baby. A hiccup. A baby called hiccup!'

'Hey, don't worry about it.' Beth put her arm around Isabel. 'I've always thought of you and Michael as the most married people I know.'

At the end of the week Isabel prepared to drive back to London, having agreed that Beth could stay a few days longer. Beth had dared, as she put it, ring Simon and tell him. It felt bold, putting her needs first. Why? she wondered. What had happened over the years to her assertiveness? Subject to wear and tear, like the rest of her, she thought.

She carried Isabel's bag out to the Volvo. Jasper followed, sensing what was happening.

'I'm so grateful you've let me stay on, Izzy. Hopefully I'll feel inspired to do some drawing, or even some watercolours.'

'Just relax. Don't feel you have to do anything. And no need to be grateful – remember our deal?'

'Yes. Beth Marcus, birth companion, that's me!'

Last night she had agreed that if for some reason Michael could not or would not be with Isabel at the birth, then she would be there.

'Great! I'm off now. You'll give the key back to Connie and Erica?'

'Yes, don't worry, I'll make sure everything is secure and switched off.'

Isabel settled Jasper in the car then turned to her friend. They hugged carefully across Isabel's bump, and Isabel promised to call when she arrived home.

She gazed at the cottage, a little wistfully.

'You are so lucky to have this retreat,' said Beth.

'I never thought of it like that. I suppose it *is* a retreat. Yes, I am lucky.'

She waved as she reversed into the lane, trying to overcome

her reluctance to return to London, to Michael, to family life. Despite the fighting talk she had indulged in with Beth, she felt she must return before the others, to shop for food, be welcoming. Wasn't that what she did? It wasn't necessarily being meek or subservient, she thought, not really. Just practical. And fair – for after all, Michael and the children could hardly stock up on food at Geneva airport or at Heathrow, could they? But she envied Beth the next few days – the solitude, the quiet, the cosy teas and chats with Connie and Erica. The independence.

30

Michael tapped gently on the children's door. Neither of them had appeared for the hotel breakfast – that wasn't unusual, but he wanted to make sure that Gemma was all right before he went off skiing.

No answer. He knocked louder.

'Gemma! Dominic! Gemma!'

The door opened, just slightly, and Gemma stood there in an oversized T-shirt, rubbing her eyes. How young she looked, thought Michael.

'Oh, hi, Dad.' She opened the door wider.

'I came to see if you were OK. How are you feeling, love? How's the head?'

The bruise was coming out on her forehead, a deep purply blue. You could barely see the stitches, half hidden in her hair. Dr Lutz had needed to cut away a little around the wound, although he'd assured her he'd remove as little as possible. Dominic had thought that very amusing and had teased his sister, saying it was typical of her to go to a Swiss doctor for a haircut.

'I'm all right. It feels a bit sore. And I've got a headache. I think I'll go back to bed for a while.' She got back under the covers.

Michael followed her into the room. 'Good idea. Take it easy today. Would you like me to stay with – hey, what's this?'

He was staring at Dominic's bed. Untouched, obviously unslept-in.

'Gemma, where's Dom?'

'Oh. He's not here.'

'Obviously! Didn't he come in last night?'

'Doesn't look like it. Sorry Dad, I hadn't noticed. I went to sleep really early, haven't woken up since. Those painkillers –'

'All right, Gemma, all right.' He sat down on Dominic's bed as if it might give him inspiration. 'So where can he be? Has he done this before? Has he stayed out all night without my knowledge?'

'No, he hasn't. I'm not sure where he could be.'

'You must have some idea. Where was he going last night? Did he tell you?'

'I think he said something about going to a bar, but what with everything that happened yesterday I didn't pay much attention.'

'Me neither.' Michael stood up, running his hands through his hair. 'So. What now? I'd better go and look for him.'

'Oh Dad, I'm sure he's all right. I expect he'll turn up soon. He probably got drunk and is sleeping it off at someone else's place.'

'I wish I had your confidence, Gemma.' But he knew that was the difference between being a sister and being a parent. 'And "someone else" – who might that be?'

'Um. Not sure.'

'Gemma, please!'

'Dad, I'm not covering up or anything! Why do you immediately assume I am? It's not fair.'

'I don't assume that. Don't get upset – look, I'm worried about your brother. Can you think of anyone he might be with?'

Gemma held her head. She could do without this right now.

'There's a crowd of snowboarders we hang out with and some chalet staff, you know, chalet girls – they work for Inghams, I think. We usually meet up somewhere in the village, sometimes the North Wall. Oh, yes, he did mention that last night.'

'I'll start there, then.'

'But it won't be open.'

'I'll see. I can't just sit here and do nothing. If Dom comes back while I'm out, tell him to stay here and wait for me.'

'OK.'

Her father left and Gemma slid back down inside the bed. Bloody Dominic, she thought. She supposed he'd got lucky last night – he'd been trying all week to get off with that blonde chalet girl, Zoë. Perhaps he'd managed it at last. All this fuss, with Dad going on at her in his lawyery voice and rushing off to find him. Dom was practically eighteen, for God's sake.

Her head hurt and she felt weepy. If only Mum was here to give her a hug.

Michael sat outside a café in the main street with his second cup of cappuccino. It was opposite the station and he reckoned that Dominic would have to pass by here whichever way he walked back to the hotel. Michael was tempted to buy a copy of yesterday's *Times*, but if he were reading he might not notice his son.

He'd calmed down a little, despite finding no trace of Dominic. There had been no messages at the hotel desk – he'd checked, just in case. The North Wall bar had been closed, but there was an Australian guy there taking out rubbish who remembered a crowd of English snowboarders, regulars he said, from late last night. He'd thought they were staying up at Winkelmatten. Probably not the right snowboarders, Michael thought, as he walked away, or Dominic might not have been with them . . . Or maybe the guy had just told him anything to get rid of him.

He'd wandered around the village, keeping a look-out, peering in cafés, not sure what to do next. Go to the Inghams office – did they have one? – and make inquiries? But what would he say? He could imagine how this might look or sound from the outside – ridiculous, no doubt. Dominic was old enough to look after himself, in some situations anyway. And this was Zermatt: nothing bad ever happened here, did it? Apart from people dying on the mountain. It was safer here than most places, including most of London. Gemma was probably right. Dominic would turn up. Michael just wished it would be soon.

It was ten thirty. At some point, if Dominic still hadn't reappeared, he'd have to consider the situation and decide what to do next. The police? God, he hoped not.

Michael sat back and sipped his coffee. It was a beautiful morning, bright sun, blue sky, clear air. He watched the plumed horses that pulled taxis or the fancy carriages for the more expensive hotels, waiting outside the railway station. Occasionally they tossed their heads but otherwise stood still, obedient and dignified. Their drivers hung around in groups nearby, chatting, smoking. At times like this I wish I still smoked, thought Michael. I could sit here in the sunshine and blow smoke rings . . .

Once again he felt the lack of Isabel. What would she do in these circumstances? What would they both have done? Would it be like the good-cop/bad-cop scenario? Her distraught, him calm. Or vice versa. And how would she treat Dominic when he showed up? Relieved, of course, but angry, disappointed? Would she discipline him, ground him? And what will I do? thought Michael. Wait and see, was all he could decide on.

As he scrutinised the crowds of skiers marching purposefully by, the colours of their clothes and equipment vibrant in the sun, hearing snatches of German and French and Italian and American and Japanese, he understood that if Isabel had been here he would hardly have been involved. To his shame, he realised that he would have reassured her that there was nothing to worry about. He might even have gone off up the mountain in a determined and macho sort of way, leaving her to it.

A shadow fell across his table. The sun had gone in. His coffee cup was empty. He shivered and experienced an awful sense of responsibility. How could he explain this to Isabel? He had brought the children away on holiday and now one of them was missing.

He glanced up the main street, towards McDonalds. A boy was loping along, hair tousled, smiling as he looked around him, smoking. Smoking?

Dominic. It was Dominic. And there was a relaxed air about him, as if he didn't have a care in the world. Michael waited until his son was approaching the café then stood up.

Dominic suddenly noticed him. 'Hey, Dad, what are you doing here? Thought you'd be skiing.'

Part of him wanted to hug his son, part of him wanted to

shake him, shout at him. Michael resisted, clenching his jaw, taking control. 'I've been waiting for you. You stayed out all night, I didn't know where you were. But I don't wish to discuss it here. I suggest we go back to the hotel.'

'But Dad –'

'The hotel, Dominic, now!'

Michael strode off, Dominic silently hurrying behind him. That muscle twitching in his father's cheek was always a bad sign.

Despite Dominic's pleas that he needed a shower and a change of clothes, Michael insisted that they went into his room. 'You'll have to wait, like I've been waiting for you,' his father told him. 'And I don't want to disturb your sister.'

Dominic slumped into a chair. Here we go, he thought.

'So, what have you got to say? Where were you last night?'

'Out.'

'Oh, for God's sake, Dominic, I know that!'

'You didn't let me finish, Dad. I was out with friends, at a bar.'

'Which friends? And *all* night? The bars close at some point.'

'Does it really matter? I'm here now, aren't I? I'm OK.'

Dominic wearily watched his father pace the small room. This reminded him of a TV courtroom drama. All he wanted was a shower and a kip (he'd got hardly any sleep last night) but he had to endure this stupid inquisition.

'Yes, it damn well does matter. You stay out without telling me, or even asking me, and I've been bloody worried, having no idea of where you were.'

'But I didn't *know* I was going to be out all night, it just happened! I got a bit drunk and went back to – to someone else's place and must have fallen asleep . . .'

'Ah. And whose place was this? Where were you?'

Dominic sighed. He knew his father wouldn't give up until he felt he'd extracted the truth, the whole truth and anything else that was on offer. Anything to cut this short. 'I was with a girl. I went back to her place.'

'I see.'

'But that's all I'm telling you because it's nothing to do with you.'

'Who was she? A chalet girl?'

'Yes, she is. But it's none of your business!'

'It *is* my business when you don't come home and I'm worried. And I hope you practised safe sex.'

Dominic leapt to his feet. 'For fuck's sake! Who are you to lecture me?'

'That's obvious, I would have thought.'

'And yes, we used precautions, which is more than can be said of you.' He made for the door but his father's arm barred the way.

'What on earth do you mean? If you're referring to the sixties, things were different then.'

'The sixties? What's that got to do with anything? The *sixties*? Get real, Dad. I'm *referring* to you and Mum.' For once, he had temporarily silenced his father. Seizing the moment, he continued, 'And you don't really care. If Mum was here you wouldn't have been bothered about me. You just thought you should be. And we all know why she isn't here. *The baby*.' He almost spat the words out.

Michael looked shocked. All he could say was, 'Don't be silly, Dominic.'

'You always say that if we ever have a row! *Don't be silly*. Well, I'm not silly or being silly. And what do you know about me, anyway? You're always working, you're hardly ever at home.'

'That's not fair.'

'You're not interested in me, not the *real* me. All you ever really want to talk to me about is schoolwork and I've had it with that, I'm sick of it. What's the point of A levels and university? Just to be like you? Why should I want to be like you?'

Michael squared up to his son – luckily he was still taller – and held up his hands. 'Enough. That's enough! How dare you talk to me like that? You seem to forget that it's *you* in trouble here!'

Dominic looked his father in the eye then stepped back. The moment passed. He turned away abruptly and sat down on the bed, his head in his hands. He sounded tearful. 'I was so happy last night. And this morning. I had such a good time and now you've spoilt it.'

Michael sat down carefully next to him. 'All I've done, Dom, is show a father's concern.'

'Nothing's right. Everything's going wrong.'

'What do you mean?'

'Things aren't the same at home any more. Mum being pregnant, it just doesn't make sense. I mean, what's the point of it? You've got me and Gemma. And it's so weird, seeing Mum like that, getting huge.'

'Dom, she's hardly getting huge!' He spoke softly.

Dom sniffed back tears. 'Well, she will soon.'

'Listen, Dom, about the baby. No one's pretending that it's ideal. But it's happened and we have to make the best of it. It's not a disaster – no, it's not, Dom. The main thing is that Mum – and the baby – are healthy. I'm sorry if it's embarrassing for you, but that's how it is. Sometimes we just have to accept things with good grace.'

Dominic nodded, head down. Michael continued, 'But I can understand how you feel. We all have to make adjustments. But about the other things you said, I'm sorry you feel that way. I *am* interested in you, Dom, and I only want the best for you.'

'I know, Dad, I know,' Dominic mumbled.

'But maybe you don't agree with what I see as best for you. We should talk about that. You don't have to do law.'

'I'm not sure what I want to do. It's all so –'

'Overwhelming?'

'Yeah.'

'Everyone feels like that sometimes, whatever age you are.'

Michael squeezed his son's shoulders, a one-armed sideways hug. It was a start. They looked at each other, then quickly looked away again, avoiding the emotions showing on their faces.

They stood up and Michael said briskly, 'Why don't you go and have that shower, Dom? You look a bit the worse for wear!'

'Oh, thanks a lot, Dad!' But he managed a grin.

'And then I'll take you out for breakfast – or is it lunch? We'll see if Gemma feels up to coming, if not we'll bring her something in. Off you go.'

While Dominic showered next door Michael stood on his

balcony, with its partial view of the Matterhorn. The remaining snow on the surrounding rooftops sparkled and shone in the sun. A dog barked, the church bells resounded across the village, and water dripped from nearby gutters as icicles melted. Michael took deep breaths of fresh air and realised that he probably wouldn't be going skiing today. What the fuck? he thought. There were other things in life. More important things. He must talk to his son, make sure his daughter was all right.

Being a parent, being a full-on, involved parent, meant putting your own needs and wishes aside, he recognised that. (Not that he had always been a fully involved father, he recognised that too.) No thoughts of skiing. No thoughts of Ellen. Especially her. Not now.

But he thought of Isabel. He wished that she were standing by his side. They'd joke about having to lean over and twist their necks to catch a glimpse of the mountain through a gap between buildings. They'd discuss where they'd eat tonight. He'd probably have his arm around her, she'd reach up to give him a kiss. They'd chat about the children, list their good points and agree what terrific kids they were, really. And they might even talk of the baby . . .

Isabel. She represented a sense of wholeness. Things weren't complete without her. This family, his family, needed her. And, he understood, so did he.

31

Michael's big yellow notepad was covered in doodles. They'd started in the margins and had spread all over the page like a virus. Straight lines, dots, angles . . . They looked vaguely scientific, he thought, or mathematical maybe. What did that signify, he wondered, recalling an article he'd seen that analysed people's scribblings. Was he searching for order, for control? Probably.

He eased his tie away from his neck and loosened his collar. It was too hot in here. Was something wrong with the air-conditioning? He must mention it to his secretary who would notify the office manager who would tell – whoever.

Law books lay on his desk, pushed aside. His mind was on other things. He'd been trying to make some notes about this fictional conference next weekend. Mad, really, he knew that. Making notes about something that wasn't actually happening? Well, *something* was happening next weekend: he was booked into a hotel in Sussex for two nights with Ellen. He didn't really have the energy – did he even want to go? – but he felt he owed it to her. And he had committed to it, as Ellen would say. There hadn't appeared to be any choice: spending two nights away together seemed to have assumed monumental significance for her.

So here he was, doodling, attempting to prepare what he was going to tell Isabel. He wanted his story to be convincing, hence the so-far non-existent notes. A conference that he had to attend as a substitute for someone else, which was why he hadn't been able to inform her earlier? A bonding session with fellow partners at the firm? It had to be coherent, it had to sound real.

There was a possibility that he was worrying unnecessarily. Maybe Isabel wouldn't care, or even be interested. Her mood was hard to gauge, these days. Often she had a faraway look. On the few occasions when they were together he'd watch her and she didn't seem to notice. It was as if she were in a world of her own. Separate. Closed-off. Perhaps she was. A female world, a pregnant one. Somewhere he couldn't enter, even if he wanted to try.

He'd been so eager to see her on returning from Switzerland. In the taxi from Heathrow, squashed in with the children and the luggage, he'd gazed out at the lack of landscape along the M4, the greyness, and had found himself thinking of Isabel with a rush of anticipation. Isabel will be there, he'd thought, Isabel will be at home.

He'd wanted to talk, to share all that had happened. Suddenly there had seemed so much to say: how he'd felt when Gemma hurt herself, how anxious then angry then relieved he'd been when Dominic appeared to be missing. How close he'd felt to them both, closer than he had for quite a while . . .

When they'd entered the house Isabel had been in the kitchen. Hugs for the children, who'd promptly raced off to make phone calls. A smile for Michael. Her new haircut was disconcerting. Oh, sure, he'd seen it before the holiday, but he'd forgotten how it looked on her and he wasn't used to it yet. As she'd turned towards him, for a moment he'd thought of Ellen. Isabel's shorter lighter hair had brought her to mind for a second, just a second. Perhaps that had showed on his face, for as he went to embrace her, she merely pecked him on the cheek. Disappointment flooded through him.

She'd gone to bed early that night, as she so often did, leaving him making a sandwich to have with his whisky. As he'd sat alone in the kitchen he felt weary – and something else. Lonely.

In the weeks since then the feeling he'd had of wanting to talk to his wife, to be close to her, began to fade. He tucked it away, ignored it – that was easy, really, as there were so many other things he had to do and think about. Sometimes, just sometimes, it would surface as he watched her in the kitchen or in the garden. Then he'd wait for the right moment but it never seemed to come. Once, lying alone in bed (Isabel was in the spare room) he wondered if she did the same thing: watching him, wanting to talk, waiting. It could be that they were unknowingly engaged in a kind of ritual dance: as he stepped forward, she stepped back; as she moved towards him, he turned the other way . . . They were out of sync. Of course they were.

Isabel wandered around the garden with a glass of orange juice. It was a glorious morning, warm and bright, the kind that takes you by surprise, signalling that summer was on its way. Buds were opening on the white climbing rose – it always flowered first, before the other roses. There was much to do in the garden, she could see, but this year it was being a little neglected.

She lowered herself onto the bench, closed her eyes and lifted her face to the sun. Just a few rays, she thought, that won't hurt.

Life was pretty good, she decided, all things considered. The 'all things' being her pregnancy, and Michael, and the children, she supposed. Things that were important and could be wonderful, but weren't always.

Yet they were all co-existing comfortably enough. In a moment of whimsy it occurred to her that at the moment the Turner family were rather like lines on the tube map: Michael could be the Central line, straight and purposeful (although didn't it zoom off somewhere in the east?). Gemma and Dominic – the Northern line, branching into two at Camden Town? Or the District, dividing at Earl's Court? And I'd have to be the Circle line, she decided. We meet, we join, we intersect, sometimes at the same time and place. Otherwise we go our separate ways.

This is daft, she thought.

The baby stirred languidly in her belly. A reminder of what she should be thinking about?

Time was a strange thing when you were pregnant. It had been passing slowly, lazily, as if she had always been pregnant and always would be. That was fine with her for lately she'd been experiencing a great sense of well-being. One thing she did remember from her previous pregnancies was this enjoyable lull at five months and more.

But now she'd reached nearly six months and it seemed to be speeding up (although she guessed that towards the end it would slow right down again). There were rushes of things to do. Oh, my God, she'd think, and add something else to the list, either the one in her head or her notebook or both.

Things to buy, research to do. She'd had to start completely from scratch. Things had changed so much since she had Dominic. How could she buy a buggy or a car seat until she'd found out which one was best? She pored over *Which?* reports in the library. All these products, all this equipment. What sort of cot should she get? What kind of mattress was the best? A quilt or sheets and blankets? Decisions, decisions. Towelling nappies or disposables or both? Then there was feeding . . . She planned to breastfeed but should she get bottles and formula and a steriliser – *all that* – just in case?

Something had sprung into being called baby transport. Car seats for babies which you put in the *front* of the car facing *backwards*? Could that be right? Prams no longer seemed to exist. There were multi-function pushchairs and travel systems, even something called a Shop'n'drive. And baby joggers – Isabel had seen a woman jogging in Richmond Park while pushing her baby in a triangular-shaped buggy with big wheels. Then she began to notice more of them – they were quite the thing, she realised, but maybe not for her. Slings were now 'carriers' or 'cuddle-ups'. Confusing. It went on and on. Her notebook filled up. But at least she could afford all this stuff, she told herself. She was lucky. And the baby was fine and healthy, touch wood, so far. Lucky again.

Preparing for a baby, let alone having it, could be a full-time job if you allowed it to be, Isabel thought.

She'd sorted some things out. The birth plan was done, although the midwife, Sheila, stressed that she could make changes, it should be flexible. It wasn't written in stone. Isabel just wanted things to be as natural as possible, with the emphasis on the possible. Sheila was practical and reassuring, and didn't show any surprise when Isabel announced that her birth partner might be her friend Beth rather than her husband. She's probably seen and heard everything, thought Isabel.

Meanwhile she went to check-ups and classes – not ante-natal classes yet, although she was booked to start in a couple of weeks, but keep-fit classes for mums-to-be at the local church hall. She reckoned she was the oldest there, one of the oldest certainly. Some of the women were in their twenties, having their first babies. They were bright and shiny and enthusiastic, with smooth skin and supple bodies. Isabel would smile and attempt to feel serene, or at least to appear so, and most of the time it worked. She tried to give the impression – in case anyone cared or noticed – that having a baby at her age was a perfectly natural thing to do.

Once or twice a week she went on solitary expeditions, making preparations in her own way. She marvelled at the fresh baby food in Waitrose. (And again she thought how privileged she was to be able to consider buying it – expense was never really a factor.) She bought more new bras and big comfy knickers and clothes, not necessarily maternity clothes, enough to last her until after the birth when she'd be back to normal, whatever that was. And she indulged in buying baby clothes, convincing herself that this had to be done. Well, it did.

Every time she went into John Lewis or Mothercare to suss

out cots or baby baths, practical necessities, she'd buy something, vests and socks, bodysuits or rompers, a little velour hat. Mementoes of an event yet to happen. She secreted things away, like a squirrel, she thought, in a drawer in the spare room. Soon it would be the spare room no longer: it would have to become the baby's room. At times she just stood in there, clutching a pair of tiny towelling socks or a Babygro, planning where the cot would go, and the changing table (purpose-made, these days), imagining things to come. The baby to come.

And when she saw babies close up in shops, in the street, she sometimes felt a little faint. Tiny babies, bonny babies, pretty babies, even ugly babies: they all had the power to move her.

She roused herself and went into the kitchen. Gemma was cramming bread into the toaster. 'Want some, Mum?'

'No thanks, darling. I had breakfast earlier.'

'Are you sure? Remember, you're eating for two.'

'No! That's been discredited. Pregnant women aren't meant to gain too much weight.'

'That's a shame. I thought it would be a good excuse.'

Isabel laughed. She enjoyed these times with her daughter. Every day now, after Michael had left for the office and Dominic had hurtled off to school – both in a rush, saying little – she and Gemma would reclaim the kitchen. Gemma was no longer working as she was going to Greece next week: she'd got the summer job at the beach club, and could barely contain her excitement. Isabel was going to miss her.

It was good to have Gemma to talk to – not in any major way, just chatty, easy, everyday stuff. She'd become used to the idea of the baby. And as it became more of an actuality than an idea, as Isabel's stomach grew, she seemed to become more interested. Of course, thought Isabel sceptically, it could be something to do with the fact that she was going away, leaving this behind, managing to avoid the event.

Dominic's behaviour had not really changed. He steered around his mother and kept his distance, probably embarrassed by her developing size, she thought. She tried to be patient and understanding, putting it down to his age, his hormones, the pressure of revising for his exams. And, of course, some of it was due to him being male: he couldn't help being influenced by his father's example, his lack of interest.

It saddened Isabel that the household seemed to have divided along gender lines but she wasn't going to waste energy worrying about it. Perhaps it was inevitable, pregnancy or not. She was determined to stay calm and relaxed for the baby's sake. And meanwhile she enjoyed her daughter's company. Her *elder* daughter's company. For it appeared that another daughter was inside her.

The cat attempted to jump on to Isabel's lap, but failed, slipping to the floor, then proceeded to lick herself as if nothing had happened.

'Willow, you silly cat! You'd think by now she'd realise I don't have much of a lap any more. She will keep trying.'

'She's displaced. Aren't we all?'

'Gemma –'

'Only joking, Mum, you know that.'

She watched Gemma carefully spread honey on her toast, thinking, Shall I tell her or not? She was dying to tell someone.

'Guess what – I've got something to tell you, Gem.'

'Oh God, it's not twins, is it?'

'No! But you know I went for another scan yesterday? Well, the radiographer was pretty sure she could tell the sex of the baby.'

'Really? So do you know?'

'Yes. It looks like a girl.'

'Oh brilliant, great!' She rushed around the table to embrace her mother. 'A girl. I'm so glad. Thank God it won't be another Dominic.'

'Gemma – now that's unfair. Although I must admit I am pleased.'

'What does Dad say?'

'I haven't told him yet. Haven't had a chance really, I hardly see him. You're the first to know.'

Gemma had left to buy things she needed for the summer – shorts and bikinis, T-shirts and sunscreen. There had been no time to show her the scan photo of the baby as she was in a hurry to meet a friend and hit the shops. 'Later, Mum,' she had said, 'OK?'

Isabel sighed, turning the picture around. It was shadowy and blurry, mysterious in its way, but the spine was clearly visible, and one arm, one leg and a foot. The face was turned slightly away. She wasn't quite sure how the radiographer knew it was a girl, but whatever she'd seen on the screen had convinced her. Probably the lack of a penis and testicles, the fact that they weren't there. What was it Beth used to say at the height of her feminist reading years ago? We women are measured against men. We're considered defective. They're the norm, we're the other.

Isabel sighed and slid the picture back into its envelope. Maybe she'd take it to the shop and show Jenny – she could be relied on to be an appreciative audience.

She returned to the garden to read the newspaper. It was quiet, apart from builders' noise a few doors away and the planes overhead as usual, one every three minutes, but quiet enough. The sun shone, the cat dozed under a buddleia bush, Jasper unsuccessfully chased a fly. The baby moved. Does it respond to sunlight? she wondered.

Isabel leant back against the bench, stroked her stomach under her shirt and talked to her baby, silently. Was this talking, she wondered, or transmitting thoughts? Either way, she liked to do it and it was important, surely? She described the garden, the plants, the grass. The baby moved again, shifting and turning. Isabel thought she could feel an elbow – or was it a foot? – pushing against her. It – she! – was often very active when Isabel rested.

She sat up and turned to the births column in *The Times*, running her eye down the names, saying them to the baby, trying them out. Hannah. Caitlin. Eleanor. Alice. Rebecca. This was going to be fun, she thought. It was so much easier choosing a name for a girl than a boy. The name book was already well thumbed.

She closed her eyes, feeling drowsy, the sun warming her face. She'd stay here awhile before going to the shop, Jenny wouldn't mind. Her female friends were being so supportive. And as for Michael . . . She was getting better at bypassing the niggle of pain she experienced when she thought of her and Michael and how it could be, should be. How it used to be. It hurt, whatever was happening, whatever he was thinking or doing, it hurt. And she felt the lack of *him*.

The shop looked good. Isabel scrutinised the window as she waited to cross the road: it made quite an impact even at a distance. People going by in cars or buses should notice it. Passing trade, always important.

Jenny was with a customer, extolling the virtues of a Workers for Freedom skirt: yes, it was nice and long, covered everything, if that's what you wanted! Isabel smiled at her over the woman's shoulder and glanced through the rail of new stock waiting to be labelled. There was an oversized cream linen shirt, which would cover her bump beautifully – she'd try it on later.

Jenny swiped the customer's credit card through the machine then wrapped the skirt in tissue paper. How different she looked from a few months ago, Isabel thought, not for the first time. It wasn't exaggerating to say she looked a different person, re-emerging as she recovered from the loss of her marriage.

As the woman left, Jenny turned to Isabel and beamed. 'Another new customer, said she'd never been here before but will certainly come again. That gives me such a buzz! And the figures are good this week so far.'

'That's great. A lot of it's down to you, you know. The window looks super, by the way. When did you do that?'

'Early this morning. Thought we needed something more summery. I remembered what you said about just using one or two items, simple but eye-catching. And do you like the flowers?'

'I do. A nice touch. Now, do you want to take a break as I'm here?'

'I don't need to go out, I brought a sandwich with me. I'll just dive into the loo. How about some tea? I'm having one.'

'Yes, please. I was planning to stay anyway. I'll help you put the new stock out.'

Isabel sat down in the wicker chair. She looked around and observed how tidy it all was – crucial for what was basically a second-hand clothes shop, not that anyone ever called it that. The clothes hung straight, separates on one rail, dresses on another, suits on another. Sweaters were neatly folded on pale wooden shelves; scarves and belts loosely rolled in a basket on the counter; hats perched just so on the bentwood hat-stand. It all looked cared for, with no hint of things being people's cast-offs. Jenny's influence was obvious elsewhere too: flicking through the stock book on the desk Isabel could see how well organised she was. Much more so than Angie had ever been, or even me, she thought. And Jenny had taken over the accounts and the VAT returns – she was good at that too. What would I do without her? she thought.

Later they closed up and left the shop together. It was working out so well, as she and Jenny kept telling each other. Mutual support, mutual benefit. Isabel wished she had more of that at home. They'd had an idea for expansion – in fact, Jenny had tentatively raised the idea and then it bubbled up in conversation as they were hanging the new stock. Maternity clothes! Surely there must be a market? Even though most pregnant women, these days, just bought larger sizes, or lived in loose tops and stretchy trousers or leggings – 'Thank you, Lycra,' declared Isabel – there were still occasions that demanded a maternity dress or a swimsuit or a jacket. Working women especially had to buy extra things. And what did they do with them when they'd had all their children? 'Or if they're like me,' said Isabel, 'when they *think* they've had all their children.'

As Jenny walked home she thought about Isabel's news, that the baby was a girl. She'd always wished she had a daughter. But after the twins were born, for a long time after, she had been so exhausted and Graham had made it clear that *he* thought their family was complete. 'Two boys, wonderful,' he'd said, over and over. So having more children had never been discussed. Maybe it was for the best, she thought. I wouldn't have been a very good role model for a girl. Although she might have made me brave.

Jenny had some news too, although she had not told anyone. She had met a man and was seeing him tonight for a drink. She hadn't intended to meet anyone, she was enjoying life on her own. Who needs a man? she'd say to herself, frequently.

Anyway, not yet. But what the hell? she thought. Let's see what happens. She was making herself brave – or bold anyway.

On Sunday morning she'd been leaning over the wall looking at the Thames, near Barnes police station. She still walked along the river for exercise, nothing else. These days she saw the water as neutral, even benign. Today everything was grey-green: the river, the stones on the 'beach', the mud. The flocks of seagulls had gone – back to the coast, she presumed. Along the wavy edge of the shore two velvety-black crows dipped gingerly into the water. Some small birds hopping and pecking near the water were grey-green too, camouflaged.

Jenny turned as a jogger pounded past and noticed a man standing close by, watching the river. He smiled. She gave him a quick once-over to see if he was some sort of weirdo. No, he looked all right, as far she could tell. Tall, with thick grey hair, strong features, twinkly eyes. Probably mid-fifties. Green polo shirt and navy chinos. The colours of water, she thought. And a dog stood obediently next to him on a lead, a black and brown collie-type, gazing up at her.

She smiled back tentatively. He spoke. 'It always surprises me the number of different birds you see here. Not that I know them all – do you?'

'No. I sometimes think I should get a bird book and bring it with me.'

'Me too!'

She pushed her hair back, tugged at her shirt, but soon forgot to be self-conscious. They chatted, leaning over the wall. She said he seemed to know a lot about the Thames and he revealed that he had been a river policeman until he'd retired early. Hurt his leg in a chase, he said. Jenny asked if he'd been based here, and gestured towards the small wooden landing-stage beyond the railway bridge. He said that he had.

She hesitated, remembering that in those dark days, not so long ago, for Christ's sake, she'd hoped that someone like him would find her, fish her body from the water, do what was necessary. He was hesitating too, then said gently, 'I've seen you here before, haven't I?'

'You may have done. I do like walking by the river.' Oh, God, was she blushing?

'This was a few months back. You always looked so – so preoccupied. I tried to keep an eye on you.' His voice dropped, he leant slightly towards her. 'Tell me, were you thinking of going in?'

Jenny stared at the river. She could have walked away, she could have told him to mind his own business, but she looked him in the eye and said, 'I flirted with the idea'.

He nodded. Later he was to say that she could flirt with him instead but now he merely suggested that they went for a coffee in Barnes village. She agreed. His name was Bill, his dog was called Molly.

They got on well, she was surprised by how easy it was. He seemed a kind man, a straightforward man, although perhaps he had hidden depths, like the river. And he was obviously observant, even intuitive – look how he'd *known* about her. (Although that could have been his professional expertise, she told herself.) She felt he was someone she could talk to, if she wished to. And she found that she did.

Over coffee he'd told her that he was a widower – he believed in being upfront about these things, he said. And Jenny had replied that she was separated. There, she'd said it. It really wasn't so bad, either saying it or being it.

And now she was seeing him *tonight*. Her pace quickened: she wanted to get home, decide what to wear, have a long bath, find some perfume, apply fresh makeup ... all those delicious anticipatory things. For she hadn't done this, whatever *this* was, for a very, very long time.

32

Mist still hovered around the edges of the hotel grounds and gathered in the fields beyond. Ellen shivered and wished she'd thrown on a sweater. Perhaps this early-morning wander had not been such a good idea. Romantic maybe, practical maybe not. The grass was damp beneath her bare feet, the paths too crunchy with gravel to tackle without shoes. Maybe she should have worn her trainers and gone jogging instead.

The old, formal English garden lay behind the hotel. She

didn't know much about gardens but she sensed that this was one to be admired. In fact, the hotel brochure almost demanded it. Planned and planted by a famous Victorian gardener and restored more recently, it was the kind of place that could be used as a setting for a Shakespearean comedy. Courtiers parading and trading witticisms; conversations overheard and misunderstood; lovers meeting and hiding behind the clipped trees . . . A place for assignations. Which is why I'm here, thought Ellen.

She turned back to go inside. The sun, still tentative at this time of day, shone a pale light on the flagstone terrace and the back of the building. It was a pleasing sight, she had to admit. Grey stone and mullioned windows, golden-hued creepers climbing the walls, tall chimneys. Apparently about a hundred years old, but designed to echo an earlier age. Medieval, she guessed. Or an approximation of times past.

Ellen picked the head of a lavender flower – there were glorious fat lavender bushes alongside the paths – and rubbed it between her fingers, inhaling the fragrance. It should be perfect, she thought. This weekend should be perfect. She'd done all she could to make it so. Reading other people's articles on romantic short breaks, *The Definitive Dirty Weekend*, that kind of thing, researching hotels . . . She'd chosen this place for its sophisticated appeal and discretion (so the literature declared), for its tucked-away location near the South Downs yet with reasonable proximity to London (just in case Michael had to return suddenly). It claimed to provide the atmosphere of a private country house – that attracted Ellen, although as she'd never been in one of those old-money places she wouldn't be able to compare it with the real thing. She was better acquainted with the Ralph Lauren version.

Michael had left it all up to her, so she'd even booked two separate rooms, at unnecessary expense (although obviously they'd only occupy one, the large room with a four-poster bed booked in Michael's name). Again, just in case. The Wife might phone, or whatever . . . Just how much more sensitive and thoughtful could I have been? she wondered.

Yet she knew the problem, whatever it was, did not lie with her. It was Michael. This morning she'd left him sleeping in the four-poster (not as old as it appeared, she suspected). She'd gone next door and mussed 'her' bed, made the room look a little lived-in. Crazy thing to do, just for the hotel staff, she thought, but as she'd initiated this artifice she might as well do it thoroughly. They probably think I'm his secretary, Ellen thought, and assume we're screwing each other anyway.

It did worry her, though, if she let herself think about it. All this catering to Michael's needs, anticipating any problems he might have . . . Not the sort of thing she associated with Ellen Linden, her real self. Did loving him reduce her, make her less than herself? Did loving anyone have that effect? she wondered. Did it happen to men?

She slipped in through the terrace door and walked across the polished wood floor to the oak staircase. Sounds of cutlery and dishes, the clatter of plates and the murmur of voices suggested that breakfast was being prepared somewhere nearby.

The wide corridor upstairs was hushed. No sign of anyone. She took her time, wanting to leave Michael to catch up on his sleep – he'd seemed so tired last night. Along one wall was a glass-doored wooden cupboard, itself a piece of merit she assumed, embellished with carved leaves and hearts, copper locks and latches. Arts and crafts movement, wasn't it called? Inside were other small objects of its time: pewter ink-wells, iridescent glass vases, a clock with an enamelled face, a silver teapot . . . She gazed at them with little interest. Everything was so damn tasteful. At first she'd welcomed it, the antiques and polished wood floors and Oriental rugs and fresh flowers everywhere, but now it was starting to irritate her. If only she'd been able to drag Michael to New York, they could have stayed at one of the giant art-deco palaces on Madison or Park Avenue, one thousand rooms or more, all glitz and glamour (but honestly ersatz, different from this), with that good old impersonal I'm-paid-to-be-polite service. None of this pretend-you're-our-personal-guests stuff.

Ellen opened the door and tiptoed in. Michael was still asleep – buried under the covers anyway. His hair looked almost black against the white bed linen. She sat down in the button-backed chair (William Morris fabric, naturally) by the window and considered what to do. Impatience began to take hold. Their precious time away and he was sleeping.

It was strange, this business of being together. All the wanting to be together, conniving to be together but now here they were and . . . what? It was less than perfect, she had to admit. Perhaps the very nature of the weekend was at fault: it was contrived, even false. A bit like aspects of this hotel, she thought.

It had begun badly on Friday evening. As planned, Michael had picked her up after work. He had to double-park outside her building and by the time she got downstairs he was involved in a shouting match with a taxi driver trying to get past.

The traffic out of London was appalling. When Ellen remarked on it, merely remarked, he'd snarled, 'Well, what did you expect? It's a summer weekend, everyone's leaving town if they can.' His tone surprised her – she'd never heard him be bad-tempered before. And it sounded as if he was blaming her for it, for everything. She was about to snap back when she took a deep breath and reminded herself that he'd had to tell lies to come away with her, he'd had to leave behind The Sick Wife and all the attendant problems, no doubt he felt tired and stressed and guilty . . . So what else did she expect?

As she concentrated on the map, even though they were heading straight down the M23 and only really needed it for the last part of the journey, down the winding lanes to the hotel (the brochure again), she stole occasional glances at him. He did look drawn and weary, but his profile was as gorgeous as ever, his dark hair falling on to his forehead, the light catching his cheekbones. He'd undone his shirt and rolled up his sleeves and she gazed at his forearm, the dark hairs lying flat against his skin, his hand steady on the wheel, and thought of them together in the hotel room.

She rested her hand lightly on his thigh and said, 'This will do you good, Michael, this weekend away.'

He sighed. 'I hope so.' He heard her sharp intake of breath and added, 'Oh Ellen, I'm sorry. I'm being a spoilsport, aren't I?' He flashed her a smile. 'It will do us *both* good. And I'll be fine, I just need to shake off my cares and worries.'

She smiled back and patted his leg, thinking, I hope you can shake them off, I hope you can.

But he wasn't fine, something was wrong, Ellen thought, as

she sat and watched him sleep. Or maybe he was just pretending, hiding under the covers to avoid facing the day – and her. Last night she'd told him it was nothing to worry about, it didn't matter, it happened to all men – 'Not to me, not ever,' he'd said. Well, it happened to all men sometime, she'd said, trying to reassure him. But he would not be reassured, he'd seemed distraught. She'd ended up holding him, comforting him like a child (she assumed that's how you comforted a child – what did she know?) and eventually they'd fallen asleep. Their first whole night together.

She ran it through her mind again. Of course she'd expected it to be different – she'd expected it to be special. Perhaps that had put pressure on him, she wondered. Even more pressure.

Once they'd been shown to their room, dutifully admired the four-poster and the window-seat with a view of the garden and approved the bathroom, Michael had announced he wanted to shower and change. Fair enough, she'd thought, resisting the urge to say she'd join him. She unpacked the few things she'd brought and waited. When he emerged from the bathroom, hair wet and slicked back, towel around his waist, she'd encircled her arms around him from behind, enjoying the lean, hard feel of his back against her breasts. He'd turned, kissed her gently and briefly, then pulled away and said, 'Let's go and have dinner, shall we? I'm pretty hungry, aren't you?'

She'd sat on the window-seat while he dressed and told herself to be patient.

Dinner wasn't bad, although they'd agreed the chef was probably trying too hard. To their surprise the dining room had been full, not just with guests but with locals as well apparently, so the waitress said. They amused themselves by discussing their fellow diners, speculating on their names and occupations, and they drank a lot, somehow finishing two bottles of wine. Michael had put away most of it, Ellen realised.

They climbed into the unfamiliar bed – it was high off the ground – and slipped naked under the sheets. He made a big fuss about banging his pillow into shape. Ellen propped herself up on her elbow and watched him fondly. The movement of the muscles in his arms. God, I could consume him, she thought. Come on, Michael.

He looked up and caught her smiling at him. 'What, Ellen? What?'

'Just you. I want you so much.'

She seized him, kissing him fiercely, holding his face, stroking his hair. Their bodies bent and stretched together, it was familiar and unfamiliar at the same time. The bed, the room, the circumstances, she thought. He murmured her name and his tongue slithered down her throat to her breasts. She groaned in pleasure and anticipation.

But something was missing. Usually at this stage – no, *before* this stage – she'd feel his erection up against her thigh or her stomach or her bottom, somewhere, depending on what they were doing. The length of it, its heat, its urgency would make an impression, But now . . . She twisted so that her hand could move downwards, down to his penis, but in this position she couldn't quite reach it. Michael applied himself even more energetically to her breasts, but all she could think of was his state of arousal – or lack of it.

'Michael?'

He paused and she grasped his head to kiss him.

What should I do? she asked herself. Do all I can to arouse him? Ignore it? But I can't.

Slipping her hand down again, she managed to touch him. His penis was soft and warm, not completely limp – semi-erect, she supposed you'd call it. She began to stroke him, hold him, but he suddenly pulled away, separating from her to lie on his back, covering himself with the sheet.

'Oh, shit,' he said, rubbing one hand over his forehead again and again. 'Ellen, I'm sorry, I'm sorry. This has nothing to do with you.'

It hadn't occurred to her that it might.

She leant towards him and stroked his hair. 'Michael, it's OK, really it is. You're probably just tired.'

'I am tired, that's for sure.'

And that's when she'd held him and tried to reassure him and said all the things that women do, and hoped they were true.

Michael stood at the top of the hill and looked across the landscape where it fell and swooped into fields, punctuated by a distant village marked by a tall church spire. It was a beautiful day, they'd both remarked several times. The sun shone, a few fluffy clouds dotted the expanse of blue sky, the air was tangibly fresh. Ellen was by his side. Yet he was plagued by the feeling that he shouldn't be here.

They'd set off after breakfast, resolutely cheerful, neither of them mentioning last night. He was grateful for that. God, how humiliating. He couldn't bear to think about it. If he did, apart from the pain of reliving it, he'd start worrying about whether it would happen again tonight. So they'd looked at the map and planned the day – or, rather, Ellen had made suggestions and he'd agreed. A walk on the South Downs, lunch in a country pub, then perhaps some shopping: there was an antiques fair on not far away.

It was good to be with her, of course it was. He loved her, didn't he? He certainly wanted her, despite what had happened in bed last night. Yet it was odd to be here with her. They'd never spent so long alone together before – yes, yes, he knew that was the whole idea. So why did he feel so ill at ease?

He turned away from the view and there was Ellen watching him, smiling. She put her arm through his and they continued walking. As it was the weekend the path was more crowded than they would have liked. Frequently they had to separate and walk single file so that other people could pass. Families with trailing children and dogs racing ahead; serious ramblers in serious boots; elderly couples taking care how they walked. And there seemed to be this polite convention of saying good morning or at least nodding and smiling at everyone who passed. It was getting to be exhausting, all this unwanted social interaction.

It was as if he and Ellen had been dropped on a mission in the heart of the English countryside. Like aliens, he thought. He wondered how they appeared to all these strangers – do they suspect we're illicit lovers? Probably not, he decided, we fit in as long as we keep nodding and greeting and smiling.

A dog bounded by, very similar to Jasper. He couldn't help thinking of Isabel and the children, the countless family walks just like this. Memories filled his mind, thoughts of home. And before Jasper, that other dog they'd got from Battersea Dogs' Home when the children were quite little, which had got run over near the park – it had been difficult to control, he mustn't blame himself, Isabel had said. Gemma had been more confused than upset: she couldn't understand where it had gone. What the hell was its name? Ah, Tinker, that was it.

'Michael? What are you thinking?' Ellen asked, then laughed. 'Oh, God, how trite. I can't believe I just said that! Forget that I did, please.'

He laughed and kissed her quickly, saying nothing. As they continued down the hill he tried to shrug off his mood and jettison all thoughts of Isabel, the children and family dogs past and present. Switch that off, he told himself, switch track. He put his arm round Ellen and they walked in tune, side by side (for the moment). There was a symmetry about them; they seemed to be a couple.

33

Waiting and watching. Watching and waiting. I do too much of it, Isabel thought. Waiting for the right moment to approach the subject of antenatal classes with Michael – the partners' preparation class was coming up in a couple of weeks. She really couldn't envisage him there, sitting on the floor among giant cushions, listening to slightly patronising explanations (even she found them so), encouraging her to breathe correctly, rubbing her back. But she felt she should offer him the opportunity. And then there was the follow-up question of whether he'd be there at the birth . . . At times she thought, To hell with it, Beth will do it, Beth will be there. But really she wanted Michael with her, at the classes, at the birth of their daughter. She still hadn't mentioned that either, that the baby was a girl . . .

So she watched him, waiting for the right moment, waiting to see if there would *be* a right moment . . . It wasn't that his moods changed. It might be better if they did. Lately he appeared to be the same more or less the whole time. Subdued, distracted. He made an effort when he spoke to Dominic, asking him about his exams and actually listening to the replies. And he'd say, 'Never mind, I'm sure you've done better than you think. And if not, well, we'll deal with that when we have to.' He was being a model father, Isabel had to admit.

But with her . . .

It was easy to watch him as he seemed reluctant to look her in the eye. It had been like that since his weekend away. He'd barely spoken of it, which was odd. Two years ago, when there'd been a similar company weekend, brainstorming bonanza, bonding exercise, whatever they called it that year, Michael had talked and talked about it. Complaining that he had to go, disagreeing with the rationale behind it, cross at the loss of his weekend . . . And on his return, he'd regaled her with the highlights, the lowlights, the revelations people had made about themselves, inadvertently or not . . .

This time, nothing. Nothing before he went, except the last-minute announcement that unfortunately he had to be there, duty called. And when he came back on Sunday, no anecdotes or gossip, even though she attempted to show an interest. Michael muttered something about the traffic and a headache and said all he wanted was a shower then a quiet read of the papers.

Suspicion had risen like bile in her throat, mingled with fear. If it hadn't been for Dominic revising upstairs, requiring peace and tranquillity around him (and the baby, of course, must keep calm for the baby), she might have let it all come to the surface – the questions, the doubts. Round and round they went, finding no outlet. She struggled to keep control, gritting her teeth. She could not ask him. Would not.

Even now, more than a week later, she found herself sitting in the kitchen in turmoil, trying to relax and unclench her jaw by using the breathing she'd learnt in antenatal classes. She kept telling herself that worst fears did not always come true. Suspicions did not necessarily reflect reality. But she still felt one step away from – from what? That catastrophe thing again.

With good timing the phone rang. Isabel moved towards it, hoping it was Gemma, who usually called once or twice a week from Greece, reversing the charges. It always lifted Isabel's spirits to hear her daughter. As she chattered on Isabel would imagine her looking well and fit against a backdrop of turquoise sea and blue sky, although when she rang she was usually about to go to a bar or taverna or club. Isabel wondered who she went with.

It was Angie. 'Isabel, how are you? Sorry I haven't rung for a while.'

'Oh, I'm fine. And don't worry. I do often think of ringing you but I'm never sure whether to or not.'

'Don't want to disturb the love nest?'

Angie laughed but there was a hint of tension in her voice, Isabel thought.

'Angie, no! Well, not exactly.'

'Anyway, Izzy, I'll keep this brief. Look, I'm coming back to London for a few days, perhaps a week. There are some things I need to sort out, things at the bank, stuff like that. I'm coming on Thursday.'

'Are you all right? Is everything OK?'

'Yes, absolutely. Everything's great. But this is a good excuse to come over, which means I can catch up with people, especially you.'

'Good. I'd love to see you. Where will you stay? With Jenny?'

'Well, I'd like to. It is still my home, sort of. It's a bit strange though as I've let it to her. What do you think?'

'I'm sure it will all right. Jenny seems to take everything in her stride, these days. And it would be a bit strange if you *didn't* stay there.'

'That's true. Look, can you mention it to her? Then it won't come out of the blue. And I'll call her later.'

Angie stood in the office, thinking for a few moments, then went off in search of Max. It was lunchtime so she wouldn't be with a painting group. The fierce midday sun made even the keenest students retreat inside for a siesta or to the village bar.

She crossed the courtyard, the light bouncing off the white walls and tubs of flowers into her eyes. The stable, of course. Max's voice, talking to Dali and Rocco, carried through the still, quiet air. Surprise, surprise, thought Angie. This is a first for me, having horses as rivals for my lover's time and affection.

It took a few moments for her eyes to adjust to the shade inside the stable block. Max looked up from brushing Dali's mane, her dark hair shiny and glossy, the same colour as the horse. Her eyebrows were raised in a question.

'I've booked my flight, Max. I'm going to London on Thursday. And I've spoken to Isabel, told her . . .'

Max said nothing and turned her head into the neck of the horse. It was solid, warm, reassuring.

'Maxi? Look, I've told you, it will only be for a few days, a week at the most.'

'Are you sure? You may decide not to come back.'

'I don't understand you, I really don't. Why on earth would I do that? You know I want to be here with you. It's just that there are some things I need to do.'

Angie didn't say that one of the things was to experience some distance, to test her feelings for Max. To be sure.

'And *I* don't understand why can't you do these things, these financial things, over the phone. Or by e-mail or something.'

'I can't, that's all. Max, please, trust me. It's no big deal.'

Max bowed her head. 'I do, I'm sorry, Angel. Take no notice of me.'

Angie went to her side and put her arm around her, pulling her close. 'Max, come on, this isn't you. Where's my big strong Maxi?'

Max laughed and kissed Angie on the top of her head. 'It's the effect you have on me, you reduce me to –'

'To what?'

'A quivering heap, a little girl, a jealous lover.'

'No more,' Angie murmured, and stopped her with a kiss. They leant against the stable wall and kissed some more. Seriously, needily.

Dali snorted and stamped his foot.

'Another jealous lover,' Max said, as they drew apart.

Angie laughed, 'God, I hope not.' She pushed Max's hair off her forehead. 'Now, why don't you and I go and have a little siesta together?'

Arms entwined, they headed quickly for the cool hush of their bedroom.

Jenny gave the cottage a quick inspection (she'd begun to think of it as a cottage too). She'd dusted, she'd hoovered, she'd attacked every surface with Mr Muscle, she'd put fresh flowers wherever she could. Yes, it looked fine, probably cleaner than when Angie had vacated it.

She'd even brushed Desdemona.

The bed in the tiny second bedroom was ready – Angie had insisted on the phone that she'd sleep there. She'd been effusive in her apologies and concerns. She didn't want to put Jenny out, was it an awful cheek to descend like this? Jenny would be doing her a favour.

At first, when Isabel had warned her that Angie would be paying a flying visit, the old insecurities had flooded over her. Was Angie – her landlady, after all – checking up on her? Was she in fact coming back for good, to reclaim her property, even though their six months' agreement wasn't yet up? Would Angie take over again at the shop? Would it be the end of that too?

It hadn't taken long for the panic to subside. There was no room for such anxieties in her life, her new life, she told herself. Even if those things were to happen – *if*, which was unlikely – she still had choices. She had money in the bank, her share from the sale of the house. A tidy sum, as her mother would have said. Jenny preferred to think of it as untidy – big wodges of cash, banknotes bursting out of rubber bands, spilling out of a briefcase, like a great hoard of treasure . . .

Anyway, she could move, she could get a job (Isabel would give her a glowing reference) or she could run the shop with Angie and give Isabel a break (lately she'd been looking as if she needed one). Lots of alternatives. Yes, she thought, I can choose, I can decide.

She was independent now, she was in control.

She'd already made a decision about Bill. It had all been tantalisingly teenage so far, with goodnight kisses that increased in intensity and complexity as the weeks went on. Embraces that became closer, hotter, when clothes began to get in the way. His hand on her breast, his erection growing hard to ignore. Maybe it wasn't teenage, she'd thought (didn't they just get to it, these days?), maybe this was courtship. What did she know? It had been so long since she experienced anything like this, so long since she had felt the pull and tug of sexual desire.

On Saturday night she'd decided to do something about it.

234

She sensed Bill was being sensitive, that he was waiting for a signal from her. Well, it was time, she thought.

They'd gone to Pizza Express in Richmond. Jenny had left half her Veneziana: she didn't want her stomach to be too full, she wanted to feel comfortable. She *was* more comfortable with her body than she'd ever been, but still . . .

'Let's skip coffee and go home, Bill,' she'd said, leaning across the table towards him. 'Let's go to my place.'

Lucky he's such a sweet man, she thought, otherwise he might laugh at such a clichéd line.

But all he did was look at her with surprise, then delight.

It had been a bit of a romp really, they agreed the next morning. They sat up in bed and looked at each other, grinning with satisfaction. For it *had* been a very satisfying night. Rushing and fumbling at first, laughing as they tripped over clothes, both trying to explain how long it was since they'd had sex, shuddering with anticipation as their skin touched . . . Later, during the second, slower time, Bill had said how gorgeous she was, what glorious breasts she had, such a generous body . . . and had anyone ever told her how good she was in bed?

What a treat he was, she thought, as she locked the cottage door and set off for the shop. A lovely, delicious treat. If this is a sample of the uninhibited post-menopausal sex I've been reading about, then I'm all for it, Jenny decided. Post-menopausal, post-marriage, post-everything life.

34

Ellen perched on an aluminium stool in the health-club café and leant on the counter, sipping her vegetable juice. She'd hoped to see Michael in the gym today but he'd left a message on her voice-mail early this morning. She'd been in the shower, the water pounding as hard as she could take it. Impossible to get away from work, he'd said, he'd ring her later.

Things had been strained recently, there was an almost indefinable awkwardness between them. It was since the weekend away. That hadn't been a success, she had to admit.

The second night had somewhat made up for the first, at least Michael had been back on form, although she'd had to work pretty hard. They were both relieved – one less thing to deal with – though neither of them had said anything. Delicacy was needed, Ellen had decided. Sunday had been a waste of time. Michael had been edgy, not wanting to do anything or go anywhere, preoccupied with leaving the hotel early to beat the traffic. She'd smiled, imagining Michael beating traffic into submission, as if it were a foe. Or an addiction. Her smile had irritated him. And that set the tone for the rest of the day.

Funny, really, she thought, the weekend that was going to be so wonderful, that was going to bring us together, had the effect of pushing us apart. It was probably naïve of me to think otherwise, she decided.

Ellen sipped more vegetable juice, wishing she'd had coffee, and tried to focus on the day ahead. There was masses to do: research for the article she was writing on air pollution in European cities; edit the piece on healthy living, UK style, more like unhealthy living she thought, and try to make it more amusing, then fax it to New York. Calls to make, payments to chase . . . The joys of a freelancer, she thought. The trouble was, she wasn't really in the mood for any of it. Michael preoccupied her.

She gave in and ordered an espresso, feeling cross with herself. Somehow she'd got herself into this situation: wanting him but not being able to have him. It was oppressive. And there seemed to be nothing she could do about it, except wait for him to act. How she hated that, having to be passive, not being in control. All she could do was ask herself questions, the same old questions: Why wouldn't Michael make a commitment to her? What was the matter with him? Were things going wrong between them? And why wouldn't he tell his wife, however sick she was? Just how sick was she? Questions, questions, but no answers.

'Ellen? It is Ellen, isn't it?'

A male voice too close to her shoulder. It was James, a work colleague of Michael's, his hair wet, a towel around his shoulders. He grinned and eased himself on to the stool next to her.

'Oh, hi.' She wanted to discourage him. Michael had

reluctantly introduced them some months ago in the gym, and she'd seen him a few times since. Ellen didn't like the way he looked at her, up and down, all over, nor did she like the amused, teasing tone he used when speaking to her. Like now.

'Hard morning on the machines? Did you give them hell?'

'I did my best.' She concentrated on draining her coffee cup.

'Would you like another?' He laughed. 'I mean coffee or that rabbit juice!'

'I know what you mean, and no thanks, James, I should be off, lots to do. Shouldn't you be at the office?'

She gathered her bag up off the floor, bending carefully so that he couldn't gaze at her bottom.

'I'm going in late.' Still he persisted. 'So, no Michael today, then?'

'Should there be?'

'No, no. It's just that I often see you here together.'

'Well, he's not here, is he? Now, I must go.'

'Of course, he does have a lot on. Hectic at work at the moment, some big cases, plus family life, and another on the way! Mad dog!'

He gulped his diet Coke, the ice banging in his glass but kept his eyes on her. Ellen was suddenly acutely aware of every sound . . . Everything had slowed down, including her brain. She gripped her bag tightly and managed to say, 'Oh? What do you mean?'

'Michael and his lovely wife Isabel – they're having another kid. She's expecting. Bit surprising, really, at their age. Didn't you know?'

'Er – no. But then I don't know him very well.'

He smiled and a cruel satisfaction lit his face. She muttered goodbye and fled.

Walking home was a blur. No point in taking a cab – the streets were completely snarled up. Ellen couldn't have handled speaking to a cabbie anyway. She strode through the streets in a rage, blinking back furious tears, hurrying, going faster and faster but barely seeming to make any progress. Squeezing through lines of cars and buses, bumping people with her gym bag, almost knocking a workman off a ladder. 'Hey, slow down, darlin'. What's your hurry?'

'Shut up, you stupid fuck.'

Now she started running, devouring the pavement with her feet. At last she slammed her front door behind her and threw herself on to the long pale linen sofa she'd recently acquired. Sobbing, she pummelled the cushions and kicked her heels, cursing and shrieking.

'You shit, Michael, you bastard. How could you do this to me? Liar. Cheat. Telling me stories about your wife being sick, while all the time she's fucking pregnant! And you said there was nothing between you. I thought you didn't even have sex with her any more . . .'

Not once did she stop and wonder if it was true. Her gut feeling told her that it was – there was something about The Wife being pregnant that fitted. It made sense. It explained all sorts of things, including Ellen's own unspoken and unadmitted doubts.

Eventually her sobs subsided and she lay more quietly on her back, her head throbbing, looking up at the expanse of ceiling high above. Was it floating or was she? Her anger was on the wane, pushed aside by other emotions. Michael had let her down. All those promises: yes, he would tell his wife, he would leave, they would be together. Lies, all lies. Or if not lies, then signs of weakness. She couldn't work out what was worse – Michael being a complete bastard or merely being feeble and inadequate.

She felt drained yet full of disappointment. Searching back through the relationship for clues to help her understand, scanning the good times, the sex, she found that she could no longer see it clearly. Everything was out of focus, like a visual in a newspaper when a colour was wrongly overprinted. Things had shifted, moved sideways. And where am I? Ellen needed to know.

She forced herself off the sofa – how messy and crumpled it looked now – and went to the kitchen corner to get some water. She trailed her hand along the zinc counter, for once unable to appreciate its qualities, and took a bottle of Evian from the refrigerator. Standing at the window, looking down at the street below, empty except for an old man walking slowly with a stick, negotiating the bumpy pavements, she drank the water from the bottle and finished it. For the first time she found the view from her windows depressing. Run-down buildings awaiting redevelopment, sooty brick walls, rubbish in the street, a half-demolished house . . . Why had she never noticed the desolation before? She pressed her head against the window; the glass felt damp and grimy. That just about sums it all up, she thought.

She paced up and down the flat. Nothing made any sense.

She ran to the bathroom and threw up.

Hours passed.

What now? She would have to help herself. There was no one else.

Water gushed into the bath. She rarely used the tub, but right now felt the occasion demanded it. Higher, deeper, she wanted it. Total immersion. The restoring powers of water. Hadn't she written an article with that title?

She tipped something soothing, so the jar said, from Aveda into the water. The fragrance drifted around her, gently melancholic and reminiscent of interiors of old churches in Greece. She stripped off her clothes and slid into the water, running her hands reassuringly over her body while she thought about what to do. Some reassurance – she was trembling.

She lay back and tried to do that thing, imagining you are in a safe place. Where was her safe place? It didn't work.

Should she confront Michael? She supposed she ought to hear what he had to say. But she didn't want to see him or talk to him yet, not while her mind was in such confusion. It was as if her feelings for him – her love? – had been liquidised and new ingredients added: a touch of contempt, anger, of course, suspicion, fear, and more, all mixed in with a great dollop of distress.

She went over the scene with James. He was a slimeball and was probably jealous of Michael and after his job. He may just be a spiteful sod. Should she question what he said? Why would he lie? Perhaps she should investigate further, to confirm – and she thought it would be confirmed – if Isabel (how she disliked to think of her by name) really was pregnant.

She had an idea.

Ellen sat at her desk in her robe, typing a list of ideas, a plan of action. She'd had a bowl of oats and some peppermint tea and then got down to it. This required a lot of thought and careful organisation.

She felt a little better now that she was *doing* something. The hum from her computer, the whizz and whine from her printer were comforting and she was beginning to feel more in control. *Fighting back*, she named the file on screen.

The phone rang and she heard Michael leave yet another message, his fourth or was it his fifth?, sounding no longer just irritated but desperate. He was used to her being there whenever he managed to be available. That's how it had been.

And who are you, anyway, you voice on the machine? Do I know you? Did I ever?

Let him stew for a while, she thought. It's the least he deserves.

Michael was finding it hard to concentrate on work, partly because a long lunch with clients was taking its toll. He'd recently accepted this case and was beginning to wish that he hadn't. A couple of musicians, partners in all senses of the word, who made a lucrative living composing TV theme tunes and advertising jingles wanted to sue a competitor for plagiarism. Their agent had persuaded Michael to take the case and they'd all met for lunch in Joe Allen's. He wasn't really hungry, but he consoled himself that it was billable time. After half an hour of listening to their bitching and ranting Michael had had enough, but there were still several courses and bottles to sit through. He felt increasingly distanced, his thoughts straying to Ellen. Something was happening between them that caused him disquiet. What was it? Or was it the fact that nothing much was happening between them?

When they staggered out of the restaurant at half past three he declined the offer of a shared cab, deciding to walk back to work. The air and exercise would do him good. As he made his way through the crowds in Covent Garden, he determined to make time to see Ellen today. He needed to hold her, to find reassurance. Sod the rest: the files, the cases to read, the people he should talk to. In his position he should be able to do what he liked – sometimes, anyway. He'd worked hard enough for it. He bought a copy of the *Big Issue* (not that he ever read it) from the guy on the corner of Neal Street and hurried on.

Back at his desk Michael read his messages and gazed at the piles of work in front of him without taking any of it in. He felt uncomfortable, full of food and drink. He drank some Alka-Seltzer and rang Ellen but could only talk to her machine. He kept trying at regular intervals. Damn. If she was at home working she'd pick up the phone surely – she usually did when she heard his voice. So where was she?

No wonder he couldn't focus on his work. At times he experienced his predicament as pain: as if he were in a vice that was being steadily tightened. Pain in his chest, deep tension in his neck and shoulders. Did he deserve this?

He rocked gently backwards and forwards in his chair. If only I could square it somehow, make it all better, he thought. For everyone. But how? Realistically it was impossible, he knew that. Even if he were to be open and honest, wouldn't that make things worse? Take Ellen. Supposing he admitted that he was unlikely to leave Isabel, not *now*, what would that do to Ellen, to their relationship? But maybe she'd already accepted that he wasn't going to leave: she had stopped mentioning it. No doubt she was disappointed in him. Then there was Isabel . . . His marriage. His family. Where would he begin? And what would happen then?

Guilt. It swamped him. A double dose. No, more than that. He felt guilty about cheating on Isabel, lying to her; guilty about misrepresenting her to Ellen; guilty about the children and, yes, even guilty about the unborn baby. Plus he felt guilty about Ellen: he had misled her, lied to her too . . . Lies upon lies, like strata of rock. More like shifting sands in my case, he thought.

Suddenly he thought of his son and his delight yesterday when Michael had handed over the money for a student railcard. (Dominic wanted to go off around Europe for the summer with a few friends. Inter-railing, they called it.) Michael realised this was about his approval as much as his money. I haven't been a bad father, he thought. For God's sake, I've been a good one, considering the so-called role model I was given. But a good husband? How about that?

It was all too much. There was no clarity in any of this, no clear course of action, no clear purpose, he decided.

Creating a space among the law books and files on his desk, he put his head down on his arms and closed his eyes.

35

Dusk was creeping up on the day. Isabel gazed at the sky streaking with gold and pink and purple over the rooftops, the great wash of colour infusing the clouds. She was watering the pots and flower-beds behind the house – thank goodness there wasn't a hose-pipe ban – and it was a calming experience. The garden was full of the lushness you get in June. Full-blown roses hung heavily from their branches; they looked so solid, yet one slight touch and the petals began to fall. Fragrance from the honeysuckle tumbling over the fence sweetened the air. Voices murmuring from a neighbour's garden merged with the steady sound of the water spraying the plants. So peaceful. And no planes today: the flight path had been switched to somewhere else. Isabel sighed, feeling content. It seemed as if everything in the garden was lovely, everything was coming up roses . . . *Everything?* She could be lulled into believing so.

The flow of water stopped suddenly. Looking behind her Isabel saw there was a kink in the hose where it had twisted back upon itself. All the water was banked up behind, unable to get through. She bent down with difficulty and managed to straighten it out. Now, why did that make her think of Michael? Was it because his emotions were so tightly con-trolled that nothing could get through?

Water flowed again and Isabel pulled the hose down to the very end of the garden, aiming at the scented geranium and trailing lobelia planted in a Victorian chimney-pot, which always reminded her of a giant chess piece. Nearly done, she thought. Her back was beginning to ache. Looking back at the house she could see Dominic silhouetted at his bedroom window. He caught her eye and waved then turned away.

Things had been a little easier between mother and son lately, just in the last few days. The gap was being bridged, the demarcation lines of gender were being fudged. Or so it seemed. Perhaps it was because she'd been trying not to fuss or make conversation . . . There was no point in trying too hard, she understood that. Let him be. Maybe it was also because his exams were ending and he was going away, like his sister. At the weekend he'd be off with his friends, somewhere on a train in Europe, heading south, or east. I'm glad he's not going further afield, Isabel had thought, to South America or Thailand. Not yet.

A few nights ago in the kitchen, with Michael not yet home, she'd realised that talking to Dominic was less awkward when it was just the two of them. When there was no audience they managed somehow to edge towards the easier relationship they used to have, when he was younger, smaller. As he'd sat toying with his supper, she ventured, 'Cheer up, Dom, only two more exams.'

'I know.'

She'd kept quiet, waiting. Sometimes you just had to listen.

He pushed away the plate of spaghetti. 'I just keep wondering if it's all worth it. For what? I don't even know if I really want to go to university. Gemma hasn't.'

'But I thought you were keen to go. You liked the idea of going to Bristol.'

'I like the idea of going *away*. But university – that's what everyone expects, isn't it? You and Dad, and school. All these expectations . . . And no one has ever talked to me about what *I* want, all the other things I could do.'

Let him thunder on, she thought. It had to be healthy for him to let it all out. She wondered about the emphasis on going away. Was it because home had become difficult? Were the problems between his parents affecting him, even though they were unspoken and unacknowledged, at least to Dom? But, she told herself, *away* – somewhere else – was inevitably attractive to a boy of his age, whatever the circumstances at home.

Eventually he ran out of steam. He looked exhausted, with dark shadows under his eyes. Too many late nights doing last-minute revision.

She made a gentle suggestion. 'Dom, what about postponing the decision, having a year off?'

'But I've always wanted to do that! Bloody hell! Does no one listen to me? Everyone has a gap year. I wanted one too but when I mentioned it ages ago Dad said he definitely didn't think it was a good idea so I didn't mention it again.' He pushed his hair back and rubbed his eyes.

'I didn't know that,' Isabel said quietly. 'You should have tried again or talked to me. Anyway, it's not too late. You can defer entry to university, I'm sure. We can raise it with them after you get your results. I think you – we – should speak to your father about it. Especially if you tell him that otherwise you may give up the whole idea of university. What do you think? All right?'

Dominic looked at his mother in surprise. 'Yeah, OK, Mum. Absolutely. Thanks.'

They had reached some sort of understanding. She'd wanted to go to him, give him a hug, but she was very aware of her bump: he might recoil from being held against this big pregnant stomach. A pat on his shoulder, that would do, that was something.

As darkness began to take over the garden she relinquished the hose and went inside to find Dominic in the kitchen making himself a tuna sandwich. The smell of the fish made her feel queasy as she threw away the empty tin he'd left by the sink.

'Mum, I was about to do that.' He looked hurt, as if she hadn't given him the chance to prove himself.

'And I could have made you something to eat, Dom. We could have had supper together,' she replied, as she gazed at the contents of the fridge for inspiration. Ouch, she thought, that came out all wrong, I sounded petulant, needy. That wouldn't do.

'But I'm meant to be eating out tonight, remember I told you? This is just to keep me going.'

'I do remember. How could I forget? Your last exam today, you deserve to go out and celebrate. So where are you off to?'

She waited while he wolfed down a mouthful of bread.

'Not sure yet. We're all meeting at Hammersmith, probably go into town somewhere, a pub or a club . . . So don't wait up.'

'OK. But take care, won't you? How will you get home?'

'Night bus, probably, but I'll be with Ben and the others so don't worry.'

As he dashed off Isabel pressed a twenty-pound note into his hand, saying it was emergency money, for a taxi or whatever. He kissed her cheek then was gone. Isabel's eyes filled with tears. A sign of affection from her son, freely given with no sign of hesitation or embarrassment! No wonder she was moved.

A whiff of aftershave lingered in the air. There are probably girls involved, she thought, or he hopes there will be. Strange, she thought, there's my son, he's finished his exams, he's effectively left school, ready to leave the nest, almost, and here am I about to start all over again. She rested her hand on her stomach and whispered, 'Give me an easy time, will you, baby? Please?'

Alone in the house again. She wished she could ring Gemma but the phone was in the club office in Greece and was rarely answered in the evening. She just had to wait for her daughter to call her. Anyway, she thought, Gemma was fine. She'd last rung a few days ago – 'I'm loving it Mum,' she'd said. 'It's brilliant and sunny, hard work, too many brats but still great . . . So don't worry!'

That's how it was going to be from now on, she thought. Dom and Gemma heading off into their futures, getting on with their own lives. I'll be less and less involved – and only when they want me to be. What a contrast with the baby when it – sorry, she – comes. That day and night, minute by minute involvement, doing everything for her, being there . . .

No wonder it was so hard to adjust, both when babies were born, then when they left you. We move forward whether we like it or not, she thought.

Isabel forked over the bulghur wheat salad, left over from yesterday, and ate slowly, wondering when Michael would be home. It was as if they were existing in different time zones, leading different lives. Lately, if and when they found themselves together, they spoke amicably enough about practical matters, renewing the car tax disk, mowing the lawn, walking the dog . . . Or about the children: what did Gemma's insurance actually cover, how were Dominic's exams going, what about his plans for the future? The conversations tended to be brief. Michael would occasionally ask how she was feeling and she would invariably say she felt fine, sometimes adding that the baby was fine too. Apart from that Isabel no longer made any effort to talk about *it*, about their situation. She didn't have the energy for it. All the things she might have wanted to share, the baby, the future, the fact that it was a girl, all her concerns, her thoughts, she kept inside. Tucked away.

With practice she'd found it surprisingly easy. After all, she did have a role model: Michael. For wasn't this his usual mode of operation? She had always told herself, and others, that Michael didn't waste words, he did not fritter them as others did. He could, of course, be eloquent at work where he was paid handsomely to talk and give opinions. But he stayed buttoned up when it came to emotions or anything approaching them. (Were all men like that? She didn't know.) She had always believed that he had no option, that was the way he *was*. Now she wondered if perhaps this was the way he had chosen to be.

The rest of the evening stretched before her. A bath? Or a very early night? She stood in front of the bedroom mirror for one of the frequent scrutinies of her body. A work in progress. It wasn't that she was self-obsessed, it was more that she was fascinated by the whole process and liked to be convinced that it was for real. 'You little one, you,' she said, as she pulled up her shirt and placed her hands on the taut drum of her belly. 'Burgeoning, bursting, beautiful belly!' She had to say these things to herself – no one else did. Who was there to admire her pregnant self but her?

The doorbell interrupted her. Just as well, she thought, the slippery slope of self-pity was a bit too inviting. Could it be Michael, forgotten his key? As she approached the front door tentatively, a voice reverberated through the letterbox. 'Coocc, Isabel, it's me! Your dearest friend from across the sea!'

It was Angie, using her exaggerated actressy voice.

Isabel's spirits lifted. 'Angie, what a lovely surprise! I didn't realise you'd arrived!'

They embraced, laughing at the great bump that came between them.

'Well, here I am, kiddo. Just dropped my stuff at home – at *Jenny*'s, I should say – but look at you!'

Isabel did a slow twirl as they entered the kitchen. 'And how do you find me?'

'Your hair, Izzy! You look so different – and the size of you!'

'God, I know, less hair, more of the rest of me.'

'I love the hair.'

'You know, I suddenly thought I'd had the same style for so long – could it be since I was a *child*? It really was time for a change.'

'Good for you. You *have* had that bob as long as I can remember, so goodbye bob!'

'Let's drink to that. Would you like some wine or something, Ange?'

'*Would* I? You know me. Any colour will do. But are you drinking, with the baby?'

'Occasionally, just a little.'

Isabel took a bottle of rosé from the fridge, put it on a tray with some glasses and asked Angie to carry it into the living room. 'I spend too much time in the kitchen. Sometimes I think it's a bit like a comfort blanket.'

'A room as a comfort blanket? That's a new one!'

Isabel lit a scented candle (one of those expensive French ones, but why not? she'd thought. Why shouldn't I treat myself now and then?) and Angie opened and poured the wine. Then they settled together on one of the sofas.

'You've certainly grown since I last saw you. Can I feel?'

Isabel nodded. 'Be my guest.'

Angie reached over and tentatively placed her hand on Isabel's stomach, letting it rest for a minute.

'Wow. It's impressive. Strange to think you've been growing a baby while I've been away.'

'You've been busy too – starting a new life, building a relationship. You seem happy.'

'I'm happy to be back. It's good to see you.'

'It's good to see you too. But you're happy in Spain, aren't you?'

'Oh, yes, don't get me wrong. I do love being there, I do love Maxi . . .'

'But?'

'But it's good to be here!' She smiled at Isabel, acknowledging that there might be something else she wanted to say, but not yet. 'And it was so great to see Desdemona again even though she was a bit snooty at first. You know what cats are like. Jenny's her servant now.'

Isabel leant across and refilled Angie's glass. 'How was it with Jenny?'

'Fine, actually. The cottage looks great, so clean and tidy. I'm so glad she's there, she's the perfect tenant.'

'And she's a marvel at the shop too.'

'Well, aren't we lucky bunnies? You know, it's funny I never really noticed her before.'

'Well, you only met her a few times. But I know what you mean. In a way I didn't notice her either, not truly . . . She probably didn't notice herself, not until recently.'

'Now you're getting all deep on me! Enough. I want to hear all about *your* news, Iz. Tell me all. Especially any gossip.'

Isabel sipped her wine. 'No gossip, not about my life!' She laughed, then brought Angie up to date on the baby, the fact that it was a girl ('Yes!' exclaimed Angie), on developments with Gemma and Dominic, how the shop was doing, the idea to expand it . . .

'You haven't mentioned Michael.'

Isabel looked down at her wine.

'Izzy, is everything all right?' Angie leant towards her.

'Not everything. Some things are all right, but other things – oh, I don't want to talk about it.'

'Because you think I won't understand?'

'God, no, Angie!'

'So what is it?'

'It's to do with me and Michael. Started with the baby, him not being keen, but now . . . Hard to explain, really. It's as if we've run aground.'

'The call of the sea again!'

Isabel giggled. She didn't laugh enough, these days. But then she had always laughed with Angie.

'Run aground, but not yet on the rocks?' Angie persisted.

'Stop it, Angie. I'll get the full-blown giggles in a minute.' She took a deep breath. 'We're going through what you might call a difficult patch, every marriage does. Every relationship. Doesn't it? But I do think at times that it's Michael being difficult.'

'Have you tried to discuss it with him? I always thought you and Michael talked things through.'

'I thought we did too. We used to. I've tried but not recently. I suppose I've given up for now. You see, I haven't got the energy for it. I don't want to keep challenging him and having rows. At some point I decided I'd conserve my energy, whatever, for other things – and I do have other things to think of!' Her hand went to her stomach.

'Fair enough. You say Michael's being difficult, do you think it's just about the baby?'

'God knows.'

'It may be his age, some sort of crisis brought on by you being pregnant.'

'I start to imagine all sorts of things but then I won't let myself.' She tried to smile.

'Isabel, you don't mean an affair? Not Michael, surely not?'

'Well, even the most unlikely people . . . Talk to Jenny, she has stories about middle-aged men you'd find hard to believe!'

'I'll take your word for it. But why do you think –'

'I don't necessarily *think* anything, Angie. It's more a sense of unease, which, let's face it, could be down to all sorts of things, like having a baby at my age . . . Anyway, I don't think about it, whatever it is. I don't want to. And I don't want to talk about it, even with you. As for Michael, I don't ask him, I don't want to know. Not yet. Does that sound pathetic?'

'No, not pathetic. Pragmatic, more like. But if it were me, if I had suspicions – all right, you don't call them that – I'd find it hard to ignore them. I'd want to scream and shout and make the bugger tell me!'

Isabel laughed and shrugged. 'That's you, Angie. Hell, whatever works for you, whatever gets you through the night . . .'

They were silent for a moment.

Angie sighed and said, 'Relationships, they're all the same. Men, women . . .'

Isabel shifted her position and looked at her friend. 'Yes, how is it with Maxi? You haven't told me. Isn't it easier with a woman, all this relationship *stuff*?' She waved her hand vaguely.

'I thought it might be but – I don't know, some of it's down to personality, isn't it? Is it because a person's male or female or is it just the way they are?'

'Now, that's an enormous subject.'

'Don't I know it! But one thing I've realised lately – it's nothing new – is that in a relationship you have to decide how much you're going to compromise, how much you're going to give up.'

'Relinquish.'

'Yes, relinquish. Almost a sexy word, isn't it?'

'Possibly. For women born when we were.'

'Yeah. Hopefully other words are sexier now, like independence or strength.'

'Let's drink to that!'

'Amen. But you know what I mean, Izzy. All that stuff people see as issues in relationships, whose place you go to, where you live, who does what in the house, who pays, it seems to me to be more to do with how much of yourself you slice away and say, "There that doesn't matter." But what's left?'

'Angie. That sounds as if it comes from the heart.'

'It does. Now I'm getting deep! But with Maxi, well, I'm sure she is making adjustments too, compromises, even. But how do I know? Part of the problem, if there is one, is that I don't know her very well.'

'You trusted your instincts, Angie, that's how you are. Perhaps you've got to carry on trusting them.'

Angie sighed and lifted up her hair, rotating her neck. 'That's probably all I can do. God, I'm missing her already. But the trouble is, when I'm in Spain with her, I sort of miss myself. Whoever that is!'

A key in the front door. 'Hi,' Michael called

Isabel called back, 'We're in here.'

We? thought Michael. Surely Dom's out celebrating. He put his briefcase down in the hall and went into the living room.

The light of a large candle illuminated the faces of Isabel and Angie turned towards him. Ah, Angie.

'What are you two doing sitting here in the dark? Hello, Angela.' And he switched on the light.

She got up and kissed him on each cheek. He did the same.

'Michael, how are you?'

'OK, and you? You look well.'

'Oh, I'm fine and dandy, thanks.'

Isabel started to rise from the sofa with difficulty, her hand at her back.

'Would you like something to eat?' she asked.

'Thanks, but you stay there. I'll have a shower first, then see how I feel. It's been a long day.'

He walked upstairs slowly. Their voices resumed. How he envied them their shared confidences and chatter and laughter.

At bedtime Isabel rubbed cocoa-butter lotion into the taut skin of her stomach. She did this every night – who knew if it made any difference? – but she liked the smell anyway. Smells didn't affect her adversely as they had earlier in the pregnancy, most smells anyway. For small things I am grateful, she thought.

'Well, baby, thirty-one weeks now. It goes on going on. You may be causing backache and indigestion and tiring me out, I may feel more and more like an elephant, but I love you anyway,' she murmured.

As she brushed her teeth she reflected on what Angie had said about Michael. How tired he looked, how pale. Gaunt, that was the word. Was he ill? Angie had asked. I don't know, was all Isabel could say.

She climbed into bed and tried to get comfortable. She was running out of sleeping positions. Take things as they come, accept things as they are, she thought, turning and turning again. The baby joined in. Tomorrow is another day and all that. Why *was* she thinking these things? Were they mantras to help her fall asleep?

In fact, tomorrow might be a different sort of day – it should be interesting: a journalist was coming to interview her about the experience of being an older mother. My fifteen minutes of fame, she thought, as drowsiness took over. She'd been going to mention it to Michael – it would help to have something new to fuel their exchanges of dialogue – but the right moment hadn't presented itself. He probably wouldn't be interested anyway.

'Sleep. Sleep, baby, sleep. Sleep with me,' she said.

36

Isabel was expecting the journalist at any minute. Where would they talk? The kitchen? Checking it over she found things to do. She wiped the table, swished some bleach around the sink, poured fresh water into the vase of flowers, shooed the cat off a chair.

If the sky stopped threatening rain they could go into the garden, but out of the window the clouds were grey on grey. It looked like, felt like, the calm before the storm.

The cab stopped. For a moment Ellen's legs felt like jelly and she stayed where she was until the driver looked round at her. 'This is it, love. The address you said.'

Yes, this was it, she thought, and made herself get up and get out and get on with it.

She walked slowly up the herringbone-tiled path, smoothing down her dress. Dress? What on earth had made her buy this then wear it? She felt more than uncomfortable.

The house was much as she'd expected. A family house, well looked after, in a road lined with others just the same or very similar. Solid, attractive, unpretentious. Roses around the front door, masses of them, in a deep red. All very English.

She took a deep breath and rang the bell.

It was answered by a very pregnant woman. So it is true, thought Ellen. Not that she'd seriously doubted it.

'Come in! You must be Ellen Linden? I'm Isabel.'

She smiled and put out her hand. Ellen shook it.

How tall she is, thought Isabel, and so American-looking, or at least what I think of as American: sleek blonde hair, good teeth, long tanned legs. Young and gorgeous. The dress she was wearing – a short black linen shift – made Isabel think of Jackie Kennedy, Onassis, whatever. Her shoes were flat backless loafers made of what appeared to be real snakeskin – no doubt very expensive. Well, I don't often meet people like this, she decided.

Ellen listened as Isabel chattered away, offering coffee or something cold – such a warm day, wasn't it? – though it looked like rain, so why didn't they start off in the kitchen? Ellen opted for a glass of water and followed, thinking, This is Michael's wife. A real flesh-and-blood person. More than that, there's a baby too. More flesh, more blood.

And definitely not ill, no trace of sickness. (How *could* he say that? How could he?) This woman was blooming and full of life.

And was Isabel how she expected? No, but then she'd deliberately created an unfavourable image of The Wife. Isabel was younger, prettier, livelier, *nicer* than she'd imagined. Even quite stylish, with a sharp haircut. Naturally. Michael wouldn't have married anyone less than this, would he? How could she have thought otherwise?

Ellen sat down at the kitchen table, wanting to clasp her stomach as a painful knot had formed inside it. She tried not to look right or left. Usually in these interview situations her antennae were out, she'd be noticing everything, anything that might be useful. Details that would make the interviewee and her life seem more real. Not today, not here. She didn't want to witness the minutiae of Michael's family life. Up to now she'd tried to deny its very existence and here it was staring her in the face.

She'd obtained this interview through false pretences, of course. Several ideas had been deleted or hit the wastebasket along the way. In the end she'd had a few vodkas and rung Isabel, pretending, explaining that she'd got her number from a magazine's database. And Isabel had accepted that. It could happen, for Isabel had filled out coupons in mother-and-baby magazines, she'd put herself on mailing lists, she'd sent off for catalogues, she had included her phone number.

So Isabel is a trusting person, thought Ellen. That much I knew already.

'Ellen? May I call you that? Here's your iced water.'

'Thank you. And call me Ellen, of course.'

God, she hoped the other woman hadn't noticed that her hands were shaking. Be calm, be calm. She made a big deal of getting her tape-recorder out of her bag – she wanted to postpone looking Isabel in the eye. Talking to her briefly on the phone was one thing, this was a whole new ball-game. It was going to take all her self-control and every ounce of any acting ability she might possess.

'Is this OK? You don't mind being recorded?'

'Not at all.'

Ellen checked the batteries and sound levels and said, 'I'll ask you questions and you – well, just be yourself. Talk as much as you like, say what you like.'

'I won't find that difficult!'

They began. Ellen pretended she was doing this for real – she even had a list of prepared questions in her mind, the ones she would have asked if this had been a genuine article.

Isabel was enjoying this. She had lots to say and assumed she was giving Ellen what she wanted. It was hard to tell – Ellen seemed somewhat distracted, even a little nervous. Unless she was always like this: after all, Isabel didn't know her.

She was recounting other people's reactions to her pregnancy when Dominic came loping into the kitchen, yawning, looking rough. At least he was dressed, in an old T-shirt and tracksuit trousers.

'Dominic! I didn't expect you to be up yet – oops, sorry, Ellen.'

'No problem.' Ellen leant forward and turned off the machine.

Dominic suddenly noticed there was a visitor as he headed for the fridge. 'Oh –'

His mother got up and bustled about. 'Dom, this is Ellen Linden, the journalist I told you about – at least, I think I did.' To Ellen she said, 'This is my son Dominic. He was out last night celebrating the end of his exams.'

Dominic raised his hand in Ellen's direction as he drank some orange juice.

Ellen got up abruptly. 'Could I use your loo?'

'Of course, the cloakroom is down the hall, second on the left.'

As Ellen hurried out Isabel asked her son, 'So did you have a good time?'

'Yeah, a bit too good.' He threw back his head as he

swallowed some aspirin, followed by gulps of water. 'God, my head hurts.'

'Why don't you go back to bed?'

'Yeah, I do need some more sleep. I'm going round to Will's place in a while to go over our Inter-railing routes, work out where we're staying . . . stuff like that. But not yet.'

Isabel said she'd see him later.

Ellen stood in the Turners' cloakroom running her hands under cold water. Anything to stop her shaking, stop her heart beating so fast.

She did not want to see that boy who looked so like his father.

She did not want to see these family photos on the wall, crammed collage-style into a large frame, younger versions of Michael and Isabel and the children smiling out at her, looking for all the world like a happy family.

She did not want to walk out of here, past the foot of the stairs, which led up to the bedrooms. She did not want to imagine Isabel and Michael in their marital bed. She did not want to think about his suits hanging in a closet, his shirts in different shades of blue, his shoes waiting neatly underneath, his ties on some fancy hanger.

She did not want to think about the bathroom where his toothbrush and his shaver stood on the shelf, or the basket where his laundry was tossed.

No more. This was too much. It was a form of torture.

This was Michael's *home*. She did not belong here.

She looked at herself in the mirror: her face was flushed. 'I'm not a bad person,' she said to her reflection. 'I can't do this.'

Isabel was standing looking out of the kitchen window when Ellen returned.

'It's started to rain. We were right to stay inside.' She turned towards her. 'Are you all right?

'I'm OK. Isabel, please sit down. I need to talk to you.'

Isabel sat down very slowly, sliding on to a chair, puzzled. 'What is it?'

'I've deceived you.'

'What? What do you mean? Aren't you a real journalist?

Why are you here?' Her eyes widened, her hand flew protectively to her stomach.

'Yes, yes, I am. Please – I mean you no harm. Oh, shit. But I haven't told you the truth. I came here specifically to see you, I wanted to meet you.' Ellen put her face in her hands. 'God, this is difficult.'

Isabel was standing now. 'I think you'd better tell me what this is all about, and quickly.' She gripped the back of a chair. Was this it? Was this what she'd been avoiding? A sense of doom invaded her.

'You see, I know Michael –'

'*Michael?* My husband? What's he got to do with this?'

Something clicked in Isabel's mind. Like a machine being set in motion. Click, whirr. Wheels turning, cogs interconnecting. She held her breath.

'I'm having – I've been having a relationship with Michael.'

Isabel sat down again suddenly, holding on to the table.

'What? *What?* No. Michael –? An affair? Oh, Jesus Christ.'

An undeniable whoosh of recognition thumped her in the body. She stifled a sob with her fist and continued to stare at Ellen, transfixed.

'Yes, with Michael. I'm sorry, I didn't want to alarm you, but I had to tell you. I had to tell the truth. I can understand –'

'I don't think you can understand anything about me.'

'Isabel, please. I am not treating this lightly. It *is* true. If you want I can tell you all about it, tell you things that will convince you. But I don't want to rub your nose in it – this is a completely appalling situation already. And now I know that you're pregnant, actually pregnant – well, that changes everything. You see, I've only just learned that you are.'

Part of Isabel wanted to hear more from this woman, part of her wanted to scream and shout and throw her out. Part of her wanted to look her over, at the colour of her eyes, at her breasts, at the details of her body. Her and Michael? She fought against nausea.

Slowly, she got up and poured herself a glass of mineral water then sat down again. Remember to breathe. Deep breaths. At last she said, in a small voice, 'Tell me about it – not everything, just enough. The things I need to know.' This had to be done.

Ellen started to talk. Her voice was low and hesitant. Every now and then Isabel asked her a question, When? How long? Where? But they both knew what Isabel would not ask and Ellen could not answer, the big question: Why?

Isabel heard the words but they seemed far away. They made her flinch, she wanted to stop it but she had to know. She was determined not to cry in front of her, *Ellen*, but it was so very hard.

The baby kicked. Oh no, not now baby, please. And Dom was upstairs – please, make him stay asleep. She sat up as straight as she could and managed to regain some composure, some dignity, she had the feeling that was important.

Until Ellen said something that threw her even further off-balance.

'Michael told you *what*?'

'His excuse for not leaving you was that you were ill. He implied it was serious, he gave me the impression it was gynaecological – you know how men do. I imagined you might have cancer, ovarian cancer or something awful like that. But, of course, instead . . .' Ellen gestured towards Isabel's bump.

'Oh my God.' Isabel dropped her head into her hands. When she looked up her face was white. 'That is sick. What a thing to say. How could he? How could he?'

It seemed like a double betrayal.

'I'm sorry, I'm so sorry.'

'Sorry? You're sorry?' But as she said it she knew that, rightly or wrongly, she felt little towards this girl. Her feelings were focused on Michael. He was the cause of her distress. 'I think you'd better go. I can't take much more, not now. I don't feel too well.'

'Is there anything I can do?'

Isabel laughed, a small bitter sound. 'Haven't you done enough?'

'I'm sorry, I didn't mean – Can I do anything about you not feeling well? That's what I meant.' Ellen fought back tears.

Isabel noticed. 'No, there's nothing you can do. Just go. I need to be alone, think this over. But one thing – what will you do about Michael?'

'I'm not going to see him any more, if that's what you mean. It's finished. I haven't told him yet. I wanted to see you first.'

'In a way that was brave.'

Ellen shrugged. 'Not really.'

Ellen left. Isabel stayed exactly where she was, sipping another glass of water. Time passed, of course it did, life went on. How long had she been sitting here? It could be five minutes, it could be an hour. She had to stay very still as she felt queasy and dizzy, as if she had just got off a roller-coaster. A nightmare ride. But it was no use waiting for everything to get back to normal, for the world to right itself, because there was no more normal, not now.

She must go and lie down. She switched on the answering-machine then wrote Dominic a note, telling him she was having a nap, and left it in a prominent position on the table, propped up against the bowl of apples. Hopefully he'd see it and not cover it with a cornflakes box.

Climbing the stairs she felt so very heavy, not only because of the baby. It was an effort just putting one foot in front of the other.

Isabel slipped into bed. Sadness settled upon her like a blanket. At last she allowed herself to cry. 'Sorry little one,' she said. 'I don't want to upset you.'

She must have slept. The bedside clock said it was half past three. It had stopped raining and she could see the afternoon sun through a gap in the curtains. As she stretched out, stroking her stomach, it came to her that she was experiencing some sort of relief. Now she knew what she hadn't wanted to know. What she had recoiled from she now had to face. The truth, thanks to Ellen Linden.

Surprisingly, she didn't hate this girl, her husband's lover or girlfriend or whatever she was – no, *had been*. In fact she thought that in other circumstances she would have liked her. Did she hate Michael? She couldn't describe how she felt about him at this moment. Did she even know this man? Who was he? After all their years together, marriage, children, family, how *could* he behave like this, behave so badly?

Anger was the prevailing emotion. She felt so very angry that she wanted to get hold of him and do something to him, something unexpected and violent. It wouldn't happen. Good old Isabel, wife and mother, just didn't do things like that, did she? Maybe I'll start now, she thought.

She did have to consider what to do next. She had to decide what was best for her – and the baby.

37

Isabel splashed her face again and again, trying to clear her head and reduce the puffiness from crying. She took a clean towel from the airing-cupboard and buried her face in the sweet smell of it, wanting to blot everything out. When had she ever had to deal with anything like this? I've been fortunate, she thought, I've led a charmed life.

What was she going to do? The question would not go away. Not just long-term, or even short-term, but what was she going to do *today*?

Earlier she'd rung Angie. Someone to tell, someone to confide in. No answer. Then she remembered Angie had said she was going into town today, clothes shopping, stocking up on underwear at Marks and Spencer's. 'Something I do miss in Spain,' she'd said.

Isabel considered calling Beth, but she was probably at work. Jenny was at the shop and it wouldn't be appropriate to talk there. OK, so some customers shared their problems, but she wasn't a customer, was she?

No, she decided, she wouldn't tell anyone, not yet. Not until she'd confronted Michael. This was between them.

Michael sat in a meeting in the conference room feeling disconnected, his thoughts elsewhere. All around him men in suits blaahed on. Once or twice he joined in automatically, his voice sounding as if it belonged to someone else. Two women came in, one pushing a trolley with coffee pots and cups, the other bearing aloft a large oval platter draped in clingfilm. She carried it seriously as if it were a sacrificial offering and she a handmaiden. Sandwiches. Neat little triangles with their crusts cut off (Little boys, are we? he wondered), nestling together in a bed of watercress. He'd avoid the tuna – he couldn't stand the lingering smell of it on his fingers.

He was so pissed off: he couldn't get in touch with Ellen. It had been like this for days. Her machine was on the whole time and she hadn't called him. Just before this meeting he'd tried her number again and there was her voice with a new message saying that she'd had to go to the States urgently. And that was it.

Could this be true? Why hadn't she contacted him? Or maybe her silence was significant, a way of trying to tell him something . . . What had he done? Perhaps he'd go round there and keep ringing her bell and see what happened.

It would have to wait until tomorrow. The meeting went on and on, then there were still things to do – he'd have to work late again. (It had happened a lot recently, so he'd actually been telling Isabel the truth about where he'd been.) Eventually he staggered home exhausted. Home. A place to sleep.

The lights were all out except for the one in the hall. There was a note from Dominic on the table, saying he'd gone to Will's, back late. Michael assumed Isabel was in bed.

He went into the kitchen to hunt for something to eat.

A noise behind him.

'Oh dear, did I make you jump?'

Something in her voice – an unfamiliar edge? – whipped him round.

'Isabel! I thought you were in bed.'

She appeared from the darkness beyond the room and stood there holding her robe close to her. Christ, how pregnant she looked – he still hadn't really got used to it. Vulnerable, too, he thought. Bigger, yet smaller. And her eyes were red, her face crumpled. He began to move towards her, 'Isabel, what's the –'

She held up her hand, as if to stop him. 'I've had a little surprise today. A visitor. Ellen Linden.' She said the name very slowly.

'What?' He crashed on to a chair. She knew. Oh, Jesus. What could he say? This is what it would feel like to be sucked into a maelstrom. Male storm, he thought. Female storm.

'I hope you're not going to try to deny it.'

No words would come anyway, for his mind was whirling trying to take this in. What was Ellen doing, telling Isabel? And how come she'd been here today, when her phone message said she'd had to go to New York? It didn't make sense. Oh, shit. He put his face in his hands.

'Yes, Michael, hide your face. You should. You're lucky that I'm too tired and too upset – no, too angry – to discuss this now. Obviously I know what you've been up to. *Ellen* filled me in. A big mistake was to tell her that I was ill. In a way I find that harder to take than the – the affair. It upset her too. I –'

'How did she find out?'

'Is that all you've got to say? *How did she find out?* Is that what you care about? You have to know, you have to have all the facts – you're such a fucking control freak. God, even now. What about me? What about this baby? You fucking bastard.'

She held on to her stomach and sat down heavily on a chair opposite him.

He was shocked – Isabel hardly ever swore.

'Surprised, Michael? Shocked by my language? Good old Isabel, such a good girl, docs what she's told, does what's expected of her, always so well behaved.'

'I think you're confusing me with your father.'

He regretted it as soon as he said it. Where had that come from? Stupid, stupid, stupid. And cheap, he thought, cringing inside.

She slammed her hand down on the table. Her voice grew even louder. 'That's it! I can't find words enough to express how contemptible you are. Even now you have to be the smart-arse.'

'I'm sorry, Isabel, I'm sorry.'

'Oh? Sorry for which bit exactly? How many sorries can you possibly say?'

She fetched herself a glass of water. He remained silent, an ache gnawing away at his stomach. Was it hunger or fear? He was desperate for a drink but did not dare move.

'I've had hours of thinking about this, Michael. I don't want any pathetic explanations, I don't want any more lies. What I've decided for now is this. So listen: I want to go away to Devon. I don't know for how long, maybe a week or two. I'll let you know when I'm coming back – and I think it would be best if you weren't here. Does that funny expression on your face mean you think you can go to Ellen? I think you'll find she has other ideas!'

What the hell did she mean? Jesus, it was as if he were being torn apart. Half of him wanted to know about Ellen, what she'd said, what she was doing, the other half knew he should be paying attention to Isabel, dealing with her shock, her hurt ... Rent asunder. That was him. A biblical phrase, how appropriate. All he needed now was some sort of divine intervention, wreaking vengeance upon him. But this was like a scene from hell already, the worst nightmare. He would never have wished it, never have started it – yet, of course, he had caused it, he knew that. Witnessing Isabel sitting there shaking, more upset than he'd ever seen her, he feared for her. Supposing this brought on the baby prematurely? Oh, God –

'Michael! Are you listening to me?'

'Yes, yes. Isabel, please, you can't –'

'Don't tell me what I can and can't say or do. Don't even try it. How dare you? Surely you've thrown away any right to do that?'

'Oh, Isabel.'

'I'm not surprised you're speechless. After all, where would you start? And I'm glad because I don't want to *talk*.' She spat the word out. 'I don't want to discuss it, at least not yet. Or hear any paltry excuses from you. I'm trying to hold on here, keep myself together. That's all I can do right now. I have no energy for anything else.'

'So you're saying you want me to go ... Temporarily or what?'

'Yes ... No ... I don't know, for God's sake!'

'How will we explain things to the children?'

'Oh, you're thinking of them *now*, are you? We don't have to explain anything yet. Luckily Gemma's away. As for Dom, I think we should behave as if nothing has happened for the few days before he leaves.'

'Isabel! Is that –'

'Don't look so shocked, Michael. I'm sure we can keep up a front of some sort of normality until the weekend, it's only a day or two. And you're good at it, remember? Lying, pretending, faking it ... You've had lots of practice.'

'You seem to have all this worked out.'

'Don't be ridiculous, I have nothing worked out! How could I? I'm struggling here. My instinct was to flee to Devon, be on

262

my own, try to sort it all out in my mind. Then I thought I couldn't let Dom down, I should be here until he goes away. I would have liked to leave you to deal with things . . . but I found I couldn't.'

Michael groaned, involuntarily. He was trying to remain silent and stoical in the face of her onslaught, but it was overwhelming, all of it.

'Oh dear, Michael. Is this too much for you? Just remember this whole appalling situation is of your making.'

'Is it? Entirely of my making?' Despite a small voice in his head telling him he had no case, let it go, he continued, 'Well, what about you getting pregnant? And insisting on having the baby, regardless of how I felt? Marginalising me?' He refrained from saying that he hadn't wanted another child, Ellen or no Ellen.

'Oh, please. That won't wash. It's no excuse for what you've done.' She wearily pushed herself up from the chair and said, 'I'm pregnant by *you*, remember? Look at me. It's unfair of you to use that – how could you? I'm going to bed.'

'So . . . that's it, Isabel?'

'For now.'

Michael sat immobile. He was lost for words. Lost. There were no words to describe this situation . . . His lover had been to see his wife. He shuddered as he attempted to imagine it. They had talked in some sort of way; he had been discussed. Now Isabel knew everything – or most of it, he presumed. And what did it mean that Ellen had other ideas? What did Isabel know about Ellen that he didn't?

In bed Isabel lay as still as she could, hoping that would encourage sleep to come. It didn't. Her mind was a jumble, thoughts raced through it, disordered, confused. Thank God I've already been sleeping here in the spare room, I've got a safe place, I haven't got to share a bed with him. But did *that* drive us apart? *Was* it the pregnancy?

Wait a minute.

She remembered what Ellen had told her about the seeming seriousness of the affair . . . about how long it had been going on. Long before she got pregnant, months before. So why did he do it? Why? What was wrong with her? Or with the marriage?

Wait a minute.

If it had been going on that long, it meant he'd been having sex with them both. The bastard. She could weep at the humiliation of it.

The baby stirred gently inside her. All this turmoil couldn't be doing her daughter any good, thought Isabel dismally. Only recently she'd read about more research which showed that stress and arguments and maternal distress could adversely affect unborn babies. The thought of that was enough to make her even more distressed.

Enough, she decided. No weeping. I'm all right, the baby's all right, we'll come through this. And she thought of women all over the world, past and present, having babies in dire circumstances. Refugee women; homeless women; women in prison; deserted women; starving women; women alone; women in war; women whose partners had disappeared; women whose husbands had been snatched by death squads; women who could do nothing to help themselves.

'So we're all right, my little one,' Isabel said.

Count those blessings – would it work?

Gemma and Dominic were fine, they'd be all right – she'd done a good job with them, hadn't she? She had a home (two, in fact), she had money, she had friends, she was healthy. She had a lot to be grateful for.

Practical matters: she turned to those, and took refuge in making lists in her head of things to do before she left for Devon.

Speak to Dominic about his trip – did he need any supplies, clothes, things she could buy? Check antenatal appointments, ring the midwife. Talk to her friends . . . Tell Angie and Jenny and Beth what had happened. Obviously she would share this with them and feel the strength of their support but . . . But she wanted to keep the commiserations and wailing and screaming to a minimum. And somehow she felt it would be better, for her and the baby, if she didn't discuss the awfulness of Michael at great length. With anyone.

She sighed and closed her eyes and it was as if some of the

264

anger and the hurt was seeping out of her, like blood from an open wound.

Soon after dawn Michael crept out of the house. He hadn't slept, he couldn't eat any breakfast. He understood the word turmoil.

There was something he had to do. Ellen. The message on her phone was the same but he knew it wasn't true, she couldn't be in New York – after all, she'd visited Isabel yesterday, hadn't she?

He drove to her street and took up position outside her flat. It was half past six. London was still pretty empty. There was a strange quiet that he wasn't used to, but it would all come to life soon. For now he would wait, he would do this for as long as it took. He was on watch.

It wasn't like in the movies, though – she had no regular routine, no office to go to. There was no doorman he could quiz, no neighbours he could ask. But she'd have to go to meetings or the gym or shopping, wouldn't she? That is, if she was in there. But he was sure she was, he just felt it.

How he wished he had some coffee and a newspaper. But he couldn't leave his post.

A little before eight Ellen appeared in the doorway of her building. Stepped on to the pavement, looked at the sky, turned left. He could see that she was dressed for the gym. She began walking fast, head down, carrying her sports bag.

He leapt from his car and ran in front of her.

She was forced to stop. 'Michael. Get out of my way or do you want a scene on the street?'

'Ellen, please. I need to talk to you. Can't we talk?

'No, we can't. I have no desire to speak to you, to go over it all with you. I just want to *get* over it.'

'Please, can't we just go upstairs?'

'No! I don't want you in my home. And there is no *we*.'

She moved to one side slightly as if to walk past him.

He blocked her. 'What do you mean?'

'Isn't it obvious? "*We*" no longer exist. *Finito*. You cheated and lied – and not just to your wife.'

Early office workers were walking by, giving them a wide berth or crossing to the other side of the road.

'Ellen, please, whatever I've done –'

'Whatever you've *done*? Oh, you've done plenty! Did you really think you could come to me and expect us to carry on? Did you imagine we could ride off happily into the sunset? You've been cheating on your pregnant wife, for Christ's sake! Pregnant by *you*! So much deception, Michael. How could you? And she – Isabel's not even the kind of person you made her out to be. I liked her . . .'

As she faltered he stepped towards her. If only he could touch her, if only he could hold her, get her upstairs, explain . . . But explain what exactly? And how?

Ellen swung at him with her bag, hitting him on the shoulder. 'Now do you get the message, you sad man? Leave me alone!'

As she went to push past him she took something from a pocket of her bag and thrust it into his hands. A micro-tape. 'A little gift. Listen to my so-called interview with your wife. You could get off on it, who knows? I've been carrying it around in case you sprang out at me – I thought you might. Now, go away. Don't try this again – I'm going back to New York soon. For real. OK?'

She was gone, running. He put the tape in his pocket and got back in the car. I am a sad man, he thought, but not in the way she means. What the fuck? Probably in that way too.

38

Folding sweaters had a certain satisfaction, Jenny had decided. Shake, flatten and smooth, line up, fold and fold again. It left your mind free to wander and the tidy end result was pleasing. Lately she often thought about Bill when she did this, their developing intimacy, how much they laughed together, the surprising ease of it all. Today, however, Isabel was on her mind.

She looked up to see Isabel and Angie approaching the shop. Why is my heart thumping? thought Jenny. Ever since Isabel had rung this morning and she'd learnt about Michael, what he'd *done*, she'd experienced this weird feeling. She didn't want to admit it, even to herself, but it was a kind of excitement. So, it had happened to Isabel too! Even she wasn't immune. Michael had betrayed Isabel in the same tawdry, banal way that Graham had betrayed her; Michael was as pathetic as the countless other middle-aged men who behaved in the same way. She slammed the grey sweater she'd been folding on to a pile. Let it go, she told herself. Who knew what really happened between a couple? Who knew what the real story was? If there *was* one real story, more likely several versions of several truths.

They came through the door, talking quietly. On seeing Isabel, looking tired and so very pregnant, Jenny felt a twinge of shame, that she should have found any gratification, however fleeting, in her friend's predicament. She rushed towards her to give her a hug.

I've joined the club, Isabel thought as Jenny's sympathy enfolded her.

Angie and Jenny fussed around her, putting the Closed sign up on the shop door, making tea for her and coffee for them, all the while darting concerned glances in her direction.

This is Day One, she thought. This is how it is now. Was it really only yesterday that she'd had the visit from Ellen and her confrontation with Michael?

She looked from Angie to Jenny, sipping coffee, waiting for her to talk. They knew the bare facts, that was all. She hadn't yet revealed the extent of Michael's deception, of what he had told Ellen about her being ill. That stuck in her throat, she might never tell anyone that nasty little detail, and maybe in the future it would seem as if he'd never said it, had never piled trickery on treachery.

She smiled at her friends. 'I am OK, *really*. I've got to be, for the sake of the baby.' She patted her bump.

'You're being very brave,' whispered Jenny, words and emotions catching in her throat. Angie murmured her agreement.

'Look, people have far worse things happen to them than this.' Isabel tried to sound cheerful. 'No one's died or anything.'

They all reached for the counter to touch wood.

'Even so,' said Angie, 'it must have been an enormous shock. Having her come to see you, telling you like that.'

A sharp intake of breath from Jenny. 'I can't imagine such a thing.'

'Well, in a way it made it more real, meeting her, seeing her. Rather than Michael telling me half-truths or whatever . . .' Her voice trailed away. Her mouth had gone dry. She didn't want this, to tell the story, let the drama unfold. To allow her life to be pored over by others, even with the best of intentions. She got up suddenly. 'Must go to the loo.' She actually did need to, the baby was probably pressing on her bladder, it wasn't just to escape.

As Isabel came back into the shop she could hear Angie and Jenny talking about her. Of course they were, she'd do the same.

'. . . that's Izzy for you, always good at bearing up.'

'. . . think she's being amazing. Anyway, I can look after things here while you go to Devon with her.'

They turned. Angie said, 'I was just explaining to Jenny about you going away for a bit.'

'Yes. Can you manage here, Jen? I won't leave until the weekend but I don't know how long I'll be gone, at least a week probably.'

'I'll be fine. Don't worry about a thing. Oh, you know what I mean.'

'I do, Jenny. It's OK. You don't have to watch everything you say to me you know, I won't break!'

They smiled, not quite reassured.

'But listen, Izzy,' Angie said, 'We don't think you should go off on your own. I'm going to come with you. I insist.'

Isabel could not argue. Suddenly she felt full of weariness.

Her sights were fixed on the next few days, that was enough. All she had to do was get through them. She kept telling herself that she mustn't cry, just hold on. It became a refrain. Isabel imagined that when she got to Devon she could collapse and let it all out, although there would still be the baby to think of. Her constant companion.

The sympathy and kindness of her friends was unexpectedly hard to take for it knocked her off track, threatening her resolve to hold back the floodtide of emotion. She gritted her teeth and carried on.

She'd switched to automatic pilot, that seemed the best way of dealing with things for now. Michael got up early, went to work as usual, and came home late. They avoided each other. So what's new? she thought.

Dominic was wrapped up in the anticipation of his imminent departure, so he didn't seem to notice that everything was not as it should be. And why should he? Things hadn't been as they should be for some time, even longer than she'd realised. And had *she* noticed? If she had, she'd opted to ignore it.

Her son was a welcome distraction. She insisted that he sat down with her to run through a list of things he was going to take on his trip. (Lists, what would she do without them? They shaped her life, gave it some sort of meaning.) At first he protested that he didn't need her help, he'd got things sorted, but after ten minutes or so he relaxed and admitted there might be some things he hadn't thought of.

They went shopping together (something they hadn't done for ages) to get a first-aid kit and toothpaste and traveller's cheques, and some basics from Gap. Incredible, she'd thought, as they drove to Richmond, he doesn't seem to mind being seen with me, with his pregnant mother. One step forward . . .

On Saturday morning Dominic banged down the stairs, tugging his huge rucksack. The pockets bulged, the drawstring barely tied.

'You OK, Mum? Come on, you're not getting tearful about me leaving?'

'Not really.' She smiled at him. 'Anyway you're only away for the summer.'

'Not even that. Got to come back for my A-level results, remember?'

'Of course. Now, don't worry about those. Just go and have a good time. But be careful!'

'Yeah, yeah. If I can have a good time while being careful!'

'Don't tease! And try to ring us occasionally. You've got that international phone card, haven't you?'

'Dom! Are you ready?' Michael called from the hall. He was taking his son to the station to meet the others.

''Bye, then, Mum.' Isabel hugged him as best she could without squeezing him against her bump. Over his shoulder she saw Michael through the doorway, their eyes met for a second before he bowed his head and pretended to examine his car keys.

Her bag was packed, she was ready to go. Jasper had to come too – he couldn't be left here on his own all day while Michael was out. Or when Michael was gone. 'Come on, Jasper old thing, move yourself.'

As she was about to leave Michael returned. Damn, she thought.

'So you're off to Devon now?'

'You know I am.'

'Are you sure you're all right to go on your own?'

'Isn't your concern for me a little late?'

'Oh, Isabel . . .'

'Anyway, I'm not going on my own. Angie insists on coming with me.'

'I see.'

He looked at her and looked at her. She sensed that he wanted to talk, to tell her things, but she was not going to listen, not now.

'I'm going. Jasper's coming with me but you'll feed Willow?'

'Of course I'll feed the bloody cat! Isabel –'

'I'll ring you from Devon. And I do think it would be better if you moved out while I'm away.'

'Jesus Christ.' He ran his hands desperately through his hair. 'And who will feed the cat if I do that?' Another stupid remark – why do I do it? he wondered. Substituting sarcasm for what I really want to say.

Isabel chose to take his words at face value. 'Jenny. Just ask her. Goodbye, Michael.'

Isabel drove slowly, trying to keep her mind on the road. Angie sat next to her and resolutely kept her company, chattering about nothing much. 'Oh look, Iz, we've just passed three Belgian cars in a row, do you think they're together?' Then, trawling through their mutual past, offering up incidents for Isabel's amusement, 'Remember that time with those boys from Exeter?' Switching to Spain and the landscape there and Maxi's horses . . .

Whole swathes of motorway flashed by without Isabel registering any of it. How did I get here? she thought, as she drew up to the service station at Taunton Deane. The car park appeared to be full of dusty Volvo estates piled with stuff, not luggage but indiscriminate *stuff*. Perhaps they were all antiques dealers.

Angie insisted that Isabel should have something to eat and went off to queue with a tray while Isabel sat in the non-smoking section and waited. Who are all these people, pouring tea and eating doughnuts? she thought, and felt depressed.

The last stage of the journey. She was getting tired, her back ached.

'Are you sure I can't drive?' Angie asked.

'Best not. I don't think the insurance covers you.' And, Isabel *didn't* say, 'Your driving is erratic, Angie, you take your hands off the wheel too often to make gestures while you talk.'

The red field, her red field, came into view. Could it be the same one that she'd seen in the spring, or was it a subtle substitution?

The sun shone in a wide, wide sky. It was a beautiful day. She'd only just noticed.

'Do you know, I'm looking forward to this, Izzy? It's been a long time since I was down here.'

Isabel was about to reply that she was glad she'd given Angie an excuse to come, but she stopped herself. What's the matter with me? I mustn't let what's happened make me bitter. If she didn't deal with this, if she tried to shut it away, it could curdle and sour inside her. But I'll deal with it in my own time and my own way, no one can tell me how or when.

She concentrated on the road ahead. Dartmoor lay in the distance. A wonderful big white cloud sat in the sky and her eyes were pulled to it, in appreciation of its shape and texture. Fluffy but solid. It made you want to roll in it. Can you fall in love with a cloud? she wondered.

The cottage at last.

'You go and sit down,' said Angie. 'I'll bring the bags in.'

'I'd rather stretch my legs in the garden. Come on, Jasper.'

Everything was in full bloom. The grass needed cutting. She wandered, deadheading flowers, Jasper bounding around her. The sound of bees, a distant tractor, the panting of the dog, that's all. Isabel sighed.

Angie called out of the kitchen window, 'Izzy, do you mind if I phone Spain? I want to tell Maxi where I am.'

'Course not, go ahead.'

She'd sit in the garden for a bit, close her eyes in the sun. As she struggled with the old steamer chair, pulling it out of the shed with difficulty, trying to unfold it, shouting, 'Come on, open up you bastard,' she began to cry.

Angie stayed for three days. While Isabel struggled with the reality of what had happened to her marriage, her life, while she attempted to come to terms with what she'd lost, Angie tussled with her lover on the phone. Maxi wanted to know what she was doing, who she was with . . . Above all, she wanted to know when Angie was coming back. How could a relationship prosper if the couple weren't together? And she needed Angie, she said, she really did.

Isabel and Angie went for a walk on Dartmoor, they mingled with the summer crowds in Dartmouth and on impulse embarked on a river trip up to Totnes. They talked of old times, they laughed a little, but their hearts were not in it. They both had other things to think about.

Eventually Angie said, 'I'm going back to Spain, to Max. I do miss her, I even miss the place. I want to give it a try, see how it works out. We all have to compromise, don't we, Izzy?'

Isabel took her to the station, then drove slowly back to the cottage. Solitude beckoned. After all, she thought, we have to cope with all the major life events on our own: being born, giving birth, dying . . . We may have people around us, but fundamentally we're on our own, we have to do it ourselves.

Solitude is what I need, she thought. A time to weep, a time to wallow, a time to please myself.

She slowed right down, slept a lot, sat in the garden, walked by the sea. Beth rang, and Jenny, and she reassured them that she was coping, whatever that meant. Next door Connie and

Erica were there if she needed them. Sometimes she did. They cosseted her and made her feel important but tactfully did not ask too many questions. 'We only want to know what you want to tell us, my dear,' Connie had said. She gave them the bare bones of it, that was enough.

Michael had once jokingly suggested that they might be witches. Perhaps he was right. She could ask them to put a spell on him. But to what end?

And as for Michael, what should she do?

She would do nothing, not yet.

He had rung her, twice.

To see how she was, he said the first time. She'd assured him she was fine – *without him*, she could have said, but didn't. He'd wanted to linger on the phone, she could tell. There was a reluctance to say goodbye (ironic, she thought, like a young lover), he'd kept trying to spin out the conversation, repeatedly asking if she was sure she was all right.

He's probably lonely, she thought. No me, no Ellen. And miserable – she could hear that in his voice.

What she did not know was that he had been desperately unnerved by listening to the tape that Ellen had thrust at him. He'd kept it in his pocket for days, wanting to throw it away but finding himself unable to. Discarding this small piece of Ellen, this piece of Isabel, would have been too much, another small betrayal. Of them both. One evening at home (what an empty place it was, just him and the cat) he had gone into his study with a large glass of whisky, found the mini-cassette recorder in his desk drawer and played it. Ellen's voice, clear and efficient, brief questions. Isabel's voice – and there was much more of Isabel's voice – talking about being pregnant, laughing, being self-deprecatory. And honest. He froze as he heard Isabel talk about her doubts, about her age, about her fears . . . It was revelatory. He hadn't credited her with half of those feelings, he hadn't tried to *understand*. Too concerned with my own agenda, he thought.

It was painful hearing Isabel being so open, talking like that to Ellen, of all people. To her husband's lover. Her innocence pained him. And it was additionally excruciating, knowing that she was about to find out . . . Like those poignant photographs of soldiers in the First World War relaxing in the trenches, having a smoke and a chat, reading letters from home, caught in that moment of time before they were ordered to go over the top. No, not so bad, Michael thought, Isabel wasn't about to *die* . . . But she was about to have her life undone.

Meanwhile, he heard her laugh and say that being pregnant wasn't so bad, babies could be delightful . . . and you felt strong and powerful and it was good to be female sometimes . . . Ellen had laughed too and he sensed that a warmth, an intimacy was developing between them – he replayed parts of the tape and listened more acutely. How did women do it? he wondered. Making contact, feeling sympathy for each other, whatever the circumstances. It made him feel inadequate.

He heard Isabel refer to him, saying that her husband wasn't too happy about the pregnancy, that she hoped he'd come round. Ellen was silent then.

As the tape continued, ending with a click after Dominic had obviously entered the room (Dom? There?) Michael had felt himself wilting under more and more layers of emotion. Shame piled on guilt, misery on anguish, self-pity on regret.

He had to ring Isabel in Devon, to hear her voice directly, to see how she was.

The second time he rang, a few days later, Isabel had asked when he was leaving. He'd mumbled that he was taking care of it. (He'd done nothing yet.) After he rang off, he knew that he must take action – this was the one thing she had asked of him. He had to respect that. Moving out would be a lonely and dispiriting thing to do, but he knew he had to start serving a real apprenticeship of pain.

One bright morning Isabel awoke feeling stronger. As she listened to the birds singing outside she waited for the usual mist of misery to hover over her but it did not appear. Heaving herself out of bed she went downstairs to the kitchen, which was filled with sunlight. And tranquillity. Everything was still and quiet; only Jasper stirred in his basket in the corner. Through the window she could see small brown rabbits hopping across the lawn, nibbling the grass. Hop, nibble, hop.

She smiled, although they could decimate the garden, strip the plants bare. So be it. She felt a certain tolerance towards the world today. And optimism, she felt a spark of that too.

She knew that she had to go forward – that was one thing pregnancy made you do, as it advanced slowly but relentlessly. A flash of memory: in labour with Gemma (it was taking so long), when she'd been shouting and insisting that she didn't want to do this, she wanted to go home, in a lucid moment between contractions she'd suddenly realised that there were few things in life that were inevitable. The fact that the baby would come out, sooner or later, one way or another, was one of them.

Back to the baby, this baby. That was where her focus should be.

'You and me, babe,' she said to her unborn daughter.

It was time to return to London, she decided, to pick up the pieces and move on. There were responsibilities: the shop, the house, everything. Most of all she had to prepare for the birth of her baby, only six or seven weeks away.

Time to get on with her life, the life she had.

39

Michael ripped open the bag of pre-washed gourmet salad and let the leaves fall into a bowl. Some of them, with red stalks, he didn't recognise. He shook the bottle of ready-made vinaigrette and struggled with the top, then poured that on to the salad. In a minute the microwave would ping, telling him he could eat his Indian-influenced medium-hot meal for one. For him, this was cooking. Instant meal, instant dressing, instant salad.

Instant, easy. Wasn't that how he'd imagined life with Ellen would be? (Now he'd never know, but he thought about it, when he wasn't thinking about Isabel.) It was a fantasy life, he understood that much. But Ellen herself? He was finding it difficult to recall her with clarity, he couldn't summon up her face, it blurred in his mind. Had he ever seen her clearly? Was she instant too, an instant introduction to a new life?

So many things he didn't know; so many things he was

trying to understand. There had been sexual chemistry between him and Ellen, that was for sure. But what else? He suspected he'd been drawn to her otherness, her American-ness. She didn't come with all that baggage of the English, the class-ridden snobbery, the attention to backgrounds, accents, schooling . . .

Yet she must have had baggage of her own. He realised that he'd known little of her life. Maybe he hadn't wanted to, that instant thing again. Perhaps he hadn't cared enough.

His meal was over quickly – eating alone didn't take long. He couldn't help being reminded of family meals, Sunday lunches when the children were small. Cutting up food for Gemma, playing that game with a spoon as a train – or was it a plane? – encouraging her to try avocado or broccoli ('Tree, tree,' she'd said); Dominic in his high-chair, messy and noisy, his bib all crooked and covered with puréed carrot or mashed banana . . . Trying to conduct a conversation with Isabel at the same time, ending up laughing at the merry chaos of it all. Long ago. Vivid details, sharp slivers of memory brought the past alive, although it was as if that past belonged to someone else. It *was* me, he thought, and I was happy.

He remembered suppers with Isabel, spaghetti Bolognese or a simple risotto. The children were in bed, and they'd sit at the kitchen table and eat and talk and drink and he'd tell her about his day at work . . . How he'd look forward to coming home, to the warm, bright house – and his wife. He shuddered. What had happened? How did he – they – get to this point? It wasn't just because of the affair with Ellen, was it?

Michael sighed and put a plate or two and some cutlery in the dishwasher, wiped the worktop, threw away the food packaging – clearing up didn't take long either.

The flat was small, the kitchen was a corner of the open-plan living area. It may be an efficient way to live but it meant the smell of Chicken Pasanda still hung in the air.

But I'm lucky in some ways, he thought. He'd found this place quickly enough: all it had taken was a phone call to the agents, a flash of a card, references, a signature on an agreement and a direct-debit form. Arranged in a day. Easy, instant. That's because he was a middle-aged man with good credit rating; a solid, respectable person. So here he was in a small rented flat. *Paying rent.* It seemed bizarre to him: it was so long since he'd done that. But, then, his whole life seemed bizarre now; nothing was as it should be.

The evening yawned in front of him. He seemed to have so much time on his hands now. No commitments. No family life. What used he to do when he wasn't working late or seeing Ellen? Before that? Help Dominic with his homework, talk to him about sport or driving lessons; discuss the rights and wrongs of animal rights or legalising cannabis with Gemma (and probably end up arguing), try to pin her down about her future . . . Those suppers with Isabel. And doing the crossword together – he'd forgotten how they used to do that. Always Isabel, always there. She was – had been? – part of the very fabric of his life. And he missed her, how he missed her. He even missed the things he used to complain about, the irritations and aggravations of family life, minor things, he could see that now. He missed the whole damn thing.

He debated whether to load the washing-machine as its noise reverberated throughout the flat and made it hard to watch television or listen to the radio. But there was no arguing with the pile of dirty laundry. He still wasn't used to this: scrutinising the labels on his clothes, squinting to read the small print of the washing instructions, decoding the dials and numbers on the machine, trying to work out how much powder to use . . . A grown man, an educated man, yet he found these tasks taxing. Pathetic, he knew that, but Isabel had always done these things. And he'd taken it for granted – taken *her* for granted. She'd done so many things for him, that much was becoming obvious. Little things, big things. He was beginning to understand how much, the extent of it, the depth. Not just the damn washing, for Christ's sake, but all manner of things, supporting and encouraging him, listening, loving . . . The things that bound a marriage together. And kept him together, he suspected.

He stood and looked out of his fifth-floor window. Nice and secure up here, the agent had said. Michael had agreed, not wishing to discuss the various meanings of 'secure'. But now he felt far from secure: at times he felt as if he'd been cast adrift. Floating, just, with no map or compass or resources on a sea with no horizon . . . Lost.

Dusk – a melancholy time, he thought. The walkways of the Barbican lay below, and he just had a glimpse of the ornamental stretch of water and the fountains, not that they were functioning at the moment. There were few people about. He snapped the blinds shut and turned to the sofa and television, just a few steps away.

The flat wasn't so bad. Recently decorated, already furnished, to what the agent called an *executive* standard. That had made Michael smile, briefly. But it was impersonal, rather like a hotel room. Smart, serviceable. He supposed he could jazz it up a bit, *personalise* it. But he'd brought very little with him from home (*home*), mainly clothes, that was all. He wasn't about to go out and start buying things – that would mean admitting that he was staying here, that *this was it*.

He slumped on the sofa and switched on the television to try to avoid the questions that had taken up residence in his mind, questions about him and Isabel and the future, to which he had no answers.

All these channels and nothing to watch. He pressed the remote control again and again, creating a mad montage of quick-change images, which horribly began to make some sort of sense, then eventually settled for a rerun of *ER*.

Isabel had always liked this programme (maybe she was watching it now). She knew who the characters were, what their history was. Sometimes he had half watched it with her. Oh, no, the story-line concerned a pregnant woman, a very pregnant woman, who appeared to be in danger of losing both her baby and her life, for reasons he couldn't quite grasp. Noise and confusion and shouting.

He turned it off.

Functioning wasn't too much of a problem, and Michael managed it day by day. He went to work, did his job, earned the money – wasn't that what he always did? He was still paying the mortgage on the family home (of course), his salary still went into the joint account, which Isabel continued to use. They hadn't discussed money, but then they hadn't discussed *anything*.

He rang her every day or so and they had unsatisfactory, awkward exchanges, but he needed to hear her voice, to reassure himself that she was still there. It eased his feeling of being lost, just a little. As she spoke he would imagine her at home, in the kitchen or bedroom or wherever. Once he'd asked where she was, and when she'd replied, 'At home, of course,' in a snappy way, he'd insisted she told him which room, where exactly. Her tone suggested she found the question intrusive. He didn't ask again.

He did keep asking how she was, he tried different ways of saying it as he was becoming repetitive. For he found he worried about her. After all, she was pregnant, she was living alone. Suppose she slipped in the bath, suppose she tripped on the stairs? So he had to keep ringing, and asking. One night he dared mention that he was concerned and her reply was that it was a bit late for that. He understood.

Their conversations ran dry. Isabel would relay news of Dominic and Gemma but otherwise ignored his efforts to open up the conversation. He tried to talk about practical things, he tried to discuss possible ways of proceeding, to decide what they were going to tell the children. Things they had to do jointly. Surely that was reasonable? But she was resolute: she did not, would not, talk about it yet. He got nowhere. That's where I am, he thought, nowhere.

There was no one else he could talk to. When he looked about him he realised that he had no friends. Acquaintances, colleagues, but no friends. Not of his own.

People at the office seemed to know about his new circumstances: he'd given his secretary his new address and number, so of course they knew *something*. They looked at him differently, they smiled sympathetically. James smirked at him and Michael suspected that he had been instrumental in telling Ellen, but he had no desire for confrontation. James had no significance, not in the wider scheme of things.

He'd been living in the flat for almost a month when Henry, the most senior partner, invited him to a summer party, a Sunday daytime thing he called it. 'Do you good, Michael, come and socialise,' he said.

Perhaps it would, thought Michael. His social life, if that's what it was, had lately comprised going to a couple of films at the Barbican, and a concert. He hardly even went to the gym any more – it was too demanding, he didn't have the energy. So he'd go to this party. Anyway, office etiquette made it hard to refuse.

Michael stood on the stone terrace of Henry's fine Hampshire home and looked at his glorious garden dotted with antique statuary, discreetly chained down. He sipped a glass of champagne and watched two small children chasing each other around the neatly clipped bushes, shrieking with laughter. He thought of Dominic and Gemma, how they used to love playing hide and seek in Richmond Park among the trees, how he'd kept a discreet but constant eye on them, just in case. He swallowed hard as he remembered how Dominic used to hide behind young trees, their trunks too thin to conceal him, his hair or an arm or leg showing, but Michael pretended anyway . . .

And he thought of Isabel, of how it must be nearly time for her to have the baby. Christ, he didn't actually know the projected date. Why didn't he? Had she ever told him?

A woman came and stood beside him. 'Hello,' she said, in a husky voice. 'I'm told that you're Michael.'

He turned to look at her. Tall, attractive, late thirties probably, a generous mouth. She wore a long straight column of a dress, in lilac, which looked more like a slip to him.

'Yes, I'm Michael. Hello.' Better go through the motions, he thought, be polite. Remember to smile.

'I'm Georgie, well, Georgina actually.'

'But everyone calls you Georgie?'

'How did you guess?' Her eyes narrowed. Maybe because of the sun, maybe something else, Michael thought.

She told him she was a friend of Julia, Henry's wife, she told him she was an interior designer, she told him lots of things about herself. It was clear that she wanted to flirt. She *was* flirting. Michael knew that he'd forgotten how.

'I'm divorced,' she said. 'How about you?'

He hesitated. She waited, smiling at him.

'Er, I'm married.'

'Oh. I heard that you were separated.'

'Did you now? Was I being set up?'

'Only in the nicest possible way.' That wide smile again,

showing lots of big strong teeth. They transfixed him. 'Michael?'

'Sorry. I'm sort of separated, I don't know. It might be temporary, might not.'

'Tough, isn't it? It'll get better.'

Separated: is that what I am? he was thinking. Detached, displaced. I'm a sad man in limbo, but you couldn't say that to attractive women at parties, could you?

'Hope so. Anyway, you must excuse me.'

'Oh, are you off already? We've hardly got to know each other.'

'Yes, sorry, something in London, got to go.'

'Let me give you my number, maybe we could get together for a drink.' She fished a card out of her beaded bag and pushed it into his hand. He glanced at it, she lived (worked?) in Fulham.

'Thanks, nice meeting you, 'bye.'

As he drove fast up the M3 the panicky feeling in his chest began to subside. If only there really was something bringing him urgently back to London.

He stopped at a Tesco superstore off the motorway and bought a pile of Sunday papers, food, and a bottle of Scotch. That should fill the rest of the day. Georgie's card he dropped in a rubbish bin in the car park. He wasn't ready for flirting or sex, for anything.

Late in the evening he looked at the whisky bottle and saw that it was half empty. What now? Drink the rest, drink himself into oblivion?

God, how he wanted his old life back. Isabel, his children, his home . . . What had he done? Had he thrown it all away? Not really, he thought, lucid for a moment, it's all still there, but I can't have it.

He rang Isabel. At last she answered and said he'd woken her. When he tried to express himself, to say how sorry he was, truly he was, she told him he was getting sentimental and that he'd drunk too much. Then she was gone.

He struggled with the weight of the phone directory and the print danced before his eyes. Eventually he found the number he wanted.

'Hello?' A young female voice answered. Must be Beth's daughter – God, what was her name? He felt ashamed that he couldn't remember. Why didn't he know these things? He asked for her mother.

'Beth, it's Michael. Michael Turner.'

'I know who you are, Michael.' She waited, listening.

Michael let his self-pity, misery and regret stream down the line. Eventually he said, 'So will you, Beth, will you? Try to get Isabel to talk to me – you know what she's thinking.'

Beth said she could understand what he was feeling, but it wasn't appropriate to discuss Isabel with him.

He began to shout. 'Bloody female Mafia, that's what you are!'

'Michael, if you're going to be abusive I'm going to put an end to this conversation.'

'I'm sorry, Beth, I'm sorry,' he mumbled. 'Please . . . It's just so frustrating, Isabel not wanting to talk to me, I can't tell her how I feel . . . How sorry I am. I know it sounds lame . . . Oh, fuck, I can't get the words out, not the right ones. What am I going to do?'

'Well, it sounds as if you've had too much to drink. Why don't you go and sleep it off?'

'You're right,' he said, and put the phone down.

He crawled into bed. So alone. His face was wet, the pillow was damp. But I never cry, he thought.

He felt crushed by the sense of what he'd lost. He hadn't known what he had, not really, and now it was gone.

40

Beth and Isabel sat at the end of the garden, enjoying the last rays of the day. They had to keep shifting their canvas chairs to stay in the pool of sunlight.

Beth had come over to go through the breathing exercises and discuss the plans for The Day – the day (or night) when Isabel would go into labour.

'More wine?' Isabel proffered the bottle.

'Thanks. Sure you won't join me?'

'No, I'm fine with my lemonade.' Officially, the baby was

due in three weeks but, as Sheila the midwife had warned Isabel, two weeks either side of the due date was considered normal, so . . . Hope it's earlier rather than later, she thought. 'God, look at me, I'm gigantic,' she said. 'You could balance a drink on this belly of mine, use me as a table.' She leant back and tried but the glass wobbled. They both burst out laughing.

'It's more like a drum – I remember that feeling, so tight and stretched,' Beth said. 'Anyway, I think you look magnificent, like a ship in full sail.'

'Thank you. Is that part of your duties as birth partner, keeping up mother's morale?'

Isabel had been teasing Beth for taking her duties so seriously – Beth had even produced an article she'd found about alternative birth partners, as in not the husband. But, of course, she was glad her friend was rallying to her side, and grateful. At times the thought of giving birth was daunting. At times she was downright scared, even though she'd done it before, even though it would be a relief, even though she wanted to meet her baby face to face.

'So how *is* your morale?' Beth leaned forward. 'How's it been living here on your own?'

'My morale is OK, most of the time. Not exactly high, but all right. And do you know? I have to admit I like having the house to myself. Pleasing myself . . . Besides, Dom's back next week, so I'll be alone no more. For a while, anyway.'

'Have you decided what you're going to tell him? About you and Michael?'

'Not exactly. But I must tell him something, obviously.'

Beth was about to say that perhaps Michael should be involved in telling the children but decided to keep quiet. Earlier she'd told Isabel about Michael's phone call and the response had been explosive. Isabel had been outraged that he should do such a thing, how dare he? How selfish he was, thinking only of himself, and he was the one who'd caused all this . . . Beth had noticed Isabel's hands shaking as she'd opened the bottle of white wine and she wondered if Isabel's decision to set the whole issue of Michael aside – *to set Michael aside* – until after the baby was born was a wise one.

It must require an enormous amount of self-control, apart from everything else.

Beth could understand it but knew she could never be like this. So restrained. Although Isabel *had* thrown Michael out, hadn't she? Not so restrained, but in control. Luckily I don't have to face it with Simon, she thought. In fact, things were good between them at the moment. A lot of it was to do with the fact that he was happier, now that he was establishing himself as a storyteller. With some success. Only this week he was holding a two-day workshop for managers of an international company, his theme being '*Mythology in the Workplace*'. And for that he was earning the equivalent of a month's salary as a lecturer. Crazy money, he called it. 'Crazy man,' she'd said. Everything had improved in the Marcus household lately – Simon's moods, sex, the children's behaviour, the whole atmosphere was more relaxed. Beth was delighted, of course, but she wasn't entirely comfortable with the implication that if Simon was happier they all were.

'How do you think the children will react?' Beth asked.

'God knows. It's so hard to predict.' Isabel looked up at the sky. The sun had moved behind a tree.

Beth felt sorry for them all. Obviously poor Isabel. And poor kids – first having to adjust to their mother being pregnant and now this. And, she couldn't help thinking, poor Michael (or, as Simon called him, poor bastard). She couldn't see how it was going to work out, for one thing she'd noticed was that Isabel never mentioned the F words . . . forgive and forget. Maybe it was too soon, or it was too much to ask.

They went inside. Back to practicalities.

'So we're all set, Izzy? We've done the breathing.'

'Been there, done that.'

'You wish! So, as soon as you think you're in labour, you'll ring me straight away? And we know that, traffic permitting, et cetera, et cetera, the quickest I can get here – or to the hospital – is about fifty minutes. If it's rush hour it will be more like an hour and a half.'

'I'll try to hold on.'

'I've got alternative routes planned, in case there are roadworks or anything. That seems wise.'

'You are efficient, Beth, I'm impressed.'

'Thank goodness it's the summer holidays – you've timed it well.'

'Glad you didn't say planned it, that would be pushing it a bit.'

'Anyway, I'm spending most of my time at home drawing and painting so you should be able to get hold of me easily. The furthest I'll go is Sainsbury's.'

'That's reassuring. Thank you, thank you for everything. I'm truly truly grateful.' They hugged each other, Beth held her tight, and they stayed like that for a moment.

'I told you I'd be here for you, Izzy. That's what friends are for.' She said nothing about husbands.

'Beth, I suddenly thought, the reason you're not going away on holiday, it's not because of me and the baby, is it?'

'No! Honestly it's not. The kids are of an age when they want to do their own thing. Daniel and Hannah want to go to pop festivals all summer it seems – we're still negotiating terms – and Leo is happy to potter around at home with his friends and his computer. Simon is busy, the workshop this week, then he's doing a summer school later in the month. Did I tell you about that? It's really taking off.'

'Watch out, he could turn into a guru yet!'

Isabel stood in the spare room. Early-morning light streamed in – the curtains were in the wash. There weren't many more preparations she could make. Not long now. Soon it would be the baby's room. And hers too, of course, she'd been sleeping in here for months and would stay in here with her daughter. Until . . . until what, she wasn't sure.

Looking around, she checked off the necessities. Cot near the window. Mobile ready to be hung above it. A changing unit with a cupboard underneath containing towelling nappies and disposables, baby wipes, cotton wool and cream. A chest of drawers with baby towels, neat piles of baby clothes. Most of it had been delivered by John Lewis in boxes. Jenny had helped her carry them upstairs; then the unwrapping and discovering began. It had been like Christmas. Look at this . . . Oh, isn't this sweet? How things have changed . . . They'd squealed with excitement and oohed and aahed over the tiny rompers and T-shirts . . . It was exciting, it was definitely exciting. When she heard the baby's heartbeat at her check-ups (that determined rhythm, a sound she summoned whenever she felt low), when she felt her daughter's strong movements inside her, when she looked at all *this* . . . Yes, she was excited.

There was a sense of caution too. Maybe she was just superstitious, but she didn't call this room the nursery, she hadn't decorated it with friezes of bunnies and teddies, she hadn't gone overboard with equipment and clothes, even though the shops and catalogues were tempting. (Tempting you to enter a light, bright, sunny world of gorgeous babies and gorgeous young mummies and daddies, everything clean and happy and sparkling.) Maybe it was also because of her age . . . Maybe it was all the other stuff going on . . . The context, as Beth would call it.

The phone was ringing. She moved slowly to answer it in the main bedroom, the bedroom where once she and Michael slept, then just Michael, but empty now. 'Hold on, I'm coming,' she said.

'Mum?'

The line was crackly. 'Dominic! Where are you?'

'Waterloo. Just got in.'

'I thought you were going to say Istanbul or somewhere, the line's bad. So you're back!'

'I'll be home soon, needed to make sure you were there. Can't find my key, it could be at the bottom of my rucksack.'

'Don't worry, I'm here.'

Dominic was hungry, of course. She made him an omelette while he slumped at the kitchen table. Already the house seemed full of him. Rucksack filling the hall, things spilling out of it. Trainers sprawled at right angles; plastic carrier-bags with his overflow. And he seemed older, bigger. Could he have changed so much in six weeks? Or was it merely because she hadn't seen him? But he did look taller, broader in the shoulders, though thinner too. Rangier. Bloody hell, she thought. Her son was beginning to look like a man.

His voice – deeper too? – filled the kitchen. He was talking, talking, telling her things, not everything, she knew that, an automatic censor was in place, but all sorts of things. What the

French police had said and done to Will, what happened when Ben mislaid his passport, the forests in Germany, the wonderful buildings in Vienna, the bars in Barcelona ... A whirlwind whistle-stop tour of Europe. The differences in trains, sleeping out, poverty ...

She sat across from him and smiled.

'What, Mum?'

'I'm pleased to see you, that's all.'

'I'm pleased to be home, in a way. Can't wait to sleep in my own bed.'

'It awaits you!'

'Think I'll have a sleep now, even though it's morning. I've been travelling all night.'

He stood up from the table, yawning and stretching. She noticed how brown he was, that outdoorsy sort of tan he used to get when he was a child.

'Thanks for the food, Mum. And how have you been?'

'I'm fine, thanks.'

'When – when's the baby due?'

He has changed, she thought.

'A couple of weeks.'

'Ah.' A pause. 'Anyway, I'm off to bed. See you later.'

Isabel relieved Jenny for a few hours in the shop and when she came back Dominic was in the shower. I can't avoid it, she thought, I've got to tell him about Michael. Then tell Gemma somehow. But when? She turned possible words, possible scenarios over and over in her mind. Obviously she'd tell them the truth, but *all* of it?

He came downstairs in shorts and a crumpled T-shirt and began pulling things out of his rucksack. Probably piles of dirty washing coming my way, she thought.

'Oh great, here it is. A present for you, Mum.'

Isabel unwrapped the coarse brown paper, keeping her head down so that he wouldn't see her eyes filling with tears. It was a wooden box, roughly carved and coloured, naïve but charming.

'Dom, thank you. That was very sweet of you.'

She leant forward to kiss him.

'It's from Slovakia. Hey, what's up?'

She shook her head. 'Just being sentimental, you know, what mothers do.'

He laughed and said he'd make them some tea. Then the question came. 'So how's Dad? I haven't even spoken to him for ages.'

When Dominic had rung briefly from various places in Europe Isabel had said, truthfully, 'Dad's not here.' But now?

'Dom, there's something I've got to talk to you about.'

'What is it?' He left the mugs and tea-bags and turned to face her. 'Mum, is everything all right?'

'Well, yes and no. Sit down.'

She kept it as simple and straightforward as she could, trying to tell him with the minimum of emotion. It was difficult as her son kept interrupting with questions, demands for explanations, exclamations of his own. Swearing, running his hands through his hair (like Michael). His father was living elsewhere, she said, in a flat in the Barbican. No, they hadn't split up, not exactly. It might be permanent, she wasn't sure. Who was going to decide? Well, they both were, she supposed. She explained when this had happened. Dominic wanted to know why he hadn't been told. There was anger in his voice. And did Gemma know? Well, she should be told too, he said. All right, over the phone wasn't ideal, but this wasn't ideal either, was it? It wasn't fair, they should have known. It wasn't fair . . .

Isabel agreed. Lots of things weren't fair.

Then he asked, Why?

Isabel said he should speak to his father. No, it wasn't because of the baby. He should ask his father.

Dominic stormed from the room. Isabel heard him banging about upstairs. When he returned there were tears in his eyes and he came to her side, put his hand on her shoulder. Suddenly he seemed young again.

She began to feel nostalgic for the quiet days when she'd been alone. Dominic demanded his father's new number, and she gave it to him reluctantly – Michael had insisted she have it.

She turned up the radio in the kitchen as she didn't want to overhear this. Let them deal with it between them, she thought.

*

Days of drama followed. Noise, shouting, the phone either ringing or being slammed down. Michael arrived, waited outside the house – Isabel peeped from an upstairs window – and took his son out for a drive. They parked near the river and Michael told Dominic the truth, confessed that it was all his fault. Dominic got out of the car and walked home.

He spoke of his father with contempt – at least, he tried to. He went out and got drunk, he spent ages on the phone to his friends. Sometimes he thought what the fuck, it didn't fucking matter. They'd made a mess of their lives, he had his to live. He'd be gone soon, one way or another, wouldn't he? Sometimes he cried.

When Gemma rang from Greece he snatched the phone and told her all about it, then handed the phone to his mother.

Isabel heard Gemma crying down the phone, wanting to know why she hadn't been told (her too), saying she'd come home, she'd get the next flight . . . Isabel drew on her dwindling reserves of energy to calm her daughter. It wasn't necessary, Gemma would be home next month anyway, she mustn't worry, these things happened, everyone was all right . . . As she comforted and soothed she realised that she was putting a certain spin on the situation, presenting it as probably temporary, implying that maybe it could be sorted out. But was she doing that merely for the sake of the children?

Dominic's A-level results arrived. The envelope lay on the table, looking less significant than it should, waiting for him to get out of bed.

Isabel sat in the garden, trying to relax. She felt so very tired these days. The baby was moving less than before, she mustn't worry, she knew that it didn't have much room to manoeuvre . . . And I don't either, she thought.

Dominic came into the garden, his feet bare, his hair tousled, waving the decisive pieces of paper. He was smiling. Thank God, thought Isabel.

'So, Dom? Tell me.'

'Two A's and a B.'

'Darling, that's great.' She stood up to give him a hug. 'Congratulations! Well done.'

'Don't know what happened with history, should've got an A.'

'You've done very well. *Really* well. And those grades will get you in – so what are you going to do? Ask them if you can leave it for a year?'

'God, Mum, I don't know.' He lay down on the grass and gazed up at the sky. 'I just don't know, what with everything . . .'

'Anyway, we must celebrate.'

'Oh, really? How?' He sat up abruptly. 'We can't as a family, though, can we? In ones and twos? You and me, then me and Dad.'

'Dom. Please.'

'Sorry. But you know what I mean. Anyway, I must go and ring people, see how the others did.' He ran back into the house.

Isabel leant back and breathed deeply.

That evening Michael rang.

'Isabel, how are you?'

'I'm fine. Do you want to know about Dom?'

'Yes, that's why I'm ringing – well, not just that. Anyway, how did he do?'

'Really well. Two As and a B. But don't be disappointed that he didn't get all As. Or if you are, don't show it, please. These are excellent grades.'

'I know that! What do you think I am? Some kind of monster? Oh, please. I'm delighted, I really am. Do you think he'll speak to me?'

'I'll ask him. Hold on.'

Michael waited. Maybe he *had* expected his son to get that magic triumvirate of As (wasn't that what the school was renowned for? Isn't that what parents paid for?) but what the hell! He may have missed by only a few marks. And if there was one thing Michael had learnt lately, it was that nothing was guaranteed. Some things you couldn't predict – or control.

'Hi, Dad.'

'Congratulations! You've done so well. I'm proud of you. But tell me more, I don't know what you got for each subject.'

Dominic's resolve not to have anything to do with his father began to fade. He found that he was glad to hear his voice, even though he'd been such a bastard to Mum. But he'd bothered to ring, hadn't he?

Dominic talked. About his results, and his friends' results and who had got what, about why he thought he'd slipped a grade. And he was relieved when all his father had to say about that was that the examiner was probably having a bad day, it happened. Never mind.

'Dom, will you let me take you out to celebrate? We could have dinner somewhere, anywhere you like. Then we can talk about what you're going to do this year – or, rather, you can tell me what *you* want to do. What do you say?'

Dominic hesitated. His father sounded different. Certainly more understanding about everything . . . Dominic wanted to go, he thought he did, but felt a tug of loyalty towards his mother. Did that make sense?

'You can think about it. Do you want to discuss it with Mum?'

He experienced a rush of affinity with his father. 'Yes. Well, I'll tell her. I would like to come. When?'

They agreed to meet next week. Dominic said he'd leave the restaurant up to his father. 'Surprise me, Dad,' he said.

Waking early, Isabel heard the clatter of birds in the garden, chattering at each other, announcing the day. Was that what had woken her? Or the planes? (There was one now, droning over the house.) No, she needed to pee. And she had a backache, a nagging, low ache. This could be it, she thought. Baby, are you on your way?

She checked the small case she was taking to hospital. Yes, everything was there. As it should have been, she'd only checked it yesterday. I'm ready, she thought. Ready in some ways.

She had a shower, then went carefully downstairs. Fed the cat, let Jasper into the garden. What was that? The pain. It came, it went. Yes, it seemed to have started.

Dominic came into the kitchen to find his mother standing

with her back against the wall, one hand under her stomach, breathing in an exaggerated way. 'Mum?'

She nodded and exhaled. 'The baby's coming, Dom. Could you do me a favour?'

Showing him the list of phone numbers on the board, she asked him to ring Beth, then the midwife, tell them what was happening. And should I phone Dad, he wondered, for a second, but kept that thought to himself.

When he got off the phone his mother was leaning over a chair, gripping the back, doing that breathing thing again.

'The midwife – Sheila's on her way. Beth said good luck and she'd meet you at the hospital, she'll get there as soon as she can. Now, what can I do, Mum? Surely there's something?'

'No, thanks, sweetheart. But thank you.'

'Shall I call an ambulance?' He looked frightened.

'No, no, it's OK. I'm going in Sheila's car. That's the plan.' She began to walk around the kitchen. Walking was good. Between contractions she smiled at her son. 'Don't worry, Dom. Everything will be all right.'

41

Late-summer sunshine streamed through the window.

Isabel held her daughter in her arms. She was perfect, she was beautiful, everyone said so.

Isabel held the moment too – she kept doing this, wanting to freeze the frame, stop time. Treasure this, she'd say to herself, this won't come round again. Stroking the warm forehead, the downy dark hair, nestling her nose at the back of the baby's neck, that special place. Gazing at the long eyelashes, the eyebrows barely there, the miniature hands with their pearly nails . . . Isabel marvelled at her. And adored her.

The birth had been fast and straightforward. 'Thank you, thank you for that, whoever you are,' Isabel had said. And how quickly we forget the pain, she thought. That's what women do. Who wanted to dwell on it when you had the end result in your arms?

Beth had made it in time, had breathed with her, encouraged her, held her hand. The delivery room had been full of women.

Sheila the midwife, Dr Finch towards the end. Jenny was there too. As Isabel held her daughter for the first time, feeling tired and sweaty, sore but elated – she'd done it, everything was all right, the baby was fine – she looked up and saw smiling faces, some wet with tears.

It had been a bit like that ever since. She'd come home later that afternoon and had hardly been alone. Dominic was there, waiting. He seemed overwhelmed. As he put it, 'It's weird, off you go to hospital, then you come back with a *baby*.' She laughed. 'You know what I mean, Mum.' She did.

At times it was like a party – there was plenty of champagne, and flowers and cards and presents everywhere. Beth announced she was staying for a few days, Jenny dropped by every day, Sheila came to check on her and the baby (and said how well they were both doing). Angie had phoned from Spain, excited and envious too, so she said when she heard the news. *Envious*? What could she mean? thought Isabel.

On the second day, while the baby was sleeping, she came slowly down the stairs and found Beth and Dominic in the kitchen, talking intently. They looked up, a little embarrassed. 'What are you two up to?' she asked, smiling.

They glanced quickly at each other. Beth spoke first. 'Oh, we were just discussing who else there is to ring, to tell them the news. I rang Connie and Erica. They were delighted, said to send you congratulations.'

'And I spoke to Granny,' Dominic joined in eagerly. 'And I've been trying Gemma in Greece, the office there anyway. Someone said they'd get her to ring back.'

'Good. Thank you.' Isabel opened the fridge. 'It's strange, I have this desire to drink a tall glass of cold milk. I thought you were only meant to get cravings when you were pregnant.'

'Mum! We think we should let Dad know about the baby. I want to ring him. Tell him the news. Don't you think we should?' His words came out in a rush.

Isabel looked from Beth to Dominic. So that's what they'd been discussing. She took a deep breath. They watched her, waiting.

'Yes, all right. If you want to, Dom.'

'OK, then. I'll do it now, right now.'

Isabel heard him bounding up the stairs, taking them two at

a time. She sat down at the table with her glass of milk. Its appeal was waning.

'You know, Iz, you should be proud of your son. He's handling things really well,' Beth said, sitting down with her.

'You know, Beth, I think I am.'

Days passed in a dream. Isabel realised that she hadn't got dressed since she'd come home: she'd been living in nighties and her robe. Tomorrow, tomorrow would do. Meanwhile she adjusted to having a new baby, a baby in the house again. Sleeping when her daughter slept; getting used to changing nappies; breastfeeding – the thrill of the first time. Bathing her, oh, so carefully; dressing her, fitting the tiny limbs into sleeves and legs, easing things over her fragile head. Gushing with love and milk and anxiety. And at every step getting to know her. Every inch, every detail. This living, breathing baby, small but solid, the compact body vibrant with life. In a way, she felt she'd known her for ever.

Gemma rang, shrieking with excitement. So happy, so glad, she couldn't wait to see her new sister. She told Isabel she was going to come home earlier than planned, she'd arrive at the weekend. 'Are you sure?' Isabel asked.

'Absolutely, then I can help you,' Gemma said. 'Do the shopping and the cooking, stuff like that. Especially as Dad isn't there to do it. I'm so pissed off with him, Mum.'

Isabel said she had to go. She was touched that Gemma wanted to be supportive, but she didn't want to think about Michael, all that, not now. She wanted nothing to disturb the enchanted state she was experiencing. Euphoria.

It was as if she were in a bubble. Time was disappearing too quickly.

The baby puckered up her face and began to cry. Isabel lifted her shirt, unhooked one side of her bra and eased her daughter on to the nipple, already dripping with milk. The baby's nose nearly disappeared into the swollen breast.

'Ooh,' said Isabel. Deep, noisy sucking. It felt good, complete, almost sexual with a deep tug reverberating inside her.

'Beth? I've been thinking about her name. I think I'll call her Beatrice, after my great-aunt.'

'Beatrice. Beatrice. I like it. A serious name, but that's good. Do you think you need to consult Michael?'

'I don't think so. Why?'

'Oh, Izzy. Never mind.'

Beth continued to stir a spaghetti sauce – she was cooking supper – and thought of her own children. And Simon. She really ought to go home soon.

A postcard arrived. It was from Guatemala, a photograph of women in a market wearing exuberantly bright colours. Isabel thought it would be for Gemma or Dominic, from one of their friends who was travelling but it was addressed to her in handwriting she didn't recognise.

It was from Ellen. She waited for the anger to return, although it had always been directed more at Michael than Ellen, but she felt surprisingly calm. Perhaps the birth of Beatrice had rendered her immune.

> *I wanted to wish you well and say I'm sorry. I've learnt a lot from the whole thing. It shouldn't have happened. Now I'm on a long trip with my best friend Grace. We've got a commission for a book on women around the world, I'm the words, she's the photographs. So how's the baby?*
>
> *Yours, Ellen.*

Isabel smiled and propped it up on a shelf in the spare room, Beatrice's room, against the baby-care books and jars and tubes of cream and lotion.

Michael kept phoning. He said he wanted to come to see her – and the baby. He spoke to Beth, and Dominic. Once Isabel overheard Dominic saying, 'Mum's resting. She can't talk to you now, Dad, really she can't.'

As Michael put down the phone he pressed his head against the wall of the flat, weighed down by sadness. The feeling of being excluded was difficult to cope with, especially as he knew it was his own fault. He'd screwed everything up, there was no doubt about it. Perhaps not quite everything – at least there was some progress with his son.

They'd met for the meal as arranged, at a new restaurant in Clerkenwell. No, Dominic had insisted, he didn't need a lift, he could find his own way, and no, he wouldn't come to the flat first. Michael had made sure he arrived early and sat at the table, with a large gin and tonic, waiting for his son. The young man who approached the table surprised him. Dominic? Looking older, more solemn, more cautious. At first it had been awkward, Dominic had even seemed a little shy, but Michael kept up the flow of words, anything to make contact. After they'd given their order to the waiter he had handed over a Waterstone's bag, saying, 'Dom, I got you something which might be useful, help you sort out this gap year of yours – if that's what you're going to do.'

Dominic pulled out the hefty book, a directory of ideas and contacts for travelling, community work and voluntary service abroad. 'Oh, Dad, cool. Thanks, thank you.' He grinned at his father. Michael smiled back, wanting to hug him. A look of acceptance passed between them.

Since then they spoke on the phone – Dominic even rang him, initiating contact. Michael was grateful, not just because he wanted it to be all right between him and his son but also because he could have news of Isabel and the baby. He needed to know. And, surprisingly, Dominic was quite happy to answer his questions and talk about them, especially his new baby sister. (He had to admit she was cute, he added. Now that she was here, it didn't seem so bad.)

We must have done something right, thought Michael. Look at the way Dominic's protecting his mother, looking after her. Which is more than I did, he thought.

Beth went home, taking with her a sketchbook full of work – 'A bonus of being your birth partner!' she said to Isabel. Drawings of Beatrice while she was asleep, of Isabel feeding her, holding her . . . Inspirational, Beth thought, and decided they were really rather good. She gave one to Isabel as she left. 'Now, are you sure you'll be all right?'

'I'll be fine. Dom's here, and Gemma arrives tomorrow. I've only had a baby, women do it all the time!'

Brave words, thought Beth, for they both knew that that wasn't all Isabel had to deal with.

Gemma was back. The house was fuller, even noisier, more untidy. But it was good to see her, Isabel thought. Like Dominic, she'd changed over the summer, tanned obviously, but leaner, more muscular. 'All that exercise,' she said. 'Non-stop sailing, windsurfing and swimming, playing with those hordes of kids.'

When she'd arrived home she'd almost knocked Isabel over as she hugged her and held on tight, then she'd insisted on seeing Beatrice, even though she was sleeping. 'It's love at first sight,' she told her mother.

Isabel was impressed with how helpful Gemma was being. 'Well, I'm experienced in childcare now,' she said. 'You can leave her with me, if you want to go out. Why don't you, Mum?'

And Isabel did go out, although not far and only briefly. It was good to have a break from the full-time, full-on, no let-up mother-and-baby experience, permanently attached. As soon as she'd fed Beatrice, Gemma took over and Isabel went to the shop, surprising Jenny. They started to plan the new 'department' – 'Aren't we grand?' Jenny said – of maternity clothes for resale.

'We can start with mine, the few I've got,' said Isabel.

'Oh,' said Jenny, smiling. 'So you won't be needing them any more?'

'Ha bloody ha. I hardly think so!' Isabel replied. Her breasts began to feel tender and milk was leaking through her bra. Time to go home, she decided.

Gemma and Dominic were talking in the kitchen. They'd been to Waitrose and were unpacking bags of shopping.

'I can't believe you actually know where things go,' Gemma teased her brother. 'You never used to. Come to think of it, you never used to go shopping or help.'

He flipped her playfully with a bag of spinach leaves. 'So, what do you know? Maybe I've changed. Lots of things have changed around here.'

'That's certainly true.'

'And I think Dad's changed too, you know.'

Gemma snorted, a dismissive, angry noise.

'What are you going to do about him Gem?'

Gemma was stacking tins of petfood in the cupboard and took a while to reply. Eventually she turned to her brother and said, 'I really don't know. Part of me thinks *I* shouldn't have to do anything, sod him.'

'I felt like that at first. Angry with him. And it was hard believing it. *Dad?* Doing that?'

'Best not to go down that road, Dom.'

'Yeah.' He sighed. 'But he's still our father.'

'I know, I know. It's so hard. At least Mum isn't slagging him off, or asking us not to see him. That's a relief.'

'So what *are* you going to do? We could see him together.'

'Let me think about it. Part of me doesn't want to have anything to do with him, part of me wants to see him so I can tell him what I think of him, and another part –'

'How many parts is that?'

'Don't be facetious, Dom. You know what I mean. Part of me does want to see him, just to see him . . .' She shrugged and pulled a face.

Isabel had been coming downstairs after feeding Beatrice and settling her for a nap. She'd paused, hearing her children in the kitchen. Actually talking. They continued to surprise her . . . being supportive, shopping, cooking, occasionally even cleaning and ironing. And this *talking* to each other in a reasonably civilised way. She stood on the bottom step, leant against the wall and listened.

'Yeah, it's confusing. It's easier in a way since I've seen him and spoken to him . . . And he's being great about me having a year off and everything.'

'Oh, big deal, Dom.'

'Well it is, because before he was dead against it. Before –'

'Before the baby or before the affair?'

'Shit, I don't know. But he is trying, I'm sure he is. It's not just to get me on his side or anything, it's not like that, believe me. I think he feels really bad about – about what's happened.'

'And so he bloody well should.' Gemma slammed the freezer shut and asked, 'So what's it like to be disappointed in him instead of him being disappointed in us?'

'Gem, that's not fair.'

'Maybe not. But none of it seems fair, does it?'

Isabel stood very still, tears running slowly down her face. What should she do?

She heard the sound of the kettle being filled. Any minute one of them would probably call her for some tea.

Dominic said, 'You'll have to see Dad sometime – or at least talk to him.'

'I suppose I will. Maybe I'll ring him, perhaps even tonight.'

'He's probably scared to talk to you.'

'Huh. Now, there's a thought. Make the tea, little brother, and I'll call Mum.'

'Hey, not so little. Look how much taller I am than you!'

A few mornings later Isabel walked around the garden with Beatrice in her arms, telling her about the last of the roses, describing the cat asleep under a bush, the bees searching for end-of-summer flowers. Showing her the world.

Gemma came to join them. 'Did you used to do this with me, Mum?'

'Yes, as a matter of fact, I did. Hey, you're looking rather smart today, Gem.'

'Actually I have made an effort.' She gestured at her white cap-sleeved top and black skirt. 'I'm taking a cardigan as well, but you don't think the skirt's too short, do you?'

'Depends what for, darling. Where are you going?' Isabel sat down on the garden bench, gently rocking Beatrice against her shoulder.

Gemma perched next to her. 'Oh, didn't I say? I'm going for a kind of interview – not an interview exactly, as they know me from the summer – but for a chat about being a chalet girl this winter, in France.'

'Good, if that's what you want to do.'

'Oh, hell. It's not only that, Mum. You see, I'm meeting Dad for lunch too. You don't mind, do you?'

'Gemma, please. It's all right.' She put her spare arm around her elder daughter and squeezed her. 'Don't feel you have to choose between us – you don't. And just because I'm not seeing your father at the moment doesn't mean you can't.'

'I know. But it's difficult.'

'It is. But he's still your father. Obviously I understand that. So off you go, and have a good time.'

*

Gemma came home as Isabel was loading soggy cot sheets and babyclothes into the washing-machine. 'Jeez! Mum, how can such a small baby make such a lot of washing?'

'I know, it's one of the facts of life. But tell me, Gem, how was your day? No, wait, let me finish this and wash my hands first.'

This is weird, thought Isabel. I want to ask Gemma for news of Michael. I want to know what he said, how he is.

They sat in the kitchen undisturbed. Dominic was out, trying to get a temporary job to earn some money for travelling ('Wonders will never cease,' said Gemma). Beatrice slept upstairs. (Thank God she's an easy baby and sleeps a lot. It gives me time for reflection, thought Isabel.) She switched on the baby-listener, just in case.

Gemma needed little prompting to talk about Michael. Isabel could see that her daughter was trying to be tactful and temper what she said. She doesn't want to hurt my feelings, she's sensitive to my position, thought Isabel. But in the end it came out in a rush: how Gemma found it hard to stay being angry with him when she actually saw him face to face, how awful he looked, really he did, Mum . . . And how sorry he was, for what he'd done, so very sorry, Gemma could see that. 'This is dreadful for everyone, all of us,' she said.

Isabel took Gemma's hands in hers. She was about to ask if Michael had suggested that his daughter should plead his case when Gemma said, 'And he didn't ask me to tell you anything, or try to persuade you to see him, honestly he didn't. Mainly we talked about me, my summer, and the idea of me being a chalet girl, and skiing, stuff like that. It was me that made him talk about it . . . Even then . . . Mum, look, he doesn't want me and Dom to be caught in the middle any more than you do! Though, of course, we are.'

As Isabel held Gemma while she cried, feeling tearful too, she made a decision. This bubble of hers was about to burst. Maybe it was time to see him, maybe he was ready. She wouldn't keep Michael at a distance any longer.

42

Michael stood on the doorstep, clutching a bunch of flowers. Feeling a little strange, he rang his own doorbell.

He thought Isabel looked wonderful when she came to the door. He'd expected her to look otherwise. He stepped inside.

'Dom and Gemma are out shopping for clothes. Together. Amazing, isn't it?' she said as he followed her down the hall.

The baby started crying, as if on cue.

'I'll just go and get her,' Isabel said, and climbed the stairs without looking back. He went into the kitchen and put the flowers in the sink. Home. It looked just the same as always. Isabel didn't seemed to have changed anything but, then, what had he expected? That she'd redecorate and buy new furniture? Most of this had been of her choosing anyway. There was little of him here, and there was little of him in the flat.

He heard her calling from the stairs. 'Michael? Let's go into the living room.'

She was carrying a bundle. White blanket with a dark fluff of hair peeping out, making whimpering noises. 'Meet your new daughter,' she said. Gently she pulled down the blanket and said, in a softer voice, 'Here we are, darling. This is your daddy.'

Thank you, Isabel, thank you, Michael thought, for saying that. He leant forward and saw a cross little face, pink and heart-shaped. His heart thumped. He hadn't anticipated experiencing such a lurch of emotion. He found it hard to speak, swallowing whatever it was blocking his throat. 'She's beautiful, Isabel,' he whispered.

'Yes, isn't she? Her name is Beatrice.'

'Oh. I see. After your aunt?'

'*Great*-aunt, remember? Haven't decided on a middle name yet. Maybe she doesn't need one.'

He was about to ask if he could hold her – *Beatrice* – when the baby opened her mouth and cried loudly.

'She needs feeding. Do you mind?'

Michael wasn't sure if Isabel meant did he mind her feeding, or would he mind leaving the room. Hesitantly he sat down on the sofa. Isabel settled in a chair by the window, putting a cushion behind her back, bending her head over the baby, murmuring softly. Sunlight fell on them. Perfect, he thought. If things were normal – would they ever be again? – he'd be taking a photograph for the family album. Of his wife and child.

The baby fastened on quickly. 'We're old hands at this now, aren't we, little one?' said Isabel.

Michael gasped, then words flowed out of him as if a dam had burst. He was so, so sorry . . . No excuse . . . Selfish . . . Preoccupied . . . No reason . . . Didn't know why. Hadn't appreciated what he had until he'd lost it . . . His voice broke into sobs.

Isabel only half listened, she was paying attention to the baby, but this was more or less what she'd expected him to say. Now he was covering his face with his hands as he cried.

She said nothing and moved Beatrice to the other breast, watching the dust dance in a shaft of sunlight.

Michael left the room. She heard him go into the cloakroom, sounds of him blowing his noise, then running water.

Oh Beatrice, what are we to do? Isabel thought. She did feel some pity for him. Not much, but he was obviously suffering. Some people might say he deserved to. But he wasn't a *bad* man. What he'd done, he'd done. Now he was troubled and confused – more than she was, she could see that. And he *was* the children's father.

Her nipple slipped out of Beatrice's mouth. The baby was asleep.

Do I want him back? She thought, as she carefully lifted Beatrice on to her shoulder. In some ways living without him was no different from living with him, except that it was easier. And how much had he ever really been here, she asked herself, physically and otherwise, especially towards the end?

The end? Was it the end?

Michael returned. He did look wretched. Thin and drawn, with dark shadows under his eyes.

Isabel said, 'It's a beautiful day and Beatrice has finished feeding for now. Shall we go for a walk?'

'Yes, I'd like that. If you want to.'

Isabel could hear the anxiety in his voice, could see his

eager-to-please expression. It's up to me, she realised. It's up to me what happens next, what happens between us. I'm in control, I can decide.

'I'll just put Beatrice in her sling. Won't be a minute.'

'Do you need any help?'

'I can manage on my own, thanks. But you could get Jasper organised.'

They headed towards Richmond Park, making small talk, Michael asking polite questions about the birth. They skirted around each other.

Inside the park Isabel turned on to a path, taking a different route from the old one they had used, back then. Michael followed, Jasper bounded ahead. Beatrice slept in the sling, snug against her mother's chest.

Michael looked down at the sandy path then sideways at his wife. 'What are we going to do, Isabel?'

'We?'

'All right.' He sighed. 'What are *you* going to do? What do you want to happen?'

'I really don't know. I'm not just avoiding the issue –'

'And avoiding me? You prefer to do that too? I don't blame you.'

'In some ways it's easier, I admit.'

'I can understand that. Don't look like that, please. I think I can understand a lot more things now than I ever did.'

They walked on in silence. Then Michael said softly, 'There are so many things I want to say to you, Isabel. Please listen. Those things I said at – at the house, they were all true, but I'll try to be more coherent now. Isabel?'

She nodded. She'd let him speak.

This was a different Michael, she thought, as she listened. Maybe the children are right, maybe he has changed. He's less sure of himself, more tentative, even occasionally searching for the right word. He sounded like a man who had learnt that there might be more than one way of looking at things.

'I have to say it again, and it's trite, I know, but I am so sorry for doing what I did. All the things I did. I am ashamed. If I could undo it, I would. Turn the clock back . . . All the hurt I've caused, the damage. Believe me, Isabel,' and he stopped and looked into her face, 'believe me, I could not be more sorry.'

'Let's sit down,' was all she said, motioning to a bench by the path, one of the few in the park. She adjusted Beatrice as she sat down, moving the weight.

Michael continued, 'And, of course, I keep asking myself why I did it. Why did I jeopardise everything we had?'

'Perhaps it's better if you don't try to explain it all away.'

'I know I can't do that, not explain it *away*. Isabel, please, I'm not correcting you – oh, damn. I – I should try. I owe it to you, surely?'

'Oh, Michael . . .'

'It seems too easy to fall back on the old male mid-life crisis thing, but there could be some of that . . . I look back and I wonder if things had become too much the same, perhaps I was weary, tired of things – no, not of you, Isabel, not consciously.'

She snorted.

An elderly couple walked slowly by with their dog, a small terrier on a lead, also elderly. Michael held Jasper by the collar and they sat in silence until the three had passed – it seemed to take ages.

'Perhaps it can't be explained,' Isabel said, looking down at Beatrice, her dark eyelashes curving on her round pink cheek. She added quietly, 'But remember – I met Ellen.' There, her name had been said. 'I would think she – the way she was, is – could be reason enough, Michael.'

He pushed his hair back from his face, repeatedly, as if that would help.

'Oh, God.' He tried to keep his voice on track. 'I suppose her being American may have had something to do with it,' he said. 'I wonder about that. You know, I never went in much for self-analysis, but I've been thinking that it could be because she was different, she wasn't part of all this, everything . . . It meant I could step outside myself . . . Leave behind the strain of being me, trying to be me. That was what I was weary of.'

'What do you mean?'

'This is hard to put into words. I've – I've always felt that I had to invent myself, make myself into something –'

'You have! You did! You've done incredibly well.'

'Thank you.' He smiled at her; she smiled back. There, that was something. 'But I don't just mean in material terms, Isabel, I mean as a person. I always had to keep things reined in – myself, I mean – otherwise I felt I was teetering on the brink . . .'

'Brink of what?'

'Oh, chaos, disaster. Unformed, unnamed things. That's why I had to keep control. I've always felt very – very uncertain about myself. Things bothered me, scared me, made me angry, things you probably weren't aware of . . . Snobbery and class, the English disease. It never quite went away. And because she – Ellen – was American, I could shed all that, like a skin.'

Isabel was thinking, why was I not aware of this side of him, this insecurity? Why did he feel he had to pretend with me? I should have known, she thought, I should have understood.

She shifted the baby slightly and said, 'Michael, I'm not trying to change the subject, but I think she needs changing. Let's go home.'

He helped her up off the bench and said, 'That's probably enough of that, anyway. Maybe I should talk to someone about it, get some help.'

Isabel did not disagree.

They walked back along the path, side by side. A cyclist zoomed up behind them, riding too close. Michael took Isabel's arm as she jumped in surprise. 'Stupid sod. Why doesn't he use the road?' he said.

She was looking up at him. After a moment or two he let his hand fall away. 'Michael, you haven't said what you want to happen?'

'I didn't think that was an option, considering what I –'

'You can still tell me.'

'Oh, Isabel, I want to come home.' His voice faltered. 'One thing – one of the many things I've realised since we've been apart is how much it matters to me . . . you, the children, home. The family. What we built together. It sounds so clichéd, doesn't it? But I miss it all so. Don't think, Oh, he's just missing his home comforts – though, of course, I am. And, by the way, I think I now understand how much work there is in keeping it going, how much *you*'ve put into family life, into making home *home*. Am I making sense? It's hard to express the complexity of it, the layers . . .'

'It's OK, Michael. Carry on.'

'And another thing I realised was how little I did, not enough . . . I'm not just talking about the washing and ironing, the housework, I don't think you ever expected me to do more . . . It's the commitment, I suppose. It was there to begin with, for a long while, in fact, but maybe I took things for granted . . . I wasn't putting enough into it, maybe I wasn't paying attention.'

And maybe I wasn't either, thought Isabel. Maybe there were things I should have done, or things I shouldn't have done. Perhaps *I* should have been paying more attention too . . .

'I want us to be together, I want us to be a family again, all of us,' Michael was saying. He looked down at Beatrice, to include her.

His honesty touched her. And his vulnerability – of course, that moved her. Isabel couldn't deny that his words pulled her towards him, towards what he wanted. Part of her wanted it too, she knew that. But it wasn't that simple, was it?

'So you want me to forgive and forget?'

'Isabel. Have I any right to ask you? And is it possible to forgive? Or forget?'

They turned into their street. It held so many memories, from so many years. And there was still so much unspoken, Isabel thought. We've barely begun.

As they approached the house she said, 'Do you remember that Victorian vase? It belonged to my grandmother.'

'The blue and gold one that got broken?'

'Yes, Dom knocked it down when he was little.'

'But you got it repaired. That ceramics expert managed to glue together all the pieces . . . Ah, I think I see what you're getting at.'

'You could say our marriage is broken. Fragmented. Perhaps it can be put together again, but it would never be quite the same.'

'What are you saying?' Sadness and regret were in his voice, on his face.

'I'm not sure. But those hairline cracks, they'd always be

there. We'd know they were there. We should think about that.' She fished her key out of her pocket. 'Meanwhile, we can be in contact. You should see the children, in any case.'

He nodded. It was too much to expect – had he expected it? – that she would take him back with open arms. Of course she wouldn't.

And he had to accept what she said. Whatever happened would be on her terms. Humility. Another thing I've learnt, he realised.

'So, Michael, let's see how it goes, shall we?'

Isabel took Beatrice upstairs to change her, leaving Michael in the kitchen talking to the children, who'd returned from their shopping. (The carrier-bags of evidence lay in the hall.) She could tell from the sound of their voices that they were pleased to see him, and to see him *here*.

Presumably he'd go back to the flat – *his* flat – soon. 'I need time, I need peace', she murmured to Beatrice, as she removed the wet nappy. 'I have just had a baby, for Christ's sake.'

But whatever happens, I can do it. I can live without him. At some point I can probably live *with* him again, if I choose to.

'Choice, Beatrice, there's the thing,' she said, as she wiped the soft little bottom.

The baby looked up at her with her dark blue eyes. Isabel could have sworn she smiled. She beamed back at her daughter. 'I know what we can give you as a middle name,' she said. '*Hope*.'